Brandon's throat constricted as he watched her strip away the last of her clothing and stand naked in the semi-darkness of the hut. He wanted to look away, but he couldn't tear his eyes from her.

Sweat trickled down the back of his neck. "What are you about, woman?" he demanded. "Must you torment me with . . ." His mouth felt dry and he longed to seize her in his arms and taste those sweet breasts. He reached for her, and she stepped away, leaving the scent of honeysuckle.

"Not here," she answered. "Come to the river."

His chest felt tight; his heart was pounding. "You know what I want from you," he persisted. "What I've wanted from the first."

She caught his broad hand in hers. "Come to the river, Brandon-mine." She stared up at him from beneath thick, feathery lashes.

"Will you?"

"Yes," she murmured.

Moonfeather

JUDITH E. FRENCH

AVON BOOKS ◭ NEW YORK

AVON BOOKS
A division of
The Hearst Corporation
105 Madison Avenue
New York, New York 10016

First Avon Books Printing: December 1990

AVON TRADEMARK REG. U.S. PAT. OFF. AND IN OTHER COUNTRIES, MARCA REGISTRADA, HECHO EN U.S.A.

Printed in the U.S.A.

RA 10 9 8 7 6 5 4 3 2 1

PART 1

America

Prologue

Maryland Colony, Spring 1706

Pale moonlight filtered through the thick canopy of tangled branches and whispering green leaves to illuminate the child's tearstained face. "Father," she pleaded in a soft, lisping tone. "Father, do not go and leave me." Her small fingers grasped the folds of his faded tartan as she pressed herself tightly against him. "I know—"

"English, lassie," Cameron prompted. "You know I dinna ken your Shawnee when ye cry."

Smoothly, Moonfeather switched to fluent English, delivered with the burred accents of the heather-covered Scottish Highlands she had never seen. "I try nay t' be bad, Papa. I promise I'll be a good lass if ye stay." Her lower lip quivered, and the tears that welled up in her huge, dark eyes spilled down the dimpled, honey-colored cheeks.

"Shhh, shhh," he crooned, rocking her warm body against his chest. "Dinna think you are the reason, bairn. Never, never think it." He swallowed hard, blinking back his own tears. "It breaks my heart to

3

leave you, darlin', but my place is across the sea with my own people.''

She buried her face in his neck. "Take me with ye, Papa. Please . . .''

"Nay." Shaken, Cameron rose to his feet, unclasped his five-year-old daughter's fingers, and held her at arm's length. " 'Twould break your mother's heart, love. You are Shawnee, little Moonfeather. This unspoiled forest, this untamed wilderness—this is your world." Gently, he lowered her to the ground and shook his head. "Ye'd nay be happy in my land.''

Her small hands perched defiantly on tiny hips, and her heart-shaped face took on a look of stubborn determination. "But ye said I be Scot . . . a Stewart, ye said. Leah Moonfeather Stewart, ye said to the black-frocked priest. He wrote it in his holy book when he sprinkled me with water.''

Cameron dropped to his knees, bringing his eyes level with hers. "Aye, that I did say," he agreed, "and 'twas true. You are as much Scot as Shawnee, but . . .'' He trailed off, fumbling with the chain around his neck.

The child stared wide-eyed as her father removed his pendant necklace and laid it across a rock. "Aiyee," she hissed. Never had she seen him take it off before. Her mother had told her that it was powerful medicine. The amulet glittered in the moonlight . . . beckoning her.

Moonfeather held her breath and tiptoed close to see. She glanced up at her father for permission. He smiled, and she cautiously extended a delicate finger to touch the beautiful necklace. Suspended on the bronze chain was a flattened oval pendant, wider than the palm of her hand. Four linked sections were covered with strange designs etched into the beaten gold. Together, the pieces formed a giant eye, complete with staring pupil.

"The Eye of Mist," Moonfeather whispered.

"Pictish gold," Cameron said. "Made when the world was young and innocent . . . so my mother told me." He drew his dirk from its embroidered sheath and laid the steel blade carefully against the top link that held the right section of the amulet to the whole, then bore down with all his weight.

The link parted and Moonfeather gasped. "Papa, no!"

Quickly he repeated the process with the lower length, then slid the triangular-shaped end piece off the chain. "Listen to what I tell you," he said urgently. "Listen and remember well." He slipped an arm around his daughter and pulled her so close she could feel the prickle of his beard against her cheek.

"The Eye of Mist has been handed down from mother to daughter in my mother's family for two thousand years. I had no sister, so when my mother died, she gave the necklace to me to give to my true daughter." He stared into the child's almond-shaped obsidian eyes. "This is hard for you, I know, but you must try to understand. Do you remember that I told you I had another family across the sea . . . another daughter?"

Moonfeather nodded. "Aye, Papa, ye said I had a sister bigger than me."

Cameron's lips tightened into a thin line, and he

drew in a deep, ragged breath. "If . . . if I give you all the necklace, there will be nothing for your sister." He put the end section of the pendant into her tiny hand and squeezed tight. "My mother told me that the necklace is magic, and that I must tell you a secret. She said you must remember to tell your own daughter when you pass it on to her. Can you?"

"I swear to thee I shall remember," she said solemnly, lapsing into the formal Shawnee tongue. "So long as the earth gives forth grass and the heaven rain."

"The legend says that whosoever possesses the Eye of Mist shall be cursed and blessed. The curse is that you will be taken from your family and friends to a far-off land. The blessing is that you will be granted one wish. Whatever you ask you shall have—even unto the power of life and death."

Her golden charm glowed hot in her fist. "If I get a wish, I want ye t' stay with Mama and me forever and ever," Moonfeather proclaimed stoutly.

Cameron chuckled. "The wish is not for the bairn ye be, but for the woman ye will become. The Eye of Mist will not work for a wee lassie like yourself." He kissed the soft fringe of hair on her forehead beneath her beaded headband. "Like as not, the legend is no more than tales told around a winter fire—just a story, no more."

Moonfeather uncurled her hand and stared at the gleaming amulet. "When I am big, I'll wish ye home again."

"Aye," he answered hoarsely. "Do that, little Moonfeather. And mayhap, if the magic be strong enough, your wish will come true."

May the warp be the white light of morning,
May the weft be the red light of evening,
May the fringes be the falling rain,
May the border be the standing rainbow.
Thus weave for us a garment of brightness.

Song of the Sky Loom
Tewa—Native American

Chapter 1

Maryland Colony, Summer 1720

Moonfeather moved from the shadows of her wig-wam into the glow of the orange-red firelight, then slipped silently beneath the overhanging boughs of the ancient cedar tree. No one glanced her way; no one took note of the sleek hickory bow clenched in her left hand—or of the feathered shaft she notched into the bowstring. All eyes were on the fierce, painted warriors that circled the captive bound to the blackened stake in the center of the clearing and on the victim—the hated *Englishmanake* who would soon writhe in the flames of Shawnee vengence.

War drums muted the thud of pounding feet as the young men danced and chanted themselves into a white-hot frenzy. Already the women had gathered their children, retreating to the shelter of their dark-ened wigwams, covering the little ones with blankets despite the heat of the summer night, trying futilely to shut out the chilling war whoops that resounded through the encampment.

Moonfeather's intense gaze was focused on her yellow-haired enemy. The Englishman faced his tormentors bravely, refusing to cry out, despite the blood that trickled down his half-naked body from a dozen wounds—despite the threat of a steel war axe hurled into the post beside his head by a howling Delaware brave.

Unconsciously, she swallowed the lump that knotted the back of her throat and moistened her dry lips with her tongue. Moonfeather had witnessed a man's death by burning once before, and the sights and sounds had haunted her dreams. It was a cruel death, even for an *Englishmanake*.

Pity for the prisoner clouded her vision, and she blinked back tears. The man bound so tightly to the tree of death was tall and well muscled, a young man in his prime. She could not see the color of his eyes, but the taunts of the war party echoed in her ears. "Sky Eyes!" they called him. She drew in a ragged breath, remembering the vivid blue of her father's eyes.

Heedless of her own safety, Moonfeather raised the bow and drew back the arrow. A brave man, even an enemy, deserves a warrior's death, she thought. Such courage should not earn the agony of crackling flames. I would do as much for a dying wolverine.

In the split second between her decision to end the war party's sport and the release of her arrow, the captive turned his head in her direction. His defiant gaze met hers, and in that heartbeat of time, Moonfeather's compassion conquered her common sense. She raised the bow a fraction of an inch and let the feathered shaft fly.

The arrow sped past a startled Delaware brave's ear and grazed a furrow along the prisoner's neck as it plunged into the post. The Delaware screamed in rage and whirled toward the unseen bowman. The war drums stopped.

Head high, Moonfeather stepped from the shelter of the cedar and walked slowly across the hard-packed earth toward the prisoner, bow in hand.

The Delaware raised his fist in anger at the intruder. "Whose woman is this?" he cried. "To interfere with—"

A Shawnee warrior laid a hand on the Delaware. "Take care, brother," he cautioned. "She is no ordinary woman."

Moonfeather's almond-shaped eyes narrowed in silent warning as she slung the bow across her back. The force of her gaze struck the Delaware. Fishmouthed, gasping for air, he stepped back to let her pass.

The captive raised his head to stare at the slight figure in fringed white buckskins coming toward him through the circle of warriors. Firelight illuminated her heart-shaped face, her dark, waist-length braids, and the glittering gold pendant suspended around her neck.

A gray-haired Shawnee brave challenged the woman loudly. "What do you do here? This is not your affair, *equiwa*. This man has been tried by the council and sentenced to death by burning."

Moonfeather stepped past the grizzled warrior and stopped directly in front of the prisoner. For a long minute, she stared into his face, her own features as expressionless as though she were carved of rose granite. Then she laid a small hand on the arrow that protruded beside his head and glanced back at the crowd. "I claim this man," she stated clearly in Algonquian. "By my right as widow, I claim him as my own." She turned again to the captive and spoke in English for his benefit. "I take ye, Englishman," she said, "as my husband. Will ye accept, or do ye choose to wed the flames of hell instead?"

The prisoner blinked and tried to form words with his cracked lips. "Do . . . do I look mad?" he croaked. "I'd take that"—he raised his chin in the direction of the scowling Delaware brave—"that painted devil to wife if it would cut me loose from this stake."

Heated shouts of "No" and "She has no right" rose from the warriors as they pressed tightly around the prisoner. A lone drummer beat a frenzied rhythm, then let his drum fall silent.

One brave pushed his yellow and black painted face close to Moonfeather's and delivered a volley of insults laced with English curses. She ignored him, and within seconds an older warrior seized the young man by the arm, berated him loudly, and dragged him away.

The gray-haired leader who had spoken earlier raised his hand for silence, and the protests faded to a muted grumbling. "Are you men or beasts," the warrior demanded, "that you would forget the law?" He turned hooded eyes on Moonfeather. "You claim this man to take the place of your husband who fell in battle?"

She cast her gaze demurely down toward the toes of the honored speaker's quill-worked moccasins. *"Kihiila."*

"Louder, that all may hear," he commanded.

She raised her head. "I, Nibeeshu Meekwon, Leah Moonfeather Stewart of the Wolf Clan, take this captive as husband. My claim is greater than the stake.

Give him to me, or risk the wrath of Inu-msi-ila-fe-wanu.''

An hour later, Robert Wescott, Viscount Brandon, only son and heir of the Earl of Kentington, lay face-down on the floor of Moonfeather's wigwam with his hands tied behind him. Blood oozed from the fresh gash on his neck and from the wound to his head. Welts on his arms and legs ached, and his bones felt as though he'd survived three score years instead of barely half that.

Lifting his head required a major effort, one Brandon wasn't certain he was up to. It was easier just to lie there and try to suppress the waves of dizziness that assailed him. His mouth and throat were dry, and he longed to ask the woman for water when she came back into the hut, but if she gave it to him, he was certain he'd shame himself by vomiting all over her deerskin rug.

Brandon swallowed, trying to quell the queasiness in his stomach. It's been a hell of a day, he thought caustically, and I'll venture it's going to be a hell of a night.

He tried to remember why the idea of coming to America had seemed a good one. His father had suggested it. ''To keep you out of trouble, boy,'' the old earl had said. Naturally, his father had been furious about the scandal with Lady Anne, and nothing Brandon said could persuade him that it was more idle gossip than fact. Worse, the lady's husband was kin to King George. The lovely Anne, and even the danger from the king, seemed inconsequential compared to those howling savages outside the hut. What would you say if you could see me now, Father?

Someone pulled back the deerhide that covered the entranceway, and a ribbon of firelight spilled across the hut. Brandon opened his eyes in time to see the woman's form outlined against the flames. An armed warrior stood close behind her.

Brandon's muscles tensed. If they've changed their minds and want to make me the main course at supper, they're going to have a hell of a fight on their hands. His hands clenched into tight fists as he strained at the rawhide bonds. Sweat poured down his face; the salt stung his raw scrapes and bruises, but he paid no heed to the pain. He pulled his knees up under him. If he could just get to his feet.

"Nay, *Englishmanake*," the soft voice admonished. "Be still. I've not come t' harm ye. Are your wits addled that ye've forgotten so soon? I've taken ye as husband. You'll meet nay death this night, 'less ye be more stupid that ye look."

"You do speak English," he rasped. I wondered if I'd imagined it, he thought.

"Aye, I do." Her voice was low and clear, the Scottish accent oddly enhanced by a musical cadence.

Brandon felt as though he had wandered into a mad ward at Bedlam. The exotic beauty before him looked like a savage, but her voice was that of a gently bred Edinburgh lady. "You're not Scottish."

"Nay. I am Shawnee." She dropped to her knees and fumbled with something in the darkness. Seconds later a spark sprang to life. She blew gently, and Brandon heard a faint swish and a crackle. Brandon recoiled as a flame leaped up in the fire pit inches from his face. Moonfeather patiently fed a few pieces of wood into the flames. "My father was a Scot," she explained. "I learned your tongue from him as a bairn and later from Alex."

Brandon struggled to a sitting position. "I owe you thanks for saving my life, m'lady."

"It is not saved yet," she warned, rising to her feet and brushing off her hands. "There are many who would like to hang thy yellow scalp fra' their lodgepole." She circled the fire and crouched warily before him. "I will untie ye as soon as I am certain ye will do nothing stupid. Two warriors wait outside wi' full quivers of arrows. If ye try t' escape, they will kill ye. Do ye ken, *Englishmanake?*"

"I'm not certain I could stand, let alone walk." God, but his head ached. He felt as though he'd been run over by the London mailcoach. Waves of nausea made him faint. "You're safe . . . safe enough in untying me," he managed hoarsely.

She sighed. "My English name is Leah. In nineteen summers Alex has not learned to say my Shawnee name properly. It is best if ye call me Leah." She extended a hand toward his battered face, then pulled it back. "I will tend your hurts when I can."

"You need not fear me m'la— Leah. I've never harmed a woman yet." He exhaled softly. "So long as you don't try to slice the hair from my head, I won't start now."

"If you try to hurt me—if I utter a single cry— they"—she motioned toward the entrance—"would cut ye t' pieces. Slowly . . . very slowly." Her expression grew solemn. "Ye must believe me, Sky Eyes. I dinna trust ye—and I know ye dinna trust me, but I am your only hope of seeing tomorrow's sunrise."

"Why?"

She ignored his question. "Where were you two moons . . two months ago?" she corrected. "Were you among the English soldiers who attacked the camp of our cousins the Delaware, beside the Sweet Water? Were you one of the white men who burned women and old people in their wigwams? Did you crush the heads of Delaware babies to save your musket balls?"

Brandon's mouth tasted of ashes. "No," he replied honestly. "Two months ago I was in Annapolis, beside the Chesapeake, and I wish to God I was still there."

She stared at him intently for several minutes, then nodded. "Ye tell the truth. I'd know if ye lied."

"How would you know?"

She sniffed daintily. "A liar gives off the scent of evil." Moving behind him, she began to untie the leather thongs that bound his wrists. "Rub your hands together," she ordered when he was free. She retreated to the far side of the fire. "Quick, before the pain comes."

He did as she told him, as common sense would decree, but the numbness in his hands gave way to agony as blood surged into his cramped fingers. Sweat broke out on his forehead, and he clenched his teeth together to hold back the moans that rose in his throat.

"There has been peace between us and the English for two winters," Leah said softly as she unhooked a basket from its peg along the far wall. "Most of the Delaware braves were hunting a bear. They thought the village was safe because many of the people in it had converted to Christianity. Forty-one were slain, forty-two if you count the unborn babe that was cut from his mother's belly." Her voice grew hard. "The

English soldiers did not kill the young women right away. They left their bodies one by one beside the trail when they were done with them."

Brandon shut his eyes. "I tell you I was in Annapolis. I know nothing about this . . . this atrocity. I'm not a rapist, and I'm not a murderer."

"If I thought ye were, I would have lit the wood at your feet myself," she answered coldly.

He continued to rub his hands and wrists. The pain was easing now, the numbness slowly dissipating. "We heard nothing in the Chesapeake colonies about war on the frontier."

She made a small sound of derision. "Perhaps the death of forty-two *savages* is not important to the English king."

"You can't blame me for what the soldiers did."

She sighed again. "No. And ye canna blame me for the warriors' anger. In war, many suffer. Will ye weep for those four who were with you?"

Brandon's eyes snapped open. "Hayden, Lynch, and the others? They're dead?"

"Aye. They did not die well."

"Damn." He shuddered inwardly. Scum they were and common thieves, but he'd not wished their deaths at the hands of these savages. He'd wanted to kill them himself; he'd fought, but there were just too many. He'd managed to land a few good punches to the ringleader's face before they'd beaten him insensible. Brandon supposed that Lynch had carried the marks of his fists to his death. "I hired Lynch and the other three to guide me into this country. A man in Annapolis said they were experienced woodsmen." Brandon shook his head slowly. "I was a fool to trust them. They jumped me when I was asleep, beat me, and left me for dead. They took the horses and the muskets and everything I had.''

The gold could be replaced once he got back to Annapolis—if he lived to get back. But my surveying equipment . . . By the bloody wounds of Christ! I'll not find the match of those instruments in America.

Leah held out a tiny wooden dipper. ''Drink this. I do not know what it is called in English, but it will dull the pain.''

Cautiously, Brandon accepted the potion and raised it to his lips.

''Drink,'' she urged. ''If I wished to kill ye, I'd find a cleaner way than poison.''

He took a tiny sip; the musty liquid tasted of bark and damp places. Grimacing, Brandon swallowed it in one gulp, and it burned a trail down his throat. ''Arrhhh,'' he sputtered. '' 'Twill never take the place of a good brandy.''

''It will bring healing sleep.'' Leah motioned toward a low platform covered with skins. ''Lay down there.''

''You've not asked who I am.'' For some inexplicable reason, he wanted to hear her say his name in that peculiar accent of hers. ''I'm Robert Wescott— Viscount Brandon. It goes without saying that I'm deeply in your debt . . . and if I get out of here in one piece, you'll be suitably rewarded.'' His words sounded slurred in his ears. Deliberately, he continued, speaking slowly and precisely as though to a backward child. ''I'm a wealthy man of status . . . powerful . . . in the English colonies and across the sea. You do understand what wealth is, don't you?''

''Viscount Brandon? Viscount is a title like Earl. Much the same?''

Brandon lowered himself onto the bed. The dizziness was worse. Had she poisoned him? "Not quite," he said. "An earl is greater than a viscount. My father . . ." He rested his head against a roll of fur. "My father is the Earl of Kentington. When he is dead, I will inherit the title. For now, I am called Brandon."

She snorted. "Ha. So ye be not *so* important an Englishman. My father also is an earl, an earl of Scotland, and that is much better. Alex said so. He says English titles be for sale like hot cross buns, and English lords be weak and cowardly."

Brandon blinked. The softness of the furs and the clean smell of pine and tobacco made his eyelids heavy. "English lords are not . . ." he began, then the absurdity of what he thought he'd heard sank through the layers of cotton batting that clouded his mind. "I'm sorry," he murmured, chuckling. "I must be hurt worse than I realized. I thought you said that *you* were the daughter of an earl."

"Aye. And he proved as faithless as most men." Slowly she began to unbind her braids, shaking loose her heavy mass of silken black hair. Next she stood on one foot and tugged off a moccasin, then took off the other. Barefoot, she padded silently close to the bed.

Honeysuckle, he thought absently. She smells of honeysuckle. He breathed deep of the sweet scent and extended a hand to touch her, no longer certain if she were real or an illusion. "Why are you—"

In a single fluid motion, she slipped her deerskin dress over her head and stood before him stark naked.

Brandon's breath caught in his throat as she let her only garment drop to the floor.

"I told you," she said, "I have taken you for my husband." With a low chuckle, she lay down beside him and nestled her bare bottom against his loins. Before he could utter another word, she caught his left hand in hers and pulled it over her shoulder to rest against a full breast. *"Tauwun,"* she cried out loudly. "Open the door. *Yu undachqui*. Come and witness that I have taken this captive as husband."

Chapter 2

"**W**hy did you do such a thing?" Moonfeather's round-cheeked aunt dipped stew from her cooking pot and ladled it into wooden bowls for her family. "Matiassu is angry with you. You shouldn't have taken the prisoner to husband after you refused the war chief. The *Englishmanake* deserved to die for what his people did to the Delaware village beside the Sweet Water."

Moonfeather raised a finger to her lips and glanced toward her chubby three-year-old son sitting cross-legged on a wolfskin. His round little face was only a shade darker than her own, and his glossy, chin-length hair was as black as a crow's wing. "Not in front of Kitate." she cautioned. She smiled at the boy, and he grinned back at her with an impish giggle that never failed to touch her heart.

Her aunt grunted her disapproval, and Moonfeather looked away to hide the amusement in her eyes. She'd expected her aunt's tirade, even looked forward to it in a perverse way. *She's saying everything I should have said to myself before I claimed the sky-eyed stranger.*

Her mother's younger sister, Amookas, had given

her a home when Moonfeather's mother died in child-birth. Among the Shawnee, blood ties were strongest with the mother's people; clan and tribal status came from the female line. Duty would have forced Amoo-kas to adopt Moonfeather, but her aunt had always given more than what was required. She had been teacher and friend, instructing Moonfeather in the proper behavior for the only daughter of a deceased Shawnee peace woman. Amookas had loved the grieving, half-white child with a fierce passion, de-fending Moonfeather's actions to the other women no matter how outlandish her behavior might sometimes seem.

A warm rush of emotion brought moisture to Moonfeather's eyes. Dear Amookas, I do love her. She's always opened her arms wide for me to run to, and this will be no exception. No matter how she fusses, she'll stand with me. She always has.

Smiling, Moonfeather glanced around her aunt's spacious wigwam. Baskets of dried fish, bags of pem-mican, and bundles of herbs hung from the roof poles. Fur robes were neatly rolled and stacked on the sleep-ing platforms, and her aunt's grinding stone and pes-tle were in their accustomed niche. Some wigwams seemed cluttered when the family gathered around the fire pit, but never her aunt's home. Everything here was clean and orderly. Moonfeather inhaled deeply, savoring the sweet smells of wild mint and drying tobacco. My mother's wigwam was the same, she remembered fondly. I'll never smell drying mint without thinking of home.

"How do you expect to hide what you've done from him?" her aunt continued. "Is the boy deaf and blind that he does not hear what everyone is saying? You've insulted the war chief Matiassu and taken an enemy—perhaps even the slayer of your own husband—to bed." Amookas Equiwa, Butterfly Woman, blew on her fingers and added a choice piece of meat to Alex's portion. Usually the family ate outside the wigwam in summer, but today everyone had taken shelter from the rain.

"Don't you agree with me, husband?" Amookas urged. Her tone softened as she handed Alex the heaped-up bowl and several corncakes.

Moonfeather shrugged. "Anyone who believes that is a fool. Kitate's father has been dead for two winters. The scalp of the man who shot him is stretched on a Delaware hoop." She nibbled at a sweetened corncake. "And I do have respect for Matiassu—he's a brave man and an able leader. I just don't want him as my husband. I have the right to choose a husband. Any Shawnee woman does."

Alexander Mackenzie accepted the bowl from his grumbling wife and settled against the elkbone backrest, stretching his single leg out before him. His green belted kilt was faded and much mended, but the good wool of the great plaid covered his shrunken thigh to the knee. "Let there be an end tae bickerin' in this house. Are we nay kin? I say the lassie be of age. Let her do a' she wishes—she weel anyway." He ignored Amookas's frown and began to spoon the delicious stew into his mouth, taking care not to spill any on his full red beard.

"I'm only thinking of the child," Amookas fussed in her native tongue. "It is not safe for him around such a barbarian."

"The English are barely civilized, that much I give ye, wife," Alexander replied in English. Chuckling good-naturedly, he reached out to ruffle Kitate's hair. "But there's nay guid reason the bairn can't stay wi' us 'til we see which wa' the wind blows."

"I gave him enough of the black drink to make him sleep for hours," Moonfeather explained. "His wounds were not grave, but he lost a lot of blood. He had been injured by the English before he was captured by the war party." She stopped to wipe a bit of gravy from her little son's chin. "Slowly, slowly," she admonished. "No need to gobble like a beaver. Auntie has plenty in the pot."

Kitate licked his fingers and flashed a wide smile at his mother. "Uncle said I can go fishing with him tomorrow. I'm going to catch the biggest fish you've ever seen."

"Don't go far from the village," Moonfeather cautioned in English. She usually spoke to the boy in Algonquian, the Shawnee tongue, when she was in her aunt's home. Amookas understood English well enough, but she never used it. Uncle Alex was fluent in Shawnee as well as French, but he used English with his wife to tease her. The result was that Kitate and Moonfeather's cousins, Amookas and Alex's twin sons, were bilingual.

Alex wagged his balding head. "We'll fish fra' yonder bank, lass. I'd nay put the wee laddie at risk. Dinna trouble yer mind wi' it. Besides"—he motioned toward his tall brawny sons, both silently eating—"my clan weel protect us."

"I'll keep Kitate with us again tonight," Amookas said. "I'd not sleep a wink, thinking of him near that bloodthirsty Englishman."

Moonfeather nodded her agreement. She'd feel better knowing that the child was safe with Butterfly

Woman and her uncle. She was certain she could protect herself from the blue-eyed Englishman, but she'd take no chances with her only child.

Alex fixed Moonfeather with a hard gray stare. "It's nay too late tae change yer mind," he said. "Mayhap we could persuade the council tae trade him tae the French instead of killin' him."

"Nay, old friend," Moonfeather replied in English. " 'Twas too late when I called the warriors to witness our bedding." She rose gracefully to her feet and offered formal thanks to her aunt for the meal. "I'd best see to him now."

Moonfeather bent and hugged her son, nuzzling his soft neck until he giggled and squirmed free. "Mind Alex, love. If you're not good, he'll tell me." She gave Kitate a final pat and glanced at her identical cousins, trying to decide which was Niipan and which was Liiuan. They were growing into manhood and already taller than any other man in the village. "I'll have your scalp locks if Kitate falls into a deep spot in the river," she threatened lightly. The twins were good-natured and fiercely protective of Kitate. If they were watching over her son, she knew she need not worry.

The nearer twin grinned. "The boy swims like an otter. If we fall in, he'd be the one to pull us out. Right, little warrior?"

"Aye," Kitate proclaimed, puffing out his small chest. "I swim faster than an otter, faster than—"

"And brag like Uncle Alex," Moonfeather teased.

She ducked her head and stepped out into the rain. Heads poked through the openings of wigwams, and low murmurs of women's gossip followed her as she hurried through the village. Moonfeather ignored the comments and met the angry stares boldly.

The enormity of the step she had taken troubled her. Suppose the Englishman was dangerous? Had she put her tribe at risk as well as herself and her child by saving Brandon's life? The thought was unnerving. Kitate's smallest finger was worth more to her than the blue-eyed foreigner. And yet there was something about him . . . She sniffed. Common sense told her that she was being sentimental over him because of her father.

No, she decided firmly, it wasn't that. Her father was a Scot and the prisoner was English. They were nothing alike. Hadn't Uncle Alex pounded that fact into her head with his years of teaching?

The wind shifted direction, and the rain fell harder. Drops pelted her face, and she ducked her head against the downpour. As she rounded the last wigwam before reaching her own, Matiassu suddenly appeared in front of her.

Startled, she stared up at him, noting the smudges of yellow and red warpaint that still marred his stern countenance. The war chief's nose was broad and hawklike, his thick black hair streaked with premature gray. Even with his features taut with anger, with raindrops running down his face and soaking his hair, Matiassu was still a handsome man. She wondered if she'd been a fool to turn him down.

"Why did you do it?" he demanded loudly. "Everyone knows I asked you to become my wife."

She tried to step around him, but he barred her way with an outthrust arm. "You have a wife," she said. Her heartbeat quickened. *I should have known he'd not give up so easily.*

"I would have made you my first wife." The hand at his side knotted into a tight fist. "You shame me by taking an enemy—a white man—in my place."

She forced a thin smile. "You're a good man, Matiassu," she soothed, "but I don't want you for husband. We're not for each other."

He seized her shoulder and yanked her close against his bare, muscular chest. "I will have you, Moonfeather. I will have you, and I will have his scalp. I swear it!"

Ripples of fear spread through her body; her breath caught in her throat. *Don't struggle against him,* her inner voice cried. Knowing it was useless, she stood rigid. "You have the strength of a bear, Matiassu. I won't fight you, but neither will I yield."

His mouth descended on hers in a hard, demanding kiss. His fingers twisted in her hair as he crushed her against him. Anger rose from the pit of her stomach to beat back the fear. *Don't let him best you,* her spirit voice insisted. Moonfeather concentrated on that small voice, offering no resistance to Matiassu's kiss, giving him no more response than if she were a woman carved of cedar.

When he released her, his eyes were clouded with shame and remorse. "Moonfeather," he managed, "I . . ." He trailed off and stepped back away from her. "You invade my dreams, woman. I cannot eat or sleep. By the blade of the Great Hunter! What do you want of me?"

She met his eyes for an instant, then let her gaze flicker past him to focus on the green rim of the encroaching forest. The boughs of the great hemlocks swayed in the wind. Water dripped from their dark green needles to soak the rich humus beneath. The air was heavy with the scent of the damp earth and the smoke of cooking fires.

"What do you want, Moonfeather?" he repeated. His deep voice cracked with emotion.

"To be left in peace."

He shook his head. "You ask what I cannot give. Ask something else of me."

Color stained her cheeks as she tore free of his grasp. "Take care, Matiassu," she warned, "that I do not seek vengeance against you for slighting my honor. A woman is not game to be hunted."

"What greater honor can I offer than to ask you to marry me?"

"I'll be no man's second wife."

"Then I'll put Cawasque aside. I'll divorce her."

"And your children? What will they say when you discard their mother for a younger woman? She's a good woman and a loyal wife. She deserves better!"

"And what of your own son, Kitate? Doesn't he deserve better?"

Her eyes darkened to glittering ebony stones. "It's my right to choose," she replied. "I've taken the Englishman for my husband, and you'll never have me. Not today, not tomorrow—not so long as the spring sun melts the ice of winter."

His answer grated like bone against bone, chilling her more than the cold rain. "You will," he promised harshly. "You will lie beneath me, and you will bear my sons—if I must kill a hundred white men to accomplish it."

"In your dreams, Matiassu!" She met his challenge without flinching and flung back her own. "The *Englishmanake* is mine now, and I will fight to keep him."

* * *

Brandon woke to the sound of rain on the bark roof above his head. For an instant, he wondered where he was. Then everything that had happened since his capture by the Indians came flooding back in a rush of tumbled, frightening memory. Painfully, he raised his hand to his head, gingerly exploring his cuts and bruises, gauging their severity. His seeking fingers found the arrow wound on his neck; it was covered with a greasy substance. He sniffed the sticky ointment—it smelled strongly of mint.

Head spinning, he sat up slowly and looked around the hut. The open doorway and the coals glowing in the fire pit gave enough light to see the interior of the wigwam at a single glance. The woman was nowhere in sight.

He blinked, trying to focus with one swollen eye. He couldn't tell what time of day it was. It had been dark when . . . "Damn." He exhaled softly. It had been night when the woman had called the warriors into the hut. He'd seen a painted brave lift a war club over his head. The bloodstained club had plunged down, missing him by inches.

"Hours ago," he murmured, rubbing his head again. "I must have passed out." If the Indian had clubbed him, he would have been dead. What demented game were they all playing? And where was the woman?

As if in answer to his question, she ducked through the low doorway. "You're awake," she said in English. "How do ye feel?" She began to pull off her moccasins; they were soaked through by the rain.

Brandon stared at her. Dripping wet and dressed in animal skins, she was still a beauty. Her wide brown eyes were fringed with thick, dark lashes, and her nearly classic features were enhanced by a flawless complexion and perfect white teeth. Seen in the light of day, she was younger than he'd believed her to be before. Much younger, but definitely not a girl. No girl ever exhibited such a lush, womanly figure. "Is it . . . Leah?"

"Aye. Do your hurts trouble ye?" Her huge liquid eyes watched him warily as her deerskin skirt followed the moccasins. Under the skirt, she was wearing nothing more than a narrow loincloth of dark smooth fur. Still eyeing him cautiously, she tugged her sleeveless vest over her head. Brandon caught a quick glimpse of her shapely breasts before he turned his head away.

"Damn you, woman!" he said, flushing with embarrassment. "Can you do nothing but strip yourself bare in front of strange men?"

Leah's mouth dropped open in astonishment. "Have I insulted ye?"

Brandon glared at the broad stitches that held two sections of bark wall together, his back rigid.

She laughed softly, and he heard the faint pad of her bare feet on the deerskin rug. "I did not mean to offend thy honor, Englishman. But my clothes be wet. What would ye have me do? Catch my death?"

His head snapped around, and the breath caught in his throat. She was wearing a white fringed skirt that fell to mid-thigh. Her breasts were bare.

She smiled at him, and he felt heat rise to his hairline. "Would you have me treat you as a common streetwalker?" he demanded roughly. There was no denying the familiar tight sensations in his loins. He swallowed hard, remembering the stake. This woman had snatched him from a fiery death . . . but it could be that her own flame burned hotter. Instinct told him that a misstep could cost him his life.

Her brow furrowed as she crouched before the fire pit. "I do not know this word . . . this *streetwalker*. It be bad?"

"I've not had personal association with your race before, but it can't be the usual practice for respectable Indian women to offer themselves to the enemy."

Leah's eyes narrowed, and her voice took on a thread of steel. "I've offered ye nothing but your life, Englishman. As ye say, you be the stranger here. Do not judge what ye dinna ken."

"When a woman climbs into my bed, I assume that's an offer," he replied hotly. "That's what happened last night, unless my head wounds are worse than I think."

"Ye be in *my* bed," she corrected stiffly, "and in *my* wigwam. I took ye from the stake to save your life, and"—she sighed—"and for reasons of my own. There was no other way but to make ye my husband." She took two corncakes from a basket and laid them on stones before the fire. "It may be that we will both regret what I did, but if I had not"—she spread her hands gracefully—"your soul would be wandering on the endless river this day."

"If I'm to play your game, m'lady, at least be good enough to tell me the rules. Am I permitted all the usual rights of a husband?"

It was Leah's turn to blush. "A Shawnee husband has no *rights,* as you call them. The pleasures of the mat are the gifts a man and woman give to each other. I have no wish to share pleasures with a barbarian."

"Damn you, woman! Speak plain! What in the

name of all that's holy are you about? Is this some new kind of torture?'' He stood up, ignoring the ringing in his head, and took a wobbly step in her direction. She tensed, and he sensed her fear. Another second and she would spring up and flee. ''Don't run from me,'' he said. ''I told you I wouldn't hurt you. I just want to know the rules before I break one and end up with my head on that bloody stake out there.''

''I'm not afraid of you.'' She averted her eyes and busied herself with the corncakes. Her hands were trembling.

Brandon exhaled slowly and settled back down on the sleeping platform. He rested both hands on his knees. ''Woman . . . Leah . . . what do you want of me? Am I to consider myself your prisoner?''

Her finger touched the hot stone and she flinched, popping the burned finger in her mouth like a child.

Leah's eyes met his, and he sensed the force of emotion behind her gaze. Damn, but she's a rare beauty, he thought. Any other time, any other place, and he'd . . .

''It be our custom,'' she said softly, ''when a woman has lost a husband or a bairn . . .'' She rose to her feet and approached him hesitantly. ''My husband was killed in battle by the English. It is my right to choose a captive to take his place. If I do so, that man . . . you . . . take his place. When I called the men to witness our bedding last night, it was . . .'' She sighed heavily. ''I am nay certain I ha' all words. 'Tis like handfasting among the Scots. Do ye ken?''

He nodded. ''A common law marriage.''

''Aye. So in the eyes of my people, we be man and wife.''

''If I'm your husband, then why did you tell me

some bloody buck was standing outside the hut ready to put an arrow through my gut?''

'' 'Twas true. Ye be my husband, but ye be not Shawnee—not yet. Ye are''—she chewed at her lower lip in search of words—''on trial yet.''

"And how do I survive this trial?"

A smile played at the corners of her lips. "Ye maun be verra good. Ye will be permitted the freedom of the village. Later, ye will hunt for this house. Ye will sleep and eat here in my wigwam. In time, if the people believe ye to be human, they will make ye Shawnee.''

"You don't look like a woman who would have to take these measures to find a husband. There must be Indian men willing to—''

Her obsidian eyes flashed warning. "Aye, there were men willing. But I was not.''

He caught the scent of honeysuckle from her hair, and he felt a sudden urge to pull her into his arms and taste those ripe, rose-tinted lips. "You know this can be no true marriage,'' he challenged.

"True enough for my need,'' she flung back.

"How long to you expect to keep me here? As your . . . your *husband?*''

"Aiyee, *Englishmanake*,'' she murmured softly. "Ye do not ken, do ye? Once ye become a Shawnee, there is no going back. So long as ye draw breath, ye maun remain here.''

He swore a foul oath. "Then I am still a prisoner.''

She shrugged daintily. "Aye, husband . . . but a live one.''

Chapter 3

Brandon's lips were firm as they pressed against her own. His eyes were open; his bold stare daring her to accept his advances. He drew back the feathered cloak that covered her naked body and let his gaze travel over her full breasts, her unclad thighs.

"Leah," he whispered, "wife." His questioning blue eyes reflected the glow of the firelight, and she trembled as the intensity of his scrutiny brought a flush of heat to her body.

"No!" she wanted to cry out. "Don't!" But the words died unspoken on her lips. Her breath came in short, tight gasps as the man scent of him invaded her nostrils, tantalizing her senses . . . forcing her to lie waiting beneath him, eager for his touch.

As if sensing her thoughts, he took her chin in one broad hand, letting his thumb caress the softness of her throat with gentle, soothing motions. "Shhh," he whispered. "Don't be afraid, Leah. I'll not hurt thee. I'd never hurt thee." His unbound hair, the color of ripe corn tassels, fell in shining ripples against her skin, and she reached up and fingered a lock, marveling at the silken texture.

He lowered his head to kiss her again, and against

her will she parted her lips and tasted the warm sweetness of his mouth and tongue. Languid desire flooded her limbs as she put her arms around his neck and pulled him down to her. Their kiss became more passionate, and she felt herself slipping deeper and deeper under his spell. Too long had she slept alone . . . too long had she watched other women go into the arms of their men. She moaned as his hand moved down her throat and shoulder to cup a love-swollen breast and tease her nipple into a hard nub of yearning.

"Leah." His breath was hot on her bare flesh. "Shall I do this? And this?" His tongue brushed her nipple, and she cried out with pleasure. "Such beautiful breasts," he murmured, "made for a man to love."

She dug her nails into his broad back and arched against him, gasping as he let his hands move over her belly and slide down her thigh. Their mouths met again, and the intensity of the kiss fanned the flames that radiated from the pit of her stomach. "Brandon," she whispered hoarsely. "Brandon."

His hard male body pressed down against her; his muscular legs wrapped around hers, and she felt the throbbing urgency of his tumescent shaft hot against her trembling flesh.

"Leah?"

She tossed her head, throwing one arm against the side wall of the wigwam. The back of her hand struck the smooth bark, and her eyes snapped open.

"Leah? What's wrong?"

She sat bolt upright and stared across the fire pit to where Brandon lay on his bed of skins on the far side of the hut. Her cheeks grew hot as the memory of her vivid dream filled her mind. She drew in a long, shuddering breath and closed her eyes to shut out the sight of Brandon's face. To her dismay, the image of his sinewy body and the sensuous feel of his golden hair came rushing back with terrifying intensity.

"Are you all right?" he demanded.

Leah opened her eyes again, flung back the feathered cover, and rose from the sleeping platform. Quickly, she pulled on her short deerskin skirt and a quill-worked, laced vest that covered most of her breasts. " 'Twas nothing," she said. "A dream." She wiggled her feet into her moccasins and tried to clear her mind of the disturbing images.

What had put such thoughts into her head? This marriage with Brandon was not a true one. She would never think of taking the pleasures of the mat with a barbaric Englishman . . . or would she? Leah inhaled deeply and tried to push the thought away.

No man had shared her blanket since the death of her husband. According to the custom of her people, a widow was free to enjoy sex with any man she pleased—at least with any man who was unwed. She was a matron, a grown woman. What she did with her life and her body was her own choice. An unwed maid might be considered unchaste if she allowed men too many favors, but no such laws restricted a widow or a divorced woman.

Sex had never been a problem between her and her late husband. It was—she remembered with a twinge of regret—the best thing about their marriage. No, she corrected herself, the best thing was their child, Kitate.

Brandon rose and squatted beside the fire pit, adding small twigs to the coals and blowing on them to make them catch fire. He wore the remains of his tattered breeches, now streaked with soot and blood-stains. He was barefoot and unclad from the waist up. His corn-colored hair was held back from his face by a rawhide thong.

Leah watched in silent approval. In the three weeks since she had brought him to her wigwam, he had learned something of building and maintaining a proper fire. "Today we must hunt," she reminded him. "Too long ha' we depended on the charity of our neighbors. We finished the last of the meat yesterday."

He looked up. "Three weeks, and they"—he mo-tioned toward the entrance flap—"haven't let me get far enough away from the camp to piss in private. What makes you think *they'll* let me go hunting?"

"It is time." She joined him by the fire. From a birchbark container, she took a little cornmeal mixed with dried berries. She measured several handfuls into a cedar bowl and added water from a gourd. In sec-onds, she had patted out several flat patties and laid them on a clean rock to bake.

"I'll be back before those are ready," he said. He went to the entranceway, ducked low, and disap-peared outside.

Leah repeated his words softly, trying to catch the rhythm of his speech. English was not spoken as she spoke it, Brandon had informed her haughtily. He had said that what Leah spoke was "badly accented Scot-tish." His mocking had smarted, and she'd made an effort to imitate his speech when they were alone. After all, if she was ever required to translate English for her tribe, she'd not want the Englishmen to believe she was an ignorant savage.

Of course, Brandon had shown his lack of proper upbringing by making fun of her speech. No Shawnee would ever think of doing such a thing. She'd reminded him that he hadn't known a word of Shawnee before his capture and that she understood more languages than he did. He hadn't been impressed. "An Englishman has no need for knowledge of an obscure Indian language," he'd said condescendingly.

"I can think of one *Englishmanake* who did," she'd snapped back.

Bringing Brandon into her wigwam and into her life hadn't been easy. Having charge of him was nearly as bad as keeping a pet bear. The women and children were afraid of him, the men hated him, and the half-grown boys taunted him. Once, she'd even caught boys throwing stones at Brandon by the river. Her son, Kitate, couldn't even sleep in his own bed. He was still living with Amookas, and Leah wasn't certain when it would be safe to bring him home.

Brandon was so different from any other man she had ever known that she wasn't even sure she *liked* him. She sighed. That was why the dream had been so disturbing. It was one thing to live with a creature of another species—a pet bear—and quite another thing to find out she was thinking of him as a desirable man.

Not that there was anything wrong with his body. Other than being too pale, Brandon was well built. His belly was taut, his legs corded with muscle, his shoulders and arms brawny. In height, he towered over most of the Shawnee men; when she stood beside him, her head came only to his shoulder. No, his size and form were not reason to find fault.

His hair was impossible. Leah had never seen a man or woman with hair that color. Her own father's hair had been dark red, the color of autumn leaves, a sensible color for a barbarian. Most Englishmen had earth-colored hair; Alex had told her so. So why did her Englishman have to be so outrageous? A man should have hair as black and glossy as a crow's wing, hair like Matiassu's or her own. A person could not take a man seriously if that man had sky eyes and white-gold hair.

And now, those eyes and that sun-tinged hair had invaded her dreams. Dreams were nothing to scoff at; they were serious. Often one could see into the future by reading dreams. Was it possible that she and Brandon . . .

"Ptahh!" Leah jumped up and brushed the cornmeal from her hands. Foolish thoughts! What had she come to, that she would imagine such a thing? If she wanted the embrace of a man, she had only to ask. There were many warriors in the camp who would be only too happy to oblige.

She shook out her feathered blanket and rolled it neatly out of the way before settling cross-legged on her sleeping platform and beginning to comb out and braid her hair. "I never meant to keep him," she murmured to herself. "It was only to hold Matiassu or some other man like him at bay." From the first, she had known Brandon must return to his own people. But it would take time—months, or even years. If he tried to escape too soon, the warriors would recapture him. If they did, nothing she could say or do would save Brandon from death.

The way out for both of them was to have patience. In time, Brandon would be accepted by the tribe and would be adopted into it. Even then, he would not be free to leave. But eventually the men would slacken their vigil. She could help her husband return to the coast, and she could still claim to be married. Matiassu would be forced to keep his distance, and she could continue her life as she pleased.

She had accepted the fact that it would be easier to live together if she and Brandon were friends. She wasn't certain if he wanted to be her friend, and she didn't know how to go about forming a friendship with a barbarian. He had angered her when he'd suggested she was a loose woman by undressing before him, and he'd made it clear he disapproved of her wearing only a skirt as most Shawnee women did in the summer. She wasn't certain what it was about her bare breasts that offended him, but she had taken pains to cover them as much as possible.

Now she was troubled. She'd believed she was treating Brandon as she would have treated one of her cousins. Was it possible that she had been enticing him, sending silent signals that she was willing to share her body with him? Instead of decreasing the tension between them, had she only made things worse?

Leah heard a rustle and turned toward the doorway. Brandon appeared with an overflowing pot of water and an armload of sticks. "I brought some more fuel for the fire," he said. He glanced back toward the entranceway. "Only two guards this morning. They threatened to skin me with oyster shells and make a drum of my hide." He grimaced. "I won't repeat what I told them."

Leah rolled her single braid and secured it with a carved bone ornament. "Pay them no heed. Young men always say such things. Besides,"—she grinned—"the women cherish their oyster shells. They ha' to coom many days fra' the sea. They'd nay gi' the men their shells for such a purpose."

"It's a comforting thought." He placed the water bowl in its accustomed spot along the far wall and covered it with a piece of hide. "And the word, Leah, is *come* as in *drum,* not *coom* as in *boom.* Don't pucker up like a dried turnip. Your English is improving." He began to stack the kindling beside the water pot.

Her face flushed with anger. "Did ye ever think, me great Viscount Brandon, that it could be my Uncle Alex who is right and ye wrong aboot the way words are to be spoken? I've only your own say-so on the matter, and I've heard the English lie easier than they break wind."

"The Scots should know about wind," he retorted with an edge of amusement in his voice. "They were always more talk than action."

Leah struggled to follow his meaning. She thought she knew English well, but Brandon twisted the words about to make a different purpose. An argument with him was like the braves' competition for dancing on hot coals. Even if you won the contest, you had doubts if you had really won anything worthwhile. "My father spoke in the manner of Alex, and he was a real lord," she insisted. Actually, it had been so long ago that she wasn't certain how her father had talked. "If he was here, ye would soon see."

"I'm sure of it," he replied mildly.

Leah glimpsed the hint of mischief in his eyes. "Ye

dinna believe me, do ye? Well, it matters nay whether ye do or dinna. " 'Tis true, and there be an end of it."

"As you will, my Highland lady, but the word is still *come.*" He reached for an oatcake, and she smacked his fingers sharply.

"They're nay ready yet."

He chuckled. "I bow to your superiority in the kitchen." He licked his burned fingertips. "What did you have in mind to hunt today?"

"Aatu, the deer." She turned the corncakes. "Did the men call you *equiwa?*"

"How'd you guess?"

"Men—married men—dinna fetch water and firewood unless their wives be sick or heavy with bairn." She rummaged in a basket and came up with a wrinkled man's vest. It was decorated across the back with porcupine quills and fringed along the bottom. "In the forest ye will need protection. Your back is tender yet. Put this on."

He frowned. "You think to make a savage of me so easily?" She held it out to him and he took it. "It stinks," he grumbled.

"Nay, 'tis ye who stink. Ye didna bathe today in the river, nor yesterday."

"In England, a man who bathes once a month is considered a milksop."

"I dinna ken this *milksop,* but a mon who doesna wash is nay human." She wrinkled her nose. "Those"—she pointed at his breeches—"are nay fit for a mon t' wear."

"Keep your hands off my breeches, woman," he warned. "They're all I have left of civilized attire. You've already stolen my boots."

"I gave ye moccasins in return. Elkskin. They will last many years. Do they not fit as your own skin?"

"They fit well enough, but they're heathen foot-wear. My boots were Spanish leather, made by the same family who does them for the duke of—" He broke off with a low oath. "Damn me, girl. They cost more than a country parson would see in two years."

She looked unimpressed. "Eat your corncakes now. If we dinna bring down game, 'tis all ye'll ha' to eat this day." She tugged on a long fringed legging and tied it to her skirt. "And wear the vest," she ordered. "I'll nay be slowed down in the forest by your complaining."

"Yes, m'lady, as you say. I'd not wish to delay your hunt."

Leah fixed him with an unwavering gaze. "Take care, Englishman. I'm nay a fool. Ye'll go wi' me into the woods and you'll do as I bid ye. There are more dangers in the forest that a Shawnee war party, and I for one intend to return to camp with my scalp intact."

"And a fat deer, don't forget that."

"Aye," she agreed. "If the spirits are wi' us."

Brandon's gaze was fixed on the back of Leah's head as he followed her down the steep incline. They'd been walking for hours without stopping, and he was surprised at the small woman's endurance. The undergrowth was thick here, and he had to duck his head to avoid the branches from trees overhead. More than once, he'd admitted to himself that he was grate-ful Leah had insisted he wear the vest.

Sweat ran down his face, and he paused briefly to wipe it away. The air was hot and sticky; the August afternoon seemed to close in around him. He climbed over a rotten log and braced himself with his left hand. Instantly, he felt a sharp stinging and looked down to see huge black ants swarming up his arm. Cursing, he brushed them away and started back down the hill.

His foot slipped, and he slammed down on his backside with a jolt. Ahead, he heard Leah's faint giggle. Damn the wench, he thought. Was she attempting to walk him to death? What had begun as a welcome respite from the Shawnee camp was fast becoming an ordeal. If the shameless baggage wanted to hunt deer, why in hell didn't they hunt them? They'd passed enough deer tracks in the last few hours.

Brandon reached the bottom of the slope and found Leah kneeling beside a tiny, fast-rushing stream strewn with mossy rocks. Her longbow lay on the bank beside her, and she cupped her hands to drink.

"It's about time," he grumbled. "My mouth is as dry as a powder keg." He squatted down and splashed his face with the icy water, then drank. It tasted heavenly.

Leah bathed her face and neck. The end of her braid came loose from the bone ornament and dangled into the stream. When she raised her head, water from her hair dripped down her vest front, making a dark stain on the supple leather. "You walk good for an Englishman," she said.

He raised an eyebrow wryly. "And how the hell would you know how an Englishman walks?"

She shrugged daintily and shifted the quiver of arrows off her shoulder. "We'll rest here until the sun begins t' go doon. Then we shall hunt. I've a broken-horned buck in mind. He has yet to see his second winter, and his flesh will be sweet."

Brandon settled down with his back against a pine tree and his long legs stretched out in front of him. "I see," he murmured lazily, folding his arms across his chest. "We've come hunting for a particular deer. I should have guessed. That's why we walked past enough deer sign to satisfy the king's hunting party." He snorted in derision.

Leah raised her head and stared at him.

Her eyelashes are black as soot, Brandon thought. Thick and long, they framed large, liquid eyes—eyes that glowed with an inner flame. No lovelier creature ever graced a sultan's harem, he decided.

"Ye nay believe me?" she protested indignantly. "I wouldna fash ye wi' lyin' aboot such a thing. I know the tracks o' this deer."

Brandon deliberately closed his eyes. Salome of the Seven Veils with the speech of a Scottish brigand, he thought. Seconds later, Leah splashed a double handful of water in his face. Gasping at the shock, he jumped to his feet. "What in God's name . . ." he sputtered. "Why did you do that?"

She stood a few feet in front of him, hands on her hips, stubborn chin high. "You'll nay laugh at me," she warned. "You are an ignorant barbarian. Ye ken nothing, and withoot me, ye'd probably slip in yonder burn and drown."

Brandon's anger became amusement as he realized how foolish he looked. This slip of a girl—a wench he could lift over his head with one arm—had bested him again. "Truce," he offered with a grin. "Don't torture me further, and I'll believe your tall tale about the broken-horned buck."

"But 'tis true," she insisted. "In summer, we hunt far fra' camp so that the animals nearby dinna fear us. In bad weather, when 'tis hard to walk sae far, we can kill game nearby. Surely ye can see the wisdom o' it."

"I'll believe it when I see your maimed buck."

Leah sniffed and retreated to sit on a flat rock. Pointedly ignoring him, she began to remove her steel-tipped arrows, one by one, from the beaded quiver and inspected them carefully.

He sat down in front of the tree again and let his eyes drift almost shut so that he could watch her without her knowing. He sighed loudly. The woman was an enigma, and she was fast driving him out of his mind.

As long as Brandon could remember, he'd had a good relationship with women. He liked them, all sizes, all ages, and all types. He liked their laughter and the way they swayed when they walked. He even liked talking to them and listening to what they had to say. Best of all, they liked him.

Contrary to popular opinion, he didn't believe that women were less intelligent than men. True, their minds worked differently, but no one could compare the intelligence of a dog to that of a cat. You never knew what a cat would do in any given situation, but he'd known cats that he would have sworn were smarter than most dogs. Women, he'd decided long ago, were cats. They were emotional and unpredictable, but they were certainly capable of logic.

He'd always gotten along well with his mother and his female cousins. And he'd never lacked for the other kind of female company since his voice had changed. A chambermaid had introduced him to the

joys of sex when he was fourteen. He'd been delighted
with the procedure, and he'd not found reason to
change his mind in the years since then.

Brandon had always taken his good relationship
with women for granted. He knew they considered
him handsome, and he was somewhat vain about his
appearance. Still, he worked hard to maintain his
body, scorning the flabby gentlemen who lounged
around King George's court. He'd coaxed women out
of their maidenheads, and he'd even bribed a few, but
he'd never forced himself on a wench. He'd never had
to. Most women, highborn and servant alike, were
quick to show him their interest. So why was Leah
an exception to the rule?

He exhaled again, softly, between his teeth. Leah
was the key to his escape. She'd saved his life, as
she'd reminded him often enough, and she was protecting him from the wrath of those bloodthirsty
Shawnee warriors. If he played his cards right, he
could convince her to help get away. The problem
was, how to play cards in the dark?

Leah seemed impervious to his many charms. He
was no closer to her bed now than he'd been the first
night he'd been led to her hut. She was a beautiful,
exotic, desirable wench, and he was a healthy, red-
blooded Englishman. They were sleeping ten feet
apart, and all they were doing was sleeping.

He peered at her through his lashes. She'd replaced
the arrows in the quiver and was staring intently down
into the fast-moving water. The front of her vest was
damp enough to cling to her perfectly shaped breasts;
he could glimpse a patch of honey-colored skin between the bottom of the vest and the top of her skirt.
A copper band encircled one arm, and tiny earrings

dangled from her ears. Her face was smooth and expressionless; her hair was neatly braided into a thick, glossy rope. She didn't look like a woman who'd just led him on a six-hour march through a trackless forest.

Brandon swallowed, trying to dispel the dryness in his mouth. She was exquisite. He'd find her enchanting even if it hadn't been months since he'd made love to a woman. Being near her twenty-four hours a day was wearing on his nerves. Her skin was soft and warm; he knew that much from the times they'd accidentally touched.

He remembered that first night when she'd lain beside him and put his hand on her breast—when she'd called out to the war party to witness that she'd taken him as her husband. He'd been too hurt and dazed to appreciate that sweet handful at the time, but he'd gone over and over the scene in his mind since then.

What would she do now if he took her in his arms and kissed those full, tantalizing lips . . . if he slipped a hand into that clinging vest? Would her mouth taste of wild honey? Instinct told him that Leah was a woman made for love, a woman who would give and take passion with wild abandon.

She had nerve enough to captain the king's guard. She'd come alone into the wilderness with him, armed with a knife, a bow, and a quiver. He could take weapons from her without raising a sweat; he could take her body and her life if he was that kind of man. Yet she trusted him, acting as though they were still within earshot of her protectors. It would take a harder-hearted man than he was to use force against such womanly courage.

"Leah," he murmured, startling himself that he had spoken her name aloud.

She turned those dark, haunting eyes toward him, and her lips curved upward in a smile.

"Why do you find me distasteful?" he asked.

She chuckled, covering her mouth with her fingertips in a gesture he'd seen her use so many times before. "Do I?"

"You seem to."

It was her turn to look suspicious. "I ha' made ye my husband. Would I do sae, did I find ye, dis—distasteful?"

"It appears so."

She laughed again. "Ye be smarter than ye look, *Englishmanake*," she teased. "But I promise I will like ye better if ye can shoot yonder bow. Have ye the skill t' hit a running deer?"

Brandon flushed and glanced at the hickory bow. It was not unlike the English longbow, and he'd practiced many an hour to master that. "I've not used your bow and arrows before," he said, "but I think I could bring down a deer."

"Good. Ye shall ha' the first shot. The camp will be pleased if you find meat to share."

He got slowly to his feet. "No," he replied. "They won't be. We have a problem, my Highland lady."

Her expression hardened. "What then?"

"I don't hunt deer. I don't hunt any wild game at all."

Her eyes dilated in astonishment. "What? What kind of mon be ye, that ye dinna hunt?"

"A soft-hearted one, I'm afraid," he admitted candidly. "I find no sport in killing animals. Bloodletting is distasteful to me. I kill nothing at all, if I can help it, let alone helpless deer.''

Her brow wrinkled. "You make a joke with me.''

He shrugged and spread his hands. "I'm afraid not.''

"But ye eat my venison wi' a right good will.''

He grinned sheepishly. "I've no aversion to meat, once it's dead. It's the killing I don't have the stomach for.''

For long seconds they regarded each other in silence as color suffused her cheeks. Nostrils flaring, she rose and snatched up the bow and quiver. "I knew ye were different when I chose ye for husband, but I dinna know how different. I thought I ha' chosen a mon!''

Brandon stiffened with anger. "Hold your tongue, woman. You go too far.''

"Do I?'' she taunted.

"If you were a man—''

"If ye were, we'd nay be havin' this conversation, would we?''

Brandon swore a foul seaman's oath. "My manhood, or lack of it, has nothing to do with hunting your damned deer!''

"Nay?'' She dismissed him with a withering glance and began walking away down the stream bank.

"Leah!''

"Coom if ye like,'' she called over her shoulder, "or stay here until the moss grows over ye. I came for venison, and 'tis clear t' me that if our cooking pot needs filling, 'tis me who maun fill it.''

Chapter 4

$\mathbf{B}$randon paused to catch his breath and shifted the dead buck's weight to ease his aching shoulder. True to her promise, Leah had stalked and brought down a young male deer with a broken horn. She'd waited for the animal at a natural salt lick and slain the beast with a single arrow from a distance of thirty yards.

Leah had field dressed the deer on the spot, working quickly to take advantage of the fading light. The job of carrying the venison home fell to him, and she'd given him a few terse instructions on securing the animal's legs together with thongs to make the burden easier to bear. They'd barely spoken since their sharp exchange by the stream, and Brandon's temper was short.

Leah kept walking ahead of him through the thick woods, and he muttered a few choice words under his breath and balanced the buck across his shoulders. Brandon guessed the weight of the carcass to be eight stone or better, and he was dreading the hours of steady march back to the village. "Wait for me, damn it," he called after her, "unless you'd like to take turns carrying this."

She didn't answer, but the fading sound of rustling leaves told him that she hadn't stopped.

"Slow down, or I'll leave your buck for the scavengers," he threatened. He set off in the direction she had gone, fighting to get the deer's head and horns through the briers and ducking when his load wouldn't fit under low tree limbs.

A branch slapped him across the face, and he began to swear again, soundly cursing the tree, the forest, and the entire North American continent. "I should have stayed at Westover." His father's country house in South Wessex was enchanting at this time of year; if he shut his eyes, he could visualize the herds of dun cattle grazing on rolling green pastures and the deep blue surface of the Frome River. "I could have pleaded the wasting sickness, or married Lord Warsham's hairlipped daughter. No, I have to cross the sea to these godforsaken colonies and fall in with a feathered madwoman."

Leah materialized from the gathering darkness and laid a small hand on his arm. "Shhh," she cautioned. "Would ye ha' us killed?"

Brandon swallowed the reply that rose in his throat, and they continued on without speaking until they reached the edge of a stream. He didn't know if it was the same creek they'd stopped at before, and he wasn't about to ask. Leah motioned for him to set down the deer, and he complied gratefully.

"It be too hot to carry it back this night," she explained. "We'll cool the meat in the water 'til dawn. Lower it there." She pointed to a curve in the stream. "Be sure that the water covers it completely. Ye may need t' pile up rocks t' make a . . ." She struggled to find the correct English word. "A dam. Wash yourself free o' the blood, and I'll cook a wee bit o' the liver for our supper."

By the time he'd gotten most of the blood off, Leah had used flint and steel to build a tiny fire and was grilling fresh venison over the coals. "We'll douse the fire as soon as the meat is done," she said. " 'Tis a dangerous time for a campfire."

"Why? It rained only a few days ago, and the leaves are still damp." He crouched beside the flames and held out his hands to warm them.

" 'Tis nay forest fire I fear."

"What then?"

She shook her head, and it was clear from her stubborn countenance that he'd get no more from her until she was ready to talk. They ate in silence, then Leah doused the campfire. She led the way up the hillside to a rocky outcrop. There they took shelter in a niche in the hill too shallow to be called a cave.

Leah showed Brandon how to break pine boughs and piled them up to make a bed. "The pine scent will keep away insects," she said softly, "but 'twill do nothing for snakes. Ye maun take your chances with them."

She made her own nest of pine needles inches from his and curled up and went promptly to sleep. Brandon lay awake for hours, massaging his aching shoulder and listening to the howling of wolves.

It would be a simple matter, he thought, to take the bow and arrows away from her. He was certain he could even get Leah's eight-inch skinning knife without hurting her. Was he a fool to pass up this chance to escape? He knew enough about direction to travel north, and if he went far enough, he'd reach French territory. Since the Triple Alliance in 1717,

England and France had tolerated each other. If war hadn't broken out between the two countries since he'd left home, he could arrange passage back to Europe or at least to the English colonies on the coast.

He'd have to take Leah with him, of course. He couldn't leave an unarmed woman tied up in the wilderness, and if he left her free, she'd have a war party on his tail within hours. For one brief instant, he considered killing her, but the thought was so repugnant it turned his stomach. He rolled over and stared at the star-strewn heavens. He was a prisoner, and now that he had an opportunity to get away, he was too soft to take it. Maybe Leah hadn't been far off when she'd questioned his manhood.

How in the hell had things gotten so mixed up? He wanted to get away from the Shawnee before they murdered him—probably in a particularly painful manner—but he wanted to do it without putting this woman in danger.

She was sleeping as soundly as a baby; she hadn't stirred once or altered the soft rhythm of her breathing. Asleep, Leah seemed so tiny and defenseless. If he betrayed her trust and made her his captive . . .

Brandon sighed. Could he do it? Or would she put up such a fight that she might be hurt in the process? Would he be able to face her, to look into those luminous eyes if he betrayed her faith in him? He rubbed his face with his hands and closed his eyes. I'd be no better than Hayden and Lynch, and no amount of reasoning on my part could make it right.

Leah moaned faintly and burrowed down into the pine boughs. She lay on her side with one hand curled over her head, the other half hidden by her body. In the concealed hand, she held her unsheathed hunting knife.

No, Brandon decided. If he played by the rules, he might be able to stay alive until a better chance to escape came along—a chance that didn't involve risking Leah. His first plan had been the best one; he'd win her confidence, and she'd help him get back to civilization.

At last, his eyelids grew heavy, and he relaxed enough to drift off. When his breathing slowed, Leah crept from her bed and moved off into the forest as silently as a shadow.

A primeval growl wrenched Brandon from his sleep. He leaped up, realized that Leah was no longer beside him, and peered frantically into the pitch blackness. A second roar shattered the quiet night, and the hair rose on the back of his neck. Bear! He'd never heard one before, but no other animal was capable of uttering such a chilling sound.

A low, foreboding rumble seemed to shake the trees. Brandon looked about for a weapon, uncertain whether he should run or stand motionless where he was.

"Brandon!"

It was Leah's voice.

"Machk! Witschemil! Help me!"

His mouth dry and fear numbing his limbs, Brandon ran down the brush-covered slope toward the source of her cry—toward the snarling bear. As he stumbled into a small clearing, he caught sight of Leah, torch in hand with her back against a tree.

"Here," she cried. "Over here. *Lachpi!* Ha' care! It is *machk.*"

"Where is—" His feet froze to the ground as he stared through the trees toward the stream bank. Clouds parted overhead, and moonlight filtered through the blackness to illuminate a small mountain rising from the creek.

The bear reared up on his massive hind legs, threw back his head, and roared.

Brandon felt his stomach drop through his knees.

"Brandon!" Leah screamed. "Here!"

The bear tossed aside the bloody deer carcass and waded, still on two legs, out of the stream. His small, piglike eyes glowed red in the torchlight; his teeth loomed like white spears in the gaping cavern of his open mouth. His growl rumbled out of his belly, low and ominous.

Brandon made a mad dash for Leah's side. "What the hell—" he began. She thrust the torch into his hand and began to light a second branch from his.

"Where's your damned bow?" he demanded. Her torch burst into flames, and he saw the blood on her face and arm.

The moonlight dimmed, but the bear kept coming, step by ponderous step.

"Matchemenetoo," Leah cried out. *"Matchele ne tha tha!"* Shrieking a Shawnee war cry, she rushed toward the bear, waving the burning brand.

"Son of a bitch!" With only a heartbeat's hesitation, Brandon leaped after her. "Back! Get back!" he yelled at the bear. A putrid stench hit Brandon full in the face and his gorge rose. "Yaaa!"

The beast faltered and stood still. He dropped to all fours and snarled at the two humans advancing on him. Leah hurled her torch, and it bounced off the bear's head. Brandon smelled burning hair as the animal reared up again, then turned and lumbered back across the stream.

"Palli aal!" Leah shouted. "Go away! Get!"

The bear stopped and looked back at them, rearing up and giving a final snort. Then the animal lowered himself to the ground and ran off into the woods.

"N'gagelicksi!" Leah seemed to be laughing and crying at the same time. "We did it! We saved the deer! Did ye see *machk* run?" She clapped her hands and twirled around Brandon. "I thought he be Match-emenetoo, the devil beast, but he wasna. 'Twas only a bear." She threw her arms around Brandon's neck and kissed him full on the mouth.

He dropped the torch and tightened his arms around her, clinging to her warmth, meeting her eager kiss with his own.

"Ach, Brandon—" she began.

A twig snapped sharply beside his head, and a feathered shaft buried itself in the tree beside him. With a cry, he shoved Leah to the ground, protecting her with his own body. Stunned, they lay still.

"Get off me," she protested. "Ye be crushin' me."

"Shhh, listen." He strained to hear, but there was no sound other than the wind in the trees. He rolled aside and pointed silently to the arrow over their heads. She nodded, pointing toward a patch of thick brush.

They crawled into the thicket and hid there until dawn. When the first rays of morning light lit the forest floor, Leah wiggled free of Brandon's embrace and ventured out of the undergrowth. Cautiously, he followed her.

The buck lay half in and half out of the water, where the bear had thrown it. There was no other sign of life, human or animal. Even the birds seemed strangely hushed. Brandon noticed that the musty scent of bear was still strong in the air.

Leah went to the tree and examined the arrow. She tugged at it, but the arrowhead remained firmly wedged in the wood. She pointed to the feathering at the end of the shaft. "Seneca," she said.

He grunted. "I was afraid at first that maybe it was your bear devil come back to finish us off."

She sniffed. "A small war party. One warrior, one arrow." Snapping the arrow in two, she rolled it between her fingers. "A small, stupid war party—one that would nay finish off two unarmed enemies."

"Doesn't make much sense, does it?" Brandon spied Leah's broken bow on the ground a few yards away and went to retrieve it. The strong hickory had been splintered in two.

"Save the bowstring," she called. "The bow is useless." He glanced at her questioningly. "The bear. He came at me too fast to get off a shot. I beat him off with the bow."

For the first time, he remembered the blood on her face and arm. "Are you hurt?" By the light of day, he could only see a few dried smears of blood, nothing fresh.

"Only a scratch. I maun care for it. *Machk*'s teeth be bad medicine. The old women say demons live in his mouth."

"Why didn't you let him have the damned deer?"

" 'Twas ours, not his. Let *machk* hunt for himself."

"By the wounds of Christ, I've never seen anything that big."

"Aye, but ye showed courage for an *Englishman*-

ake.'' She smiled up at him, and he saw a mischievous twinkle in her eyes. "Ye showed courage for a Scotsman." She unsheathed her knife and tossed it to him. He caught the handle. "Skin the buck," she said, "whilst I check for sign. I want to see what I can find out about the war party that attacked us last night." She pursed her lips. "Ye do know how t' skin a deer, do ye not?"

"After a fashion."

"Good. Leave the head. As a rule, we use every wee bit o' the beastie, but we maun travel fast this day, so we will take only the choice meat." She smiled at him. "And when we reach the camp, ye must scrape your face again. I dinna care for the porcupine quills sproutin' there. Yellow it may be, but 'tis not human for a mon to grow a pelt on his chin."

Leah crossed the stream and followed the bear trail long enough to be certain the old boar wasn't lurking in the bushes to charge them again. Then she circled back to the area she felt the arrow must have been launched from. After a few moments' search, she found the tracks she had been searching for—those of a lone man. She located the spot where he had waited and watched their fight with the bear and the log he had braced his right foot on when he loosed the arrow.

The forest floor was thick with leaves; there was no bare earth to make her task easier. If she had found a complete footprint, she would have known instantly if the man was wearing a Seneca moccasin or not. The man had not crossed the stream, so there was no chance of finding his tracks in the mud near the water. She did find a freshly broken twig and several crushed ferns—a trail a child could follow—leading off uphill away from the bear's path.

Satisfied that the man wasn't in the immediate area, Leah climbed a tall pine. From the highest branch she could reach, she looked out over the forest. To the north, she saw a red hawk circling; to the south was the deer lick where they had slain the buck. She waited and watched as the early morning mist lifted off the trees. There was nothing to alarm her.

The sun rose hot and bright; the heat felt good on her throbbing arm. She had told Brandon the truth; the scratch would heal fast enough if she found the right medicine to cleanse the wound. Still, it was nothing to ignore. She had seen men die from smaller injuries.

Leah laid her cheek against the rough bark of the tree trunk and thought of the kiss she and Brandon had shared. Why had she done it? One minute she was laughing at the running bear, and the next . . . She had thrown herself into his arms. She had kissed him. No, she corrected herself, they had kissed each other. It had been a very satisfactory kiss if she remembered correctly. Brandon's mouth was clean and tasted of mint.

She moistened her lips with her tongue and swallowed. Brandon's manner was arrogant, but his kisses were not so. She had been kissed by enough men to know the difference. Brandon was forceful without being overpowering. He desired her—that was plain— but there had been no insistence in his demands. It was clear that he had been willing to go as far or as short a distance as she wished. That was right and proper for a man.

She chuckled, wondering how far she would have

allowed matters to go. Apparently, she had been so involved with his kiss that she had ignored an arrow flying past their heads. "Aiyee," she murmured softly. There was more to her Englishman than she had first realized. Perhaps it was not necessary to have such a distance between their sleeping mats. She shut her eyes and let the delightful dream images of Brandon surface again.

"Leah!"

She opened her eyes. What was he shouting about now? She wondered why the English were so loud. Quickly, she began to climb down the tree.

"Leah, where the hell are you?"

She dropped to the ground, landing lightly on the balls of her feet, and picked up her quiver of arrows. Slinging it across her shoulder, she hurried down to the stream bank where Brandon was washing his hands.

"Oh, there you are. I thought maybe the bear had eaten you." He stood up and dried his hands on his breeches. "Did you find out what you wanted to know?"

She shook her head. "Nothing more. The bear be gone, the man be gone."

"Do you think it was a Seneca who shot at us?"

She spread her hands palm up before her. "The arrow was Seneca."

"But you have doubts?"

"The dead ha' no doubts."

Brandon scowled. "Can you for once say what you think, woman?"

Her eyes clouded with perplexity. "I do. 'Tis ye who speaks in riddles, Englishman."

"And it's *the dead have*," he instructed, "not *the dead ha'*. And it's *you*, not *ye*."

"*You*," she said sharply, "ha . . . *have* made a mess o' this deer." She pulled the knife out of the ground and examined his butchering job. To Leah's dismay, there were several cuts in the deer hide other than those made by the bear. One front quarter of the venison was ruined, but both hindquarters were virtually untouched.

"At home, we have huntsmen to do this sort of thing," Brandon explained.

"Ye—you dinna have to apologize."

His jawline firmed. "I didn't intend it as an apology, merely a statement of fact."

"No matter. We'll wrap the meat in the hide. Your load will be easier than yesterday. I'd not linger here longer than we have to."

"And your Seneca? What if he comes back?"

Leah sliced the deerhide into pieces and began to divide up the venison. "A man alone could be a scout or an outcast from his tribe."

"We're hunting. Why couldn't he be doing the same?"

"This is Shawnee land. An Iroquois hunting here is hunting scalps."

"You said Seneca." He squatted down beside her and helped her make a bundle of part of the meat.

"The Seneca belong to the Iroquois League of Nations. Sometimes. You never ken what a Seneca will do."

"Like a woman."

She ignored his comment. "One Seneca I can deal with. A war party would be verra bad. We dinna wish t' meet them without Shawnee warriors at our back."

"But why would this Indian shoot once, then run away?" Brandon persisted.

"I dinna ken, Brandon mine, and that is what frightens me."

They set out without eating; both of them carried a portion of the venison on their backs in packs made of the animal's hide. A short distance from the stream, Leah stopped to cut off a young sapling. As they continued walking, she stripped the bark from the wood and shaped a crude bow with her knife.

"It will not shoot as well or as far as my hickory bow," she said, "but it will give us more than our empty hands to fight with if we do come up against an enemy war party."

Brandon rolled his eyes; it was obvious to Leah that he had little faith in her hastily constructed bow of green wood. She couldn't blame him; green wood had no strength. She paused again long enough to notch the tips and tie the bowstring, then slung it over her back, and they continued walking.

I should have armed Brandon when we left the village, she thought. Then we wouldn't be defenseless. But she hadn't trusted him—she still didn't. She trusted him more than she trusted the Iroquois, she admitted to herself. One thing was certain, she'd not be taken alive. The Iroquois were rumored to have adopted the white man's disgusting habit of rape. She'd fight as long and hard as she could, but if capture seemed imminent, she wouldn't hesitate to take her own life. In that case, Brandon would have to look after his own skin.

They entered a section of very old oak forest. The massive trees formed a canopy overhead, nearly shutting out the light. There was almost no underbrush,

and the walking was much easier. Brandon lengthened his stride and caught up with Leah.

"You're a widow."

"Aye."

"What happened to your husband?"

"Among the Shawnee, it is not good manners to
speak of the dead."

"We're not among the Shawnee. You haven't even
told me his name."

She felt her cheeks grow hot. "I canna speak his
name. That be an even greater taboo." She walked
faster.

"You're educated, Leah. Surely you don't believe
in primitive superstitions. How did he die?"

"An Englishman shot him."

"I'm sorry, I didn't know."

"Why should you be sorry if you didn't kill him?"

He stopped and caught hold of her arm. "Leah,
don't be like this. Last night we—"

She stared up into his sky eyes. "I be not in
mourning for my son's father, if that what ye—you—
wish t' know. We were nay good for each other. If
he had lived, I would have divorced him."

"Somehow, I didn't think you were." He let go of
her arm and brushed her chin with the tip of his index
finger. "I've never met a woman like you, Leah . . .
and that's truth, not—"

"Not what a man tells a *wench?*" Amusement
flickered in her dark eyes.

"I can't stay with the Shawnee forever," he said
huskily. "We both know it."

"Aye," she admitted. She gazed into his dep blue
eyes and felt suddenly breathless, as though she had
been running.

"But . . ." His finger traced her lower lip. "While I'm here . . ."

She smiled and stepped back out of his reach. Her lip tingled where he had touched it, and there was a warm, bubbling sensation in her chest. He was still very close. A lock of his yellow hair had come free of its rawhide thong, and she had a strong urge to tuck it back into place. *"Taktaani,"* she said. "I've nay decided yet."

"I want to kiss you."

She laughed. "And I would like to be kissed." He reached out to her, and she shook her head. "But not enough to lose my scalp for it. Come, Brandon. Let us go while we can. There will be time enough for kissing when we smell the smoke of my village campfires." She whirled around and set off at a steady pace. With a shrug, Brandon followed.

It was late afternoon when Leah led the way into a gully, made a sharp turn to the left, and motioned him to get down. "We're being followed," she said. She'd suspected it for an hour. Then, a few minutes ago, she had heard a flock of crows behind them fly up and call out in alarm.

"I didn't hear anything."

"Nay. You'd not hear bagpipes unless they were under your chin." She slipped off her pack. "You wait here while I—"

His fingers closed around her arm. "If there's danger, you're not going out there and face it alone." He caught her other arm and forced her to sit down on the ground.

"And what help would ye be against a Seneca war party?" she hissed. Fear made her heart pound in her chest, but she was determined not to let him know how scared she was.

"More than you suppose." She tried to struggle up, and he pushed her down again. "Give me that damned excuse for a bow."

"What would ye do wi' it?"

"More than you, girl."

"But ye dinna have the stomach for blood, remember?" she taunted.

"That's hunting. This is survival. Two entirely different situations."

"Ye ken nothing of—" Leah froze and clutched at Brandon's hand as a bone-chilling war whoop rent the still morning air. "Iroquois," she whispered.

"Great. I was hoping it was only the bear."

Chapter 5

The seconds became minutes as Leah and Brandon waited motionless. The ground beneath them was damp, and the air still and hot. Leah listened intently, separating and identifying the woodland sounds that filtered down to her hiding place. Overhead, a squirrel scurried back and forth, padding its nest with leaves and barking to an unseen companion. To the right, at the top of a beech tree, a woodpecker drilled into the bark searching for insects. The *rat-ta-tat-tat* echoed through the tall trees, drowning fainter rustlings of birds and animals.

Brandon leaned close and whispered in Leah's ear. "What now?"

"We wait." She tried to keep her tone light, masking her fear. She had almost convinced herself, earlier, that the man who had shot at them by the stream was not an Iroquois. Now, raw terror threatened her ability to think clearly.

Since Leah had been a child, she had heard stories of the Iroquois and their atrocities. Mothers used the tales to frighten children into staying close to camp; old warriors relived past glories by relating spine-chilling feats of battles against the Iroquois. The difference between those tales and the ones about Matchemenetoo, the devil beast, was that Matchemenetoo was a legend. The Iroquois were all too real and more terrifying than any imagined demon.

Leah's aunt, Amookas, had been captured by the Iroquois when she was wed to her first husband. Amookas's infant son had died on the trail, and her husband had been killed trying to get her back. Amookas still bore the scars of running an Iroquois gauntlet, and she had told in brittle words of seeing her dead husband's heart sliced from his warm body and eaten raw by Iroquois warriors. Leah's grandfather had led the Shawnee war party that later rescued Amookas. Her grandfather was gravely wounded in the ensuing battle and had died of his injuries the following winter.

When Leah was eight, Iroquois had attacked her village. She'd come face to face with a painted Mohawk brave, and he'd seized her by the hair, ready to dash her brains out with his war club. Alex had gotten off a snap shot, putting a musket ball neatly through the enemy brave's forehead and saving her life.

"How many do you think are out there?" Brandon whispered, pulling her back to the present with a start. "Just the one, or a war party?"

She shrugged. "I dinna ken. We're close to the camp for a single brave to stalk us, but . . ." She shook her head. "Seneca, they dinna think as we do. I canna tell ye."

"Do they know where we are?"

She shrugged again. "If ye'd give me back my bow, I'd—"

"Forget it. You're not going to—"

A covey of quail flew up a few hundred feet to their

right. The sudden burst of noise sent Leah to her feet. Catching Brandon's hand, she ducked low and began running down the gully away from the quail. *"Kschamehella,"* she cried. "Run."

The matted roots of a fallen tree blocked their path like a wall of solid earth. Leah ducked to the left and scrambled up the bank.

"Drop the venison," Brandon ordered.

"Mata!" She slipped on the wet moss, and he caught her around the waist and boosted her up.

Something hard struck him in the back, and he dropped to one knee.

"Are you hurt?"

"No." He caught hold of a sapling and pulled himself up the last few feet. They dashed toward a clump of hemlocks as another arrow sped past.

Hidden by the low-hanging boughs, Brandon yanked off his pack and notched an arrow into the bowstring. Cautiously, he parted the feathery green foliage and scanned the forest. Nothing moved. "I don't see him," he said.

"There was only one mon."

"What makes you so sure?"

Leah peered through the branches. There was no sign of their pursuer. "We be alive." She tugged at his arm. "See. I was right nay t' drop our venison."

Brandon glanced down at his pack. An arrow protruded from the bundle of meat. "That's why it didn't hurt when I was hit." He chuckled. "And I thought it was because I was so tough."

She laughed softly. "Ye be tough enough . . . for an Englishman." She looked out at the woods again. "We maun wait a wee bit, but I dinna think he will trouble us again this day."

"Why do you say that?"

" 'Tis a feelin', Brandon mine. I canna explain, but in the same way I ken his coming, I ken the leaving." Absently, she fingered the amulet at her throat.

"Spells? Witch sorcery?"

"Nay," she replied sharply, letting go of the triangular-shaped bauble. He reached out for the amulet, and she jerked away. *"Mata!"* She flushed. " 'Tis no witchery. Just a charm my father left me when he went away."

"And you've worn it ever since. You must have loved him deeply."

"Aye." Her tone grew cold and distant. "But I was *geptschat,* a fool. He left me and my mother to return to his English wife, his white-skinned child." Unconsciously, Leah's small hands tightened into fists at her sides. "My father went awa' in the time o' new leaves, and when the first snow fell, it cast a winter pelt on my mother's grave. She carried his bairn—a son, but they buried him wi' her. Born too soon in a river o' her blood." Leah shivered. "I could have stood my father's leavin', but did he have t' take my mother wi' him?"

"I'm sorry," Brandon said. "Life is hard for an orphan. My mother and father took in my cousin Charles when his parents died of the plague, but it was never easy for him. Nothing we did or said could make up for the loss of his family."

Leah stiffened. "Among the Shawnee, there are no orphans. Each child is cherished, a gift from Wishemenetoo. I had Amookas and Alex." She rubbed the back of her neck. "Alex is a Scot. He was a soldier and my father's friend. He chose to remain among us—to stay with his redskinned sons and his

Shawnee wives, after he lost his leg in battle against the Iroquois.''

''Wives?''

''Here a man often has more than one wife. Alex is married to Amookas and to her sister, Tahmee.''

''At the same time?''

''Of course.''

''Must be a cozy arrangement.''

''Each wife has her own wigwam.''

''And where does Alex live?''

''Sometimes with one wife, sometimes another. Usually, he stays with Amookas. He likes her cooking best.''

''This Alex must be an interesting gentleman.''

''He is a great man, verra wise. It is Alex who taught me French and kept up my English.'' She inclined her head slightly. ''My Scot. He taught me sums and the history of war. I can tell ye the manner in which the great sachem, Alexander of Macedon, made war against the Persian tribes on the plains of—''

Brandon threw up a hand. ''Enough!'' He grinned at her. ''I had tutors enough to hear something of Alexander's exploits. Are we to stand here until your Iroquois comes back with his entire nation, or shall we make tracks while we can?''

''Aye, ye speak sense, Brandon mine.'' She shouldered her pack once more and set off at a quick pace eastward. With a final glance behind them, he followed her.

A village sentry caught sight of them and signaled the boys keeping crows out of the cornfield. The youngest slid down the pole from his stand and ran toward the village, shouting the news that Moon-feather and her English captive had returned from the hunt bearing meat.

By the time Leah and Brandon reached the edge of the town, half the village, including the children and the dogs, had come out to meet them. Leah called warm greetings to her friends and relatives, all the while scanning the crowd for one particular naked child. "Kitate?" she asked an old woman. "Have you seen my—" She broke off with a cry as a small brown body hurled himself between a brave's legs.

"Mama! Mama!" the boy cried.

Laughing, Leah caught her son in her arms and spun him around. She hugged him tightly against her and showered him with kisses. "How's my pump-kin?" she murmured. "Have you been good for Alex and Amookas?"

"Did you shoot a bear?" Kitate demanded, cling-ing to his mother's neck.

"No, but we saw one, didn't we, Brandon? The biggest bear you ever dreamed of." She lifted Kitate high and nibbled his warm belly. "Big enough to eat you in one bite," she teased. Kitate giggled, and she lowered him to the ground. He held tight to her hand and walked along with them as they continued toward the central clearing.

Leah raised her voice, speaking formally in Algon-quian. "Behold, my husband brings fresh meat for the village. Bring your bowls. You are welcome to whatever we have. Share with us the bounty of the forest."

Matiassu came from behind a wigwam and blocked their way. He glared at Brandon with hate-filled eyes and muttered something under his breath.

"You must speak English if you want him to understand," Leah said. "He doesn't understand our tongue."

"And he'll not live long enough to learn it," Matiassu replied harshly.

Brandon smiled innocuously. "Grant us the favor of the path, you trug-moldie sprag."

Matiassu's dark eyes narrowed suspiciously, and his hand moved toward the knife at his waist. Leah's head snapped up, and she stared at Brandon. He was still smiling.

"Matiassu," Leah said quietly. "Let us pass."

Someone in the crowd whispered loudly, and Leah heard her name linked with Matiassu's. An old man craned his head to see. Matiassu's muscles tensed, and his scarred fingers tightened around his knife hilt.

"Leah, lass!" Alex called out heartily. He hobbled toward them on his crutch, his tall sons flanking him on either side. "Welcoom home. We were worried aboot ye when ye didna coom back last night." Alex slapped Matiassu on the shoulder. "Fresh meat. Be certain ye take some for yer lady. She's been fussin' aboot the lack o' it in yer pot."

Amookas squeezed her ample body between Matiassu and Brandon. "Moonfeather, child," she cried in Algonquian. "I've been worried out of my mind. What were you thinking to spend the night in the forest with a barbarian?"

With a final sullen glare, Matiassu stalked away.

Alex motioned with his head. "Ye've nay seen the last o' him, lass," he warned. "Take care." He turned his attention to Brandon. "And well for ye, ye didna harm m' lassie," he said. "She trusts where she shouldna. There be ways and ways for a mon t' reach the gates o' hell. Do ye bring hurt t' Leah, I'd find a way t' make certain ye—''

"Brandon will nay hurt me, Alex," Leah assured him. "He is my husband. And English or not, he is a good man. He had plenty of chances to run in the forest, and he didna. He helped me drive off a bear and fight off an Iroquois."

"Iroquois?" Amookas frowned. "What is this of Iroquois?" Her two sons crowded close. "Tahmee!" Amookas called to a tall, thin woman scraping a deerhide. "Come quick, sister, and hear what's happened."

"Someone shot at us in the forest," Leah explained. "We saw Seneca arrows last night and again this morning. And we heard an Iroquois war cry, not an hour's march from here, at the place of *Thee-po-a-thee*. I think it was one man, rather than a war party, but our warriors must be alerted."

"Aiyee!" Amookas raised her hands in shock. "To come so close." She glanced anxiously at her sister. "Iroquois," she repeated for Tahmee's benefit. "Moonfeather and the *Englishmanake* were attacked by Iroquois."

"Oooo." Tahmee's eyes widened in disbelief. "Those butchers! They dare to come again to our hunting grounds!"

"Let us sit," Alex said. "Coom to the house and let us hear this tale from beginning to end. Aye, wife?"

Amookas nodded vigorously. "Yes, yes. Come to my fire and eat. I will divide the venison, and we can all hear of these evil happenings."

Niipan, Alex's son, went to fetch the council members who were present in the village. In minutes, nearly everyone in the camp had gathered around the entrance to Amookas's wigwam to listen to Leah's recounting of their encounter with the bear and the unseen Seneca.

Matiassu volunteered to lead a scouting party of young braves to search for sign of the intruder, and Tuk-o-see-yah, the sachem, ordered a heavy guard set around the village.

"No women or children are to leave the camp or cornfield areas," Tuk-o-see-yah ordered in Algonquian. "This Seneca may be a lone warrior seeking to win honor by taking captives or scalps, or he may be an advance scout for a major attack. We will risk none of our people."

Leah respectfully repeated her suspicion that the unseen attacker might not be an Iroquois at all, but someone using Seneca arrows. The sachem refilled his pipe with tobacco, lit it, and puffed slowly while he considered her idea.

Brandon took a hard look at the old man. Even though he'd understood almost nothing of what had been said, it was obvious to him that Tuk-o-see-yah was some sort of chief or man of great importance. The sachem was short and bony, his sagging face a mass of leathery wrinkles. His hair was white as milk and hung in two braids to his shrunken thighs. The aging leader wore a mantle of silver-tipped fox fur despite the heat of the August day. His leggings were of scarlet trade cloth, adorned with silver bells; his leather moccasins were worked with red, blue, and silver beads in an intricate floral design. Copper disks dangled from his ears, and a small cap woven of turkey feathers crowned his receding hairline.

"What you say is so, daughter of a peace woman,"

Tuk-o-see-yah admitted finally. A small girl-child wiggled into his lap, and he bent his head to kiss the back of her neck. The child's mother called her away, and Tuk-o-see-yah focused on Leah again. "The Seneca may not be a Seneca at all."

"What if it was not a man?" Tahmee called, gathering her small sons into her arms. "What if the bear was really Matchemenetoo in the skin of a man?"

"Woman's fancies," a grizzled warrior muttered. "Let us seek out this Seneca, I say. Let us ask him why he has brought violence to Shawnee land."

"Manese speaks true!" another woman shouted.

"Yes! Yes!"

"Find the Seneca!"

Tuk-o-see-yah raised his wrinkled hand for silence. "Iroquois or demon, we will seek out this intruder and drive him from our hunting ground. Women, cease to frighten your children with tales of Matchemenetoo. Men, sharpen your spears and tighten your arrowheads. We are Shawnee. We fear nothing that walks by day or flies by night. Is it so?"

"It is so!" Amookas answered stoutly.

"We are Shawnee," echoed another woman.

Gradually, the crowd thinned. Families went to their own wigwams and young braves to their guard posts. Leah remained seated on the ground near the old sachem and Alex the Scotsman with her aunts, Amookas and Tahmee, beside her. Leah's son, wearied by all the excitement, had fallen asleep in her arms.

"Does Tuk-o-see-yah speak English?" Brandon asked Leah.

"The sachem understands your tongue," she replied quietly, "but he won't speak to you." She sighed and glanced at Alex for help.

"Tuk-o-see-yah canna see or hear ye," Alex said, taking a puff of the sachem's pipe and passing it back to the old man. "Ye be a captive, the lowest form of life." The Scotsman grinned. "He wouldna recognize a Mohawk prisoner. 'Twould gi' him status, ye ken. And as an *Englishmanake . . .*" He shrugged. "Ye would need t' rise a great deal to coom equal wi' an Iroquois warrior."

Brandon scowled. "I'm a lord of the realm, a viscount, and, if I live long enough, I'll be a belted earl."

"And Tuk-o-see-yah is a sachem of the Shawnee. Were he born English, he'd be a prince or a king. This old mon is general, ambassador, judge, and ruler. If he nods his head, he can set ye free or ha' ye chopped into wee bits for fish bait. Tread lightly, me haughty English laird. If ye insult Tuk-o-see-yah, Leah canna save ye."

"I had no wish to offend your . . . their chief. I just wanted to ask—"

"Shhh," Leah said. She shook her head. "Amookas, would you take him?" The older woman lifted Kitate into her arms and carried him inside the wigwam. "Honored sir," she said, addressing the sachem in Algonquian. "My husband made no attempt to escape. He showed courage against the bear and against the man who attacked us. I would make of you two requests, first that he be permitted to carry weapons, and second that I might seek out a sponsor to adopt him as a member of our tribe." Leah laid a hand on Brandon's arm and repeated in English what she had said.

"Just don't expect me to be his foster mother," Amookas said as she emerged from the entranceway. "I've no use for *Englishmanake,* and I'll have none at my campfire."

Leah chuckled. "No aunt, I'll not ask you. For if you 'gave birth' to my husband, he'd be my clan brother. If I wish to share my bed with him, he must be adopted by a woman of another clan." She glanced meaningfully at Tahmee.

Brandon's eyes clouded with confusion.

"Tahmee is not my mother's sister," Leah explained. "She is the sister of Amookas's first husband, my aunt by marriage. All the women of my mother's blood, including me, are born into the same clan. I am a Wolf. Tahmee is a Turtle. If she wishes to, she may sponsor you for adoption."

Tuk-o-see-yah closed his eyes and puffed on his pipe. Alex propped the stump of his amputated leg on his good leg and began to whittle on a piece of cedar. Brandon noticed that the Scotsman seemed amused.

"Dinna look this way, Englishman," Alex said. "I be of the Turkey Clan myself, but a mon canna make ye a Shawnee. The power o' sech things lies wi' the lassies. Were it up to me, I'd lift your scalp."

"Hush then," Amookas scolded in Algonquian. "If Tahmee wants to adopt Moonfeather's husband as her son, she can. As you say, mighty warrior, the power lies with the women. Men had best tend their own business and leave such things to women. There is no need for you to be here at all, Alex mine. Did you not say that you would finish assembling that musket this afternoon?"

Tahmee shifted restlessly. Her youngest boy, a toddler, crawled in her lap and began to nurse. Smiling, Tahmee began to rock the child and croon softly to him. Another boy, a year or so older than Kitate, leaned against Alex's shoulder and watched intently as the cedar block his father was carving became a bear.

Brandon's legs cramped. Finally, when it seemed he could sit still no longer, the shaman opened his eyes.

"Someone is restless," Tuk-o-see-yah said. "Someone may wish to become a human being, and who would not. But it is too soon. One who is not yet a human being may be tempted to do evil if he carries a weapon. He might hurt himself or another. Who knows what that kind might do? We will wait, and we will watch. When the time of planting comes, it may be that Moonfeather will ask again. That might be a better time." He smiled at Leah. "You have a forgiving heart, and that is a good thing. It pleases me, and it tells me that the seeds of a peace woman lie within you. If your . . ." He grinned. "If someone proves himself worthy, this one will ask the honored Tahmee to sponsor an adoption in the moon of new leaves."

"Thank you, my shaman," Leah said in formal Algonquian. She nodded respectfully and crossed her hands over her chest. "As you say, sir, the time of planting might be a better time." She rose to her feet and motioned Brandon to follow.

When they were far enough away that the others couldn't hear, Brandon stopped her. "What the hell was all that about?"

Leah reached for her bow and arrows. "I didna think Tuk-o-see-yah would give permission for you to carry weapons yet, but it was worth asking. Now we must wait until spring. Your adoption must wait, too.''

''What makes you think I want to be adopted?''

She grimaced. ''Do ye ken nothing? Until you become Shawnee, you will be watched. Every eye will be on you. No one will trust you. And if you try to escape, 'twill mean your death.''

''And if I was adopted?''

She caught her lower lip between her teeth.

''Well?''

''Some who are adopted leave.''

''Then you lied before, when you told me that once I was a Shawnee, I was here forever.''

''I dinna lie!''

''No, you said one thing, and now another. Both statements can't be true. Either you lied then, or you're lying to me now.''

Leah walked away toward her own wigwam.

Brandon kept pace with her easily. ''There's no way I'm staying here for the rest of my life, woman. Make up your mind about that. I'll get you of here, or I'll die trying.''

''There is nay need for ye t' die, but ye maun ha' patience,'' she flung back. ''Trust me.''

''As you trust me?''

'' 'Tis different.''

''Yes, I can see it is. You're playing some kind of game, and no one will explain the rules to me. That damned Scotsman knew it. He was laughing at me!''

''Alex doesna like Englishmen.''

''He's a white man. He should support me against—''

Leah whirled to face him. ''Aye, your skin is whiter than mine. But dinna think for an instant it makes ye better. 'Tis only that the Creator took your kind from his bakestone too soon. Cut your white skin, Brandon viscount, and your blood is no redder than my own.''

"I didn't mean it that way.''

She gave a snort of derision and ducked into her wigwam, Brandon following. "Aye, but ye did,'' she said. She pulled off her vest and leggings and tossed them into a heap on the floor. "I dinna hold it against ye,'' she said coolly. "Ye know nay better. My father said that it was so, that the English all believed their piss smelled sweeter than that of mortal men. Ye be an ignorant barbarian.''

Brandon's throat constricted as he watched her strip away the last of her clothing and stand naked in the semi darkness of the hut. He splayed his fingers against his hips and drew in a long, shuddering breath. He wanted to look away, but he couldn't tear his eyes from her.

Leah's breasts were full and ripe, the color of warm honey; her waist was tiny, her belly too flat for a woman who had borne a child. His gaze lingered on the dark, silky down at the apex of her thighs, and he felt the growing hardness of his loins. Sweat trickled down the back of his neck. "What are you about, woman?'' he demanded. "Must you torment me with . . .'' His mouth felt dry, and he longed to seize her in his arms and taste those sweet breasts, to lay her back against the bed and cover her with his body. Could she be innocent of what she was doing to him? "Must you flaunt yourself in front of me?'' he asked hoarsely.

Abruptly, Leah's mood changed. She laughed. "I'm going to bathe,'' she said lightly. "Ye need to scrub off that blood and dirt yourself. Ye be as filthy as a badger." She wrapped a short doeskin skirt around her middle and took a bundle from a basket on the floor. "Leave the vest here," she said. "You willna need it at the river." She tugged at one shoulder, and he raised his arm to let her remove it.

"Leah . . ." he said. "I can't . . ." He reached for her, and she stepped away, leaving the scent of honeysuckle.

"Not here," she answered. "Come to the river."

His chest felt tight; his heart was pounding. "You know what I want from you," he persisted. "What I've wanted from the first."

She caught his broad hand in hers. "Come to the river, Brandon mine." She stared up at him from beneath thick, feathery lashes.

"Will you?"

She pulled him out into the hot August afternoon. "Yes," she murmured. "No . . . maybe."

Chapter 6

The riverbank was deserted; none of the villagers swam or played in the cool running water. Even the mud slide downriver was bare. Not a single child's voice rang out with laughter. With the threat of an Iroquois attack, mothers had called their children into the comparative safety of the inner camp circle.

Leah paused by the edge of the water, then motioned to Brandon. "Come, we will go upriver." She led the way through a grove of willows and across a small rocky stream that fed into the river.

Brandon glanced around. The thick forest seemed no different than on any other day. Squirrels chattered in the trees overhead, and bright flashes of color heralded the clear sweet songs of multitudes of birds. Leah turned and beckoned to him as she followed a faint path beside the bank. "Where are you taking me?" She laughed and hurried on.

The river curved sharply to the left, and the current rushed faster. The willow trees gave way to oak and chestnut, and finally to beech. The path turned inward, away from the river. Brandon lengthened his stride to keep up with Leah. "Where—" he began. She stopped and turned back toward him. When he was within a few feet of her, she parted the leaves to reveal a hidden glade in the trees.

The green foliage of the thick forest formed a backdrop for a wide pool of blue-green water. At the far end, a waterfall cascaded over a sheer wall of rock thirty feet high. Spray from the tumbling water rose in a mist over the pool, lending an air of magic to the scene.

Leah caught Brandon's hand and smiled up at him. "Do ye like it?" Her eyes twinkled with the delight of a child sharing a wonderful secret. "We call it the Place of the Maiden's Kiss. Long ago, the old ones say, an enemy war party chased a Shawnee maiden to the top of the falls. Rather than be captured, she leaped to her death on the rocks below." Leah put her bundle beneath a tree and unfastened her short skirt. "The next morning," she continued, "her betrothed found her body. He gathered her in his arms and kissed her cold lips, and his tears fell on her fair, still face. Inu-msi-ila-fe-wanu, the Great Spirit who is a grandmother, took pity on the lovers. She couldna give the maiden back her life as a mortal. Instead, she changed them both into hawks, and they flew together up into the heavens. In memory of their love, the waters formed this pool below the waterfall. Only those with loving hearts, the old ones say, can find this place. To any who would do evil, it be invisible."

Brandon looked at her without speaking, his expression wary.

"Come," she said, pulling off her moccasins and standing naked before him, wearing only the gold amulet around her neck. "It be safe for us to swim. The Seneca, if Seneca he be, canna harm us here."

"You really believe that, don't you?"

"Aye, 'tis true. Ye need ha' no fear." She swallowed the lump rising in her throat as her composure faltered. "Besides . . ." She moved toward the bank. "Our warriors are combing the woods for signs of the enemy. We are well inside the circle of safety."

Brandon was still watching her, but his scrutiny had become more intimate. She turned her face away to hide the blush rising in her cheeks. What was there about his unwavering blue-eyed stare that made the space between them seem suddenly charged with unseen power? Something fluttered in the pit of her stomach and she felt light-headed, even breathless.

"Leah . . ." He reached out his hand.

With a cry, she dove into the pool, arching her body and propelling herself deep into the clear, blue-green depths. Eyes wide, she swam down to the sandy bottom, letting the tranquility of the cool water wash the fever from her blood.

She heard a muffled splash above her. Rolling onto her back, she saw Brandon swimming toward her. With the dexterity of an otter, she dodged him and swam upward until her face broke the surface. She waited, and when he came up, she scooped up a double handful of water and splashed him in the face.

He yelled and made a grab for her. His hands closed on empty mist. Laughing, Leah bobbed up behind him. He whirled around and lunged for her, but she spun and swam under water toward the foam at the base of the waterfall. Seconds later, she came up, hidden from his view by the tumbling cascade.

"Leah! Leah!" Brandon called. He rose in the water and glanced around anxiously. "Leah?" Taking a deep breath, he dove under.

Leah's heart was pounding. Brandon's voice was

barely audible above the falling water, but there was no mistaking his tone of concern. He cared for her. The question that plagued her was whether she cared for him.

I am a widow. I can do as I please, she thought. What harm can there be in sharing pleasure with this man? She blinked to clear the water from her eyes. The roar of the cataract in her ears was familiar and soothing, easier to accept than the uncertainty in her mind. *There can be nothing lasting between you,* an inner voice cried.

Brandon's corn-silk hair broke water. "Leah! This isn't funny. Where are you?"

She swam from her hiding place beneath the curtain of water and waved to him. "Here." A half-dozen strong strokes brought her to his side. "Ye dinna think I could drown here, did ye?" she teased. " 'Tis where we teach babies to swim before they can walk. I told ye, Brandon mine, 'tis an enchanted pool."

His blue eyes glared at her. "I tire of your games, woman. What would you—"

She silenced his censure with a kiss, wrapping her arms around his neck and pressing her naked breasts against his chest. At first his mouth was hard and unresponsive, but then his lips softened and his arms closed around her. She opened her mouth to let the tip of her tongue touch his. Brandon groaned, and one hand slipped down to caress her bare buttock.

Leah laughed as tingles of curious hot excitement coursed through her body. "Ye kiss nicely," she dared tell him, and tilted her face to be kissed a second time.

Brandon sank under water and came up sputtering.

"You'd drown me," he protested. He caught her arm, and they swam together toward shallower water.

"I wondered if the English kiss as we do," she said. "Alex said ye do not." She could not keep her eyes from his wide, brawny chest that tapered to a flat, hard belly; from his sinewy arms with their light sprinkling of blond hair.

Her heart skipped a beat as Brandon pulled her roughly into the circle of those muscular arms. "And how many Englishmen has Alex kissed?" His voice was light, but the pressure of his hands was like iron— not hurting, but as solid and unyielding as the oaks that grew from the riverbank.

"Let me go," she ordered. "I canna bear to . . ." He released her, and she moved away through the water. It was easier to think when he wasn't so close, when she didn't feel the full intensity of those strange blue eyes. "We came to bathe," she reminded herself aloud. "Ye maun learn to swim every day as 'tis proper for a Shawnee."

He stretched his arms over his head and leaned back against the bank. In the clear water his nakedness was as obvious as hers. "Even in winter?" he said.

"Aye, especially in winter. We break the ice to bathe in the time of bitter cold."

He laughed disbelievingly. "I wonder that any of you live to be a danger to the colonists."

She shook her head as she unbound her hair and let it fall around her shoulders and over her breasts. " 'Tis nay enough to swim," she replied. "Ye maun scrub away the dirt and man smell, lest the animals ye go to hunt smell ye long before ye come into bow shot." She scrambled up the bank and went to the spot where she had dropped her bundle. "I have herbs that will make a lather to clean ye, Brandon mine. 'Tis time, for I canna sleep much longer in the wigwam wi' ye if ye willna wash."

"No woman ever complained of my smell before!"

Leah laid a gourd on the bank and slipped back into the water. "Turn around so I can clean that great back of yours," she instructed. She kept her eyes down so that he could not read the amusement she knew must show there. It was true what Brandon had said—he didn't smell badly. But it was also a truth that he soon would if she didn't rid him of the stench of dried blood and sweat they'd acquired on the dear hunt. From the shallows she took handfuls of fine sand and proceeded to scrub his back and shoulders vigorously.

"Ouch," he protested. "Gentle, wench, go gentle. You'll scar me for life."

" 'Tis a waste of my herbs do we nay do this right." When his back was done, she moved to repeat the process with his chest and arms. "The bottom half ye maun do yourself," she said, turning to retrieve the gourd containing her soap mixture. Carefully, she rubbed the green paste into his hair, digging gently at his scalp with her fingernails until she raised a foamy lather. "Now rinse," she commanded.

"I suppose that stuff will make me smell like a goat," Brandon said, ducking his head under.

"If it does, we will smell like goats together," she answered pertly. Taking more of the paste, she swam a distance away. Brandon's gaze never left her as she repeated the process with her own hair.

"I hope you're satisfied," he said when she'd finished. "I feel like a plucked goose, scalded and scrubbed for market." He held out his arms to her. "Come here, love."

Laughing, she dove under and came up within arm's reach. "I be here." She shook her hair, spattering him with drops of water, and he sputtered.

"Closer."

Playfully, she pushed a lock of wet hair off his face, wondering at the color. " 'Tis like sunlight," she said. "Your hair . . . It is outrageous, no proper color for a man's hair."

"No man could say that of your hair, Leah. It's beautiful . . . like satin." He touched her hair, then let his fingers brush her throat. "Here in this place, you don't look real. Are you certain you're a flesh and blood woman?" He leaned forward and kissed the spot he had touched. "Are you real, Leah, or just a dream?"

She laughed up at him through the curtain of her thick lashes, pretending amusement, trying to hide the aching rush of desire that threatened to engulf her.

He nuzzled her throat, trailing kisses up to her mouth, then drew away. "I asked you before how many Englishmen Alex has kissed," he murmured.

"Alex has nay kissed any Englishmen." She sighed. "He nay be one who takes pleasure wi' other men. He was speaking in . . . in general of Englishmen when he said they kissed like crows."

He tilted her chin up with a callused thumb. His voice came low and husky. "And just how do crows kiss?"

She puckered her mouth. "As though their lips were hard, narrow beaks," she explained. "Cold lips, Alex said, cold kisses wi' out passion."

"Do you always believe everything Alex tells

you?'' Brandon was so close she could feel his warm breath and see the tiny gray specks in his sky-blue eyes. His hands on her back were faintly tremulous.

"Perhaps I shouldna." His breath was sweet in her nostrils as she traced the outline of his jaw with her fingertips, fascinated by the stubble of his yellow beard. "Ye be as hairy as Ya'kwahe, the forest spirit," she teased. "The old women say his hair is the color of dried grass. Of course, I ha' not seen Ya'kwahe myself, so ye may be even hairier." She brushed his lower lip with the ball of her thumb. "Ye dinna have lips like *hahees*, the crow, but we havna kissed enough for me to be certain if Alex be right or wrong aboot the passion."

"Would you care to judge for yourself?"

She moistened her lips and leaned toward him. "Aye, Brandon mine, I would." His mouth claimed hers, and a sweet warmth spread through her as their kiss deepened and ignited a fire that burned within. She sighed and clasped him tighter around the neck, crying out with delight as his hand cupped her breast and teased her nipple.

"Leah," he murmured, molding his mouth to hers, fanning the rising flame of desire that threatened her reason. She moaned, wrapping her legs around his waist and running her fingers through the damp tendrils of his hair.

He kissed her again, and she trembled as his mouth left hers and dropped to capture a love-swollen nipple. She felt his thick, hard shaft rising against her bare thigh. Knowing she should stop this before it was too late, she lingered, savoring the honey taste of his scalding kisses, thrilling to the possessive touch of his hands on her bare flesh.

She gasped with sudden pleasure as his fingers caressed her woman's slit.

"Leah, let me love you," he whispered. "Let me—"

"No!" Wide-eyed, she struggled free of his grasp. "I dinna think—"

"Damn you, woman!" He pushed past her and dived deep into the water. She was weeping when he came up. "Spare me the tears," he said sarcastically. "What was I to expect when you brought me here alone, swam naked with me, and let me—"

"No," she protested. " 'Tis ye who dinna understand. I thought we would kiss; I thought we would touch, but among my people it does not move so fast between a man and a woman. We are strangers, Brandon mine. How can we let our souls touch yet?"

"I'm not asking for your soul," he answered roughly. "You can't claim you were seduced. What happened between us was mutual."

"Nay, ye dinna force me to do what we did."

He wiped the water from his face. "Am I repulsive to you, Leah?"

"Nay, ye be fair."

"This marriage between us was your idea, not mine. I've done all that's humanly possible to figure you out, but there is no logic about you."

"Ye dinna ken," she pleaded. " 'Tis nay that I willna ha' ye, but I was nay prepared." She gestured toward the forest. "The moon, Brandon mine, 'tis the wrong time o' the moon. If we shared pleasures now, without taking precautions, I might quicken with child."

He scowled at her. "What precautions?"

"There is a leaf that grows in the swampy places

that I must chew. Ye wouldna ken the name if I told ye, but Shawnee women use it to keep from having babies. I canna ha' your bairn. I am a woman alone, and I already ha' a son to raise. If we were attacked by the enemy, or if fire swept through the forest, I could run with my bairn and fight if I had to. But if ye leave me wi' another babe, I couldna be sure of keeping both bairns safe from harm."

"Superstitious nonsense! There is no herb that will keep a woman from becoming pregnant."

"I dinna lie. Of course there be such medicine. How else to Englishwomen space their children and keep from having too many to feed?"

"You lie when you damned well please, the same as any other wench." Brandon turned and waded toward the bank. "Englishwomen take what children God sends them, and if there are too many to feed, they starve."

"Indeed? Then Alex spoke true. Ye be barbarians." She reached the water's edge ahead of him, scrambled out, and snatched up her bundle. "I've no more to say to ye. Find your own way back to the village, or let the wolves ha' ye."

Brandon grabbed a tree root protruding from the bank. As he heaved himself up, it snapped off, and he fell back into the water with a splash.

She stooped and picked up his ragged breeches.

"Damn you, Leah," he shouted. "Leave those be."

Ignoring him, she tossed a man's loincloth onto the grass and ran off through the forest.

"Come back with my breeches!" Brandon ran a few yards after Leah, then stopped when he realized there was no chance of catching up with her. Cursing, he turned back and kicked at the deerskin loincloth. "Damn your eyes," he muttered under his breath. "You'll not make a savage of me, no matter what you do." Still swearing furiously, he donned the fringed garment and his moccasins and set off toward the Shawnee village.

Minutes later, Matiassu stepped from the bushes directly in Brandon's path. "Where are you going *Englishmanake?*" he asked in badly accented English. "Did you think to escape so easily?" The war chief raised the muzzle of the French musket until it was level with Brandon's midsection. "Or do you plot with our enemies to attack our village?"

Cautiously, Brandon raised both hands, palms open so that the Shawnee could see that he was unarmed. "If I was trying to get away," he answered, "wouldn't I be heading away from the camp, instead of back toward it?"

Matiassu smiled coldly and eased back the hammer on the flintlock. "Turn around, Sky Eyes," he ordered. "Turn and run. I give you a chance—the same chance I would give a Seneca."

Brandon stood motionless, his gaze locked with Matiassu's. Brandon swallowed hard as sweat began to trickle down the back of his neck. He's going to shoot me, he thought. No matter what I do, this bastard redskin's going to kill me.

Matiassu's eyes narrowed. "Run, Englishman. Run like the dog you are."

"Is this Shawnee honor—to kill an unarmed man? Drop that musket, and then we'll see which of us is the dog," Brandon taunted. "You're afraid of me. If you weren't, you wouldn't need to kill me this way."

"I fear no man, let alone a pale-skinned Englishman," Matiassu lashed back. "In single combat I have killed four men. I do not need to prove my courage with one such as you."

"Talk's cheap." Brandon's heart was beating so hard he thought it would burst his chest. The sweat was running into his eyes, and the back of his left leg was cramped from holding it locked in place. "You're afraid of me, and you know it," he persisted softly. "You're a coward, a man who needs to hide behind a gun."

"Nee nin dauw," Matiassu replied harshly. He tossed his musket aside and advanced on Brandon. The Indian's right hand closed around the bone handle of a ten-inch hunting knife, and the gleaming blade slid from its fringed leather sheath with an ominous hiss.

Brandon relaxed his muscles and stepped backward, balancing on the balls of his feet. He'd been trained in the art of fencing, but now his hand was empty and his opponent carried a lethal weapon.

"Now who is the coward?" Matiassu asked. "The musket ball would have been quick."

"Still full of talk."

The Indian lunged at him with the knife, and Brandon sidestepped the blow. He snatched a length of broken branch from the ground and swung it at Matiassu's head. The Shawnee dodged the stick and slashed again. The tip of the knife gashed Brandon's right arm, and he spun away with bright red blood running from the wound.

"I'll cut out your heart, Englishman," Matiassu threatened.

Brandon backed away a few steps, holding the stick up to protect himself. Out of the corner of his eye, he spied Matiassu's musket lying on the ground. If he could get his hand on the flintlock . . . "What are you waiting for? If you're going to kill me, come on and do it."

The Indian circled to the left, and Brandon moved with him, keeping a safe distance from the naked steel. Brandon's mouth tasted like ashes, and the sounds of the forest—the birds and the rustlings of small creatures—had faded. The sound of his own breathing was overly loud in his ears. If I don't get my hands on that gun, I'm going to die, Brandon thought.

Matiassu feinted to the left, then leaped right and swung again. The knife bit into Brandon's bare thigh as he twisted away and drew a long, shuddering breath. He moves like a dancer, Brandon thought, gritting his teeth against the pain. He's fast and he's smart. "You move like an old woman!" he mocked the Shawnee. "Come on!" He motioned obscenely. "Come and finish me, if you can."

Brandon stepped back, and his shoulder hit a tree. As Matiassu sprang at him, Brandon slammed the branch down across the Indian's forearm. Matiassu winced, and Brandon kicked him in the ankle. Brandon seized Matiassu's knife hand, and they struggled face to face. Matiassu wrapped his leg around Brandon's, and together they fell to the ground and rolled over and over, fighting for possession of the knife.

Brandon's head struck a tree root, and he saw stars. Above him, Matiassu's face blurred. Matiassu's hand, still clenching the deadly knife, moved closer until Brandon could feel the cold steel against his throat. Brandon's muscles screamed in silent agony as he forced the Indian's hand up a fraction of an inch.

Matiassu's teeth were bared; Brandon could smell the acrid sweat from the Indian's body. He knew Matiassu was near the limit of his strength as well.

"Enough!" Leah's voice came loud and crisp in Brandon's ears. "Drop the knife," she commanded in Algonquian. "Drop it, or I'll kill you myself, Matiassu."

The war chief relaxed his hold and rolled off Brandon. He dropped to his knees, then rose to a crouch. Brandon scrambled up and turned to stare at Leah. She was at arm's length away, her bow drawn taut. Notched in the bowstring was a steel-tipped arrow, and it was pointed at Matiassu's chest.

"Throw down the knife, Matiassu," she warned.

"You wouldn't kill me for *that.*" The war chief motioned with his chin toward Brandon. "We are Shawnee, and he is enemy."

"He is mine! My husband," she said. "And I would kill you as quickly as I would a mad wolf who attacked my son." Leah's arms trembled with the strain of holding the bow. "I would kill you," she promised, "and none would know who had done it. Look closely, Matiassu. Do you recognize this arrow? I took it from your wigwam minutes ago. Look at the feathering."

Matiassu let the knife fall to the ground and turned away, his face crimson with shame. Picking up his fallen musket, he stalked away into the forest without looking back. Leah held the bow in place, the arrow aimed at his back, until he was out of sight.

Brandon exhaled loudly. "Thank you, m'lady. That was well done, and not a minute too soon." He leaned back against a tree and tried to keep his stomach from making a complete fool of him. His arm and thigh were bleeding freely, and he felt light-headed. "What was all that about?" He indicated the direction Matiassu had taken. "Why was he trying to kill me? And what did you say to him?"

Leah released the pressure on the bow and lowered it. She plucked the arrow from the string and held it out to him, feathered end first. "This nay be Shawnee feathering," she said precisely in English. "Look, Brandon mine, and remember. I have found our Seneca."

"Him? But why?"

"Matiassu wants me to be his wife," she explained starkly. "I have taken ye to husband instead."

"So he wants to make you a widow."

"Aye, and Matiassu be a dangerous man. He'll do it, if we canna think of a way to stop him quickly."

"What of the old man? Tuk-o-see-yah, your sachem. Can't you appeal to him?"

Leah sighed softly and reached out to take his hand. "Aye, Brandon mine, we can. Tuk-o-see-yah is a wise man and a great leader. We may ask him for justice, but . . ." Her eyes grew large and troubled.

"But? But what?"

"Matiassu is his only grandson."

Chapter 7

That night, Leah sat in her aunt's wigwam holding Kitate and singing him Shawnee lullabies until he fell asleep. "I have missed him so much," Leah admitted as she tucked him into his sleeping robe and put his favorite toy beside him. "My house seems empty without his laughter."

Amookas took a long draw on her soapstone pipe and sighed loudly. "Did I not warn you, child of my heart? Did I not say that the sky-eyed *Englishmanake* would bring you nothing but unhappiness?" She passed the pipe to her husband. "Alex mine, did I not say the man was bad luck?"

Alex nodded solemnly. "Yes, mother of my sons. You said it. You repeated it loudly. I doubt that there is anyone within a day's hunting of this place who didn't hear you say so," he said in burred Algonquian.

"The child could have been with his mother if she'd left the captive where he belonged. If she wanted another husband, why didn't she choose one of the good men who offered for her? Why not take Matiassu?" She shook a finger at Leah. "Being one of two wives

97

of a good man is not a punishment. Haven't I shared Alex with Tahmee? Did it do me harm?''

Leah made no reply. It was Amookas's way to complain bitterly. When her aunt had said all that was on her mind, she would be in a mood to offer help.

"Not that we haven't enjoyed having Kitate with us, you understand," Alex said. He was busy rubbing oil into a new musket stock he had carved from cherry. The barrel of the musket lay on a deerskin in front of him. Alex's skills as a gunsmith were well known on the frontier. His muskets brought top prices to Indian or white man, and the proceeds made his extended family wealthy. "Kitate is as welcome here as our twins.''

"And who said otherwise?" Amookas protested. "Moonfeather knows that we love Kitate as we love her.''

"I know this," Leah said. She looked around the snug wigwam. The house seemed larger tonight with only the four of them inside. Her cousins were playing the bone game with some of their friends, and Tahmee and her children had gone to their own wigwam for the night.

Alex switched to his native tongue. " 'Tis a serious accusation ye make again' Matiassu. If he's guilty, it could mean loss of his station wi' the tribe. 'Twill cause great strife among us. Clan weel stand against clan. I've seen tribes break apart for less cause.''

Leah brushed a lock of hair from Kitate's face. "Aye, so I've said to myself. It pains me that such a man has come to this because of wanting me as wife." She left her son's side and moved close to her aunt. " 'Tis why I didna go to the council. 'Tis why I broke the Seneca arrow and buried it in the forest.''

"While the matter remains hidden, there may be a way to mend the pot before the stew is lost," Amookas said. "Your sky-eyed husband must go far from this place. If he is gone, and you say nothing of Matiassu's shame, it will be forgotten. If anyone learns what has happened, Matiassu will have to kill the Englishman to save his own honor."

"So I have thought, sister of my mother," Leah replied. "Brandon must go, and he must go at once. If there is a scandal, he will never be permitted to become adopted. And . . ." She took the older woman's worn hand and squeezed it tightly. "And he will die."

Amookas peered into Leah's face. "You have allowed yourself to care for this foreigner. I can see it plainly."

"Aye," Alex agreed. "She has. And she speaks true. Matiassu will not rest until he lifts her mon's hair, that's certain."

"You know that if the captive is caught trying to escape, the council will put him to death." Amookas's kindly features creased with concern. "You could be in danger too, daughter. Matiassu may try and kill you both."

"I mean to take him away tonight, while the young men still search for Seneca . . . before Matiassu returns to camp," Leah said. "Brandon would be as helpless as a newborn elk calf in the forest. I'll have to guide him back to the white settlements. I need to know that my wee son will be safe wi' ye while I go, and I need your blessing."

"Aiyee," Amookas cried softly. She rocked back and forth and moaned. "I see great danger for you.

Would it not be better to wait until the men relax their vigil?''

"Nay," Alex said. "The lass be cunning as an old fox. The warriors watch for those who would sneak up on the camp, nay those who'd flee fra' it. She kens the woods as well as any mon. If any can get the Englishman free, 'twill be she.'' He set the stock aside and massaged the stump of his bad leg. "If I stood on two pegs instead o' one, I'd see t' the matter myself. But I canna. Sech be life, Amookas mine. Dinna fash yourself, wife. Nay harm weel coom to her. She wears her luck aroond her neck.'' He nodded. "Aye, 'tis a good plan, lass. Dinna worry aboot your bairn. He'll be safe wi' us, or we'll all be in heaven together.''

"The Englishman knows the risk he takes, if he tries to escape?'' Amookas asked. "You're certain his wounds won't slow him down?''

Leah looked up into her aunt's eyes. "The wounds are painful, nothing more. And he knows the penalty if we're caught.''

"Go then, with our blessing," Amookas said. "You'll listen to my warnings no more than you did before, no more than your mother listened when I told her not to wed your father.''

Leah embraced them both, kissed her sleeping son, and turned toward the door. "I'll be a few weeks on the trail, a moon at most. Keep Kitate safe for me.''

"Inu-msi-ila-fe-wanu protect you,'' her aunt whispered.

"God go wi' ye, lass," Alex murmured.

Eyes clouding with tears, Leah ducked out of her aunt's wigwam and hurried toward her own house where Brandon waited impatiently.

* * *

Fluid ribbons of incandescent violet spilled slowly across the gray eastern sky. As Brandon watched, the purple streaks gave way to coral and shimmering gold so vivid that he paused and motioned to Leah to look up at the magnificent sunrise. "I don't think I've ever seen one so beautiful," he said.

"Kesathwa, the sun," she said. "He comes to light our way."

"You didn't seem to need light last night," Brandon replied. "Even without a hint of moonlight, you kept going."

She shrugged. "I prayed that Tupexkee-keethwah, the moon, would hide her face behind the clouds and that the fog would make us invisible."

Brandon looked down at his mud-encrusted leggings and dirty moccasins. His arms bore the scars of branches and briers, and his hair was tangled with leaves and twigs. "While you were making us invisible, couldn't you have done something about the pain? I feel like a fox that's been chased all night by hounds."

She laughed. "But the hounds didna catch us, did they?"

The two had left the Shawnee village within minutes of Leah's return to her wigwam. Carrying packs, they had circled around through the west cornfield and entered the river. Instead of crossing, they had waded and swum upriver, going ashore on the same side as the village. They'd walked along an ankle-deep stream for nearly an hour, not speaking, listening for any sound of the men from the village. At one point, Brandon had been certain he'd heard the falls, but he'd never caught sight of it.

They returned to the river at a spot where rocks spilled into the water. Again, she had led him along the riverbed, sometimes walking; other times, when the current permitted, they had swum. Without moonlight, the night had been so black that he couldn't see Leah an arm's length ahead of him.

In the middle of the night, a thick fog had settled over the river. It was then that Leah left the water for the last time and led him directly into the forest. After a time, she changed direction, following what she whispered to Brandon was a game trail. He could see little difference between the untracked woods and the path.

Once, they'd come upon a herd of sleeping deer. The animals had panicked and fled before them; one doe whirled and leaped completely over Brandon's head. He and Leah had been so frightened by the sudden burst of noise that they'd laughed like errant children when they realized it was only deer and not a charging bear or a war party of Shawnee braves.

Leah had left the trail where the deer had bedded down for the night. She'd dragged him through a green-brier thicket and into a low, marshy area. They'd not stopped to rest once through the long night, and now, at daybreak, he was tired and hungry.

"We haven't seen or heard a living soul," Brandon said. "Don't you think we could take time to eat something and catch a few hours' sleep?"

She shook her head. "We sleep when we are safe, Brandon mine. You are slow in the forest, and I canna travel as fast as Matiassu. When they take up our trail, we maun be far enough away. We canna rest yet."

"Maybe he won't follow us at all."

She laughed softly. "Matiassu will follow. He will

have to. If we make a mockery of him, they will take away his badge of office and make another man war chief in Matiassu's place. To lead warriors into battle, a chief must command respect. He canna be publicly bested by an English captive and a woman.''

Leah rubbed the back of her neck and adjusted her quiver of arrows. She was dressed in a laced-up vest and leggings, much as she had worn when they went on the deer hunt. Her fringed skirt was cut short, and her heavy elkskin moccasins rose under her leggings to tie at the knee. Over one shoulder, she wore a cape despite the heat. Her hair was plaited into one thick braid and held back off her face by an intricately beaded headband.

Brandon's leggings and loincloth were still damp from the river, and his vest was hot and sticky. A blister had risen on one heel and broken; the sore spot rubbed every time he took a step. Leah looked as though she had just strolled out of her wigwam; her hair wasn't even tangled. "I'd give the price of a coach and four to see you in a proper lady's gown with hoops and stays." He grinned. "If I took you to the theater, none would watch the play—you're that lovely, m'lady.''

"Why do ye call me m'lady? I'm not your lady," she protested. "I be my own woman. A Shawnee woman is nay a thing to be possessed like a pair of moccasins or a French musket. You make fun at me, and I dinna like it.''

"Why do you call me Brandon mine?''

"*Ahuttch*, 'tis nay the same." She slung her bow across her shoulder and set off through the trees. "I dinna laugh inside when I call ye so. I'll nay be sport for the likes o' ye, Brandon viscount. I be the daughter of a peace woman.''

"I don't *ken* this peace woman. What does it mean?" He ducked his head to avoid a low-hanging branch.

"I've nay time to educate a barbarian. There be sachems and council members, either men or women, but usually men. There be war chiefs, only once in a great while a woman, and there be peace women. A peace woman be always female, never a mon . . . a man. She has power that comes from above and great wisdom, wisdom of a different sort than that of a sachem. A peace woman must be born wi' the power. It be magic. No woman can decide she wants to be one—she either is or she isna. In battle, a sachem may be killed by an enemy, but not even an Iroquois would dare murder a peace woman if he knew what she was.''

"And your mother was such a one?"

"Aye, Brandon mi—. Aye. On her word, the Shawnee would lay down their tomahawks and take up the hoe, or they would don warpaint. She was first in the council, and she was honored among the Delaware and the Menominee, as well as the Shawnee. She was born the granddaughter of Mo-na Mskee-yaik-wee, the greatest of all peace women. Usually, there be an unbroken line, mother to daughter, but my grandmother—my mother's mother—died in childbirth when she was still a young woman. My mother and her sister were raised in the wigwam of Mo-na Mskee-yaik-wee.''

"So your mother and your grandmother both died giving birth." For some reason the thought disturbed him greatly. His eyes rested on Leah's slim hips, her delicate frame, and he couldn't help wondering if she would meet the same fate.

"Aye."

"Did you have a difficult time when Kitate was born?" he persisted. At home in England, women died every day in giving birth. There they had benefit of midwives, and proper medical care. Here . . . Brandon glanced away from Leah, his mouth suddenly dry. Here in the wilderness, Indian women probably went off into the brush like animals to give birth alone and unattended.

Leah sniffed. "This is not a thing of which I care to speak with an Englishman. Enough talking. We waste breath, and we have far to go."

Brandon wasn't listening. From his memory, a girl's face appeared . . . blond and blue-eyed and laughing. Cecily. He hadn't thought of her for years. How old had he been that summer he'd loved Cecily? Fifteen . . . sixteen?

Leah thumped him hard on the chest. "Brandon viscount! Do ye sleep on your feet? I tell ye, we ha' far to go."

Cecily's face vanished, replaced by Leah's very real one. He forced a chuckle. "You're the walkingest woman I've ever seen," he said lightly. "Since the first day I laid eyes on you, you've tried to walk me to death. Haven't you people ever heard of horses?"

"I've seen them. I've even ridden one. But a horse be nay use in the thick forest. The beasties be for open places. They make a target of a man so that enemies may lift his scalp." She veered off to the left and began to follow a faint path. "The wind be in our faces," she cautioned. " 'Twill carry our voices." She held a small finger to her lips. "Shhh."

The sun was high over Brandon's head before Leah spoke to him again. "Down," she ordered, motioning urgently with her left hand. He dropped to a crouch, and then onto his stomach as she had done. Together they crawled to the top of a rocky ledge and peered over the edge.

Brandon heard Leah's sharp intake of breath as they both saw the group of Indians and uniformed white men gathered below. The wind was still blowing from east to west, and Brandon could make out a few words the officer was saying. "French . . . those soldiers are French," he said.

"Quiet. Stay down," Leah cautioned, pushing him with the flat of her hand. "Keep your head low. The Indians be Mohawk—Iroquois."

"But they're with the French. Surely we can—" He broke off in mid-sentence as Leah brought her knife to his throat.

"Shhh," she repeated urgently.

The tip of the knife blade pierced his skin, drawing a bead of blood. "Leah? What are you—" She glared at him so fiercely that he was silent.

They lay in the hot sun for a long time. Finally, Leah withdrew the knife and gestured toward a thick grove of trees. "Quickly," she urged. "Move without leaving a trail a blind bairn could follow, if ye can."

Brandon looked over the edge of the ridge again. The men, Indian and white, were gone. The clearing was empty. Tight-lipped with anger, he followed Leah back to the grove of trees. She didn't stop until they were hidden beneath the sweeping branches of a hemlock. There she signaled him not to speak. Hardly breathing, she listened for a long time.

"Ye be angry wi' me," she whispered finally.

"You're damned right I'm angry. What was that all about?" He rubbed the streak of dried blood on his neck. "Have you taken leave of your senses? Those soldiers were Frenchmen—white men. I could have called out to them."

"Aye, so ye could. 'Twas why I put my skean to your flesh."

"Would you have cut my throat, Leah, or was it a bluff?"

She shrugged. How could she tell him something she didn't know herself? "The leader of the soldiers, Roquette, we call the hair buyer. He trades guns for English scalps."

"I don't believe you," Brandon snapped. "We're at peace with the French. Why would a gentleman do such a thing?"

"The hair buyer be nay gentleman. He deals in blood and Shawnee women. If you had let them know we were hiding there, he would ha' had ye killed. He would ha' used me as a whore for his soldiers—or tried to." Her tone softened. "I didna wish to kill ye, but there was no time to explain. Even now, ye think I lie."

"I told you, we have a treaty with the French."

"Go then and tell Roquette about this treaty. Follow his trail and surrender to him, but gi' me time to get away first." She looked into his eyes. "Trust me, Brandon mine, or trust Roquette." She sank down and leaned back against a tree, suddenly overwhelmingly weary. "The Iroquois want guns," she said, "and so they provide him with scalps. Some are English, some are Shawnee, and I dinna doubt that some be French. Better Matiassu catch us than the Iroquois. Do ye ken?"

He moved to sit beside her. "It's true? The French are paying to have English settlers murdered?"

"Aye. Roquette says to kill only the Englishmen, but he pays the same for the hair of lass or lad, bairn or old one. He doesna say why he wants the scalps, and the Iroquois do not ask. I think the French want our land as badly as the British. The Shawnee and Delaware are few; the English are many. If Indians kill English settlers, perhaps they will not keep pushing west with their cabins and their cornfields. Perhaps they will stay on the coast and leave this land to the French."

Brandon slipped his arm around her. "How long has it been going on?"

"Years. Not all of the Iroquois will deal with him, but some do. And it may be that a few of our warriors do also. There are good and bad men in all races." She tried halfheartedly to push his arm away, but he kept it there. Her eyes stung, and she blinked back the moisture. "What can I say to make ye ken—"

"It's all right," he soothed. "You're worn out. We both are."

She leaned her head against his shoulder and fought back tears. A contrite Brandon was harder to accept than a stubborn one. She rubbed at her eyes with the back of a hand and tried to regain her composure.

She needed sleep as badly as he did, but he was helpless here in the woods. If she relaxed her guard— if she made a wrong choice—they would both die for it. Her eyes itched as though they had sand in them. A little sleep and I'll be all right, she thought. She was hungry and thirsty, and her mind was buzzing like a broken bee hive.

"I was wrong to doubt you," he murmured.

Her mind was clouded with fatigue. "If I sleep," she asked, "will ye stay awake and listen?" Could she trust him? She wasn't certain, but she'd reached the end of her strength. She had to have sleep.

"I'll keep watch," he promised.

"If ye hear anything, anything at all, wake me. The Iroquois may have scouts in the forest, or they may come back. When it be dark, we will go from this place, but for now . . ." She yawned and snuggled her head against him.

"Sleep, Leah. I'll listen for your Iroquois."

"They make no noise, 'tis the trouble," she answered sleepily. "They just . . ." Her eyes drooped and her breathing grew deep and regular. And throughout the long, still afternoon, Brandon held her close to him and watched over her.

Leah placed her fingers over Brandon's mouth. His eyes snapped open, and his muscles tensed. She pressed against his lips and brought her mouth close to his ear. "Shhh, listen."

The *gobble-gobble-gobble* of a wild turkey echoed through the still air. Leah pulled an arrow from her quiver and notched it into the bowstring. She paused and drew her knife, tossing it to Brandon hilt first. The turkey call came again, closer. Another turkey, a distance away, answered.

"Iroquois," she whispered.

She pushed aside a feathery bough and pointed. Through the gap in the needles, Brandon saw a tall, dark-skinned Indian loping through the trees. He was naked except for a loincloth, and he carried a musket in one hand. Strapped to his back was a war club and a powder horn. His head was shaved; what hair that remained was a spiked crest along his bare skull.

"There be two of them." Leah's lips barely moved. "Keep still. We are safe so long as he doesna see our trail."

The brave stopped and leaned his flintlock against a pine tree. He raised both hands to his mouth and gave an imitation of a turkey once more.

Leah drew back the bowstring. Her mouth felt dry, and her knees were weak. She knew she was close enough to kill the Iroquois, but then the other one would come. Worse yet, he would go for the rest of his friends.

The second Iroquois scout returned the signal, and the first man picked up his weapon and turned away in the direction of the cry. Leah stood motionless until he was out of sight.

"Will he be back?" Brandon asked after a time had passed.

Leah relaxed her bow and returned the arrow to its quiver. "I dinna think so. He didna know we were here." She was trembling. "We must find water and a place . . ."

Brandon took the bow from her hands and leaned it against a tree.

"We have to . . ."

He shook his head.

"But . . ."

He took her in his arms and kissed her. Shuddering, she clung to him, letting the fear drain out of her mind and body.

"Brandon mine," she murmured.

His lips were hard on hers. His tongue plunged into her mouth, filling her with eager thrusting. She wel-

comed his passion, welcomed the flood of desire that
drove away the terror.

"Little Leah." His words were a caress as his
strong hands moved in slow, sensuous circles down
her back. "I need you." She sighed as reason fled
and she was overwhelmed with the feeling that her
muscles had turned to water. Together they sank onto
the soft forest floor.

His hand cupped her breast through the soft deerskin, and she moaned with pleasure and squirmed
against him. He raised up on one elbow and lowered
his head to kiss her mouth, her ear, her throat. His
tongue trailed a hot flame down her shoulder to the
spot where the top lace held her vest together. Slowly,
deliberately, he began to undo the garment. She wove
her fingers through his yellow hair and pulled him
down to her, savoring the sweet taste of his kisses.

"Don't run away from me this time," he begged
hoarsely.

"Nay," she promised, "I willna."

Chapter 8

"I want to make love to you, Leah," Brandon said huskily. "Will you let me?"

Her shining eyes, fringed with heavy dark lashes, quivered as she raised her gaze to meet his. "Aye," she answered, "I will." She undid the tie to her cape and pushed that and her quiver away.

Brandon's mouth claimed hers in a searing kiss of unrestrained passion, and Leah shuddered as sweet waves of hot desire coursed through her. Boldly, her tongue met his, tasting, caressing as his roving hands stroked and teased her trembling body. They were so close she could feel the beating of his heart, and the sensation thrilled her beyond the pleasure he offered with his lips and hands.

"Leah," he murmured.

She felt his fingers fumbling with the leather tie that laced her open vest. The thong pulled free, and Brandon pushed aside the deerskin to lave her nipple with a hot, wet tongue. She made a small sound of delight and arched against him, offering her other breast to be licked and kissed, and finally suckled.

"So beautiful . . . ."

"Ummm." Joy bubbled up inside her as she pressed ever closer to him.

"So good . . . my sweet, sweet lady."

Leah buried her face in his cornsilk hair, breathing deep of the male scent of him. "Brandon mine," she murmured. "Aye . . . aye . . . dinna stop . . . dinna ever . . . ever stop." Her sighs of contentment changed to breathless moans as his hand slid up her thigh and fingered the warm wetness of her most intimate spot. "Oh," she cried. "Ohhh."

No man had ever made her feel like this before. With Brandon, she experienced more than the sexual pleasure her husband had given her; there was a deeper caring within her, a desire to know what he was thinking, a yearning to give him part of her that he would never lose.

He left her breast to taste her mouth again, and she caught his lower lip between her sharp teeth and nipped him lightly. *We have this moment,* she thought, *this small bit of time before we part forever.* Tears filled her eyes as her trembling fingertips brushed his cheekbones and his temple, drifting down to feel the line of his brows and the shape of his thin English nose. And all that she touched, each detail, she committed to memory, so that no ocean, no amount of time, could ever dim this joy.

Brandon rolled onto his back, pulled her on top of him, and showered her face with kisses. Her long, dark hair fell over her face, and he parted it gently. "Leah," he murmured again, "my Indian Salome, love me, little Leah."

Her teeth found his shoulder, and she lifted his leather vest to taste him with the tip of her tongue. The texture of Brandon's skin was not the same as that of her dead husband's. Brandon's fair English skin was rougher, saltier, and Leah found the difference exciting.

Brandon moaned as she nipped him teasingly, then brushed the ends of a lock of her hair across the muscled surface of his tanned chest.

"Leah." His tone was urgent, and she laughed softly. "Leah . . ." He found the tie at her waist and snapped the leather thong. Her skirt fell away, and then her leggings.

"Now your loincloth," she urged. "Take it off."

His breath was coming in deep shudders as he ripped the deerskin away. "Sit on me," he said. "Please . . ."

"Not yet . . . not yet, Brandon mine." She looked down at him and smiled. *"H'kah-nih,"* she teased. "Ye be a greater man than I thought."

"I want you . . . all of you."

Leah slid her body down his, taking care not to hurt his injured arm. She moved slowly, provocatively, savoring the sensations of his fair, salt-tinged skin, letting the intensity of her longing banish all fear and doubt. She rubbed her breasts against his chest, inflaming his ardor until he groaned with desire, fanning the throbbing ache within her until she felt she must satisfy it or die.

Her hand closed around his hard, swollen erection, stroking it as she pressed her cheek against his taut, muscled belly. *"K'daholel . . ."* I love you, she murmured in Shawnee, letting her breath stir the golden curls at the base of his shaft.

With a hoarse cry, Brandon seized her hips and raised her over him, lowering her until she sat astride his loins. She parted her legs eagerly, taking him within, filling herself with his tumescent love. His mouth was on her breasts, his hands clutching her, cradling her weight, guiding her. She strained to take all of him, and when he moved, she moved with him, finding his rhythm without hesitation.

The sweet aching in her blood had become a driving force, molten hot and insistent. The towering hemlocks, the needle-strewn earth beneath them, the blue sky above, all faded until there was nothing but this great golden man and the need to be one with him. Over and over, he called her name, and the sound of his voice whipped her passion to a frenzy. Finally, when she felt she could stand the agony no longer, she felt her soul break free from the earth and tumble into a bright abyss. Wave after wave of wondrous sensation broke over her, cresting and then receding, only to come again with glorious rapture.

Brandon shuddered and clasped her tighter to him. "Leah . . . Leah . . ." Breathless, damp with perspiration, exhausted, they clung to each other. He ran his fingers through her hair and whispered sweet love words. He raised a lock of her raven-black hair to his lips. "Sweetheart," he rasped. "I've never been with a woman like you, a woman so full of life."

She laughed softly, sighing. He turned onto his side, cradling her against him, and she caught his hand in hers. She traced the creases and mounds of his palm before bringing his fingers to her lips and nibbling at their tips.

"Woman, woman . . ." He groaned. "If you keep moving against me like that . . ."

She chuckled and nuzzled the golden hairs on his chest, then licked the nub of one male nipple. She stretched, rubbing her bare legs against his. "What,

Brandon mine? What will ye do if I dinna stop?'' She tasted his other nipple, then drew it between her lips, sucking lightly.

"Dare me, and you'll find out." He cupped her bare breast in his hand and teased the nipple erect. "Two can play at this game, wench."

"Aye," she answered. "Two can play, and two can win." She laughed. "Ye need not worry that ye will gi' me a bairn from this pleasure, as mightily as ye tried. Last night, before we left the village, I chewed the leaves that keep me from making a child."

"Are you telling me you planned this?"

She smiled. "Nay, I didna plan it . . . but I did give thought that it might happen." She sighed, knowing the mood was broken. "Ye needna fear. The herbs will work."

"I'm sure you believe it." He kissed the top of her head. "I think these pine needles have left me scarred for life. Either we change positions, or we find another spot."

Leah wiggled free of his embrace and recovered her skirt and vest. Unconsciously, she pulled them on and tied them as best she could with the broken thongs. "I found nay fault wi' my bed," she said. "None at all." She shook the needles out of his loincloth and tossed it at him. "And these be hemlock, nay pine. Will ye never learn?"

"Hemlock, then. But the twigs are just as sharp." He held one up. "This one went in at least three inches."

She began to rebraid her hair. "We can find water now and a place to eat. We will take the trail left by the French and Iroquois—only we will go the way they ha' come."

"And Matiassu won't be able to tell our tracks from theirs." Brandon wound the loincloth around himself awkwardly and hunted for his missing moccasin.

Leah scoffed. "Of course he will. But it willna make any difference. Once they find the Iroquois sign, the search party will forget about us." She found his missing moccasin half buried in the needles and retrieved it. " 'Tis true. That many Iroquois be a real danger. Matiassu can stop hunting us and concentrate on the enemy without losing face."

"All the same, I'll feel better when we're safe behind English walls."

"When ye be safe," she corrected. "I'll take ye within sight of your people—then I return to my own. As dear as ye be to me, Brandon mine, I be Shawnee. My place is with my own kind." She kept her voice light, hiding the pain. What she had told him was true; there was no future for them together. As for what had just happened between them . . . She drew in a deep breath and began walking quickly away. I've no regrets, she thought, *none*. Brandon would go out of her life as her father had done, and she would learn to live without him.

Leah picked up the trail of the French and Iroquois a few hundred yards north of where she and Brandon had first seen them. Following the tracks was child's play, and a brisk hour's walk brought them to a wide, clear stream. Gratefully, they drank and ate the provisions Leah had packed in the camp. Again they slept for several hours, and at dusk, they took up the trek once more.

They walked until nearly daylight, seeing nothing more frightening than a gray vixen and her two fox cubs. Just before dawn, Leah found a sheltered spot beneath a rock overhang. With cool efficiency, she made a bed of pine boughs, and they slept until mid-morning.

When they awoke, Brandon took her into his arms and they made slow, sensuous love. There was no hesitation, no denial, only a passionate sharing of the tenderness they had come to feel for each other. Leah made no promises she knew she could not keep. For her, it was enough to share with Brandon this magical time between the English world and the Indian, a world where each belonged equally.

On the afternoon of the eighth day, they came to a river large enough to swim in. Laughing, they pulled off their warm deerskin clothing and dove into the cool, refreshing current together. Once again, Leah insisted on scrubbing Brandon thoroughly with sand from the river bottom.

"To wash away the sweat," she said.

"And make certain I don't frighten away the game," he finished. "And do I get to sand away your skin as well?"

She pushed his head under, and he came up sputtering. "I know how to wash myself," she replied playfully.

The weather was perfect, the sun shining and a light breeze blowing to keep off the insects. They'd seen no sign of humans, and the forest seemed as peaceful to Brandon as Eden must have been. To his delight, Leah seemed willing to linger beside the river. They spent the long afternoon laughing and talking, and finally making love in the water.

Afterward they lay in the shallows in each others' arms. "You seem so different here," he murmured. He raised her small hand to his lips and pressed a kiss into her callused palm. "In the village you were—" He broke off, not certain how to express himself without hurting her.

"In the village you were verra rude." She shook her wet hair, splattering him with drops. "A barbarian."

"Was I?" he asked lazily. "Do you still think I am?" God, but she was warm in his arms. He nuzzled the back of her neck and pulled her into his lap. Leah's copper-gold skin was like silk, and her wet hair smelled faintly of mint. She laughed, a low tinkling sound that made Brandon shiver inside.

"Aye, Brandon mine, I do—a great brawny broth of a barbarian. But I dinna mind so much now." The tip of her tongue brushed his upper lip. "Ye have much strength . . . for an Englishmen."

He lowered his head and kissed her. Instantly, he felt heat flare up in his loins. "Damn me, Leah," he swore, "you do to me what no other has ever done." He'd wanted her sexually as he'd wanted other women—too many to count if he thought about it—but Leah was different. Once the physical act was finished and his arousal satisfied, he'd expected his desire for her to diminish as it always had before. Instead, he wanted her more than ever.

Why, in the name of all that's holy, is this happening to me now? Brandon wondered. He was thirty, long past the age of boyish fancies and romantic claptrap. He'd had his fill of dalliances with red-cheeked dairy maids and ladies-in-waiting. Wasn't he known in court circles as a cocksman of high degree? A reputation earned more by gossip than actual indulgence, he had to admit, but a distinction nevertheless.

I set out deliberately to make her fall in love with

me, he thought. It was a conscious act—an attempt to use Leah to free myself from the Shawnee. And it worked, didn't it? I'm free.

She laid her head against his chest and closed her eyes. "I like you," she murmured. "You give me content."

Brandon gritted his teeth and stared across the river into the trees without really seeing them. The closest he'd come to losing his own heart had been with the delicious Lady Anne. The scandal caused by their affair had landed him here in the Colonies—a scandal based on her infatuation with him and a few snatched kisses and some furtive handholding in a garden. Lady Anne was married; he'd known that from the start. He'd also known that her powerful husband was no man to cuckold, even if he was fool enough to neglect a wife young enough to be his granddaughter.

Brandon had genuinely liked Anne. If she'd not had a husband, she would have made a very suitable wife. Lady Anne had everything a man in his position needed in a mate; she was of noble birth, she was sweet-natured and biddable. By the king's cod! She was as pretty as an orange girl and as rich as Croesus. He would have wedded her gladly, but, since he couldn't, he would have bedded her with even greater enthusiasm. Unfortunately, Anne was an innocent, and her seduction had never materialized.

The point was, he'd been strongly attracted to Anne, and he should have been brokenhearted when they had been torn apart. But he hadn't been . . . not really. He'd allowed his father to cozen him into coming to the Colonies, and in the excitement of antici-pated adventure, he'd all but forgotten sweet Anne.

Leah put her arms around his neck and snuggled

close. "I'll miss ye," she said. "Truly I will." She touched his chin. "In time, I think I would ha' forgiven the porcupine quills on your face." Her dark eyes were luminous as she drew an imaginary line around his lips with her finger. "I believe I could ha' made a Shawnee of ye, if you'd let me."

Brandon's stomach knotted. I'll forget her as I forgot the others, he tried to convince himself. I remember their faces, but not their names. He splayed his fingers over her thigh, letting them slide over the curve of her hipbone. *Content,* Leah had said. He felt content when he held her like this, and overwhelmingly protective.

"Do ye have a mother across the sea? Brothers?"

Leah tugged at his ear, and Brandon realized he hadn't been listening.

"Do ye sleep?" She repeated her first question.

"Oh, yes . . . a mother and a father. You'll have earned my mother's undying gratitude when I tell her that you saved my life."

"More than once."

He laughed. "Yes, more than once. I'm her only child. My father was married before, but his first wife died without issue. I'm the sole heir to their fortunes and to my father's titles."

"But ye said ye had a . . . a cousin. Did not your parents raise him? Surely he will get something."

He put a finger over her lips. "Just once I want to hear you say *you.* Not *ye,* but *you.*"

"*Youh.*" She smiled up at him mischievously. "*Youh.*"

"Close. Put your lips like this." He demonstrated. "*You.*"

Giggling, Leah kissed him. *"You.* I think I will need much practice."

He grimaced. "Witch."

She leaned her head back until her hair drifted on the surface of the water. "Your cousin . . . Charles. Will he not be an heir like *you?"*

"Nay, lass," he teased in a feigned Scottish accent. "He canna. 'Tis nay the custom o' the *English-manake."*

"Then 'tis a bad custom. You said he grew in your father's house. Among the Shawnee, it would make him your brother."

"Charles has his own fortune. He doesn't need mine, although he'll be welcome to whatever I have if he ever does."

Idly, Leah fingered the golden charm she wore around her neck. "Does this Charles have hair like ripe corn tassels and sky eyes?"

Brandon shook his head. "Charles's hair is brown. He has the Wescott eyes, at least they're—"

"Aiyee," Leah cried, wiggling free. "Did ye see? A fish. Would ye . . . *you* like fish for the evening meal?"

"Fish would be a welcome break from meat, but we've no hooks or fishing lines."

Leah gave him a look of pure astonishment. "We dinna need hooks or lines. Come, I will show *you."* Holding her breath, she dove under water and swam to a place where tree roots extended into the water. Her head bobbed up and she waved to him. "Here, Brandon mine."

He joined her, and she cautioned him to silence. "Dinna move," she instructed. Only a few minutes passed before Brandon saw a shadow flash between Leah and the riverbank.

With a cry, she seized the struggling fish and tossed it up on the grass. "One more," she promised. The second fish was larger than the first. Leah pronounced them both delicious eating and climbed up the bank to dress and start her cookfire.

"You are a wonder," he said an hour later when they were nibbling at the broiled trout. She'd even thought to bring salt and herbs from the village, so their dinner was well seasoned. "If there hadn't been so many warriors wanting to roast me or lift my scalp, I think I would have liked to spend a few more months with you."

Her expression grew serious. "Nay," she admonished. "For ye might then become a habit. 'Tis best as things be."

When they had finished eating, Leah extinguished the fire and hid the evidence. They gathered their belongings and walked along the riverbank for nearly an hour before she signaled a halt for the night. "Tonight we will take turns sleeping," she said. "One will keep the watch. Beyond the river is bad country, and we maun go carefully."

"Iroquois?" he asked.

"Nay, white men. And they be far more dangerous."

Two days later, they crossed the first trail of man on horseback. Leah had sighted the smoke of a cabin earlier in the day, but she hadn't pointed it out. The hoofprints of the horse were plain enough for Brandon to read himself.

"One white man alone," she said, kneeling in the

dust to finger the print. "He passed here in early morning.

Brandon looked amused. "One man. And are you certain that it wasn't an Indian?" He grinned at her. "Or a white woman?"

"The animal wears iron shoes." She stood up and dusted off her clothing. "And an Indian woman might ride alone through the woods, but no white woman. They hide behind wooden walls."

"Have you ever seen a white woman?"

"Nay, but Alex told me."

"As he told you about the kissing."

Leah laughed. "Still, I bet you my bow against your loincloth that 'twas a white man who rode here."

"You'd like that, wouldn't you? The Viscount Brandon struts into Annapolis wearing nothing but a blush."

She shook her head. "You would nay blush; ye be too much Shawnee now. Ye maun let the women blush."

"I doubt it. How far are we from the first settlement, do you think?"

She rubbed her dusty hands on her leggings. "I dinna know. A day . . . maybe two. I have never been here. I only go by what Alex—"

"By what Alex said," he finished for her. "Leah?"

"Aye."

"This time with you has been . . ." He swallowed and looked away. "I'll miss you, more than I ever thought possible."

And I will miss you, she thought. She'd known the time they had together was drawing to an end, but she hadn't wanted to admit it. She'd deliberately camped for the night when they could easily have walked on, and she'd taken Brandon south of the smoke. "I've been away too long," she said. "My son awaits me. As soon as we find the white men, I will turn back."

"I don't want you to go." He put his hands on her shoulders. "Come with me, Leah—just for a little while. Come and see my father's plantation. It sits on the Chesapeake. You've never seen a great body of water, a bay or an ocean, have you?"

"Nay, I dinna wish to," she lied.

"You're only half Shawnee, Leah. Didn't your white half ever want to see the world your father came from? This is your chance. You'd be safe, I promise. I'd protect you and send you home loaded down with gifts for your family."

"Nay," she repeated. " 'Tis not what we agreed on. How would I carry these gifts? The forest gives us what we need." She tried to pull away from him. How had he seen into the deepest corner of her heart and guessed what she had wished as a child? How had Brandon known that she'd longed to see the great water and the canoes, the ships that flew along the water without paddles?

Again, Leah's hand went to the amulet around her neck, and she closed her eyes as she rubbed the smooth gold between her thumb and forefinger. How may times had she gone over her father's admonition in her mind? *Whosoever possesses the Eye of Mist shall be cursed and blessed. The curse is that you will be taken from your family and friends to a far-off land. The blessing is that you will be granted one wish. Whatever you ask you shall have—even unto the power of life and death.* Was it true? Was the charm magic—or was it a lie?

"I thought the Shawnee never lied," Brandon said.

Her eyes flew open, and she wondered if he had the power to read her mind.

"You're lying to me now, Leah," he said. "You want to see the ships and the towns. I can show them to you."

She twisted free and backed off a few steps, fighting temptation. It was impossible to think clearly with Brandon's hands on her. He was right when he said she wanted to go with him. Leaving this blue-eyed Englishman would be the hardest thing she'd ever done, but she couldn't go to the white settlements with him. There was too great a risk. If the Eye of Mist possessed the power her father had claimed, she might never return to her people, might never hold her precious son in her arms again.

"I promised Alex and Amookas I would return at once," Leah said.

"A week. Just come with me for another week. I can show you—"

A musket roared from the edge of the clearing. Leah turned and ran toward the forest as two mounted white men burst from the trees and galloped toward them.

Brandon threw up his arms. "Stop!" he shouted. "Don't—"

The second buckskinned rider fired. Leah cried out and crumpled facedown on the ground.

Chapter 9

The horsesmen thundered across the clearing toward Brandon. The lead rider raised his musket club-like to strike him down. Cursing, Brandon stood his ground, then dodged the horse at the last possible instant. Seizing the bridle, Brandon thrust his weight into the animal's neck, throwing both horse and man violently to earth. The rider fell sideways, struck his head, and lay as if dead. The bay horse struggled to his feet and backed away, snorting and tossing his mane. Wrenching the unconscious man's musket from his hands, Brandon whirled to meet the second assailant's charge.

Eyes rolling back in fear, the roan horse reared, and the red-bearded rider struggled to keep his seat on the startled animal. Brandon drove the musket barrel into the big man's stomach, and the stranger toppled backward out of the saddle. By the time the man raised his head from the grass, Brandon's moccasined foot was planted firmly in the center of his heaving chest, and Brandon's skinning knife was at the man's unshaven throat.

"I'm Robert Wescott, Viscount Brandon. I don't

know who the hell you are, but move a finger and you're a dead man.''

"Don't kill me," the bearded man pleaded. "Don't kill me, please. My name's Sawyer, John Sawyer from Adam's Crossing. We didn't know ye were white. We thought ye were Injuns or maybe renegades.''

"Stay where you are," Brandon threatened. Picking up the second musket, he ran to Leah's still form. He threw down the weapons and knelt beside her. "Leah." A groan escaped his lips as he saw the bullet wound and the blood staining the back of her vest. "Oh, Leah." Panic welled up in him as he gathered her in his arms and searched her ashen face for any sign of life. "For the love of God," he whispered. How could she be lying here like this when minutes before she had been well and whole—arguing with him?

He touched her cheek with a trembling hand. "Leah?"

She made no sound. Her eyes were closed; her long thick lashes lay motionless. Her head lolled back against his arm like that of a loosely stuffed rag doll. Brandon passed his fingers over her slightly parted lips, lips now paled from berry red to faint rose. Frantically, he sought to detect some faint sign of breathing, but he felt nothing.

Brandon's anguished moan became a cry of rage. "Leah! Don't. Don't die on me, damn it. I won't let you die." He pulled her body against his chest and held her tightly, heedless of the dark red blood that oozed between his fingers. Blood . . . there's so much blood, he thought. "How can there be . . ." His words died in his throat as reason flooded his brain. If she's still bleeding, she can't be dead!

Quickly, he laid her facedown and turned his attention to her terrible injury. There was a hole where the musket ball had entered Leah's back, high and to the right. There was no exit wound, so he knew the bullet must still be embedded in her flesh. In desperation, he applied pressure to the gunshot with the flat of his hand. The flow of blood lessened but continued to seep ominously around the edges of his palm.

Brandon turned his head toward the white men. Sawyer was on his feet; the first man was sitting up, holding his arm and groaning, obviously in pain. "You, Sawyer!" Brandon ordered. "Get over here. I need something to stop this bleeding."

Hesitantly, the man came closer. "It's a woman, ain't it?"

"She is." Brandon's eyes glittered with cold rage. "Her name is Leah Stewart, and if she dies, I'll see the two of you hanged for murder." He motioned Sawyer closer. "Take off your shirt and rip it into strips. Be quick about it unless you want to see an early grave."

Sawyer obeyed. "She's a white woman? She cain't be. Sure looks Injun to me."

Brandon balled a strip of the homespun cloth into a tight ball and pushed it against the wound. Next, he tied two strips together, wound them snugly around Leah, and secured the material over the makeshift bandage. "We've got to get her to a physician," he said. "How far are we from the nearest settlement?"

Sawyer pointed east. "Eight, ten mile as the crow flies. But they ain't no doctor there. Ain't no doctor closer'n Annapolis, far as I know." He looked down at Leah and shook his head. "She ain't gonna last ten minutes, let alone long enough to get back to Adam's Crossing. How was we 'sposed to know ye was white folks decked out in them Injun duds?'' He glanced back toward his companion. ''Will's hurtin' bad. Reckon his arm's busted.''

''He'll wish it was his neck if she dies. Catch those horses.''

''Ye really is the viscount, ain't ye? Folks figured ye was dead, killed by them savages. They's offerin' a reward fer ye. Will heard tell of it up to Chestertown. Me an' Will was huntin' wild cattle. They's a bull an' three cows 'sposed to be out this way. Ye ain't seen 'em, have ye?''

In one motion, Brandon leaped to his feet, seized the man by the throat, and shook him until his teeth rattled. Muscles corded across his bare shoulders as he lifted Sawyer off the ground and threw him head over heels into the dirt. ''You're not listening to me, you stupid colonial. This woman's alive, and you'd better pray to whatever God you worship that she stays that way. Now bring me that bay horse, and get your friend up on the other one. You can ride behind him or you can run alongside like the cur you are, but you're going to guide me back to this Adam's Crossing now, or you're not getting any older. Do I make myself perfectly clear?''

''Yes, sir. Yes, sir, yer honor.'' Sawyer staggered up and limped toward the nearer horse. The animal was standing, reins dangling, a few feet from the man called Will.

Brandon went back to Leah and picked her up. He brought his cheek close to her mouth and was rewarded by a faint breath of air against his skin. ''Don't die on me, Leah,'' he whispered. She stirred in his arms and whimpered, and his heart leaped with hope. "Shhh," he murmured, swallowing the choking lump in his throat. "It will be all right," he promised. "I'll take care of you."

Her eyelashes flickered, and she sighed. She raised her head slightly. "Kitate." Her voice was so weak that he could barely make out the child's name. *"N'dellemuske,"* she whispered.

"I don't understand," Brandon answered. "English, speak English."

"N'gattungwan . . . Kitate . . ."

Brandon's arms tightened around her. What was she saying? Something about the boy and being sleepy. "Hold on, Leah." He blinked back the moisture that clouded his vision. "I'm going to get you to a doctor."

Her eyelids trembled, then opened for an instant. "Brandon mine." She smiled. *"K'daholel . . .* I love . . ." Her eyes closed as she slipped into unconsciousness again.

Minutes later, Brandon was mounted on the bay horse and galloping at breakneck speed east toward the settlement with Leah cradled in his arms.

At noon the following day, a young priest arrived on horseback at Adam's Crossing, a small frontier settlement consisting of a blacksmith's forge, a log tavern, and three houses. He dismounted and handed the reins of his mount to a towheaded boy in front of the inn. The tavern owner's wife, a short, stout woman with graying hair and pox marks on her face, greeted the cleric and quickly ushered him into the low-ceilinged room where Leah lay dying.

"Viscount Brandon? I'm Father James." The priest was unshaven and dressed in common buckskins, his unwashed hair tied back with a piece of stained ribbon. "Please forgive my attire. I've been in the saddle for two days. I'd only returned from a funeral on the Eastern Shore when your urgent message arrived."

Brandon raised his head and stared across the dim room at the thin-faced priest. "Yes, I'm Lord Brandon." The man didn't look old enough to have finished his schooling, let alone be a priest. And the garments he was wearing were better suited to a huntsman than a man of God, Brandon thought wryly. He turned his bloodshot gaze back to Leah. She lay unmoving on the crude log bed, her face as pale as the homespun linen sheets, her dark hair spread around her face and over her shoulders like a curtain of night. "This is Leah Stewart. I want you to give her last rites."

The stout woman held out a basin of water and a bar of lye soap. Father James washed his hands and dried them, then removed a bundle from his saddlebag. "Is she a Catholic?" he asked. "When did she last take the sacraments?"

Brandon caught the inside of his lip between his teeth and bit down until he tasted the salt of his own blood. He clasped her small hand in his, wondering if she felt pain or if she had slipped beyond such agony. The pain in his own heart was almost more than he could bear.

"Leah is a baptized Catholic," Brandon said. As I am, he thought. Strange that he should want last rites for Leah, now that there was no more he could do for her. He'd never considered himself religious.

He'd not attended mass regularly for many years, and when he did go, he'd given his attention to other matters rather than the ritual. He wasn't certain if he had faith in an afterlife, but if there was one, he knew he wanted to be with Leah again.

"And her last confession?" Father James drew near to the bed, a small cross in his hand.

Brandon stroked Leah's hand. He'd sent for a physician as well as a priest, but the rider who'd gone to summon the doctor hadn't returned. Only one woman in the settlement, Anna, the tavern keeper's wife, professed to have any knowledge of nursing, and she'd pronounced Leah's wound beyond her skill. "She's dying," Anna had said. "No one can lose so much blood and live."

Leah had bled again during the ride to Adam's Crossing, and she had bled when Anna examined the wound.

"I try and take the musket ball out, she'll bleed t' death," the woman had said.

"Can't we just leave it in?" he'd asked.

"It'll fester. Fever will take her. Best call Father James. He's not the best priest, but he's the only one who will come so far for the likes o' her."

There was no denying Leah's Indian heritage, and the inhabitants of Adam's Crossing made no attempt to deny their prejudice against her skin color. It was clear to Brandon that if he'd been an ordinary colonial instead of British nobility, Leah would have been denied shelter and the barest necessities.

Money and power, Brandon thought. Even in this wilderness, rank mattered. His speech and manner had been enough to procure clothing for them and a bed for Leah. The fact that he had no coin on him meant nothing; they knew that in time he would pay handsomely for whatever he desired. He'd been offered food and drink, but he couldn't remember eating. The colorless whiskey they'd given him was harsh and burned a channel down his throat. He'd drained the small jug in the night and demanded another, but he wasn't drunk. Rage burned inside him, an anger checked by concern for Leah. If she died, he'd wreak a terrible vengeance on the two men who had attacked them. For now, he couldn't spare the time or energy to deal with them.

"Lord Brandon." The priest was staring into his face. "Are you ill? I asked when the woman last received—"

"I know what you said," Brandon snarled. "Say the words and anoint her with holy water. She was baptized. She's a child of the Church and she's dying. What more do you need?"

Father James's face reddened. "Control your anger. A deathbed is hardly the place for—"

"Get on with it!" Brandon moved aside to allow the priest to lean over her. Vaguely, Brandon was aware of other figures pressing into the hot, smoky room. The single window was covered with a scraped calfskin in place of glass. The cabin walls were of log, and the floor was dirt. The room stank of whiskey, and sweat, and wet wool. The priest's clothing and hair were damp. Brandon realized that the tapping sounds against the window must be rain.

Rain, he thought, it's raining. Wouldn't Leah rather be outside in the clean, cool rain than in this stifling room? This was no place for her to die.

Pain knifed through him again, and he reached out

to touch a lock of her hair, oblivious of the priest and his hastily murmured prayers. Oh, Leah, he thought. Why did you come into my life if you were going to leave me like this? The depth of his feeling shocked him. A few days ago he had been willing—no, *eager*—to return to his father's plantation without her. He'd been fond of her, he'd been grateful . . . When had those emotions turned to something far deeper? I love her, he thought. I love this woman, and I'm losing her.

Brandon lifted Leah's limp fingers to his lips. "Father," he said as the priest made the sign of the cross over her still body. "Father, we have lived together as man and wife. Can you make us so in the sight of God?"

The priest's eyes widened. "You know she is close to death?"

"That's why I'm asking you to perform the ceremony. I don't want Leah to die with this sin on her soul." God knows she wouldn't consider what we've done a sin, Brandon thought, but I don't want to tell the priest that. "We were handfasted, pledged to each other. I'd consider it a personal favor if you would marry us."

Father James frowned. "This is quite irregular, but if, as you say, Lord Brandon, the two of you were . . ." He cleared his throat. "Under the circumstances, perhaps . . ." He glanced back toward the onlookers. "I will need two witnesses of the faith."

"I'll do it, Father," Anna offered. "And my son John—he's baptized proper. Get up here, John. Father James needs us."

Brandon scowled as the red-bearded colonial sidled

forward. "I don't want . . ." He trailed off as he saw the priest touch Leah's amulet.

"What is this heathen ornament? Take it off her at once," Father James said. "I won't—" Brandon's iron grip closed around his wrist. The priest's mouth dropped open.

"Don't touch her necklace," Brandon snapped.

"But, your lordship . . ."

"It's not Indian, and it's all she has left of her Scottish father." Brandon released the priest's wrist, and he pulled back.

"Very well, Lord Brandon," he stammered. "As you wish. But I will take this matter up with my superiors. What is your Christian name?"

"Robert Wescott."

Father James stepped back to the foot of the bed. He was a tall, slender man, and his head nearly touched the overhead beams. "You are certain you wish to do this?"

Brandon knelt beside Leah's bed and lifted her hand to his cheek again. "Yes, I do." It would be the last gift he could give her, the only gift he had ever given her. She would have his name, and for a brief time this Shawnee Indian woman would be Lady Brandon. My wife, he thought, my true wife. Perhaps it would make a link between them that death could not break. "Quickly, before it's too late. Say the words, priest. Make her my wife before man and God."

"Do you, Robert Wescott, take this woman . . ."

Father James prepared to leave Adam's Crossing at noon the following day. Leah was still alive, but her breathing had become fainter, her skin paler. "I would stay for the burial, Lord Brandon," the priest said as he swung up onto his horse, "but I have other duties. I fear she—Lady Brandon," he corrected, "has slipped into a coma. I've seen dying men and women do so often, but I've never seen one recover after. A coma may last hours or days, and I fear I have no time to wait with you."

Brandon nodded. "It's not necessary. Thank you for coming. You will be rewarded once I can contact my father's steward in Annapolis."

"God bless you."

Brandon dismissed him with a nod and turned back to the tavern. His eyes were burning, and he felt light-headed. He'd spent the night sitting up with Leah; his only sleep had been when he'd drifted off for short naps. He'd swallowed a half bowl of something gray and sticky at midmorning. He wasn't certain if it had been porridge or stew. Certainly, there'd been nothing in the taste or lack of it to give him a hint.

The old woman, Anna, was coming out of the door to Leah's room. She looked up at Brandon dully and shook her head.

An icy chill passed up his spine. "She's dead, isn't she?" Brandon asked.

"Nope. No change." Anna pursed her full lips, and her lined cheeks puffed out. "Maybe the best thing might be t' try and get the lead out o' her back." Her faded blue eyes regarded him shrewdly. "Ain't dead yet. Maybe it ain't her time t' go. Folks dies in God's time, not man's."

"If the physician—"

"If ye don't mind me saying so, sir, I tole ye thet he wouldn't come." She rubbed her work-worn hands against her threadbare apron. "Ain't never come t' Adam's Crossing before and ain't gonna start soon.

Didn't come when Will's Trudie died birthin' twins, and didn't come when I had to cut off Jacob Tilman's leg what got crushed under a log. Physicians ride in fine carriages—they don't mess around in the backwoods where Injuns is likely t' lift their scalps.''

"Will you do it?" Brandon took hold of her arm. "Will you get the bullet out?"

"Nope." Anna shook her head. "I tole ye thet when thet slug comes loose, she's like t' bleed t' death. I ain't gonna have folks say thet Anna Carey killed no lord's woman. She's yer wife, Lord Brandon. It's fer ye t' do the honors. If she dies on ye, folks won't think nothin' o' it. Mary Hopkins doctored her man when the cow stove in his chest. He died, but nobody pointed a finger at her. Didn't stop her from getting a new husband a month later. No, it ain't fer the likes o' me. Ye must do it.''

Sweat broke out on Brandon's forehead. "I don't know anything about surgery." By the bones of Saint Paul, the nearest he'd ever come to medicine was when they dug a nail out of his father's bay mare's hoof on the London highway. He raised knotted fists and rubbed at his aching eye sockets. "Reason tells me to wait for the physician," he admitted.

"And Judgment Day," Anna replied. "Ye ain't in England, m'lord. Ye be in Adam's Crossin'. Ye can try t' help or let yer woman die. What will it be?"

He drew in a shuddering breath and let his hands fall to his side. "Will you help me?"

Anna sighed. "Aye, 'spose I gotta. But the harm's on yore head, does she bleed t' death. Don't do nothin' on my say-so.''

"Would you do it if she was your child?"

Anna considered a moment, then nodded. "Yep, I

would. Can't do no harm, and might do some good. Layin' like thet, she ain't hardly alive noways. Ye do the deed, and I'll stand behind ye and tell ye what ye need t' know. And I'll mix a bread and milk poultice t' draw the poison out, does she live through the operation.''

Because the light was so poor inside the tavern, they carried a scarred trestle table out into the muddy yard, covered it with a linen sheet, and laid Leah facedown on it. Anna bound Leah's wrists and ankles with strips of cloth and tied her down. ''If she be lucky, she won't feel nothin', but sometimes the pain gives them the strength o' a bull. Does she fight the knife, 'twill be hard t' hold her down.''

Brandon pulled off his borrowed shirt and washed his hands with the strong soap until his skin stung from the lye. He held a knife blade in the fire until the steel glowed red, then carried it carefully to the table. Anna pulled the blanket down to expose the terrible wound in Leah's shoulder.

''Use yer finger instead o' the knife,'' Anna instructed. ''Ye'll do less damage thet way. Ye only use the knife point if ye can't get the musket ball out.''

Two other women and four men had gathered under the porch roof with their children to watch the operation. The rain had changed to a light mist; the air was cool and damp. Brandon glanced up at the onlookers, noting that John Sawyer was among them, and swore softly under his breath.

''Better offer prayers than curses,'' Anna said. She held a basin of warm water and rags to staunch the blood. ''Get on with it, m'lord. Longer ye wait, quicker she'll draw her last breath.''

Brandon leaned down and kissed Leah's cheek. "I'm sorry," he murmured, "so sorry." She lay like a waxen image, her breathing so shallow he couldn't detect the slightest movement. "Mary help us both." With shaking hands, he undid the bandage and took a hard look at the entrance wound. It was swollen and red with only a faint trickle of blood.

Gently, he dilated the opening with his fingers and began to probe for the lead ball. Leah screamed and struggled against the ties. Tears filled Brandon's eyes as he pressed her down against the table with one hand and extracted the bullet with the other. Leah moaned and went limp as blood began to seep from the hole.

Anna crowded close to see. "Let it bleed," she advised. "There's evil in the wound which must come out or she'll die slow and screamin'."

Brandon waited for what seemed an eternity before the old woman handed him a saucer. He raised his eyes to meet her faded ones.

"Pack the lint into the wound," she instructed. " 'Tis soaked in oil t' let the poison get out. If she lives until nightfall, I'll replace it with a bread and milk poultice." She waved to the men on the porch. "Some o' you give his lordship a hand gettin' her back inside afore she catches an ague."

"No!" Brandon insisted. He unfastened the ties and gathered Leah into his arms. "Keep your hands off her. No one shall touch her but me." Already the linen pad was soaked with red. In God's name, he wondered, how much blood could she lose and still live?

Anna bustled beside him as he walked toward the

tavern. "I'll boil up some willowbark tea. If we can get her t' swallow it, it'll help with the fever."

Brandon paused and looked into Anna's plain face. "Fever . . . Leah has no fever."

"Ah, but the fever will come, sir. It always do."

Chapter 10

Annapolis, Maryland, November 1720

Leah opened her eyes and stared at the maple tree branch through the glass window. The leaves were bright orange-gold, and she didn't know why. Troubled, she let her heavy eyelids drift shut again and tried to think clearly. Her head hurt, and her throat was dry and scratchy. The mat beneath her aching body was soft, as soft as duck down, and her body was clothed from neck to ankles in a strange garment.

In the darkness, it was easy to slip into sleep; she had done it so many times. If she slept, the panther that gnawed at her body was driven back, and she didn't have to try and think where she was or what had happened to her. There had been dreams, confused and frightening . . . so many dreams that it was impossible to tell dream from reality. Most of all, there had been pain and the fire that burned her flesh until she felt as light as an autumn leaf.

Autumn . . . The leaves had turned. They were beginning to drop from the maple tree, so it must be autumn. Where had she lost the days and nights? She shivered. If the leaves had changed from green to gold, she had lost several weeks.

In the darkness behind her closed eyes she heard voices speaking English. She was certain she'd heard them before . . . Sometimes she thought she recognized Brandon's voice. He wasn't here now. The speakers were both women, one very young, and they were close enough to touch.

"Look at 'er layin' there," the young one said. "It ain't natural, I say. She oughta be dead."

"Shhh, none of that talk now. You'll be out on your ear if his lordship hears you."

"No disrespect t' Lord Brandon, ma'am, but ye heard the doctor wi' your own ears. 'Unexplainable,' he said. It ain't natural, an' it ain't right. 'Spose she's a witch?"

"Hold your tongue, Jane," the older women said. "There'll be no talk of witches and such as long as I'm housekeeper here. It's an act of God, not Satan. This is a God-fearing household. They may believe such claptrap in Boston, but not here."

"It don't make sense t' me, his lordship so handsome and all. Why would he take the likes o' her t' wife? She's an Injun, ain't she?"

"Jane, I'm warning you!"

"Yes'm, Miz Briggs, I'll mind my tongue. But ye don't like it neither. I see ye watchin' her from the corner of yer eye. Ye're scared o' her, too."

"My feelings are none of your concern. I mind my own . . ."

Their footsteps receded, and the older woman's words became fainter until Leah could hear them no more. Leah was alone again. Slowly, she opened her eyes.

She was in an English house. She had guessed as much when she'd seen the glass window. She'd never seen one before, but her father had told her that most houses in his land had them. The younger woman had mentioned Brandon's name. Was she in his father's house?

They'd been arguing, she and Brandon. She remembered that clearly. He'd wanted her to come to his father's plantation, and she'd refused. Then there had been a shot. She remembered running toward the safety of the trees, and then . . . And then something had hit her in the back, hard. After that, there had been only blackness and dreams.

Brandon had been part of her dreams. He'd held her hand and told her he loved her . . . He'd begged her not to die. Sometimes, in the dreams, he'd rocked her in his arms. Death had tracked her through the dream world and the waking. Leah had felt the hot breath of the shadow demons, but she'd never once believed that she was dead. Those who pass over the river know no pain, and she had never ceased to feel pain. The pain had given her a reality to cling to, an enemy to fight. She had come to respect the pain because without it and without Brandon's presence, she would have surrendered to the Dark Warrior.

Leah looked around the unfamiliar wigwam. Standing against one wall was an tall, upright chest of polished wood on narrow twisted feet. Along another wall were two more enormous glass windows, and on the third was a fire pit surrounded on three sides by curious red stone. Logs crackled merrily, and the smoke rose straight up to disappear through a hole in the red stone. The logs were held in the fire pit by two small soldiers of iron, and in front of the fire, on the wide plank floor, lay a rug of bright-colored woven cloth.

The sleeping platform that she lay on was high off the floor. It stood free from the wall, supported by four carved posts and covered by a roof of shining red and blue material. The bed was heaped with blankets, all of cloth, very light and warm, sewn with tiny, neat stitches.

Suddenly a shiver of fear ran though her bones. Leah clutched at her throat, then relaxed as her fingers closed around the Eye of Mist. "Father," she whispered, "help me." She squeezed her eyes shut, ashamed of her weakness. She was no longer a child to cry out for her father. What if her amulet was as empty as her father's declarations of love? What if there was no magic in the necklace—if the Eye of Mist was just cold metal, a superstitious tale to soothe an irritable child?

The moment of panic passed as she rubbed the golden charm with her fingertips. She drew in a deep breath and moistened her dry lips with her tongue. A small chuckle rose in her throat; her lips turned up in a faint smile at her foolish doubts. The amulet wasn't cold—it was never cold—it was warm. It was magic, a magic so powerful that she had been unable to outrun or outwit her fate.

The curse is that you will be taken from your family and friends to a far-off land . . .

"Why?" she whispered into the empty room. Her cracked voice sounded as harsh as the scrape of bone against bone. "Why did you give it to me, Father?" But she knew as she uttered the words that Cameron Stewart was only following his own fate.

The Eye of Mist has been handed down from mother

to daughter in my mother's family for two thousand years. Her father had said that, too.

But why? Leah gripped the hem of the fine linen sheet and twisted it in her hand. Why? she agonized. Among the Shawnee, a child took the mother's clan. I am the daughter of a Shawnee peace woman. Why must I carry a Scottish curse?

The answer came from a small voice of reason in her head, unspoken in words, but as plain as though it had been shouted by a Shawnee orator. *You are only half Shawnee. Your father's white blood runs hot in your veins, and among his people inheritance comes from the male line. You cannot escape his legacy.*

Something wet trickled down her cheek, and Leah touched the drop with her fingertip and brought it to her lips. Salt. Not rain, but tears. She remembered rain on her face, and with the rain had come the worst pain of all. She sighed. That was past now. The panther still gnawed at her shoulder, but the pain was no longer so terrible.

"Suppinquall," she murmured. "Only tears." She wiped her face with the back of her hand. Tears helped nothing; tears were for children. "The curse has come true. I am far from my own family and friends." She sighed again, wondering if her sister across the sea had suffered from the power of the curse.

At first, when her father left, she had been jealous of her English sister. She had been angry because Cameron left her and her mother to go back to his other family. But, as the years passed, she realized that if there was fault, it was not her white sister's, and she had wished they could meet—just once—and share laughter . . . and perhaps tears.

"Do you wear the rest of the amulet, sister?" Leah

whispered in English. "Is the Pictish gold warm about your neck?"

"Leah?" Brandon stood in the doorway.

A warm flush spread through her body as she smiled at him. He'd traded his deerskin vest and loincloth for an English coat and velvet breeches the exact blue of his eyes. Black leather boots rose to his knees, and his shirt and stock were as white as the foam at the foot of the falls at the Place of the Maiden's Kiss.

"Leah, you're awake!"

She laughed softly and beckoned to him. *"N'nanolhand,"* she said, "I be lazy. The sun is high, and I lie here upon this sleeping platform like an old woman."

He crossed to the bed in a heartbeat and took her in his arms as tenderly as though she were made of butterfly wings. He murmured her name over and over in his deep voice as he covered her face with kisses. And when she drew back to look into his eyes, she saw that they glistened with unshed tears.

"Aiyee," she said as she laid her cheek against his. Her heart sang with a joy she had not believed possible. "Brandon mine, it has been a hard trail. Without you, I'd nay be here to cause ye more trouble." She raised her head, offering her mouth to be kissed. He did not disappoint her, and the kiss was as sweet as wild grape honey.

"They all said you would die." He tightened his embrace, taking care not to put pressure on her injured shoulder. "You were shot, and I had to dig the musket ball out of your back."

"Next time, like *p'tuka-nai-thee*, the rabbit, I will remember to dodge as I run." She snuggled against his blue velvet coat and caught his hand in hers.

"There won't be a next time. I'll protect you, Leah, always. You're my wife now, and no one shall ever harm you again."

She gazed up at him. "Your wife? I've been your wife since I took ye from the stake."

He kissed her forehead. "I forgot, darling, there's no way you could know. I remembered that you told me you'd been baptized as a child."

"Aye, but what has that to—"

"When I thought you would die, I called for a priest to give you the last rites of the Church." Brandon brushed a stray lock of hair from her face and kissed her on the lips with a feather-light caress. "And I had him marry us again, in a Catholic ceremony. You are my true wife, Leah, in the sight of God and man. You are Lady Brandon now."

She laughed again, softly. "So I heard the women say, but I thought they were speaking nonsense. It makes no difference to me, Brandon mine." She yawned. "I be very sleepy." She closed her eyes. "I have hunger, too, but . . ." She yawned again. "I am as weak as a newborn fawn. First I will sleep, and then—"

"It's important that you understand, Leah." Brandon's tone was insistent. "We are wed. You are my wife, and you will be the mother of my sons."

"Aye," she murmured sleepily. "I ken. But I have a son, and . . ." Her breathing became deeper. "I must go back to my own people. Soon . . . very soon . . ." Her lashes fluttered faintly and lay still like dark wings against her cheeks.

"No, Leah, that's what you must understand. You're not going back to the Shawnee, not ever. You belong to me now. I'm going to take you to England with me as soon as you're strong enough to travel. Leah?''

She slept, unable to hear his last words.

In midafternoon of the following day, Leah sat cross-legged in the center of her bed and nibbled daintily at a square of cornbread. A mug of milk, untouched, sat on the bedside table beside a bowl of oat porridge. "I dinna like this yellow stuff on the corncake,'' she said to Brandon. "What name has it?''

"Butter.''

"Aye, so the house woman said. 'Will *you* have but-ter or jam on your bread, Lady Brandon?' '' Leah giggled and lifted the butter off the top of her cornbread with the handle of her spoon. "I dinna care for *but-ter* or for the white milk of kine.''

Brandon took another square of cornbread and spread it generously with strawberry jam. "Try this.'' He placed it on a monogrammed linen napkin and handed it to Leah. "Trust me, this you'll like.'' He removed the plate with her crumbled buttery pieces of cornbread and set it on the table.

Warily, Leah bit into the jam and bread. "Aiyee,'' she cried. "It is a marvel, this jam.'' She made short work of it and looked at the tray. "I will have more.''

He grinned. "No, you'll not have more, at least not until supper. Do you know how long it's been since you've eaten solid food? I'll not have you getting sick on me all over again.''

"You only want me well so that you can try to force me onto a sailing boat,'' she exclaimed, lying back against the pillow. Her hair was loose over her shoulders, held away from her face by a deep rose-

colored ribbon that matched her rose silk dressing
gown. "I told you this morning, I must return to my
people. I have much love for thee, Brandon mine, but
we canna stay together. I am the flame and you the
black gunpowder. Each is good, but bring one too
near the other, and there be disaster."

Brandon frowned. He had told her about their wedding a second time, when she had awakened the night
before. They had argued, and they had argued again
this morning about her going to England with him.

In the months of his absence, messages of great
importance had arrived from Westover, his family's
country estate. He'd missed his father's first letter by
only days. Another Jacobite plot to overthrow King
George and put a Stuart heir on the throne had been
discovered. A gamekeeper who had worked for Brandon's father for thirty years had been arrested, along
with Miles Chester, a neighbor and good friend of
Brandon and his cousin Charles. The gamekeeper had
been questioned under torture, and before he died,
he'd told the authorities that someone at Westover was
in league with the rebels. Miles Chester had escaped
and fled the country, and a warrant had been issued
for Brandon's arrest. The letter advised Brandon to
make himself scarce while his father tried to prove
his innocence.

A second letter from Lord Kentington, dated only
two weeks after the first, had actually arrived in Annapolis ahead of the news that Brandon was sought
for treason. Once his father had been able to travel to
London and confront Brandon's accusers, he made it
clear that Brandon couldn't have been both in London
causing a scandal by seducing Lady Anne and in Dorsetshire, more than a week's ride away, involved in a

treasonous plot. Regardless of what the gamekeeper had confessed, Lady Anne's husband, no friend to Brandon, was a solid witness for the defense. The charges against Brandon had been dropped.

"The entire matter has caused me great pain and expense," Lord Kentington's scorching missive read. "I am much ashamed of you and your behavior, and I wish you to remain in the Colonies out of my sight until you've learned conduct befitting your station in life. The fact that your affair with the lady prevented you from being sent to the Tower offers me small consolation."

A third letter was in a stranger's handwriting. It was from his father's physician, informing Brandon that his father had suffered a heart seizure and wanted his son to return on the first available ship.

A fourth letter, from his mother, assured Brandon that his father was recovering but was bedridden. "The physicians feel he will remain so," she had written, adding that Lady Anne's husband had passed away. "Therefore, my darling, you need not fear problems from that quarter. It is quite safe for you to come home. We have both missed you and look forward to seeing your dear face as soon as God's mercy permits."

Brandon sighed and looked hard at Leah. "I must go at once. You can see that, can't you? We can send for your son, Kitate. Master Briggs, my father's steward, can arrange for the boy to follow us to England. I don't want to come between you and your son. I want to try and be a good father to him."

"Kitate is Shawnee. Would you try to raise a fawn among kine?"

"Cows, not kine. The word *kine* is Scottish and

very old-fashioned.'' He folded his arms across his chest. ''We're talking of a boy, not a deer. You don't know anything about the world, Leah. You can't possibly understand what I can offer the two of you.''

''Your mother,'' Leah replied. ''She would welcome a Shawnee daughter as wife to her son, yes?'' Her dark eyes narrowed dangerously.

''Not at first,'' he admitted. ''But—''

''Ha!'' She wrinkled her nose. ''As Amookas welcomed you. Not by first, not by ever. She will look down her thin English nose at the color of my skin. She would scorn my beautiful son and call him blackamoor.''

Brandon looked away. His mother would be a problem, but, if he was still alive, his father might well have a fatal heart attack when he saw Leah. Brandon toyed with the velvet ribbon at the nape of his neck. He'd married Leah on impulse, believing she was dying, never for an instant supposing that he would have to take her home to England and present her as Lady Brandon to his family and society. But now that he had made her his wife, damn it, she'd remain so. His jawline firmed. Parents and friends be damned. She was Lady Brandon; there was no other, and as long as she lived, he'd stand by her.

''I love you, you know,'' he said quietly. He rose and went to a window, staring out at the wide cornfield running down to the river. The corn had been cut and stacked in shocks. A boy was driving a herd of pigs along the rows. To the south, Brandon could see the fruit orchard and the road running down to the plantation dock. Through the glass, he could hear the mournful cry of a flock of wild geese flying overhead. ''It took nearly losing you to make me see it.

We are wed, and I believe that neither of us would be happy if we parted.''

"Love does not always mean happy.'' She wiggled down the mattress and snatched the jam pot off the tray. Retreating to the head of the bed, she made a backrest of the heaped pillows and proceeded to eat the strawberry jam with her spoon. ''Ye would feel shame to have a wife in buckskins and moccasins.''

"I'll dress you in satin and put silken slippers on your feet. I'll drape ropes of pearls around your neck and put rubies on your fingers.''

Leah licked the jam off her fingers and studied them. ''My hands be not soft as an English lady's. They are hands meant for building campfires and scraping deerhide.'' Suddenly she threw the spoon, striking him in the center of the back. ''Where is my bow? And my quiver that took a winter to make? My arrows with points of steel? Where have ye done with them?''

"Ouch! What the—'' He spun on his heel and retrieved the fallen spoon. ''Why did you—'' He laughed. ''You've jam on your nose, Lady Brandon.''

"My bow!'' she insisted. ''What have you done with—''

"Your bow and arrows are safe, thanks to the idiot who nearly killed you. I left them lying on the ground when I took you to the settlement, but he picked them up. He thought to sell them as trinkets. I persuaded him otherwise,'' Brandon said dryly. ''Your bow and arrows are downstairs in the library.''

"I want them here.'' She licked the rim of the jam pot. ''I may need them.''

"No, my ferocious little warrior. I'll keep them for you. I'll not have you taking a disliking to cook's pork pie and using Mistress Briggs or the maids for target practice.''

She made a face at him. "Tomorrow ye will go to the forest and bring me the roots and moss I asked for. I dinna ken what medicine ye and your shaman—''

"Physician," he corrected.

"Physician have used, but I do not think it was right. I will heal quicker with Shawnee medicine. And I would like deer soup and fresh fish to eat, not *that.*'' She pointed at the milk and porridge. "I am not a wee bairn to live on such pap.''

"You are demanding, love, for a wench newly snatched from the grave.'' He came back and sat on the edge of the bed, taking her in his arms. "I will do all that you ask, Leah. But you must do as I ask. I am your husband, and it is seemly that a wife obey.''

"Aye, Brandon mine. I will play your game for a few days more.'' She lifted her chin and stared into his eyes. "I will miss you all my days, *Englishman-ake*, and I will feel your body hot against mine in my dreams.''

"Leah . . .'' Seeing the stubborn gleam in her eyes, he ceased to pursue the subject. Instead, he held her and stroked her hair. "You are not reasonable,'' he murmured.

"Nay,'' she agreed. She brought his hand to her mouth and nibbled on the tip of his thumb. "In that which ye ask, I canna be, but have I not worn these garments to please you when my skin would rather be free to breathe? So foolish are the English to sleep in cloth bags when any civilized person knows that—''

"You may sleep naked in my arms when you are recovered,'' he assured her lightly. Leah's protests still troubled him. He'd walked the floor one long night trying to come to a decision about what to do about her. When he'd decided he loved her enough to take her home as a wife, regardless of the scandal it would cause, it never occurred to him that she might have other ideas.

He'd known that she would miss her son, and he regretted that they couldn't remain here long enough for someone to fetch Kitate to the plantation. But the merchant vessel, *Dependable,* sailed from Annapolis on December first. He'd purchased passage for Leah and himself, a manservant, and a maid. Winter crossings were never pleasant, and the longer they waited to depart the worse the weather on the North Atlantic would become. If they were to be aboard when the *Dependable* hoisted anchor, he had only a few weeks to change Leah's mind.

"This sleeping mat—"

"Bed," he corrected.

"This *bed* be too—"

"This bed *is.*"

She stuck out her tongue at him. "How can I tell you what I think if ye will nay let me speak?"

He smiled at her. "Speak away, love."

She sniffed. "This bed *is* too big for a person to sleep alone. Can ye not share it with me, Brandon mine? At night I have great homesick, and I be lonely."

He cupped her face between his hands. "Nothing would please me more, darling. But I think it best if you sleep alone awhile longer. I don't know if I could resist your charms, if you—"

"So," she insisted, "this *is* another crazy custom of the English—that a man must sleep apart from his wife. I would like you beside me, even if I cannot share certain pleasures. My lips are not wounded." She looked up at him with mischief in her eyes. "My breasts have not hurt . . . nor my—"

He silenced her with a kiss. "Enough of that," he said when they parted. "You will drive me mad with your words." He kissed the palm of her hand, then licked a bit of jam she'd missed. "When you're well," he promised, "I'm going to take a pot of jam and . . ." He whispered in her ear, and she giggled.

"Aye, but that would ruin this fine linen," she teased. She traced her upper lip with the tip of her tongue. "Still," she said huskily, "I might like the taste of this jam if it was spread on—"

He kissed her again, then freed himself from her arms and slid off the bed. "Sleep, witch. I'll be back to share dinner with you."

"And my bed?"

"Soon, Leah, soon."

Her mood turned serious, and she shivered as she pulled the coverlet up around her neck. "It must be, Brandon mine," she said softly, "for we have only a short time left together. Ye maun love me enough to last all the rest of my days, and I maun give you something to carry away and cherish in your heart."

"It doesn't have to be like that!"

"Aye, *uikiimuk,* it does."

"Don't count on it." His face clouded with anger as he turned and strode from the room.

"Ye canna bend me to your will," she called after him. "I am a free woman."

"And my wife," he muttered under his breath. "God help us."

Chapter 11

Leah's recovery seemed to Brandon nothing short of miraculous. Within a week, she was walking around the manor house, and by the end of November, she was able to ride in front of him on horseback as they explored the vast Tidewater plantation.

They were mounted on a finely bred black stallion, a horse Brandon had purchased in Virginia when he'd first arrived in the Colonies. The animal was sixteen and a half hands high, with a broad chest and arching neck, spirited enough to test Brandon's riding skill, yet not so ill mannered that he would fear for Leah's safety. Even with the double weight of two riders, the black Brandon had named Caesar pranced along proudly, tossing his thick waving mane and tail.

"The waterways along the Chesapeake are far more efficient than roads," Brandon explained to her. "I can ship grain and salted beef by ship to London cheaper than it can be transported from the rural counties in England." He reined in his horse and gestured toward the virgin stand of forest in front of them. "There's a fortune to be made in lumbering here. Oak and cedar can be cut and sold for use in shipyards, and cherry and walnut for furniture. The soil is rich beyond anything I've seen."

"Aye," Leah agreed. "I know nothing of what ye speak, but I ken pretty land when I see it. I love the marsh with the flocks of ducks and geese, and sparkling waves on yonder bay."

Brandon tightened his arm around her waist. Leah's alteration of the riding habit he'd had sewn for her might have scandalized the household staff, but he had to admit her clothing was practical for riding. She'd cut off her scarlet woolen riding skirt above the knee and bullied Jane into making her a pair of loose trousers from the leftover material. Leah had cut away and discarded the bodice, but she'd found no fault with the man's style jacket stitched in brilliant scarlet with wide cuffs and silver buttons, or in the matching cocked hat with its jaunty feathered plume.

"And I love you, my beautiful little barbarian," Brandon teased. "You've managed to make even a proper riding habit into a provocative costume." He leaned forward in the stirrups and peered lewdly down the front of her jacket.

She giggled and pulled his head down so that he could nuzzle the tops of her breasts. Snorting, the horse danced sideways and laid back his ears. Leah grabbed hold of the animal's mane. "Stop," she pleaded, laughing. "You'll get us both throwed."

He gained control of the animal with a flick of his wrist. *"Thrown,"* he corrected, "and I've not been thrown since I was seven."

"Then it be time," she countered. "Ohhh, look." She pointed at the eagle circling overhead. *"Pel-al-thee,* king of the skies. It gladdens my heart to know he flies over this place, too. Whenever I see him, I'll think of our ride this morning.''

A queer tightness spread through Brandon's chest. They'd not spoken of Leah's leaving for days, but she knew that he was sailing for home soon. The thought of going without her was tearing him apart. For a few minutes this morning—in the excitement of sharing his dreams with her—he'd forgotten that they'd soon be parted. God! Losing her would be like cutting away part of his body.

Desperately wanting to regain the exhilaration he'd felt earlier, he tried to pick up where he'd left off. ''Briggs, who is father's steward here in Annapolis, has all three plantations planted in tobacco for the most part. He's allotted only a little acreage for grain. That's a mistake. Virginia tobacco is finer than Maryland tobacco, and the whole tobacco trade is subject to wild fluctuations. Tobacco is a luxury crop, and the plant robs the soil of strength. I've read that . . .'' He frowned. ''Are you able to understand any of what I'm saying, Leah?''

She stiffened. ''I'm not ignorant, Brandon. I told you, I've read Alex's books: Shakespeare, Francis Bacon, the Greek philosophers.''

''Forgive me, sweeting. I look at you, and I forget that lovely head can hold anything so serious.''

''Damn thee, Brandon viscount!'' Angrily, she slapped the horse's neck, and the animal leaped forward and broke into a run. Clods of frozen earth tore free and showered behind them as horse and riders galloped wildly across the open fields.

Leah leaned forward onto the stallion's neck, feeling the life force of the great beast beneath her. Her cocked hat flew off, and her hair tumbled free, tangling with the animal's mane as she pressed her face into his shiny black hide.

Brandon locked his arm around her waist and gave the stallion his head. A hedge loomed before them, and Caesar soared over with inches to spare. He thundered across a section of cornfield and up onto the dirt road, turning left toward the river and the prize house.

Leah's temper cooled in the rushing wind, and by the time Brandon reined in the heaving animal near the prize house, her curses had turned to laughter. Caesar slowed to a trot, then to a walk. As they rounded the corner of the building which Brandon had explained earlier was used to pack tobacco into casks for shipping, Leah saw two richly dressed gentlemen sitting on horseback by the door.

"St. George," Brandon called.

The older of the two, a man in a gray coat and cloak, scowled and nodded stiffly. "Lord Brandon."

The second gentleman eyed Leah rudely. He let his explicit gaze fall from her wildly tangled hair, over her partially exposed breasts revealed by her scarlet riding coat, and down to her trousers and beaded moccasins. "Brandon," he said curtly. "Lord Upton, at your service, sir."

It was Brandon's turn to stiffen. Leah heard his sharp hiss of breath next to her ear. "Gentlemen." Brandon's voice was as cold as the bits of earth clinging to Caesar's hooves. "May I present to you my wife, Lady Brandon."

The man Upton smiled nastily. "I'd heard you'd wed with a native, but I didn't believe it."

Brandon thrust the reins into Leah's hand and sprang from the saddle. "I'll thank you to keep a decent tone when you refer to my wife," he threatened, advancing on the horsemen.

St. George laughed. "Upton means no offense, I'm sure. You can't expect to pull something like this and not cause a scandal. It was my understanding that you were returning to England on the *Dependable*. Surely you're not planning on taking Lady Brandon with you."

Brandon's face darkened to puce. "Did you come for a reason or merely to insult me?"

Upton, splendid in a pink coat and fawn breeches, reined his horse backward away from Brandon. "St. George is interested in purchasing this plantation."

"I thought you could pass the word to your father, Lord Kentington," St. George explained. "I've sent several letters to him, but I've had no answer."

"It's not for sale," Brandon said. "None of our American land is for sale. I'm advising my father that we purchase more. Perhaps you'd care to sell your Edenton, Upton. It's a bit run down, but nothing a little money wouldn't fix."

Caesar sniffed at the other horses and shook himself; his tense muscles rippled under the sleek ebony hide. Taken by surprise, Leah pulled back on the reins until she could feel the pressure on his mouth. The animal blew air through his lips and pawed the ground with his left front hoof, but she felt an easing of the tension in his body and knew that he'd decided to submit to her control. Satisfied that he wouldn't run away with her or try to throw her off, she turned her attention back to Brandon and the two Englishmen.

What was happening was confusing. The words being exchanged by the three were not angry ones, but Leah knew that Brandon's fury was barely in check.

Another moment and he'd be at the throats of these men. She wasn't certain what they'd said that angered Brandon; the Upton man had called her a native, but that was no more than truth. The other man had said their wedding was a scandal. That too was so; her whole village had been shocked by her choice of an Englishman.

She wasn't stupid; she knew many white men hated and feared the Indians. The people in Brandon's house, the ones he called servants, were only polite to her with their words. They resented her being there, and they were afraid. But these Englishmen were not afraid of her—they had nothing to do with her. Why were they near to blows with Brandon? She wasn't sure if it was because of her or another quarrel—something to do with this land that Brandon's father claimed.

Foolish that men should fight over land, she thought, but they always did. Why couldn't they realize that land was the earth's skin, and the earth belonged to the Creator, not to the men and women who lived on its bounty. Could a man own air or water? Owning land was just as crazy. A dispute over hunting rights she could understand. The Shawnee often said, "My land." But what they meant was theirs to use, not theirs to possess as a man possesses his knife or moccasins.

The words between Brandon and the others were growing more heated. ". . . off this plantation before I seek satisfaction!" Brandon roared. The men pulled their horses around and rode off angrily. Brandon remounted without speaking to her.

"Was it over me?" she asked.

He took the reins from her hands and dug his heels

into Caesar's taut sides. The black responded eagerly as Brandon guided him back toward the manor house.

They rode without talking, but there was no silence. Overhead were birds and wild ducks; beneath them the creak of saddle leather and the comforting sounds of the stallion. Even the wind against Brandon's stiff back made a sound of its own.

I was wrong to stay so long, Leah thought. I was selfish. I wanted to be with him and I put off returning to Kitate and my family. Now, Brandon has been shamed by his own people. She sighed softly. Alex was right. Whites and Indians could find peace only in the lodges of the red men, never with the English. The English see only skin color, not the hearts that beat beneath the skin.

"It be best for us both if I go at sunrise," she said to Brandon. He pulled her hard against him so that pain shot through her healing shoulder. She gritted her teeth to keep from crying out. "This is nay my world," she continued, when she could talk without letting him know that he'd hurt her. "I be an unwelcome stranger here." He said nothing, and the cold air on her face did not stop the tears that welled up in her eyes.

When they reached the stable, a boy came to take the horse, but Brandon waved him away. "I'll see to him myself," he said, dismounting and lifting Leah down. She followed him into the barn.

A gray horse lifted his head and nickered a greeting. Two red and white oxen peered through a slat in their stall as Brandon led the black down the center passageway. It was shadowy in the barn, and warm after the cool air outside. Leah paused long enough to pet a friendly cat that rubbed against her leg. "Brandon," she said.

He threw Caesar's reins over a rail and began to unsaddle him. Leah opened the stallion's box stall door. The wide stall had been cleaned while they were out riding. Bright straw was heaped knee deep across the floor.

She turned toward Brandon. He was wiping down Caesar's hindquarters with a dry cloth. "Brandon mine . . ." she began. Her voice broke, and she began to cry. He dropped the rag and took her in his arms, kissing her face and neck.

"Shhh, shhh, darling," he soothed. "It will be all right, I promise."

She put her arms around his neck and leaned against him sobbing. *"N'schiwelendam,"* she whispered. "I'm so sorry. I wanted . . . I wanted . . ." Pain choked her words, not the physical pain of her injury, but the deeper pain of her spirit. "Oh, my Sky Eyes," she whispered.

His hands moved over her body, touching, caressing, and she felt the heat of him through their clothes. Fierce yearning curled in the pit of her belly like a growing flame.

"Leah?" It was a question, a question to which she could give only one answer.

"Dah-quel-e-mah," she answered throatily.

"Darling." His hand stroked the small of her back and cupped one cheek of her buttocks possessively. "I want you," he murmured. "I've wanted you so badly . . ."

She trembled in his arms as a familiar weakness seeped through her limbs. Light-headed, she clung to him, meeting his scalding kiss with equal fervor, urging him on with faint cries of passion. Her mouth opened as their kisses deepened, and he thrust his hard, hot tongue into her.

She moaned and squirmed against him, wanting to feel his naked flesh against hers, wanting to quell the heat of her body with his virile love.

His burning kisses moved to her ear and down her throat, driving her mad with wanting him. His hot, wet tongue caressed her again and again, moving lower and lower until the fire within her flared out of control. "Leah," he groaned, gathering her up in his arms.

She caught his face between her hands and lifted it so that she could taste his mouth once more. "Love me," she begged him. "Love me."

Brandon took two strides and lowered her into the deep, sweet-smelling straw of the box stall. She held out her arms to him as he stripped away his coat and shirt and let them fall to the floor. "Come back to me," she whispered as he lowered himself on top of her, pinning her with his weight and burying his face in her breasts. She arched against him, digging her nails into his back and entwining her legs with his. Her breathing came in shuddering gasps as desire flamed white-hot in her veins.

"I'll never let you go," he whispered. "Not now—not ever."

She cried out with wild abandon as he ripped away her riding coat and kissed one breast and then the other. He took her sensitive, erect nipple into his mouth, sucking gently, then harder, sending ripples of intense pleasure to the tips of her toes. "Yes, oh yes," she murmured. The dull ache in her injured shoulder was nothing compared to the wanting, the surging need for fulfillment inside her. She wanted him . . . wanted all of him filling her until they were no longer two but one. "Brandon," she pleaded. "Please . . ."

His tongue teased her nipples as his hands found the waistband of her shirt and trousers. He tugged, and the fabric gave beneath his fingers. Leah felt the scratch of straw against her bare skin, and then the heat of his swollen male sex as he tore aside his own breeches.

His fingertips touched her secret place, and she ran wet with desire. She raised her hips to meet his long, powerful thrust and cried out with joy as he sheathed himself again and again in her willing flesh.

"You're mine," he gasped as he spilled his seed into her. "Mine, Leah, mine."

She clung to him, lost in the splendor of her own climax, too filled with happiness to think farther than this instant, this shared rapture.

Leah held tight to Brandon's waist and stared around her wide-eyed as they rode through the marketplace of Annapolis to where the sailing ship was docked. She'd given in to Brandon's plea that she wait until he left before departing for her own village. There had been no mending her riding habit after their pleasure in the barn, so today she was wearing a proper lady's outfit, complete with red cloak and hood. In such clothing, it was impossible for her to ride astride, so she was sitting sideways behind Brandon on a little leather platform. "Riding pillion," he had called it. Leah was certain it was the oddest way to ride a horse anyone had ever imagined.

"No need to go without seeing the town," he'd

urged her, "or without taking back gifts for Kitate and your family. I'll give orders that someone escort you safely to the farthest English outpost."

They'd ridden down the dirt street that morning, and Leah had gazed in wonder at the houses that rose two and three stories. Each house had windows of glass and a chimney, most had two chimneys, and some even had three or more great piles of brick soaring into the sky. All the chimneys were spewing smoke this day, and the wide streets were crowded with people—more people than Leah had ever seen in one place in her life.

There were white men and women, and blackamoors, and even an Indian or two. Farm women bustled down the street with baskets of bread and vegetables; men lounged in open doorways talking in loud voices, and children and dogs scampered in and out of the throng. Church bells clanged, wagon wheels squeaked, and chickens squawked and scratched in the dust. There were pigs, and geese, and goats being driven up the street by farmers or running loose. Pigeons and shrieking seagulls swooped overhead and dove boldly to steal scraps of food from the ground.

One black woman was leading a skinny red cow with hipbones that stuck up like fence posts. She wore a huge white linen mobcap, and over her shoulder she carried a stick with two pails hanging from it. "Milk for sale," she called. "Fresh milk."

"Is that woman a slave?" Leah whispered in Brandon's ear. She looked admiringly at the large gold disks dangling from the black milkmaid's ears.

"Not likely. That's Mary Tice. She's a free black woman. She owns a farm outside Annapolis. She sells cheese and butter to the ships as well as to the citizens of the town. I'd imagine Mistress Tice is quite well off."

"Oh. Alex said all the blacks were slaves."

"And Alex is never wrong, is he?"

Leah giggled and laid her cheek against his back. Tomorrow, Brandon would sail, and she'd never see him again. She pushed the thought away. Today she would forget all bad things to come—today she would enjoy their last day together. "Oh, look!" she cried.

In the center of the marketplace, a dwarf was tossing colored balls in the air and catching them while a little white dog wearing a cocked hat walked back and forth on his hind legs.

"Look at the little man," she said, "and the dog. Look, Brandon, aren't they wonderful?" She laughed and drew in a great gulp of air, savoring the wonderful smells.

To the left, a woman had built a fire and was grilling fish. Just beyond her, an old man with a white beard sat on the ground with a basket of brown cakes in front of him. He was holding up the round cakes and chanting a silly song. "Cakes. Buy cakes from old Jakes. They'll cure your aches. Buy my cakes. 'Cause I bakes—cakes."

Brandon reined in Caesar and tossed the old man a penny. "Are they fresh?" he demanded.

"Aye, sir, Jakes's cakes he bakes is fresh, ever' week, yer lordship." He jumped up and hurried over with a handful of ginger cakes. "Jakes got no change, sir. No change, just cakes."

Leah giggled again, then nibbled cautiously at the cake Brandon offered her. "Ohhh," she cried. " 'Tis verra good." She swallowed the sweet in two bites and reached for two more.

"Greedy wench," he teased.

"One be for the horse, for Caesar," she said. "He deserves a treat, does he not?"

Brandon guided the horse through the throngs of sailors and merchants down the line of small open boats moored to posts. Anchored in the harbor were four large sailing ships.

"Lord Brandon!" a seaman called. "Here, sir. I'll take your mount."

"Are you from the *Dependable?*" he asked.

"Aye, sir, Second Mate Jones." He motioned for a boy to take Caesar's reins.

Leah watched as Brandon dismounted and walked a few feet away to talk quietly to the man. Mouth open, the boy holding the horse stared up at her. Leah stared back.

Brandon turned back and motioned to her. "It's necessary for me to go out to the ship. It won't take long, and you can come with me." He pointed out over the water. "It's that vessel there, the one with the sea horse on the bow."

Leah looked at the ship with its three great masts, and then at the longboat that would carry them out to the *Dependable*. Two surly-looking sailors in striped shirts waited in the small boat, their hard hands gripped on the paddles. She took a deep breath. "Nay, Brandon mine," she said. "I wait for ye here, with Caesar. Such water be not for us."

"Don't be silly," he said, lifting her down from the horse. "It's perfectly safe. We'll see the ship and be back in time for the noon meal at the inn."

She gave him a teasing shove and shook her head. "Nay, Brandon viscount. I dinna like your boats, nay the big one, nay the small. I shall stand here on solid earth until ye return.''

His face colored. "Don't make a scene, Leah.''

Her eyes narrowed suspiciously. Something was wrong. It wasn't like Brandon to try to force her to do something against her will. She backed away a few steps. "Go on. I'll wait for ye,'' she said again. Her mouth was suddenly dry. The strange way he was looking at her made her stomach do a sudden flip-flop. "Brandon?''

He moved before she had a chance to run. His fingers closed over her wrist. She screamed and struck at him with her free hand, but he swept her up in his arms and scrambled down into the waiting boat amid the laughter of men on the dock.

She struggled against him as tears of anger ran down her face. "Let me go!'' she insisted. "Let me go!''

"You're my wife,'' he whispered harshly into her ear. "You're my wife, and you go where and when I tell you.''

"Nay,'' she flung back. The tears were coming so fast that Brandon's face blurred before her. "Dinna do this,'' she begged. "Dinna.''

"Hush,'' he commanded. "Hush. You'll hurt yourself.'' She got one fist free and struck him square in the eye. "Ouch! Damn it, Leah.''

He pinned her arms against her side, and she slammed her head against his chin. "Let me go!''

"Cut it out, woman, or I'll tie you like a trussed goose. I swear I will.''

She caught the skin of his neck between her teeth and bit him hard as she could. Blood ran down his white shirt, and he grabbed hold of her hair and snatched her head back. "Damn ye!" she cried. "I'll never forgive ye for this! Never!"

Leah was still fighting and cursing him when they tied her wrists and ankles and hauled her aboard the ship in a net.

PART 2

England

Chapter 12

Dorsetshire, England, February 1721

Leah leaned her cheek against the window of the bouncing coach and stared out at the gray countryside. Chestnut, elm, and oak lined both sides of the narrow dirt lane, but occasionally there was a gap in the trees and she could see open rolling fields through the winter-bare branches.

The air was damp, heavy with unshed rain. The gloomy skies had threatened a downpour since the coach had departed from the thatch-roofed village inn early that morning. The windows of the coach were covered with leather curtains to protect the passengers against the elements, but Leah had pulled hers aside, trading a measure of comfort for the sights and smells of the outdoors.

"Leah? Are you cold?" Brandon asked.

She felt the weight of a fur robe tucked around her shoulders, but she gave him no sign that she'd heard or noticed. Ignoring Brandon had become a habit.

He leaned close to her and whispered. "How long is this going to go on? We'll be at Westover by dark,

175

and I'll not have you insulting my family with your sulking."

Her shoulders went rigid as she turned and gazed into his face. "What is between thee and me, *uiki-imuk*, concerns no other. Ye need have no fear." She kept her face expressionless, concealing the pain and anger that had nearly driven her mad in the months at sea.

"I'm not a monster, Leah," he said. "How many times must I tell you I'm sorry? I'll take you back to America as soon as I can." He glared at the maid in the seat across from them, and she averted her gaze. "You are my wife, and you must start acting like it."

"Aye," she murmured. "So ye say." She turned back to the window, shutting him out of her world, trying to shut out the memory of bitter words and broken promises.

If the English preachers were right about there being a hell, Leah had no fear of ever going there. She had already been in hell . . .

The morning Brandon had carried her aboard the *Dependable* was indelibly etched in her mind. She had fought him for hours; she had even tried to knife him with a silver letter opener. Once, before the ship had sailed beyond the sight of land, she'd nearly jumped over the side. In the end, Brandon had locked her in the tiny cabin alone and found sleeping space elsewhere.

He'd not hit her—not once—not even when she'd thrown the meal in his face. She had called him liar and deceiver, and she had sworn that she would never forgive him as long as she drew breath.

"*Cut-ta-ho-tha!*" she had spat at him, using the term given in contempt to those condemned to burn at the stake. "Better I had let them kill you." She had said those terrible words, but she had not meant them . . . not even then. In a small corner of her heart, she would always love him, no matter what he did to her. But she had said the words, and she had read the pain in his eyes. Worse, she was glad she had hurt him.

The childish ranting and the striking out had passed once the ship was so far at sea that she knew there was no chance of escaping. It had crossed her mind that there was an ultimate escape—she could take her own life. Brandon could not hold her prisoner if she wished to die. But that thought passed, too. She was many things, but coward was not one of them. She would face life . . . face the true curse of her amulet.

"I will not be defeated by my father's magic," she swore to herself in that dark cabin. "By *Inu-msi-ila-fe-wanu!* I will meet the curse without fear, and I will win!"

. . . *You will be taken from your family and friends to a far-off land,* Father had said. But he had promised more than heartache. *You will be granted one wish. Whatever you ask . . .* he had said.

If the amulet had the power to curse, it also contained the power to bless. Leah had clung to that hope, and hope had kept her from losing her mind on board ship, in a place where there were no trees, no grass, no eagles soaring overhead.

The stench of the ship would remain in her head as long as she lived. The air beneath the decks smelled of rot, and vomit, and mold. The cabin was so small she could cross it in four short steps, and there was no window. When the weather turned bad and the ship rose and fell at the mercy of the waves, the cabin became a den of misery. The backbone of the vessel creaked and groaned and threatened to snap, drowning captain, crew, and passengers in the bottomless deep.

After a few days, when she'd learned that the maid Nancy, the girl Brandon had brought to wait on her, was living in even more miserable quarters, Leah allowed the frightened girl to share her cabin. Nancy believed that Leah was crazy . . . perhaps she had been for a while. She'd gone nearly a week without eating until Brandon had taken hold of her shoulders and shaken her, forcing her to look at him.

"You're not a wild animal, for God's sake," he'd shouted. "You're an intelligent woman. Now start eating what they bring you, or I'll pour it down your throat."

She'd thought about that for a few hours, and then she'd allowed Nancy to help her dress in one of the English gowns. When Brandon had returned to her cabin to ask her to join him for the evening meal, something he had done day after day, she had accepted. She'd accompanied him to the captain's cabin and sat at the table with Brandon and the other important passengers. She had eaten a little, but she hadn't spoken to any of them. It became her custom for the remainder of the voyage.

On good days, she walked with Brandon on the deck. If he asked her a question, she answered. If he touched her, she didn't protest, but she never touched him voluntarily. Above all, she refused to let him sleep in her cabin. She would accept that she was his prisoner, but among the Shawnee even a prisoner had rights, and she would never let him forget those rights.

She had believed that the voyage would never end.

She was wrong. At last, they had begun to see birds, and other ships, and finally, far off along the edge of the world, a shoreline. The *Dependable* had sailed up a river Brandon called the Thames to a great English town.

London. Leah shivered as she remembered the crowded narrow streets and the dirty, thin urchins. Beggars crept from the alleys to hold out stumps where arms had once grown, and babies too small to walk played in fetid ditches.

Brandon spoke to her of great houses, of kings and balls and pleasure gardens. His face lit with excitement and he gestured with his hands as their coach rumbled past enormous churches and palaces. But his words fell on deaf ears. To Leah, the English buildings were only cold stone, gray and dirty, without life. She saw none of the splendor. Instead, she saw the blackened faces of emaciated chimney sweeps and heard the weeping of hungry, homeless children.

Each pitiful child reminded her of her own lost son. Kitate was only three, hardly more than a baby. How could he understand why his mother had gone away and not returned? Did he believe she had abandoned him as her father had abandoned her? Or did Kitate think she was dead? Perhaps it was better for him if he didn't think of her at all, if he forgot he had a mother. She would never forget him, and if she lived, she would find a way to return to him and to her forest home.

The coach lurched sideways, and the horses' hooves clattered across a low stone bridge. Leah raised in her seat and peered out at the meandering stream below. A skim of ice had formed in the eddies, encrusting the rocks with a silvery sheen. Beyond the bridge was a small village of stone cottages with thatched roofs.

The coachman reined in the team with a shout. "Whoa, whoa, there!" He leaned down from his box. "Herring Cross, yer lordship," he called in a hearty voice. "Nooning."

Brandon laid his gloved hand over Leah's. "We'll stop here for a while," he said. "The innkeeper serves a wonderful kidney pie, if my memory serves me. We can walk a bit beside the water, if you like."

Brandon's manservant scrambled down from his seat beside the coachman and brought wooden steps to aid them in their descent from the high vehicle. The coach was a rented one, Brandon had explained earlier, and had none of the luxuries of the private Kentington conveyances. Leah allowed the servant, William, to take her hand and help her onto the dirt road. Brandon and the maid stepped out behind her.

Leah turned back toward the bridge. She heard Brandon's footsteps, but she didn't acknowledge him until he tucked his arm through hers.

"Mind your skirts," he cautioned.

She glanced down at the yards of cream-colored satin and sighed heavily. Corsets, petticoats, and hoops made her feel like a wild creature in a trap. The English garments twisted a woman's body into an unnatural shape and made it impossible to run, or to climb a tree, or even to sit in comfort. Brandon's tight breeches, ornamented waistcoat, and wide cuffed coat with silver buttons seemed just as ridiculous.

"The hem of your gown is trailing in the dust," Brandon insisted.

She yanked the dress up, wishing for all the world she could strip away these hated clothes and ease her pinched toes into a pair of soft leather moccasins. Brandon had insisted they remain in London until a complete wardrobe of new, stylish clothing had been made for both of them. A sour-faced woman had spent days teaching her how to walk and sit without sending the hoops and the skirts over her head and exposing her private parts to anyone passing by.

She had stood for hours being pinned and pushed, tucked and tilted, and she'd accepted the torture without complaint—as she would have had she been a prisoner of the Iroquois. Her face had been painted and her hair curled. When she looked into a mirror, a stranger stared back at her, but Brandon seemed pleased.

"We'll make a great lady of you yet," he'd declared.

"But I am already a person of worth," she'd answered. "My mother was a great lady, and she had no need of English finery."

"I'm sure she was," Brandon had agreed, "but this is England. Here you must follow the customs, or people will believe you a savage."

A crow dropped out of a tree and lit on the bridge wall. He bobbed his black feathered head up and down and regarded Leah solemnly with beady eyes. She laughed.

"That's good to hear," Brandon said, squeezing her arm. "I was afraid you'd forgotten how."

A tear formed in the corner of Leah's eye, and she blinked it away. What use was it to tell Brandon how he'd hurt her by his betrayal? How could she ever make him understand that he'd destroyed their love when he'd made her a prisoner? He'd told her he was sorry, but *sorry* was only a word. *Judge a man by his actions, never his words*, her mother had told her. *Words slide off the lips like water off an otter's back.*

Leah leaned against the cold stone and stared into the icy water rushing below. "I have nay forgotten," she said softly. " 'Tis only that I have had little to laugh about."

Brandon freed his arm and dropped it around her shoulder. "That will change, I swear it. We'll make a new beginning between us. I know England is strange to you, but you'll like it once you grow accustomed to our ways. There's so much I want to show you."

She raised her eyes to meet his. "There be only one thing I want of ye—to go home."

His features hardened. "I'll take you when I can, Leah. Right now, I must think of my father and my responsibilities as his heir."

"Aye," she said coldly, "so ye tell me."

"This isn't going to be easy for either of us. You'll only make it worse if you keep treating me like your enemy."

"But ye are," she replied in her own soft, lilting tongue. "And I am held captive in a far-off land by a Scottish curse and a husband I cannot trust."

Lord Kentington snatched his wig from his bald head and flung it into his bedchamber fireplace. "Preposterous!" he roared. "I'll not have it!" Clouds of smoke and the foul stench of burning human hair arose as the wig ignited. Brandon's mother screamed and fell back into her chair, nearly squashing her small, spotted lapdog. The dog yipped as one maid began to fan her choking mistress and the second ran to open a casement window. "No son of mine shall be wed to a red Indian heathen!" Kentington shouted.

A footman pulled the blazing wig from the hearth and stomped on it. The dog ran under Lord Kentington's high poster bed, barking in a voice much too loud for such a tiny animal. Lady Kentington began to weep.

Seemingly unconcerned, Brandon stood inside the closed bedchamber door, arms folded across his chest. He and Leah had arrived at his father's country house after dark the night before. His parents had both already been asleep, and knowing there'd be a scene, Brandon had ordered the servants not to wake them. For the same reason, he'd asked Leah to remain in his chambers while he had a private reunion with his doting parents.

"I'll not have it, I say," his father repeated loudly. "Annul her or shoot her, I care not—but get the red baggage out of my house."

"Raymond," Brandon's mother wailed. "Calm yourself, for pity's sake. Remember your condition."

Brandon stepped aside to let the footman pass with the smoldering wig held at arm's length on the end of the poker. "Cease your caterwauling, Mother," Brandon said. "If he can still bellow like a bull, he can hardly be at death's door."

"You insolent young pup! I'll disinherit you! Cut you from my will!"

"If you could, you'd have done it long ago, Father." Brandon approached the great Elizabethan bed cautiously, keeping well out of reach of his father's silver-tipped walking cane and the dog's teeth. "This is hardly a fit welcome home for your only son and his bride," he said, flashing a smile at his mother.

Lady Kathryn sniffed and wiped her nose with a lace handkerchief. "A pagan woman, Brandon. How could you?"

"No more pagan than I, Mother. Leah's a good Catholic, and we were married by a priest, not a medicine man with a bone through his nose. She's the natural daughter of a Scottish earl—if that matters to you." He arched an eyebrow rakishly at Lady Kathryn. He'd only half believed Leah's romantic tale of a noble father, but he knew his mother would grasp at any pretense to quality for his bride. She'd always adored him and upheld him to his father through thick and thin. Mother had her standards, and to her, the illegitimate daughter of a nobleman was infinitely more worthy than any commoner.

Lady Kathryn blew her nose daintily and began to fan herself despite the draft from the open window. "I'm sure she told you so," she began. "You've always been too trusting."

"Leah's surname is Stewart, Mother, and she possesses a very valuable gold necklace—a family heirloom. I can trust her, I assure you. She risked her own life to save mine more than once. Without Leah, I'd never have lived to return to you."

Lady Kathryn snapped her fan shut. "Stewart, you say? Which branch of the Stewarts? Where are the family estates?"

"By the bloody head of Saint John!" Lord Kentington growled. "Am I to die of exposure? Shut the damned window!" The older maid hurried to obey, and Lord Kentington slapped the bedcovers with his walking stick. "Christ's wounds, you've no more sense than a village drunkard. Whatever possessed you to marry the wench in a church?"

"Stop your snarling, Father. You know you're glad to have me home. Leah's a real beauty—you'll like her, I promise. Nothing's ever dull when she's around."

"Have you got her with child?" the earl demanded.

Brandon laughed. "No, I have not. I married her because I wanted to. Didn't you pick mother over your father's protests?"

"He objected only because she was a cousin and he didn't want you to be born with two heads." Kentington cleared his throat and leaned forward in the bed. Immediately, a manservant propped several pillows behind the earl's back. "Should have listened to him," Kentington continued. "The lady he wanted me to wed is the mother of five sons, each one a credit to his family. Not a one involved in Jacobite plots. Nary a one has ever had arrest warrants filed against him—nor driven his father to the brink of the grave."

"Hush such talk, Raymond." Lady Kathryn protested. "Pay no heed to him, darling," she said. "Lady Dacre has the temperament and the morals of a goat. Two of her sons were reportedly sired by a stable groom, and the youngest has the nose and ears of her husband's valet. Your father wouldn't have Lady Dacre if I dropped dead this instant."

"You should have waited to wed," Kentington said gruffly. "Lady Anne is widowed, and she's been here twice asking for you. You could have had Anne and her money." He made a noise of derision. "You still could, if you'd agree to get rid of this creature upstairs."

"It's true, dear," his mother chimed in. "Anne is

smitten with you, and she would make a much better match.''

"Enough," Brandon said. "I've heard all I wish to. You've both made yourselves clear. Now, once and for all, let me do the same. Leah and I are legally married. I don't care that she's penniless. I'll inherit enough for both of us. You will treat her as a daughter in this house—as my wife should be treated—or I'll go and take her with me. I've the London town house, and the manor in Kent.''

"Mother of God! Don't think of such a thing," Lady Kathryn cried. "You've only just come. Of course you and your wife are welcome here. We only want what's best for you, dear. Tell him, Raymond. Tell him there'll be no more talk of leaving again.''

"Keep the wench if it makes you happy," his father said grudgingly. "So long as she doesn't come in here and make me miserable with her war dances and heathen practices, I'm sure I'll not slight her. Like as not the Wescott blood is strong enough to overcome even a red savage's. But if your sons are born with feathers instead of hair, don't blame me.''

"I'll take the chance," Brandon said dryly. "Now, if the servants wish to serve breakfast here, I'll bring Leah down to meet you. Mind''—he glared at his father—"I'll expect you to be on your very best behavior.''

Lord Kentington grunted as his manservant adjusted a fresh wig on his large, shiny head. "Bad enough that a man is confined to his bed without having to take sass from an arrogant young pup. Have you no pity for a dying man?''

"I crossed the Atlantic in winter storms to attend you, Father.'' Brandon turned to his mother and took her hand. "You are as lovely as ever. I was afraid tending him would wear on your own health."

"I have a delicate constitution, as you well know." She rose and embraced him. "But seeing you safely home is better for me than all the physician's medicines. Bring your bride down. If she's your choice, dear, then we shall all make the best of it, I'm sure."

"As you wish, Mother." Brandon chuckled as he took the black-veined marble staircase two steps at a time. The interview had gone much better than he'd expected. And his father looked spry for a dying man, spry enough to live for years.

He paused at the first landing where a life-sized Greek water bearer in rose marble stood guard. Absently, Brandon traced the worn right foot with his fingertips. His cousin Charles had told him that it was good luck, and, as a child, he'd never run down the staircase without stopping to rub the statue. This house held so many memories for Brandon, mostly good ones . . .

His father had always been difficult. After the loss of three babies over fifteen years, Brandon's mother had been ecstatic to have a live, healthy son. The earl hadn't been so easy to please.

Charles was older by two years, and he had already been a member of the Wescott household. Until he was nine or ten, Brandon could remember striving to match his cousin's skill in games and riding. No matter how hard he tried, Brandon could never quite run fast enough or put enough arrows in the bull's-eye to beat Charles. And the earl . . . Brandon shrugged. His father was never satisfied with his attempts, not even when Charles stopped growing and Brandon caught up with him and then passed him in size and ability.

No, nothing he ever did pleased Kentington, and, eventually, he'd stopped trying to win his father's approval and concentrated on his own pleasures.

Brandon gave the water bearer a final pat and continued ascending the curving steps, wondering just how many of his youthful indiscretions were committed to spite his father. He hoped marrying Leah and bringing her home wasn't one of them.

The maid, Nancy, met him at the door of his bedchamber in tears. "What's wrong?" he asked.

Nancy clutched her apron with both hands, balling the starched linen in utter despair. "It's Lady Brandon, your lordship."

"What is it? Has something happened to her? Is she ill?"

Nancy shook her head as a fresh flood of fat tears rolled down her blotchy face. "She . . . she . . ." Nancy pointed toward the open door leading to the balcony. "She's gone, sir. Out of the house."

"What do you mean? We're three stories from the ground!"

"Yes, sir, but it's true." Nancy wiped her nose on her apron. "She said she was goin' and she went. Over the rail of the balcony and down the side of the building." She gulped. "Wearin' nothing but her shift."

Chapter 13

Leah opened the iron gate and entered the boxwood maze. Inside, the evergreen hedge rose higher than she could reach, and she could barely see the tile roof and massive stone chimneys of Westover. The bare earth was cold beneath her stockinged feet—she'd not dared to climb down from the balcony with shoes on, so she'd borrowed a pair of Brandon's woolen stockings to pull over her own. Curious to see what lay within the passage of hedge, she shut the gate behind her and followed the neat pathway.

Brandon would be furious when he returned to their chambers and found her gone, but she didn't care. She'd not been outside alone since she'd left America. Brandon hadn't wanted her with him when he went to greet his mother and father. That was fine with her. Now he could wait until she chose to return to her prison.

She looked up at the puffy white clouds skittering across the pale blue sky and drew in a deep breath of clean country air. She'd believed that the foul air aboard the ship would smother her, and the air of London had been even worse. Gooseflesh rose on her bare arms, and she shivered. It was cool this morning, and she wished for her deerskin cloak and leggings. The satin gown Nancy had laid out for her would have been warmer than the linen shift, but the thought of trying to get out of the house in her gown and hoops made her laugh out loud.

She had learned a great deal about England since the *Dependable* docked in London. The English, she decided, were a perverse people. Custom had decreed that Brandon hire a coach and driver to bring them from London to Westover here in Dorsetshire. The journey—with servants, and baggage—took nine days. The great heavy vehicle could hardly go any distance at all before it mired in the mud or broke a wheel. It made no sense to her. There were roads leading from the city to Westover. If she and Brandon had ridden the coach horses instead of sitting on the hard seats of the teeth-jarring coach, they would have covered the distance in three days or less and avoided sleeping in flea-infested inns or being attacked by highwaymen.

On their fourth day out of London, two masked men on horseback had tried to stop the coach with a log across the road. The coachman had shouted a warning to Brandon and wheeled his coach and team around the barrier, nearly running down one of the highwaymen. The other bandit had fired a shot at the coach, but Brandon had seized his musket from the floor and shot back. Neither outlaw had cared to follow the speeding coach, and Brandon and the coachman had shared a mug of ale and laughter at the next stop.

Brandon had said it was "a pitiful attempt at robbery. Nothing to be alarmed about." He'd warned Leah not to mention the incident to his mother, who would become hysterical after the fact. "Highway-men are a nuisance travelers must contend with," he'd observed calmly as he rewarded the quick-thinking coachman with a handful of silver coins.

Leah hadn't been particularly disturbed—after all, the whole episode had been over in the time it took to skin a rabbit—but the terrified maid had sobbed for hours. It had proved to Leah that England wasn't quite as tame and civilized as Brandon liked to brag.

Continuing through the boxwood maze, Leah reached a fork in the path. One way led left, and an equally inviting trail opened to the right. Alex had once told her that given a choice, most men will al-ways take the left branch of a trail because a man's heart is on the left side. A wise trapper knows this. If he sets a snare for a human, he will hide the trap on the left fork. Leah chose the right. The pathway narrowed disappointingly, and the hedge closed over-top to make a tunnel. She continued on, and when the path divided again, she knelt and examined the earth to see which trail was the more used, then took the other.

A dried maple leaf lay in the path, its once golden color faded and dull. Leah picked it up and held it in her hand. My love for my husband has become like this leaf, she thought. Once it was a living thing, strong and green. Now . . . She crumpled the leaf in her hand and sprinkled the pieces in the air. She closed her eyes and pictured his face with his sky-blue eyes and his long yellow hair. "Oh, Brandon mine," she murmured. "Why?"

She brushed the bits of leaf from her hands. Bran-don was not the man here in England that he was in the forest. He'd not lied to her when he said he was a man of importance. Wherever they went, men bowed to him and doffed their hats. They spoke to him in hushed, respectful voices and hurried to do his bidding. She had watched and retained all these things in her memory—they made her even more confused.

Brandon was not a great warrior—by his own words, he had led no war parties and had no following of braves. There were men who obeyed his word as though it were law, but they did it for silver and copper coin, not out of loyalty. He was not a war chief or a sachem, and he certainly was no shaman. He knew little of the healing arts and still less of the workings of their mind.

Could it be possible that the English revered men such as her husband merely because of their birth? Brandon had told her that his father was a powerful earl and that he possessed great wealth. If this was true of Brandon's father, Kentington, was it not also true of her own father, Cameron?

"I have so much to learn," she murmured to the cold winter earth beneath her feet, "and so little time to learn it."

The evil that Brandon had done to her had caused a great breach between them. He knew that he had done wrong, and the more she reviled him, the colder his eyes became when he looked at her. It was possible that it was already too late for her to win back his affection. Leah folded her arms across her chest and rocked back and forth in silent misery.

"I will die rather than seek his help," she whispered. But she knew that it was her pride speaking and not the inner wisdom of her soul. If she ever wanted to go home again—to see her child and breathe

the sweet air of her forests and rivers—she must have her husband's help.

She began to walk faster down the path, taking first one fork and then another as the path split and doubled back. Finally, she was running, trying in vain to escape the truth. When she reached the little round-topped stone house in the center of the maze, she dropped to her knees and wrapped her arms around a carved stone pillar. She pressed her cheek against the cold marble and sobbed dry sobs of anguish.

After a few moments, she rose and straightened her shoulders. She was the daughter of a Shawnee peace woman; she would not shame her ancestors with cowardice or useless wailing. As the lump of frustration melted away, she was rewarded with words of wisdom from her heart. Brandon had used her when he was a captive of the Shawnee—he had sought out her love to free himself. Now, their positions were reversed. She must use him. She must gain his trust and his love in any way she could.

Her lips moved silently. "Do I want to go home badly enough to pay the price?" The answer was a great lightness that bubbled up inside her. "Yes! Yes! And yes again!"

"N'mamentschi," she said. I rejoice. And she knew that, for the first time since she'd left the Shawnee village, her heart and head were as one.

As Brandon emerged from Westover's grand entranceway, he noticed a man on horseback trotting across the enclosed courtyard lawn. Brandon shaded his eyes from the bright morning sun and grinned. "Charles!" he hurried down the curving steps. "Damn you, cousin! You look in fine health."

Charles dismounted, and Brandon threw his arms around the smaller man and hugged him tightly. "We got your message from London, but no one told me you'd arrived," Charles said. "I've been trying out this new hunter." A groom took the reins of the horse and led him away. Charles slapped Brandon on the shoulder. "It's good to see you. We thought you were lost in the Virginias."

Brandon drew back and inspected his cousin. When they were growing up together here at Westover, Charles had been a thin, sickly boy, much given to sulking. Brandon had felt sorry for his cousin's orphaned state and had fought more than one battle when the older boy's irritating manner had set someone's teeth on edge. "In truth, cuz," Brandon said, "you show no signs of ill health. You were suffering from the pox when I left for the Colonies, and I feared the worst for you."

"A light case," Charles said. "I've a few scars, but nothing like the one you gave me." For a second Charles's stare was malevolent, then he broke into a charming grin.

"You'll never let me forget that, will you?" Brandon laughed and grasped his cousin's arm again. "I was fourteen, for God's sake."

Charles's gray eyes narrowed. "Old enough to swive my sweetheart." He struck Brandon's shoulder again playfully. "No hard feelings. I've more than made up for Cecily."

"Poor chit. I've never forgotten her. Funny what sticks with you, isn't it. A shame she died. It's bothered me ever since."

"Has it?" Charles shrugged. "God's truth, Brandon, I can't remember the jade's face." He rubbed at the old knotted scar that ran up his neck. "I'd have given up drubbing you about this long ago, if the damned thing didn't stare at me in the mirror every morning." His plain face brightened. "Well, where is she? I hear you've brought home a little savage for a wife."

Brandon frowned. "Your humor is ill taken, cuz. I've had all of that I can take this morning from Kentington. And, as to where she is . . . Actually, I'm not sure. While I was making peace with the old man, she took it in her head to leave the house. I'd appreciate it if you'd give me a hand in finding her."

Charles chuckled. He removed his cocked hat and ran a hand through his thinning brown hair. "Leads you a merry chase, does she? This is one lady I'm anxious to meet."

Brandon glanced around the empty courtyard. "I don't think she'd go far." His voice took on a tone of sarcasm. "She isn't dressed for it."

"Consider me at your service." Charles laughed. "This play is becoming more fun by the moment. What, pray tell, is the Lady Brandon wearing?"

Brandon's reply was barely audible. "Her shift."

"Her shift? God's teeth! What a tale for the whist table." Charles threw up his hands in mock defense and stepped back. "Peace. I was only joshing you. You know our dark family secrets remain so." His features became serious. "I was shocked to hear you'd become involved with the Jacobites. Surely it isn't so. That route has been the downfall of far too many—"

"False, all of it. I'd rather see a good English king on the throne than a German—I've never made bones about that—but George is our lawful sovereign. I'm no traitor. You, above all, should know that. By the

Holy Shroud, Charles, you know my nights are spent arguing agriculture, not politics. And if my mind did run to treason, I'd think too much of the Kentington titles and fortune to throw them all away on dreams of civil war.''

Charles nodded. ''So I told his majesty's agents when they questioned me. There was quite a to-do. Lord Harval summoned your father, but you can imagine the answer Uncle Raymond sent back. He may not think much of you, Brandon, but since you're his son and heir, he'll defend you until the second coming.'' He nodded again. ''It was wise of you to make yourself scarce in Virginia. Two new heads went up on London Bridge, and Miles Chester lost his estates and had to flee to the Low Countries.''

''I'm sick to death of Jacobite plots. The less said, the better. Miles should have had more sense.''

''Still . . .'' Charles looked thoughtful. ''You have to admire a man like that, who'd risk everything for a cause.''

''Just be glad you're too well known for raising cups and petticoats to be considered a threat to the Crown. Too many men have coughed away their lives in the Tower because of rumors and unfounded accusations.''

Charles laughed wryly. ''A disciple of Bacchus, that's me. Now, shall we hunt for your lost pigeon or wait until we hear drums?''

Brandon swore a foul oath, only half in jest, and the two strode off toward the gardens. When they reached the first fountain, Charles set off to the right and Brandon to the left.

Brandon paused by the gate to the boxwood maze and called Leah's name. A peacock's shriek was the only answer. He turned away from the maze and searched the topiary walk and the statuary garden. He found gardeners and a stray sheep but no sign of a Shawnee woman in a linen shift. As the moments lengthened into an hour, Brandon's concern increased and his patience dwindled. Kentington would be furious, and his mother would work herself into one of her infamous fainting spells. With each passing minute, Brandon saw his chances of gaining acceptance for his marriage to Leah fading.

"Leah!" he called again. "By the grace of God, if you don't come out, I'll—"

"Up here."

He stared up at the cedar tree over his head. "Leah? What the hell are you doing up a tree?"

She laughed. "I can see far. Come up, Brandon mine. There's a field of black-nosed sheep, and a river, and a hill with a strange white dwelling on it."

"You get down here! You've kept my parents waiting and given the servants a feast of gossip. Have you taken leave of your wits, woman?"

"What is that funny white house with columns?"

"Father's architect's interpretation of a Greek temple."

"What is it for?"

"Pigeons to roost on. Now get down at once!"

She laughed again. He heard the rustle of branches, a bough parted, and Leah dropped lightly to the ground in front of him.

He scowled at her. Her shift was torn and smudged with grass stains; one braid had come loose and the other was tangled with bits of cedar greenery. Leah had a long scratch on her cheek, and her hands were dirty. He let his scorching gaze travel down over her bare, scraped knees to the damp, sagging woolen stockings. "I'll have an explanation for this," he demanded.

She shrugged and a smile danced across her lips. "I be tired of living in boxes," she said meekly. "I wanted to breath and see something other than the window of a bouncing coach."

His face grew stern. "And it didn't occur to you to ask? Or to venture forth from your chambers in proper attire?" She didn't answer. His palms grew sweaty, and he felt waves of angry frustration swelling in his chest. "You've made me a laughingstock," he said, removing his coat and draping it around her shoulders. "How the hell can I make my parents accept you if you're going to—"

"Nay," she protested softly. "None saw me but Nancy. She will na' tell. She's afraid of me." Leah caught her lower lip between her teeth and lowered her lashes, preventing him from seeing into her eyes.

"I've had it with you!" he said bitterly. "I admitted I made a mistake in bringing you to England, and I've tried to make amends. Nothing satisfies you." He took her by the arms and turned her to face him. "I've slept alone, and I've listened to your weeping and your insults. This is my country, my home, and I won't be made to look a fool anymore. If you ever want to get back to that precious wilderness of yours, we'll do things my way. Do you understand?"

Bright spots of color tinted her cheeks. "Aye," she whispered. "I do."

She looked so contrite that he wanted to pull her into his arms and kiss her, but his injured pride still pricked like a steel spur. "It's not too late to mend our marriage, Leah," he said. "Here at Westover I have my own chambers, and I hope you will want to share them with me in the near future.''

The immense black pupils of her eyes were as hard and shiny as polished jet. It was impossible for Brandon to tell what she was thinking. ''We had something once,'' he began. ''I hoped—''

''Aye,'' she agreed, ''ye may hope.'' She pushed aside his hands, shrugged off his coat, and began to walk as regally as any royal princess back toward the manor house.

''Leah,'' he called after her.

She reached down and picked up a fallen peacock feather. ''Shall I tuck this into my hair,'' she asked coolly, ''so that everyone will know for certain you've taken a savage to wife?''

Brandon swore under his breath.

''What say ye, husband?'' She tucked the feather into her remaining braid. ''Do ye approve?''

''I do.'' Charles pushed his way through a row of small cedars. ''Lady Brandon, I'm charmed.'' He removed his hat and made a sweeping bow. ''I'm your cousin Charles, and I'm happy to welcome you to Westover.''

Brandon plucked the feather from Leah's hair and wrapped her in his coat. ''You'll excuse us if we don't stay and chat.'' He glared at Charles. ''Mother's expecting us.''

Charles winked at Leah. ''Don't let him browbeat you, m'lady. He can be an insufferable prig.''

Brandon bristled, remembering Charles's biting wit all too well. ''Enough, cuz,'' he warned. ''There'll be the devil to pay if I don't get her back without Mother meeting us on the stairs.''

Charles laughed. ''For a price, I'll create a diversion that will lure every living member of the household to the back of the manor."

"What do you want?" Brandon growled.

"A kiss of greeting from my pretty new kinswoman. What say you, Lady Brandon? A kiss to save your husband from a lifetime of explanations?"

"Forget it, Charles." Brandon stepped between his wife and his cousin. "She doesn't understand your humor."

" 'Tis ye who be humorless," Leah said. She bestowed a genuine smile on Charles. "A kiss between strangers is not the custom of my people, but I would consider it an act of friendship if ye would create, as you said, a *diversion* so that I may return to my quarters unseen."

"Ah hah!" Charles cried in mock astonishment. "The beauty possesses not only speech but wisdom." He bowed again. "Your servant, madame. For this—or any other favor—you've but to ask." He arched a sparse blond eyebrow. "Give me ten minutes, and I'll give you a clear, dry track," he promised. "Until dinner, little cousin, and I've no doubt that you'll enliven our meal a great deal." He nodded and walked swiftly toward the front entrance of the house.

"I'm sorry," Leah said to Brandon. "I did not think any would see me."

He exhaled softly. "Take care with Charles. He's not the jester he'd have you believe. Beneath that light exterior is a complex, brooding personality."

"He is your clansman, yet ye canna trust him?"

Brandon shook his head. "It's not that simple. Charles is Charles . . . There's none like him. He's the closest thing to a brother I've ever had, but I spent the first years of my life envying him. And"—he frowned—"I think he's spent the remainder envying me."

She moved close and stared up into his eyes. "But do ye trust him?"

Brandon drew in a deep breath. How could he make her understand Charles when he himself couldn't and he'd known Charles all his life? Charles could charm gold from a moneylender when he wanted to, or be a first-rate bastard without blinking an eye. "I love him like a brother," he admitted finally, "but trust . . . Does any man know who he can trust?"

"Or a woman?"

Brandon's shoulders stiffened, and he felt the tightness in his chest again. "By the hounds of hell! What other man in England takes such punishment for insisting his wife goes where he does?"

"I be no Englishwoman."

"Let it rest, Leah, for the love of God. I've no wish to fight this same battle with you every hour of the day."

"Nor I with you," she answered, letting her gaze drop. "I'm sorry."

He picked a twig from her hair. What was there about Leah that made him want to kiss her and strangle her in the same moment? "If we can reach your rooms without being caught," he said as calmly as he could manage, "have Nancy dress you in the rose satin. I told Mother about your father's title—your birth makes a difference to her. Say as little as possible to her about the Shawnee. She'd be totally at a loss to understand them."

"Ye wish me to hid my Shawnee blood?" Leah drew herself up to her full height. "*Amotshiikus!* Buzzard! My Shawnee ancestors have as great value as any English. My mother's people—"

Brandon threw up a hand, palm down. "Cease. I meant no insult to your family, Indian or Scottish. I only said that my mother . . . My mother is a simple woman, Leah. Don't make things more difficult for us and for her. She will accept you if you give her half a chance."

"And Lord Kentington?"

"He barely tolerates me, so I've small expectations for you. Treat him gently, if you can. Regardless of how little we agree, he's my father."

They crossed the courtyard and started up the steps to the door. Leah hesitated for an instant and looked up at the imposing stone mansion. "I have pity for thee," she said softly.

"For me? Why?"

She sighed. "Ye be a great mon, yet ye canna trust your clansman, and there is no peace between you and your parents."

He took her arm as he opened the heavy walnut batten door. "I'd not be alone," he said, "if you were a true wife to me."

She stepped into the dark hall. "Each man must find his own trail," she replied in a hushed tone, "and it may be that Wishemenetoo means for you to walk it alone."

Chapter 14

Leah yawned behind her hand and tried to find her high-heeled satin slipper with her toe. The dinner with Brandon's mother was tiresome, and she was seated at the far end of the table near cousin Charles and away from Brandon. An unsmiling manservant in a red coat stood behind her; another man and two women scurried around the huge room bringing and removing dishes of food.

The room was so large and ornate, it was hard for Leah to imagine that Brandon's family used it only for eating. The table stretched as long as three canoes laid end to end, and the floor was painted in large white and black squares. Silver candlesticks with many arms marched down the length of the table—a table that boasted a great white strip of cloth down the middle.

Windows reached from the floor to the ceiling along one side of the room; the walls on the other three sides were cut with doors. Enormous pictures of Englishmen hung in gold frames between the doors, and under each scowling face was a chair. Leah knew she'd never seen so many chairs in one place before, either. At each end of the long room was a fireplace big enough to roast an elk. Fires burned on the hearths, but the room was still cold.

The ceiling was white and gold with carvings of naked babies and birds. She decided she would ask Brandon how the babies were fastened in the corners of the roof, and how the candlesticks that dangled from the ceiling were lit. She wondered if the great windows opened, and if real birds ever flew in to nest among the stone babies.

Brandon's mother was staring at her again. Lady Kathryn's words of greeting had been soft and sweet, but her eyes told a different story. Leah waved at Lady Kathryn. She smiled back—a smile as artificial as the powdered wig on her head. Leah sighed and tossed another biscuit to the little dog under the table. The food in this great house of cut stone was no more to Leah's liking than the clothes Brandon forced her to wear. Every dish was heavily spiced and soaked in white and yellow sauce. Butter and milk seemed to be a delicacy among the English, and Leah couldn't abide either one.

She tapped her knife absently against a water goblet. Charles shook his head in silent warning. She sighed and wiggled on the hard chair. Charles smiled at her, but his smile seemed no more genuine than Lady Kathryn's.

Leah eyed him from beneath her lashes. How she wished she could have someone paint a picture of Charles for her to take back to the Shawnee. No one would believe her when she told them how he adorned his body with false hair and bright-colored silk. Leah dropped her gaze to her gold-rimmed plate and tried not to giggle.

Charles wore an oversized wig of snow-white hair

on his head. Fat sausage curls fell over his ears nearly to the bottom of his chin. Scattered over the wig were tiny purple silk ribbons. His nose was long and even thinner that Brandon's, and his round gray eyes were small, reminding Leah of a porcupine's.

Charles's thin neck was swathed in white lace. Below that, his lawn shirt was nearly hidden by a magnificent purple waistcoat with orange and blue birds stitched into the silk. His coat was orange velvet over blue breeches, and his silk stockings were covered in a design of blue and purple clocks. Charles's short, thin fingers were heavy with rings, and jeweled buttons glittered on his coat.

Leah glanced down the table at Brandon's subdued blue coat and waistcoat of blue and gold, and she sighed with relief. At least Brandon didn't feel the need to garb himself like one of those ridiculous screaming birds in the garden.

"Patience," Charles whispered. "These dinners do seem to go on forever."

Leah nodded, feeling a little ashamed of laughing at Charles. He had helped her get into the house that morning. She didn't know what ruse he'd used, but she and Brandon had walked up the grand marble staircase without seeing a soul. Charles had done her a favor, and it was wrong to make fun of him, even in her own mind. He's been kinder to me than my husband, she thought. She retrieved her shoe under the table with the toe of her foot and wiggled into it.

Brandon had deposited her safely in her chambers and instructed her to dress in the proper clothing and wait to be called to dinner. He treats me like this pet dog under the table, she mused. Brandon says

"Come" and "Go," and I am expected to obey without question.

Later, he'd arrived to escort her to his father's bedroom to meet the earl. There she had been inspected like a broodmare. Lord Kentington had coughed and wheezed and said something that sounded like "Hrumpt." Then he'd cleared his throat and dismissed them with a haughty nod without ever speaking a word to her.

It was no wonder that Brandon had grown up a barbarian, Leah thought. No one could be normal in this house.

"M'lady?"

The servant in the red coat was offering her a large bowl of gray-green liquid. Leah looked at it helplessly.

"Green turtle soup," Lady Kathryn said clearly. "It is Brandon's favorite. I ordered it made especially for him. Surely you must like it, my dear. Turtles thrive in the sea around America, do they not?"

Leah's stomach turned over. Among the Shawnee, the turtle was a symbol of wisdom. If she was lost or confused, she might ask a grandfather turtle for advice, but eat one? The thought was disgusting. She shook her head.

"Do try it," Charles urged. "Cook's bound to have made buckets of the stuff, and Brandon and I are the only ones who like it."

"Green turtle soup gives me a headache." Lady Kathryn said, "but I have a delicate constitution. I'm certain Leah's made of stouter material." She reached across and patted Brandon's arm. "We'll soon fatten you up, darling. Your dreadful experiences in the Colonies have left you positively emaciated." She glanced at her other guests, Lord and Lady Rondale, for confirmation. "He's far too thin, isn't he? I shudder to think what he lived on in that wilderness."

"Looks all right to me," Lord Rondale said before taking another bite of his bread and butter. "Fit as a butcher's apprentice."

"Nonsense," his wife corrected. "Lady Kathryn has every reason for concern. The Colonies swarm with disease and vermin. Everyone says so."

"Cook does makes good turtle soup," Brandon said.

"None for us," Lady Rondale said. "William's gout."

Brandon looked at Leah. "It's delicious. Do try just a little."

Leah turned her soup bowl upside down and laid her butter knife across it. "No," she said emphatically.

Charles motioned to the footman. "I'll have soup." The man served Charles, and then carried the tureen along the table to where Brandon was seated.

Leah watched in horror as Charles stirred the thick soup with his silver spoon and crumbled crackers in it. The smell made her shiver. He scooped up a spoonful and raised the soup to his lips, but he barely tasted it.

"You don't know what you're missing," he said with a wink. He reached for his wineglass, and the bowl caught on his cuff and spilled. "Damn!" Charles leaped up as the hot liquid soaked his napkin and dribbled off the edge of the table onto the floor. "Beg pardon, ladies." The servants scrambled to clean up the mess and bring clean dishes and silver.

Leah watched the performance uneasily. Charles

called for more soup, and the others resumed their
meal. As Brandon took a spoonful of his soup, Leah
stood up. Brandon paused, spoon in hand, mouth
open.

"No!" she cried. "Do not eat it."

He dropped his spoon. "Leah, what's wrong?"
Blood rose beneath the surface of Brandon's fair English skin, and she knew that she'd shamed him
again.

"I have a . . . a condition," she declared. "I think
I shall faint."

Lady Kathryn clapped her hands. "Mary! Rose!
See to Lady Brandon."

Brandon rose to his feet, staring at Leah with a mixture of concern and suspicion. Lord and Lady Rondale
began to whisper between themselves. "Leah . . ."
Brandon said.

All eyes were on her. Taking a deep breath, Leah
moaned, shut her eyes, and let herself fall backward.
Lady Kathryn screamed just before Leah's head struck
the floor.

Pain shot through her head and neck, but Leah lay
still and limp, pretending unconsciousness. Strange
hands touched her . . . a man's hands. In seconds
she heard Brandon's voice, and he was picking her up
and carrying her from the room.

"Out of my way!" he shouted at someone.

"Yes, sir." It was a servant's voice, Leah decided.
She opened her eyes a slit. Brandon kept walking. He
carried her down a hall and into a shadowy room.
She heard the door slam shut, and he dropped her
onto a high-backed wooden bench.

"Now what the hell was all that about? You're not
sick, and you've never fainted in your life."

Leah opened her eyes. The room was unfamiliar. Brandon was leaning over her, his face close to hers, and he was very angry.

"I'm waiting."

"My head hurts," she said. She looked around. The dark paneled wall behind them was hung with animal horns and pigs' heads. "What place is this?"

"The gaming room," he snapped, "and your head should hurt. You've made a spectacle out of yourself and of me. You've embarrassed my mother in front of her friends and given Charles reason to bedevil me for the rest of my natural life."

Leah sat up rubbing her head and looked around curiously. In the center of the room was a table covered with green velvet. On it were small round balls and a long stick. "What is that table for?"

"Billiards. I thought your head hurt."

"It does hurt," she said. His gaze was accusing. "I be sorry, Brandon mine," she murmured contritely, "but ye were going to eat the body of a turtle."

"What?"

"The soup of a turtle. I had to stop you. Ye were going to eat it, and it is forbidden—very bad luck for a warrior. I am sorry your mother be a fool, but . . ." She looked at her fingers. They were sticky with blood. "Oh," she managed. "I think—"

"Good God, woman. You're bleeding." He went to a table along one wall and came back with a bottle of amber liquid. Using his handkerchief, he moistened the cloth with the strong smelling stuff and dabbed it on the back of her head.

It stung, but Leah gritted her teeth and kept quiet.

"There. It's not serious, but you're going to have

a bump the size of a pigeon's egg." He made a disgusted sound. "What am I to do with you?" Brandon laid his hand on her bare shoulder and stared into her eyes. "You'll never make a living as an actress, that's certain. That was the worst fainting performance I've ever seen."

Her lower lip trembled and she blinked away a tear. "I did it for you," she insisted.

"For me."

His touch made her tremble, even if her head did feel as if a tree had fallen on it. Tears welled up in the corners of her eyes. "I'm sorry," she repeated. A lock of his yellow hair had come loose and hung over his cheek. She pushed it back with shaking fingers. "I . . . I didna want . . . want ye to have bad luck. I . . . I didna want ye to eat . . ." She sniffed. "To eat the soup of turtle."

"Oh, Leah," he whispered. He leaned forward and kissed the rise of her breast above the neckline of her gown. It was a feather-light kiss, as soft as the down on a new-hatched duckling, and it made her knees weak.

She shook her head. "Nay. Dinna . . ." He kissed her again, and he let his hand caress the back of her neck. I can't let him, she thought. Not after what he's done to me. But her body cried for more.

"You've skin like rose petals," he murmured. He kissed her throat and the sensitive spot below her right ear.

His lips were warm against her skin. *Stop him!* her inner voice cried. *Stop before it's too late!*

"You're my wife, Leah," he murmured, "and I need you."

She sighed and turned her head toward him. Their

lips met, and he nibbled the tip of her tongue. She opened her mouth to receive his deep kiss. The voice in her head grew fainter as a warm delicious feeling spread through her body. The weakness in her knees intensified until she thought her bones were turning to water.

"Darling." He sat down beside her on the seat and she leaned against him, heedless of the fragile satin gown. His kisses became more urgent, and she felt her heart pounding in her chest.

"Leah," he whispered. "I do love you, little Leah." Brandon's broad hands moved down her back, massaging and stroking. He traced her eyelids and brows with his lips, and she found it suddenly hard to catch her breath.

Leah choked back a tiny moan of excitement. She could feel her breasts straining against the linen of her shift, and she longed for the sweet tugging sensation of his mouth on her aching nipples. The thought made her blood race, and she pressed tighter against him, returning kiss for kiss and tangling her fingers in his thick yellow hair.

"Englishmanake," she whispered thickly. "I need you, too."

Without warning, Brandon seized her by the waist and lifted her in the air. "Shhh," he soothed when she gave a startled cry. He lowered her onto the billiard table, then dropped on one knee and removed her high-heeled slipper. Pushing up her petticoats, he unrolled her silk stocking, then bent his head to kiss slowly the exposed skin of her ankle, and then her knee, and next the soft inner places on her thigh.

"Oh," Leah shivered with delight. With each kiss her heart beat faster. The warmth in her belly turned to liquid fire, and she longed to rip away her garments and feel his bare flesh against hers.

"Ah," he murmured as his fingers tangled in her dark curls.

Leah's hunger grew as he palmed the warm wet source of her yearning with a slow circular motion. She lay back and closed her eyes, caught up in the magic of his touch.

"So sweet." He thrust a finger into her throbbing folds, and she cried out. Her breath came in ragged gulps. He stroked her until she squirmed and tossed her head from side to side. "I want to taste your sweetness," he murmured.

She felt his warm breath against her naked skin.

"Tell me what you want," he ordered. "Tell me, Leah."

"Yes . . . yes." She clutched at his shoulders as intense tremors of pleasure rocked her body. The liquid fire bubbled up inside, flowing over and through her until she was consumed by the waves of bright ecstasy.

Brandon's laughter pulled her back to earth as his arms encircled her. She opened her eyes and stared into his. He tugged her forward until his swollen member was completely sheathed. "Sweet wife," he murmured.

"Oh." Her eyes widened as he moved slowly. "Oh," she sighed. She wrapped her legs around him, moaning softly as his powerful thrusts fanned the coiling flames within her. "Oh, Brandon," she cried.

Again the excitement grew until she thought she could stand the tension no longer. Then he gave a hoarse cry, and she felt the release of his seed within her. A heartbeat later, she shared his joy as she reached another exhilarating climax even greater than the first.

She laid her head against his chest and held him to her, unwilling to break the bond that held them, unwilling to let the world intrude on their moment of utter contentment. She could hear his heartbeat, loud and strong as he drew in deep breaths.

"Woman . . ." he began, then gave a low, satisfied chuckle. "Leah."

She raised her head and gazed into Brandon's face, noting the light sheen of perspiration over his fair complexion, the glow in his eyes.

"I love you," he whispered. Tenderly he withdrew and lifted her in his arms and kissed her. "I've missed you so much," he admitted.

She moistened her lips and kissed him, trying to hold on to the safe feeling, trying desperately to keep her mind free of everything but the sweet rhythm still coursing through her veins.

He set her lightly on her feet and stepped back. "I fear we've made a mess of your gown." He grinned boyishly and pushed down her crumpled petticoats and skirts. "It would be easier on us both if you'd let me back into your bed." He pulled his breeches together and tied them at the back, then bent to retrieve her stocking from the floor. "Let me help you with this," he offered.

Leah took a few steps and sank onto the bench, extending her legs. Her remaining stocking was wrinkled around her ankle. Brandon went down on one knee and adjusted the rumpled stocking. Then he replaced the other one and slipped her shoes onto her feet. As he wiggled the second shoe into place, they were disturbed by a sudden pounding on the door.

"Lord Brandon! M'lord! Come at once!"

Brandon swore softly and ran a hand through his hair. He picked up his coat from the floor and put it on. "I'm sorry, love," he said, blowing her a kiss. "Duty."

"Lord Brandon!"

The male voice was replaced by Lady Kathryn's. "Brandon!" she wailed. "It's Pookey."

Brandon unlocked the door and pushed it open. His mother, a footman, two maids, and Charles peered into the room. "What is it, Mother?" Brandon asked, ignoring their pointed ogling of Leah's disheveled appearance.

"It's Pookey," Lady Kathryn cried. "Something terrible has happened."

Brandon accompanied her back to the dining table. Curious, Leah trailed after them. Lord and Lady Rondale, another footman, and another maid were gathered around the crumpled form of Lady Kathryn's lapdog. Brandon knelt beside the animal and picked up his head. The eyes were glazed, and a trickle of clear matter dribbled from his mouth.

"I'm sorry, Mother," Brandon said. "He's dead." Brandon waved to the nearest footman. "Carry Pookey outside and call a gardener to bury the poor creature."

Lady Kathryn was openly weeping. "A box," she sobbed. "Poor Pookey must have a casket." Lady Rondale made sympathetic sounds and put her arm around Lady Kathryn. "He was only a baby," Lady Kathryn insisted. "Only four years old."

Leah pushed past a stout maid and halted the footman with a raised palm. She leaned over the dog and

sniffed his mouth, then pushed back the skin around
his mouth to see the color of his gums.

Lady Kathryn uttered a gasp of outrage.

"The little dog was poisoned," Leah said. "I dinna
ken—"

"Ridiculous!" Lord Rondale declared. "No one
would dare. What utter nonsense."

Lady Kathryn began to weep louder.

Leah looked at Brandon. " 'Tis true," she said.
"The dog wasna sick. I fed him at the table."

"An apoplexy," Lord Rondale said. "Happened
to Squire Grizzwald last Michaelmas. Struck down
by the hand of God. One moment the poor man was
raising a mug of stout, the next he was knocking at
the pearly gates."

"What did you give him?" Lady Kathryn demanded. "What did you feed my baby?"

Leah went to the far end of the table where she had
sat and looked underneath. There were bread crumbs,
a forgotten silver spoon, and a damp stain where
Charles had spilled his turtle soup. "Bread, esteemed
mother of my husband," Leah replied. "I gave the
dog bread and butter. It does not taste good, but I
dinna think it killed him."

Brandon turned to Lord Rondale. "M'lord, if you
would escort the ladies to the—"

A woman's shrieking cut the air. A second female
voice chimed in. Footsteps clattered down the long
gallery from the kitchen wing, and a red-faced boy
in an oversized apron burst into the room.

"Lady Kathryn!" His voice broke, ending in a
squeak, and the youth's face turned even redder. "It's
. . . it's . . ." Overcome by the illustrious audience

staring at him, the boy swallowed hard and wiped his nose with the back of his hand.

Brandon stepped forward and grabbed the boy by his shoulder. "What is it? Is there a fire?"

The boy shook his head. "No, sir. It's cook. Ye must come, sir. Cook's hung himself in the buttery."

Chapter 15

April 1721

Charles stood motionless as his valet brushed a piece of lint off Charles's new riding coat and adjusted the back curls on his wig. The servant scrutinized his master's attire and nodded, clapping his hands for a maid to carry in a tray with Charles's morning tea.

"Will that be all, sir?" the valet asked. He motioned the girl to set the tray down and poured tea into his master's cup. He added three lumps of sugar and stirred, taking care not to spill any of the precious liquid.

"Send word to the stable. I'll want the roan, and tell John to saddle the gray mare for Lady Brandon." When the servants were gone, Charles took his cup of tea and went to the window. Below, walking in the garden, he saw his aunt and his cousin Brandon.

"Damn you both to hell," he muttered. Nothing had gone right for him. The old earl clung to life with the tenacity of a fighting cock, and Brandon seemed to have his own guardian angel watching over him. Charles's brilliant plan for poisoning Brandon had gone as awry as the fumbling highwaymen's attempt on his life.

Charles took a long sip of the hot tea. The hatred he felt for Brandon gnawed at his insides and kept him from sleep at night. Idly, he ran a finger inside his lace stock and rubbed the scar on his neck. "I will have satisfaction," he promised. He reached into an inside pocket of his coat, withdrew a silver locket, and snapped it open. Curled inside was a lock of blond hair. For a moment he fingered the memento and let the memories of a long-past summer fill his mind.

Cecily. He closed his eyes and summoned her laughing blue eyes, her dimpled face, her porcelain complexion and rose-tinted cheeks . . . Cecily, the parson's daughter. He'd loved her with a passion he'd never felt for another living soul. She'd returned his pure love, love untainted by lust, until Brandon had come between them and murdered her.

Charles slipped the locket back into his pocket and drained the cup. His eyes grew thoughtful as he stared at the trace of tea leaves in the bottom. His cousin Brandon had been the bane of his life. Handsome, charming Brandon! Always surrounded by friends, sought after by women. Brandon could have any woman he wanted, but he had to have the only one Charles had ever cared for.

Scenes flashed behind his eyelids, and Charles gave an involuntary groan. The memory of that day in the barn was one he didn't want to suffer again. He'd found them together—naked limbs wrapped around each other in grotesque lewdness as Brandon pumped his vile seed into her. He'd watched them, mesmerized by the awful reality of their coupling. Finally, when he could take it no longer, he'd thrown himself at Brandon and had nearly been killed in the ensuing struggle.

Charles sighed. He'd carry the scar from the pitchfork to his grave. Brandon had lied, of course. He'd tried to convince his parents that Charles had attacked him with the pitchfork. It hadn't happened that way at all. Not at all . . .

He poured himself a second cup of tea and added sugar. There might have been a chance for him and Cecily if she hadn't swelled with Brandon's get . . . if she hadn't died in giving birth to the little bastard. But she had. And beautiful Cecily, his ruined Cecily, had been laid to rest beside her stillborn brat.

Brandon had made a pretty show of his regret. He'd forced his way into the parson's house and held Cecily's hand as her life's blood had drained away onto the sheets. He'd wept and begged forgiveness for his sin, but Charles knew it was all a farce.

Charles's resentment and envy had turned to hate that day in the barn, and he'd known then he'd have revenge against Brandon if it took him the rest of his life.

Charles gripped the fragile handle of the teacup tightly, and it snapped in his hand. Cursing, he dropped the broken cup onto the rug and wound a handkerchief around his bleeding hand. The cut was deep, and it stung. He poured water from a blue and white pitcher into a china basin and submerged his injured hand. The water in the bowl turned pink.

Charles stared at it. "Not so much blood," he muttered under his breath. The messenger he'd killed last spring had bled so much more, enough to turn the stream red when Charles had pushed his limp body over the stone bridge and into the slow-moving water.

He'd hated having to do it, of course. The messenger was one of theirs. The weary rider had just arrived from Scotland with a list of rebel supporters. The letter had begged Charles and Miles Chester, among others, to actively seek financial support for a planned uprising in the summer. But the king's men were too close and they were suspicious. They knew that someone at Westover was sending money and guns to the Jacobites. A gamekeeper had revealed information under torture, and the net was closing fast.

Charles removed his hand from the water and examined the gash. The bleeding had slowed to a trickle. He wrapped his hand in a clean napkin.

A pity about the messenger. Charles was as loyal to the Stuart cause as any man, but loyalty didn't extend to offering his head as a decoration for London Bridge. The messenger had handed the papers to him personally—he could identify Charles—and thus, unfortunately, the courier had to die.

Charles chuckled softly. It had been a simple matter to point the finger of blame at Brandon. If that ridiculous matter with Lady Anne hadn't come up at the same time, Brandon might have been one of those tried and executed for treason, and he, Charles, would be the only heir to the Kentington earldom. Not that the money mattered—he had inherited more of his own than he could ever spend. What mattered was destroying Brandon . . . utterly. Disgracing him— seeing him rotting in an unhallowed grave.

Charles picked up his gloves and walked back to the window. The garden was empty now. Brandon was probably on his way to Kentington's bedchamber, where he spent most days plodding through business matters and neglecting his wife. "A pity," Charles mused, "when bored women find so much mischief to occupy themselves."

Leah was already mounted sidesaddle on the gray mare when Charles strolled leisurely out of the west wing. "Good day, Charles," she called. He noted that her speech was losing much of the Scottish tang he'd found so distasteful when he'd first met her. He smiled and nodded a greeting. She really was quite a toothsome bit of pudding. Exotic looking, certainly, but rounded in all the right places and ripe for the picking.

"Sir Charles." A groom led the roan hunter forward, and Charles swung up into the saddle. The groom turned to mount his own horse.

"That's not necessary," Charles said. "Lady Brandon and I will ride unattended this morning. We'll be back early. You have that black mare to attend to— the one with the swollen knee. Take her down to the stream and let her stand in the cold water for an hour. If that doesn't help, I want the swelling drained. She's too good an animal to lose."

"Aye, sir." The man doffed his cap respectfully. "I'll tend to it."

As Charles and Leah walked their mounts out of the courtyard, Charles looked back at her. "If it wasn't for me, there wouldn't be a horse fit to ride at Westover. The servants are a lazy lot. They'd rather swill gin and frolic with the local jades that tend to their duties."

"Ye care for the animals verra much, don't ye?" she replied with a smile.

"I do," he agreed honestly. "Sometimes, I think, more than I care for people."

By midmorning, the two had ridden several miles from the manor house to the top of a grass-covered hill. The April sun was warm on Leah's face, and she enjoyed the rhythmic movement of the horse under her, even seated on this ridiculous woman's sidesaddle. Since Brandon's cousin had begun taking her on these daily rides, she was gaining confidence in her horsemanship, and she had come to appreciate Charles's wry wit.

She looked forward to these excursions. Without them, she knew she would have been far more depressed that she already was. Homesick and desperately missing her little son, Leah now thought she had something even worse to worry about.

Brandon had returned to her bed the night that the crazy cook had tried to murder him and his cousin and then committed suicide. She and Brandon shared the passions of the flesh, even tenderness, but she had not forgotten or forgiven the wrong he had done her. She was no closer to returning to America then she had been when she first set foot in England. And now she had missed her women's flow and feared she carried Brandon's child.

The worry that she was pregnant had kept her awake most of the night before. There were so many questions in her mind, so many unknowns. What would Brandon think? Did he want a child with her? He had mentioned children. He'd said he wanted her to be the mother of his children, but that was before they came to England—before he saw how badly she fit in here among his people and customs. His parents would be furious. They resented her and her Shawnee blood. They missed no opportunity to show their opposition to her marriage to their son. No, they would never welcome a child of her body.

"In my great-grandfather's time, this was all forest," Charles said. "The trees were cut for . . ."

Leah let his words drift away on the breeze. She swallowed against the discomfort in her throat and stomach. If she wasn't with child, she was ill. She sighed and stroked the mare's neck. Her sickness would vanish when snow fell again. Her breasts were swollen and achy, and she felt a heaviness in her lower back. Try as she might, she couldn't deny the truth— she was pregnant.

Do I want Brandon's baby? she wondered. Can I love it as I love Kitate, or will I take out my unhappiness on his child? Would Brandon let me carry it home with me, or will he expect me to leave it here in England when I go? If her husband were Indian, there would be no problem. Every human knew that a child belonged with its mother, but the English were as illogical about this as they were about everything else. Her pregnancy and the coming child would complicate her life immensely.

Charles dismounted and raised his hands to lift her down. "There's an old stone cross nearby I'd like you to see. We can walk a little if you like. Your riding is coming along nicely. My aunt doesn't sit nearly as well as you do, and she's been following the hounds since she was a child."

Leah murmured something in response and let him help her dismount. Charles knotted both animals' reins together and secured the end with a rock.

"This way," he said, taking her arm. "See, there's a little path that leads over the ridge."

Leah glanced at him suspiciously. Charles's touch disturbed her. His hands were cold, and there was something about him that made her skin prickle. She tried to pull her arm free, but he held her tightly, surprising her with his strength.

"The footing here is treacherous," he cautioned. "Brandon would have my head if you came to harm while under my protection." He smiled, and Leah's sense of danger intensified.

"No," she said. "I do not wish to see this stone." She set her boot heel into the loose dirt. "You are kind, Brandon's cousin, but I think the sun be too hot. It is time we return to the house."

Charles's open-handed blow rocked her head and made her see flashes of light. Her plumed hat tumbled to the ground. "Enough games," he snarled. "We both know why we're here." His fingers bit into her arm through the thickness of the riding coat as he dragged her down the hill after him.

In the shelter of the rise was a shepherd's hut. Doorless and abandoned, the stone-walled structure reared out of the earth beneath their feet. Charles shoved Leah through the doorway into the tiny interior. The floor had been swept clean, and a straw pallet lay along one wall.

Leah's ears were still ringing. She struggled for breath as fear made her light-headed. It was clear to her that she'd fallen into a carefully laid snare. Charles was dangerous and very smart. She must use extreme caution with him. "Why do you do this?" she asked quietly. "Do you mean to kill me?"

He unbuttoned his coat, folded it, and laid it on

the floor. "There's no need to pretend with me, slut," he replied, ignoring her question. "Brandon told me all about you—how you lived openly in sin with him in your native village." He untied his stock, folded it, and laid it over his coat. Next, he pulled his shirt from his breeches and began to shrug it over his head. "I've seen you watching me. You want it. You wouldn't have come riding alone with me if you weren't eager for it."

"Nay! Ye be wrong, Charles. I ride with you for the sky and the grass, not for desire of your body."

He laughed. "I hear you."

"Brandon will kill you," she warned, moving against the end wall. The crudely cut stones were rough and cold at her back, and the tiny room smelled of mouse nests and urine. She removed her own coat and threw it on the pallet. Charles would think she was taking off her clothes to submit to him, but it didn't matter what he believed. She couldn't move quickly enough wrapped in the heavy folds of these English garments, and she needed all her speed and agility to stay alive.

"He won't kill me, because you won't tell him. If you did, I'd say you seduced me . . . lured me into lechery. Who do you think he'd believe?" Charles's naked chest was sprinkled with patches of bristling brown hair. The old scar on his neck ran down across his collarbone. His arms were thin but muscular; his chest was thick. "Besides," he continued, "we're blood kin. We share and share alike."

"I be not a woman to betray my husband. Ye would be wise to stand aside and let me go," she advised.

He shook his head. "You know that's not going to happen, bitch." His face hardened as his eyes took on a feral gleam. "You'll like it," he promised. "I've seen Brandon's work. I'm better."

Leah let her gaze slide down over his chest to linger on his pot belly. How pale his skin was—like the flesh of a chicken when the feathers were plucked. "This be a great wrong you do," she said. "He trusts you . . . I trusted you."

"Do you like what you see?" he taunted. His short fingers found the ties at the back of his breeches. His breathing grew loud in the room as he stepped out of his last garment, standing before her clad only in his boots.

Unconsciously, Leah held her breath. His man's stick was thick and engorged; bright purple-red, it thrust into the cool air at a right angle. Charles motioned to the pallet. "What are you waiting for? Get over here. I want you facedown, so—"

Leah's hand went to her left riding boot. Charles blinked once, and she lunged across the tiny room and placed the blade of a wicked-looking knife at his throat. "Move!" she dared him. "Breathe, *kuue!*" Coward. "Do this for Moonfeather, and she will cut your throat." She raised the skean so that the point dug into the skin under his chin. A drop of blood beaded to the surface and ran down the glittering steel.

Charles uttered an oath and grabbed for the knife. Leah ducked away and slashed downward, cutting a gash in the palm of his hand. He howled with pain.

"Kipitsheoote," she whispered. "Foolish . . . very foolish." Her nostrils flared slightly as she balanced on the balls of her feet and dropped into a knifesman's stance. "I could take your ears as a trophy, *English-*

manake.'' She smiled with her lips, but her eyes were as cold as black marble. "I could take more."

Charles paled to the color of old tallow. "No!" he protested. "No, I . . ." His voice broke and he whimpered. "Please. It's a mistake."

Leah breathed deeply, fighting back the killing fury that threatened to engulf her. Every instinct urged her to plunge the knife into his heart. To slice the scalp from his head and throw it into his dead face! Instead, she took a step backward toward the open doorway. "We are enemies, you and I," she said. "From this moment. If you ever try to touch me again—if you try to harm me or Brandon . . ." She swallowed and took another step. "Never," she warned. "Never again, or ye will beg for death. By Inu-msi-ila-fe-wanu, I swear it." She seized her riding coat from the floor and ran from the hut.

When she reached the horses, she grabbed both sets of reins and tried to mount Charles's roan. The folds of her skirts tangled around her and the animal shied backward. Without hesitation, Leah sliced the clinging skirt from thigh to hem, back and front. Within seconds, her foot was in the iron stirrup and she was in the saddle. She set her boot heels into the horse's side and galloped down the slope away from the stone hut, leading the riderless mare behind her.

When they reached the green moor below, Leah urged the animal even faster. She clung to the mane as the rocks and grass flashed by under the horse's feet. The wind in her face made her eyes water, and she rubbed them with her sleeve.

A hedge barred the way, and the roan leaped over. She lost the mare's reins at the jump, but the animal followed close behind, leathers dangling. At the edge of the woods, Leah pulled in her panting steed and slid down from the saddle. She leaned against the horse, her cheek pressed into his heaving, damp side, and caught her breath.

She had made a terrible mistake in leaving Charles alive. She'd shamed him, and that would make him even more dangerous than before. If he told—and she doubted he would dare—Brandon would be forced to kill him to save his own honor. Killing Charles would be a bad thing, but if someone had to do it, it should have been she. Charles and Brandon were linked by blood, and the killing of a clansman was a very bad sin.

Charles's threat that Brandon would think she'd seduced Charles made her laugh. Brandon had a head as thick as iron, but he would never believe her guilty of whoring with his cousin. No, Brandon would believe her all too easily. He would tear his family apart by calling Charles out and putting a sword through his heart—unless Charles was the better swordsman.

"Ptahh!" She kicked a clump of grass with her toe. England was making her weak and stupid. She was beginning to think like a white woman. She had trusted Charles and let him trick her. She must stop thinking like an Englishwoman and think like a Shawnee.

Sighing, she shook her head and backed away from Charles's mount. No, she could not tell what had happened. If she said nothing, it would worry Charles more than if she screamed rape. She would hold her silence and wait to see Charles's reaction. And next time he threatened her—if there was a next time—he'd not live to grow an hour older.

It was an easy matter to catch the mare. Once Leah

had done that, she cut the roan's reins off short so that
he wouldn't tangle his front legs in them. She turned
the horse loose and tossed stones at him to make him
run away, then mounted the mare and rode back to
the manor house.

At the stables, she ignored the groom's questions
about her ruined riding habit and Charles's absence.
He could come up with some lie to satisfy the servants. Charles, Leah decided, was probably better at
lying than she was.

She left the stables and walked through the garden
toward a side entrance to the house. She had no wish
to meet Brandon's mother and face her questions. As
she hurried up the walk between the cedars, she heard
the sound of Brandon's voice. Leah hesitated and
looked around as a woman's soft laughter filtered
through the trees.

". . . thought of you often, Anne."

The woman's answer was too low for Leah to hear.

Leah started to continue up the path, but Brandon's
deep rumble drew her to the edge of the trees. Leah
pushed aside the branch and peeked through. Beyond
the cedars was open lawn, then a boxwood hedge. On
the other side of the hedge was a fountain with a
marble bench beside it. She knew because she could
see the bench from her bedchamber window.

She could still hear them talking—first Brandon's
deep voice and then the woman's reply. Her voice was
too high to be Lady Kathryn's. There must be visitors
to Westover . . . not unusual. Lord and Lady Kentington often entertained for weeks at a time. Leah
looked down at her torn riding skirt. No, this would
not be the time to join Brandon and his guest. He

would be furious with her if she appeared in such a condition.

It was easy to avoid the maids and footmen. Inside the house, Leah slipped by two servants gossiping on the staircase without them knowing she was there. Her rooms were on the second floor, but she had to pass the earl's chambers to reach them.

Kathryn's door was open, and she could hear Brandon's mother's voice.

". . . vast lands in England and France to the family, as well as closer ties to the court."

"You don't have to convince me," Kentington replied gruffly. "It's that rash young pup you've given me."

Leah moved closer to the doorway. They were talking about Brandon.

"She's obviously still infatuated with him," Lady Kathryn said. "I guessed as much when she accepted my invitation."

Lord Kentington swore, and Leah heard a manservant's soothing reply. The earl cleared his throat loudly. ". . . annulment. It's what I said from the first. It's the only solution, and he must agree quickly before that little savage gets with child."

"Raymond, really! The servants. I can't . . ."

There were footsteps coming down the hallway. Seething with resentment, Leah hurried on to her rooms. She'd known Brandon's parents wanted to be rid of her, but asking a prospective wife here to meet him before Leah was out of the house was infuriating.

She entered her apartments and closed the door behind her. "Nancy," she called to her maid. Her voice echoed in the huge shadowy room. There was no answer. The gold and white chairs and the French settee with thin curving legs and arms were as lifeless as a burned-out forest. The mullioned windows were shut tight against the soft April breeze.

Leah opened the inner door to her bedchamber and looked around. To her relief, Nancy was not there either. Leah tossed her rumpled riding coat onto a chair. It's stifling in here, she thought, going to a window and pushing it open. She needed air if she was to think. So many problems . . . What was she going to do about Charles? And now his parents had taken steps to replace her. Leah sighed.

Far below in the garden, she saw the garden bench with Brandon and the woman. They were sitting close together, and Brandon was holding her hand and looking down at it. A high tinkling laughter rose in the air . . . the laughter of a woman in love.

Pain knifed through Leah's heart. She turned away from the window, and her hand went to her belly where she believed a new life was beginning. "Oh, little one," she murmured. "What do we do now?" And when the tears rolled down her cheeks, Leah made no effort to wipe them away.

Chapter 16

Brandon turned over Lady Anne's hand and inspected her delicate, pink palm. How fragile she seemed compared to Leah. Anne's soft hands were sheltered from the weather by Spanish leather and the finest silk. No cuts or calluses marred her skin; her creamy nails were shaped and polished to perfect ovals. He smiled at lovely Anne, but his thoughts were of Leah.

When had he come to prefer a woman's hands that were hard and dextrous—hands that could draw a bow with the skill of a huntsman, or catch a fish without a net? The vivid image of Leah's copper-colored hands with their scratches and broken nails brought with it a sudden rush of emotions, and Brandon chuckled, all but forgetting the exquisite woman beside him. Leah's small hands could do more than skin an animal or paddle a canoe; she could stroke his body softly until he was driven wild with lust. She could rub his back and neck until his muscle aches and pains melted away, and she could ball those same tiny hands into fists and fight him with the ferocity of a cornered badger.

"It's been too long." Anne called him gently back from his reverie.

He blinked, realizing he'd been daydreaming about his wife as foolishly as any love-stricken youth. "Anne," he replied with enthusiasm, "you are exactly as I remember you." She gave a gentle tug, and he laughed and let go of her hand. "Beautiful and composed," he complimented.

He could never remember seeing Anne in a state of agitation—not since the day Charles had tried to drown her when they were all children. Even then, her concern had been more for her ruined dress than her near demise.

Westover's magnificent gardens were a perfect setting for her quiet loveliness. Here on this bench, they were sheltered from even the slightest breeze by the tall hedges. The warm sun was bright on Anne's translucent face, and the air was sweet with the scent of new cut grass and spring flowers. Anne and Westover—they seemed to belong together, and together they formed the elusive essence of England in his mind. When he was in America, this was the image that had wavered beyond his reach when he was overcome by homesickness.

He'd wanted this so badly . . . wanted Anne to be free of her marriage . . . wanted her here in his father's gardens. Now the moment seemed hollow, as though he were an onlooker rather than the man beside her. Anne hadn't changed, he realized. It was he who was different.

"Please don't give me false compliments," Anne answered in her low, melodious voice. "I've heard enough romantic drivel since my husband's death to fill a broadsheet. I'm not a beauty, Brandon. My mother, Barbara, is the golden-haired enchantress—I know it as well as you." Color rose to tint her cheekbones, and she looked shyly away.

He chuckled again. "Anne, Anne, you never change. When will you realize your own possibilities? Your mother is an acknowledged court beauty, I'll admit. She's as radiant and glowing as an August afternoon—but you, love, are an April morning. You have your own very special charm."

"An April sparrow, more like," she replied.

He covered her lips with his finger. "Enough of that talk. When have I ever lied to you?" It was true. He'd known Anne since she was five, and he'd always liked her. She was kind and easy to be with; she listened when people spoke and didn't talk unless she had something worthwhile to say. He'd believed he had fallen in love with her before he went to America . . . at least he'd convinced himself he had. Now . . . *I still love her*, he thought, *but she's not Leah. Anne is a quiet oasis in a desert, but Leah is the wind that whips the sands. Leah's a hunger I can't fill. The more I have of her, the more I want her.*

Anne shook her head. "You've never lied to me, at least not a lie that counted. You've always been a dear friend, even before we . . ." She blushed again. "I've made a fool of myself coming here, haven't I? Your mother wrote and told me that you wanted to see me—that you were unhappy with your . . . your new bride." Clearly distressed, she started to stand, but Brandon caught her hand and raised it to his lips.

"I did want to see you, Anne. Please wait and hear me out." He squeezed her hand gently, and she settled back on the bench, the azure satin skirts of her full sacque gown covering the toes of her kid slippers.

Brandon let his gaze travel approvingly over her fashionable attire. Around her shoulders and over her light brown hair, she wore a matching hooded cloak of azure velvet. The neckline of the Watteau gown was rounded and modestly trimmed with wide lace. Anne was, and always would be, a lady—which was more than he could say for her mother.

"I knew I shouldn't have come." Her voice choked. "When you left for America, I was desolate, and God forgive me, when my husband died, I hoped . . ." She bit her lower lip. "Forgive me, Brandon. I never meant . . ."

"Hush," he soothed. He took a handkerchief from his inside pocket and wiped the corner of her eye. "You are very dear to me, Anne. You must believe that. And you don't shame yourself by coming here. You've done me a great honor." An ache formed at the back of his throat. Why can't Leah feel this way about me? he thought. Why?

Anne took a deep breath. "You love her, don't you?"

He nodded. "I do. It doesn't lessen what we had together—what I hope we still have. I want to keep you as a friend, if that's possible."

"She must be very special . . . your Leah."

Brandon smiled. "What I've always admired most about you is your intuitiveness. We would have been good together, you and I. If I hadn't gone to America, if I hadn't wed Leah, I would have fought for your hand in marriage."

Anne folded her hands together in her lap and looked away. "What is she like, your beautiful Indian princess?"

"Wild . . . and funny, and a little sad." He

touched Anne's arm lightly. "I think I've done her a great disservice, bringing her here. I knew if I left her in America when I sailed, I'd never see her again." His features tightened. "It's a man's right to take his wife with him, isn't it? She belongs to me."

"Some women find that hard to accept," Anne observed. A robin landed on the grass a few feet in front of them and began to peck at a worm.

"I thought when she was here it would be better," Brandon continued. "In some ways, I think she's content with me. But . . . " He dropped his hand to his side, startling the robin, and it fluttered away to the safety of a tree branch. "Leah has a small son from her first marriage," he explained. "He's still with her family. I wanted to bring him, but there wasn't time. Leah misses him, and she's homesick. She needs a friend badly."

"Your mother isn't making her welcome?"

"Would your mother?"

"Barbara?" Anne laughed, and her gray eyes sparkled with unshed tears. "If I came home with an Indian husband, Mother would have him poisoned."

Brandon's gaze met hers. "I'm not sure my mother didn't try exactly that. The first day we were home, our cook put poison in the soup, then hanged himself."

Anne looked shocked. "You're not serious?" She paled. "You don't really believe—"

"Mother? No. Charles and I are the only ones who eat turtle soup. But Edgar was the cook here for twenty-five years. It's hard for me to think he happened to go crazy and decide to murder the household at my welcome-home dinner. Mother's little dog did die, and she thought more of that dog than she does me, so I believe that clears her as a suspect. I don't know who else would profit from my death, other than cousin Charles, but he doesn't need my money—he's got plenty of his own. Besides, Charles came close to being murdered too. It was his bowl of soup that killed the dog.''

"You don't think it's anything political? Those Jacobite rumors about you before you left for—"

"No. If they were anything more than rumors, I'd be in the Tower. His majesty can have my head easily enough, he doesn't need to poison me. If I was convicted of treason, the Crown would take my inheritance. But enough about me, Anne. How are you, really? Are you managing?''

She rose and began to walk down the path between the Greek and Roman style statues. "I'm well enough, I suppose," she said. "I have my books and my friends.''

Brandon walked beside her. "I'm glad you didn't go into mourning for Lord Scarbrough.''

"He wouldn't have expected it.'' She sighed. "He was good to me, you know, always very kind.'' She stopped and looked up into Brandon's face. "Henry waited for me to grow up, and when I did, he was too ill to fulfill a husband's role.''

"It was a blessing he passed on. You're too young to play nurse to an old man. It was unfair of your family to force you into wedding Scarbrough.''

Anne pursed her lips. "Mother . . . Barbara—she always wants me to call her by her Christian name now; she says it makes her feel old when I call her Mother. She said I would be a young, rich widow, and I am. Too rich, I think.'' Tears sparkled like diamonds on her golden lashes. "I am besieged by suitors, Brandon, and the only man I want, I can't have."

"You were fifteen when they arranged your marriage to the marquis. You're not a babe any longer. Choose carefully, love. You're a prize, and you can hold out for someone who will appreciate you for what you are." Brandon bent to pick a bright spring blossom and handed it to her. "Stay here with us a while. I'd like you to get to know Leah."

Anne cradled the yellow flower in her hands. "Later, maybe. For now, I think you ask too much . . . even for an old friend." She smiled. "Besides, there's Charles to contend with. He came to the funeral, you know. He wanted to be first in line."

Brandon grimaced. "You never did favor my cousin."

"He has cold hands and the manners of a drover."

"Charles?"

"I can't stand the sight of him."

"You've never forgiven him for pushing you in the moat at Chatham Abby."

"Or forgotten that you pulled me out when I couldn't swim a stroke." She laughed. "I must have been a sight. Remember how the dye ran in my green velvet? I had green legs for a month after." She cut her eyes at him. "Barbara had my nurse spank me for ruining my gown."

"Well, you owe me a boon for saving your life, and I'm claiming redemption. You must come to Mother's birthday ball in London on the fourteenth of May. She's invited all her friends, and they'll be watching like hawks hoping Leah will appear in animal skins or do something clearly outlandish. I'd like to have at least one person there on our side—other than Charles."

"Charles has never been on anyone's side but his own."

"You're too hard on him, love."

Anne tilted her head and arched an eyebrow. "It's difficult for me to imagine anyone being too hard on Charles."

"He's mellowed with age."

"Mmm," she murmured. "I'm sure." The robin returned to search for another worm, and Anne paused to watch him. "You're coming up to London, then?"

"Yes, the last week of April. At first Mother thought it was her duty to remain here at Westover with Kensington, but he wants her to go. He thinks it's better that she continue on—the physician tells him he could have another attack and go in his sleep tonight, or last this way for years."

"Lord Kentington was always so active. It must be very difficult for him to be confined to bed—difficult for you all." Anne raised the blossom to her nose. "These are so beautiful," she said. "I've always wondered why they have no scent to match."

"Promise me you'll be there on the fourteenth."

She nodded. "If you want me to."

"I do. I'm not certain when I'll be free to return to America, and I know Leah will be happier if she has—"

Anne stopped short. "You're going back, then—to America? I thought . . ."

"I promised Leah I'd take her home after Father passes away. I believe I'd stay there if it wasn't for my responsibilities here. Sometimes I'm tempted to hand it all over to Charles. Maryland's a marvelous place, Anne. The soil is so rich. I can't explain it, you'd have to see it for yourself. Father owns leagues of land there—too much to count. Most of the land is virgin timber, but some is cleared along the rivers and bay. It would be the perfect spot to try out my radical ideas on agriculture.''

''Then why don't you?''

His brow creased. ''I'll be the Earl of Kentington. I have responsibilities I can't escape. There's been a Wescott here at Westover since—''

''I know,'' she interjected. ''I've heard it all from Barbara a hundred times. 'You have responsibilities to your family . . . to your station.' Sometimes, I wish I could run away from it all too. Just once, I'd like to think of what *I* want first—not what's best for the family fortunes.''

''Wouldn't we all?''

Anne shook her head. ''No, Brandon. You say it, but I really mean it. Honestly.'' She stepped away from him. ''I'll be going now.''

''You're staying the night, at least,'' he protested. ''I want you to meet Leah, and Mother will cause a scene if you leave before tomorrow.''

''All right,'' she agreed, ''but I'll leave first thing in the morning.'' Her mouth quivered. ''I do love you.'' Her tone softened to a whisper. ''I don't want to come between you and Leah, but if . . .'' She raised her expressive gaze to his. ''If you ever change your mind, just toss a stone at my window and . . .''

Brandon took her in his arms and hugged her against him. ''If I ever wanted to throw stones,'' he murmured into her hair, ''yours would be the first window I'd try.''

* * *

Minutes later, Leah sat cross-legged in the center of her bed with the velvet curtains drawn closed around her. She had loosened her hair and let it fall around her shoulders, and she wore nothing but her golden amulet. Her eyes were closed, and her hands lay open in her lap. Her breathing was shallow.

"Kitate," she whispered. Her faint voice was lost in the heavy folds of blue and green velvet. In her mind's eye, she was floating between earth and clouds. She could see and smell nothing of the strange English house or this echoing room. Instead, she caught the scent of dew-kissed grass and deep wood-land pine. Her spirit ears heard the cry of a loon across the lake, and her heart was gladdened by the familiar trees overhead.

"Kitate," she called again. In the mist, she was certain she could see the shape of a little boy running away from her. *"Yu undachqui,"* she murmured. This way. She sucked in a short deep breath. *"N'nitsch undach aal."* Come hither, my child. But the little ghost did not wait. She heard his laughter on the wind, and then the spot where he had been was empty. "Kitate," she pleaded. "Come back to me."

Leah's head snapped up, and she found herself again in the great house at Westover. Her son was as far away as ever, and she'd not even had the chance to hold him in her arms or to smell the sweet, clean child scent of him, the scent that was his alone.

She sighed as sadness formed a heavy weight in the pit of her belly, and she threw herself backward onto the heaped pillows. How could she be the daughter of a peace woman if she couldn't transport her spirit to another place? Was it that she lacked her mother's powers, or could it be that Shawnee magic wouldn't work across the sea? She drew her knees up and closed her eyes again. If she could just concentrate . . .

Seconds later, she flopped onto her stomach. Too many thoughts filled her head—there was no possibility of weaving the spell again now. The day had begun with such promise and had dissolved into one disaster after another. Leah rubbed the triangular charm around her neck. The Eye of Mist was Scottish magic—it should work here on Brandon's island. If the necklace possessed real power, she had only to call upon the spirit of the amulet and wish herself home.

Leah undid the clasp on the chain and cradled the talisman in her hand. "Eye of Mist," she commanded. "I wish . . ." She let her speech trail off unfinished. Twice she opened her mouth to say the words, but she couldn't. As long as she didn't put the amulet to a test, she could believe in it—believe in something Cameron had given her. But if she asked and got nothing, her father's charm would be as empty as his love for her.

As empty as Brandon's love? The image of her husband and the woman in the garden formed in her mind, and with it came a strong emotion she knew was jealousy. If he wanted the pink and white English *equiwa*, then why didn't he make her his wife and send Leah home to her people? Would it make any difference to him if he learned that she, Leah, was bearing his child?

It was all too confusing. She decided that she would wait to tell him. Often, women lost children in the early months. If he really wanted this Anne, it might be wiser for Leah to keep her secrets—both of them. She would not tell him about Charles's attack, and she would not tell him about the baby. If Brandon decided to annul the marriage, he might never have to know.

I do want it, she thought. No matter what happens between me and Brandon, I want this child. The Shawnee would not care what color skin or eyes it had. Her child would be welcome in the village no matter who the father might be.

Her thoughts were interrupted by the sound of the outer chamber door opening and a man's footsteps. There was someone else, very soft—perhaps a child? She held her breath to listen and decided the man must be Brandon. He didn't walk as lightly as a Shawnee, but at least he didn't clump along as though his feet were made of wood.

"Leah?" She didn't answer. "Leah? Are you here?"

The bedchamber door squeaked on its hinges. Only one set of footfalls entered. The door closed. Leah parted the bedcurtains enough to peek out. "I be here."

He crossed the room and pushed aside the velvet draping. "What are you doing in—" His eyes widened as he took in her lack of attire. She heard his breath rush out. "Leah." His voice was deep and husky. He reached for her, and she scooted away to the head of the bed.

"I saw ye below with the Anne woman," she said. Her thick hair fell forward over her bare breasts, but she made no attempt to cover her nakedness.

"How did you know who it was?" He dropped

onto his knees and crawled across the bed toward her.
"You must get up and put something on, Leah. She's
an old friend."

Leah twisted a lock of her hair and nibbled on the
end. "Nay so old, I think. Bright feathers she wears.
Be she a great lady?"

Brandon grabbed her ankle and pulled her toward
him. "A very great lady," he murmured, planting a
kiss on her bare knee. "You'll like her, I promise."
She kicked at him lazily with the other foot, and he
caught it with his free hand. He lowered his head
slowly and kissed her right thigh.

Leah tried to ignore the delicious sensation, forcing
herself to remember that she was very angry with
him. "Thee promised I should like England."

He let go of her ankle and slid his hand up her leg
possessively. His fingers caressed her thigh and the
side of her buttock. "If we didn't have a guest waiting
in the outer chamber" he began, "the Marchioness
of Scarbrough. I'd—"

"She be here? In my rooms?" Leah sat bolt upright and glared at him fiercely. "You have bring this
great old friend to my bed?"

He chuckled and clamped a hand over her mouth
playfully. "Shh, she'll hear you."

Leah let a choice English profanity roll off her
tongue as she twisted loose from Brandon's embrace
and slid off the bed on the far side. Swearing was one
of the few white customs she approved of. In Shawnee, there were no curse words and less opportunity
to express her true feelings in a moment of white-hot
anger. "Aiyee!" she declared, too low for any but
her husband to hear. *"Shuaak."*

Puzzled, he stared at her.

"Skunk!" she repeated with venom. She tossed her head and ran her fingers through her hair. "Only a man would be so foul." She snatched up a scarlet samite dressing gown and threw it around her shoulders. Tying the neck and waist ribbons, she stalked toward the door.

"Leah," he implored. "She will be your friend if you give her a chance."

She whirled on him. "How friendly, Brandon mine? Will she take my husband? Will she raise my child?"

The door squeaked, and Leah turned back. The woman stood in the doorway, her face pink with embarrassment.

"Lady Brandon," she said. "It was wrong of me to come to your chambers unannounced. Forgive me."

Brandon put his arm around Leah. "The fault is mine. You have nothing to apologize for." His voice was tight, and Leah trembled under his hand. "Lady Scarbrough, may I introduce to you my wife, Lady Brandon. Leah, this is my dear friend, Lady Scarbrough."

Leah gazed intently into the young woman's face. Her gray eyes were kind, her heart-shaped face strained with genuine concern. Leah could read no censure in those gentle features. Taking a deep breath, she shrugged off her husband's arm and stepped forward, extending her hand in friendship. "I be Nibeeshu Meekwon—Moonfeather in your tongue—Leah Moonfeather Stewart." She glanced back at Brandon's frown. "Wescott," she finished with a flourish. "But ye may call me Leah."

Anne broke into a radiant smile that lit her gray

eyes as though with inner candles. "And I am Anne," she replied, taking Leah's hand and squeezing it. "Brandon has told me all about you, and I wanted to meet you. I'm so sorry if I've intruded."

"Nay," Leah answered with dignity. "Ye ha' not. A friend of my husband is always welcome." She motioned toward the sitting chamber. "Ye must stay and tell me of when he was a bairn." She turned her head and caught Brandon's eye defiantly. "Will ye call for tea and cakes, Brandon viscount? This Anne and I ha' much to talk aboot." Barefooted, walking proudly, she led the way into the other room.

Anne glanced over her shoulder at Brandon, and he shrugged helplessly. "You are very kind," she murmured to Leah.

"I saw Charles coming from the stables as we came up," Brandon said. "Shall I ask him to join us?"

"Nay!" Leah snapped. Her eyes narrowed to gleaming chips of obsidian. "Nay, he shall not coom here to my chambers." Her tone softened as she looked toward Anne, and the Scottish burr came strongly in her speech. "It be better if the two of us talk alone, do ye nay agree? Withoot a mon about to keep us from saying what we wish."

Anne laughed. "Yes, and yes again." She settled into a low-backed chair and spread her skirts around her. "It sounds very pleasant indeed, Lady Brandon." She glanced up at Brandon mischievously. "I do believe, sir, that you have been politely dismissed."

"So it seems." He gave a stiff bow and retreated gracefully from the battlefield. "But I fear my reputation will never recover from the attack you two will launch on it," he said.

Leah nodded. "Aye, so it may be—but I can nay think of any mon what deserves it more."

Brandon tugged on the bell pull and left the room.

For a long moment, Anne and Leah watched each other in silence, then Anne spoke. "You know, don't you?"

Leah's eyes widened, and she leaned forward. "I ken ye be the woman Brandon's parents wish him wed to."

Anne clasped her hands together to keep them from trembling. "Yes, but I am no doxy. I wish only Brandon's happiness."

"And your own . . . "

"Do you love him?"

It was Leah's turn to be stricken silent. "I dinna know," she replied honestly. "I dinna know."

Chapter 17

London, England, May 1721

Brandon sighed and lay back against the pillows.
Leah curled against his chest, her skin moist with
perspiration, her breathing deep and steady. They'd
been making love for hours—he could already see the
first glow of dawn through the east windows—and
they were both exhausted.

Once again, in the privacy of their bedroom, they'd
been able to push aside the conflicts that threatened
to tear their marriage apart and find joy in each other's
arms. Brandon sighed again and stroked her glori-
ously disheveled dark hair. If I had the power, he
thought, I'd hold back the dawn and stay here beside
Leah forever. He closed his eyes, knowing that morning would come all too soon and his problems would
be there again in full force.

Leah's unhappiness was only a part of his difficul-
ties. He had to contend with his mother and her complaints, his father's illness, and the sorry state of the
Kentington estates. Regardless of what his mother
might believe, he hadn't come to London with her to

take part in the social season. He'd come to try to straighten out a financial nightmare.

His father had placed responsibility and trust in several stewards, banking houses, and solicitors. The old earl had left more and more decisions in Charles's hands, and incomes which the estates had depended on for centuries had either dried up or been funneled off. The Kentington earls had always been conservative; they'd lived plainly, considering their position, and had never had to borrow from anyone. Now gold stores were dangerously low, and Brandon was faced with a mountain of debts.

Part of the knot had been untangled without too much fuss. Due to a mistake on the part of a clerk, the Earl of Kentington's funds had been confused with Charles's personal account, and entered there. The new accountant he'd hired, Silas Johnson, had found that error in a matter of hours. Brandon had discharged the old solicitors, hired a younger man of good reputation, and threatened to change banking houses.

Now, Brandon intended to go over every segment of his father's business affairs and learn if there were similar inaccuracies. He meant to find out if the problems were the result of his father's inattention and carelessness or if criminal intent was involved.

Because he'd been so busy since they'd arrived in London, he'd had little time to show Leah the sights he'd promised. Anne had come to his rescue and taken Leah under her wing. She'd sent the finest dressmakers to Wescott House, and she'd invited Leah to her home and introduced her to her friends. This afternoon, Anne was taking her into the city to a bookshop.

Realizing that the room had become light enough to see the outlines of furniture, Brandon rose and went to a mahogany highboy. From the top drawer, he took a red kidskin bag and returned to the bed. Leah stirred, one slim arm flung over her head. Her lovely full breasts and her shapely thighs drew him closer, and he sat on the high bed beside her.

Smiling, he poured the contents of the bag into his hand. A gleam of sunlight caught the heaped gems and set them aflame with color. Choosing carefully, he dropped a bloodred ruby onto her slightly rounded belly. Leah's eyes snapped open and he laughed, following the ruby with a sapphire, an emerald, and a dozen large pearls. "I promised you pearls, love," he reminded her. He leaned over and kissed her lips, then dropped a second ruby between her breasts. "Didn't I say I'd shower you with jewels?" he teased.

She sat up, and the precious gems tumbled into the folds of the tangled sheets. "I'm cold," she said. Her dark liquid eyes were huge in the semidarkness of the curtained bed, and her husky voice made his heartbeat quicken. Her hand brushed his naked staff, and he shuddered with pleasure.

"Leah," he whispered. She clasped him in her hand and ran her thumb along the length. "God, woman, if you . . ." He lay over her, propping himself on one arm, bringing his face close to hers as her fingers continued their teasing caress. He drew in a deep breath, savoring the sweet waves of sensation that flowed through his loins. The bed smelled of woman and sex. "By the blood of the holy martyrs, Leah," he said, "what are you—?"

Laughing softly, she wiggled down in the sheets. The tip of her damp tongue touched his hot skin, and he moaned deep in his throat, giving up all thoughts of an early breakfast and meeting with the accountant.

When he awoke again, the room was bright with midmorning light. A tray of food stood on the low table beside the bed, and Leah, clad in her scarlet dressing gown, was pouring him a cup of wine.

"Will you sleep all the day?" she teased.

He yawned and ran a hand through his tangled hair. "I didn't get much sleep last night—and that's your fault, woman. Have you no pity?"

"None." She handed him a pewter goblet, and he drank. "There be fish here, and bread and cheese. Below, a man waits. He says that ye asked him here this morning."

"Johnson. The accountant. 'Tis your fault, wench, if the family fortunes are lost." He reached under his left cheek and withdrew a ruby. "Ouch. I wondered what was digging into me."

She giggled. "Ye ha' only yourself to blame for being so foolish. What man takes his colored stones into his sleeping mat?"

"Colored stones," he grumbled, getting out of bed and pouring himself a second goblet of wine. He took a wedge of cheese and walked to the window. "A fair day for your outing with Anne." He glanced back at her. "I did promise you the jewels, kitten. The seamstress will sew the pearls onto your gown for Mother's ball. The rubies can be strung on silver or gold wires for your ears. Do you like them?"

"Aye, Brandon mine, they be pretty." Her features grew pensive. "I had a gift for you last night, but I was afraid—I couldna tell you."

"Tell me what?" He turned back toward her and smiled. "What secret are you keeping? Has Anne put you up to buying something expensive?"

"Nay," she answered quietly. "I ha' waited to tell ye until I be certain. I be with child, your child."

He stared at her in disbelief. "A baby? You're sure?" His sudden rush of elation cooled as fear curled in the pit of his stomach. He swallowed. His Leah? Little Leah swelling with a baby? Leah, whose mother had died in childbed? "When?"

She stiffened. "I thought ye would want a child. Have ye not prattled on about an heir for your English title? This could well be that son."

He turned away from her, unable to speak. Hell, yes, he'd wanted an heir from her body. It was every man's right. But thinking about a son was different from knowing she was pregnant. He'd come so close to losing her when she'd been shot that he wasn't sure he could face it again. He reached out and touched the window glass, trying to picture what a child of theirs might look like. "Of course, I want your child," he said. "Son or daughter, I'd welcome it the same." The fear became a leaden weight—Leah could die from the love they'd shared.

"Did ye not suppose that a bairn would come from what we were doing?" she demanded angrily. "Or be it the color of his skin that ye fear?"

He whirled on her. "You know better than that." He moved to take her in his arms. "I'm glad, Leah. It's just that it's a shock."

It was plain to him that she didn't believe a word he said. "Aye," she flung back, pulling free. "Ye be happy. Your lips say so, but your eyes . . . your eyes say different."

"Damn it, Leah, don't talk like that!" he managed. "I love you. It's just that having a child . . . brings a risk. I don't want to face the chance of losing you."

Cecily's dying face rose to haunt him. The black-garbed midwife's words echoed in his head like gunshots. *The child was too big—it tore her apart.* He shook his head to rid his mind of the stench of Cecily's blood—blood shed so many years ago. He'd stayed with her to the end, in spite of his family's protests, in spite of the midwife's disapproval, but it hadn't helped. Cecily had bled to death, and the child—a child that might have been his—had been stillborn.

"You're such a little thing," he said hoarsely to Leah. "I knew it could happen, but—"

She glared at him. "I dinna believe ye, Brandon. If ye feared for me before, ye have kept it well to yourself. But the problem is easy to remedy. Put me on a ship for the Colonies as I have asked. I'll give ye your annulment and ye can wed Anne if she'll still have ye."

"I said I'd take you home. I can't force you to stay with me if you don't love me, Leah. But our child—if we have a child . . ." Swearing, he shook his head. "I can't discuss this now. You've got to give me time to settle the Kentington financial affairs. Do you expect me to leave my dying father and take you home now? If you're pregnant, the worse possible place for you is at sea."

She stepped back away from him, her eyes hard. "Nay, Brandon viscount, I expect ye to do nothing. What I must do, I'll do on my own. I've waited for ye long enough. I'll find my own way home."

Fear that she might do just that made his voice harsh. "Don't try it. You're my wife. You come and go when I say. And you go nowhere—least of all to America—while you're carrying our babe." He took her by the shoulders and twisted her to face him. "I love you, and I'll care for you—both of you."

"*Mata.*"

"Yes, I will." She strained against his grip and, unwilling to struggle with her, he released her. "I'll not break my promise. I will take you . . . I just don't know when."

"And meanwhile I'm to be content with my jewels? Pretty beads to keep your Indian squaw content?" She snatched up a handful of pearls and flung them at him. "They be but cold stones, Brandon viscount—as cold as your heart."

In anguish, he turned toward his dressing room. "We'll talk later, Leah, when you're calmer."

"Aye," she taunted. "Later."

He slammed the door as he left the room.

That afternoon Brandon walked Leah down the steps to the waiting town coach emblazoned on the side with his father's crest. "I'm sorry about this morning," he said as he bent to kiss her. She turned her head so that his lips met her cheek instead of her mouth. "I am glad about the news," he added, ignoring her slight.

The footman lay down folding steps and assisted Leah into the ornate carriage. "M'lady," he said.

Brandon glanced up at the liveried coachman and spoke sternly. "You are to take Lady Brandon directly to the home of the marchioness. I place my wife's safety in your hands—do you understand?" His gaze swept over the two running footmen and the burly servant beside the coachman, including them in his command.

The coachman doffed his cap. "Aye, sir. We'll keep her ladyship safe, sir."

Brandon gave Leah a parting order. "You're not to wander off. London can be dangerous, and you could become lost." She nodded; he waved to the coachman, and the man cracked his whip over the horses' heads.

Leah caught the side of the carriage for support as the vehicle began to move over the rough cobblestones. Brandon stood on the steps of the sumptuous brick house watching until the carriage turned the corner.

Leah could still see the upper stories of Wescott House and its encompassing wall. The town house was nearly as large as Westover in Dorsetshire, but much more formal. Of the two, Leah preferred the country manor with its rolling acres of grass and parks. Brandon had explained that when his grandfather build Wescott House after the Great Fire, this part of London was open fields. Now, other fashionable brick houses lined the streets, and there was no meadow to be seen.

She settled back into the cushioned seat and tried to dispel the anger she felt toward Brandon. Anne would be hurt if she arrived in such a state. Leah's mouth softened as she thought of her new friend. The woman Leah's husband had loved—might still love— was a strange choice for a friend, but Leah had liked the shy Anne from the first hour she'd met her.

They had nothing in common except Leah's husband and a love of books. Anne did not ride—she

was afraid of horses. Anne knew nothing of the forest
or the open grassland. She did not hunt or fish. She
was modest and deferential in the presence of men.
She knew nothing about the Colonies and less about
Leah's people. Anne was everything Leah was not,
and yet Leah found a comfort of the soul in being
with the English girl. They laughed together and
traded bits of quotes from dusty tomes that became
private jokes.

Leah's mood lightened as she thought of Anne.
They had spent only a few days in each other's company, yet Leah felt as though she had known Anne
all her life. At times, it seemed as if she knew what
Anne was thinking or going to say before she said it.
Idly, she wondered if Amookas felt the same way
toward Tahmee. They shared a husband. She decided
that if Brandon had to have two wives, as Alex did,
Anne would be the best choice as second wife. The
idea tickled her heart and made her laugh. "I be too
jealous to share my man with any woman," she said
aloud.

She giggled again. If Shawnee women—some
women—were willing to be part of a plural marriage,
why couldn't she? Was it her father's Scottish blood
that made her too small to accept another woman in
her husband's life? She was still chuckling when the
coachmen reined in the team before Anne's imposing
brick town house.

"I'm sorry I couldn't come for you," Anne apol-
ogized as the footman assisted her into the carriage.
"My coachman's gone to have a tooth pulled." She
sat across from Leah and caught her hand. "Last night
I went with Barbara and Father to New Spring Gardens, and we had a wonderful time. You must have

Brandon take you there! You can only reach it by boat, but after dark when the lanterns are lit, it's a fairyland. Everyone goes." She waved her maid to a seat on the far side of the coach.

"I thank you for taking me to the shop of books," Leah replied. "I'd like to find a copy of *Paradise Lost.* I had one, but a raccoon ate it." She rolled her eyes. "Brandon sends his thanks for being my keeper."

Anne laughed." 'From his tongue flowed speech sweeter than honey,' " she quoted from Homer's *Iliad.*

Leah nodded, answering with another line from the same source. "And for me, 'Words like winter snowflakes.' We are like stones grinding against each other, Anne. He does nay speak to me in the manner he does to ye."

The maid turned her face discreetly toward the street. Anne had brought her along on their excursion two days earlier, and she'd explained to Leah that the girl was new to England and spoke only French. "This way she can't repeat anything we say," Anne had said. Leah had approved. The constant presence of servants during every waking hour of the day was an English custom she found oppressive—it was hard to find the privacy to speak with Brandon alone, or to perform the most basic bodily functions without a servant rushing forward to offer aid.

Anne squeezed Leah's hand. "It will get better between you and Brandon," she said. "He loves you."

"So he says."

"He does." Anne made a dainty moue and leaned back. For an instant, her gray eyes clouded. "I know he does, Leah. He—oh, look, there's Burlington House.''

Leah gazed in the direction Anne was pointing.

''See that carriage, the one with the white horses? That's the Duchess of . . .''

Leah pretended to listen, and as the coach rolled on through the wide streets she found herself forgetting her bitter argument with Brandon and enjoying Anne's lively description of the landmarks and the people.

''And there . . .'' Anne motioned toward another mansion surrounded by an iron fence. The coachmen slowed the horses to allow another coach to cross the intersection, and Leah stared at the high gates with a Scottish thistle worked into the iron. ''There,'' Anne continued, ''is the home of my mother's friend, the Earl of Dunnkell.''

Peacocks strolled across the lawn, and two large greyhounds were being led on a leash by a dark-skinned man in a turban and wide trousers gathered at the ankles. Two very tall blackamoors in red and white livery stood before the gate. Each man was taller than Brandon by a head, and each held a great unsheathed sword in his hand.

''The earl must be very rich,'' Leah said.

''Not him, his wife. She's much older than he is. But Lord Dunnkell's very handsome. All the women at court are mad for him. Barbara—she's my mother—included.'' Anne lowered her voice. ''It's rumored they shared a torrid romance many years ago.'' She laughed. ''Of course, Barbara is linked with all handsome courtiers at one time or another.''

''And you, are you *mad* for him too?''

Anne shook her head. ''No, not in that way. He

has always gone out of his way to be kind to me. I've known him since I was a child. He gave me the strangest present once. It was—Oh, Leah, look there. In that coach coming toward us. Don't let them see you looking. It's Lady Dunnkell. She's wearing a wig, of course, but they say her real hair is as white as wool—what there is of it."

The other coach stopped before the iron gates, and Leah saw a thin, plain woman in an elegant gown descend the steps. One of the blackamoors threw open the gate, but Leah and Anne's carriage turned another corner before Leah could get a better view of Lady Dunnkell.

They'd gone a short distance more when the coachman halted the horses again. "Sorry, Lady Brandon," he called. "There's an accident ahead. We'll have to wait until the way's cleared."

A crowd gathered as wagons and coaches stopped, and tempers flared. Passersby began to jostle one another and Leah heard a woman cry out. "Thief! Stop that boy!"

A dirty-faced urchin dodged through the knot of people and ducked under a wagon. Leah saw him roll out the far side and dart into a side street. The woman continued to shout that she'd been robbed, but no one seemed to be paying much attention.

A gentleman on horseback passed by on the left. He nodded in Anne's direction and reined in his mount. "Lady Scarbrough," he called. "Bit of trouble?"

Anne smiled. "No trouble." She glanced at Leah. "This is Lord Dunnkell. Lord Dunnkell, may I introduce my friend, Lady Brandon."

He bowed slightly from the saddle, and for a heartbeat he studied Leah's face keenly. Then he smiled, the heart-tugging smile of a man who genuinely liked women. "Lady Brandon, it is my pleasure." His cultured voice was deep and burred with the echoes of Scotland.

Leah's tongue stuck to the roof of her mouth. Her breath caught in her throat, and she could only nod and mumble something unintelligible. The hair is wrong, she thought, and his face is older, but . . . His eyes were as she remembered them.

What was Anne saying?

". . . not seen you in the city for many months."

"Aye, Lady Dunnkell has been in Italy for the winter, and I've been living rough in the Highlands. She vowed she'd cut off my allowance if I didn't make it back in time for the season. I understand—"

"Pardon me, Lady Brandon," the coachman called, "but the way's open. We must move or hold up—"

"Drive on," Leah ordered.

"I'll see you at Barbara's on Friday next, Lord Dunnkell," Anne said as they pulled away. "Good day."

Leah stared down at her hands and tried to keep from crying. That man, the one who called himself the Earl of Dunnkell, was her father, Cameron Stewart!

Leah's afternoon was a torment of confused emotions. She saw nothing of the Theatre Royal on Drury Lane, comprehended little that Anne said to her. The bookshop full of volumes Leah had only dreamed of was a blur. Leah had picked up the first book she'd come to without looking at the title and allowed Brandon's serving man to pay for it.

If Anne noted Leah's withdrawal, she tactfully did not mention it. They continued on to a popular coffee house where the two women took refreshment in late afternoon, and then Anne ordered the coachman to drive her home.

"Thank you," Leah said when they left Anne at her door. Anne nodded thoughtfully and said her good-byes.

Leah waited until Anne and her maid had entered the big house before giving a command to the coachman. "Take me back to the house of the Earl of Dunnkell," she said.

"M'lady," he protested. "I have my orders from Lord Brandon. I must—"

"Your orders were to protect me, nay to keep me from going where I wish," she replied haughtily. "Lord Dunnkell's house, at once."

The coachman obeyed, and soon they were in front of the earl's gate. Trembling, Leah clung to the inside of the door. She wanted to get out and go to the gate—to demand that the blackamoors with the swords open the way for her. She wanted to go to her father and tell him who she was, but her courage failed her.

Waves of nausea made her head spin. If she had recognized him, why hadn't he known her? "Oh, Father," she whispered. "Why?" Was it that he couldn't acknowledge a copper-skinned daughter here among the *Englishmanake?*

"Lady Brandon?" A footman stood by the window. "Did you wish to call upon Lord and Lady Dunnkell?"

"No," she answered hoarsely. "No."

"Are we to go home, then, m'lady?"

"Aye," she conceded. "Home."

When she was safely in her bedchamber at Wescott House, Leah dismissed the maids. She took a quill and ink and began to write.

To Lord Dunnkell, from his daughter. Moon-feather, greetings . . .

The ink trailed across the page as the pen dropped from her numb fingers and teardrops fell to smear the words she had written. Weeping, she tore the letter into bits and burned them by candle flame.

At a tavern near Blackfriars Stairs, Charles took his leave of two men. "You failed me before," he said sternly. "If you do so again, it will be the worse for you."

"We'll earn our silver," the taller of the two answered. "Ye've no cause to complain about the way we did in the cook, do ye?"

His companion, a stocky man with bushy black eyebrows, nodded vigorously.

"No," Charles admitted, "that was clean enough. The servants' side door will be left open. Wear the livery I've provided, and make certain you're not seen. And I want no one to find her body. I don't care what you do with it—I just don't want it recovered. Do I make myself clear?"

"I know my way around the 'ouse," the spokesman replied. " 'Ave ye forgot I worked there four months? Now where's our coin?"

"You get nothing until the job's finished." Charles leaned close to the tall cloaked figure, trying to ignore his unwashed stench. "And remember, Giles, you're to tell her that her husband hired you."

" 'Cause 'e didn't want no red bastards." Giles laughed, a sound like the rattle of dried beans. He stuck out a dirty hand. " 'Alf now and 'alf when the deed's done."

Charles shook his head. "Nothing until she's dead."

The silent man gave a rumbling grunt and slid his hand to the hilt of a knife.

"Naw," Giles said. "None of that, now, Ben. We know Sir Charles will be good fer it. We can trust 'is lordship to be fair and square with the likes of us."

"Of course," Charles replied smoothly. "A Wescott always pays his debts."

He hurried from the noisy public room and got into a hired coach waiting by the door. Now he would go home and have a private discussion with his aunt. It was time she knew the truth about Brandon's wife— at least his version of the truth. He settled back onto the hard seat and rapped on the roof to signal the driver.

A pity Leah wouldn't know who had really ordered her death, he thought. But then, one couldn't have everything. It was enough to pay the bitch back for the insult she'd offered him and to deprive Brandon of his heir in one blow.

Charles took a silver flask from the coach seat and unscrewed the cap. The liquor was sharp on his tongue, and he wiped his mouth with his ruffled sleeve. Giles and Ben would take their pleasure with the red-skinned slut before they slit her throat—he'd bet twenty crowns on it. He smiled and took another sip. Leah deserved whatever she got. He only regretted that his dear cousin Brandon couldn't witness his wife's butchering firsthand.

Chapter 18

Later that evening, Charles escorted Brandon's mother into the same coach Leah had used in the afternoon. He got into the seat beside Lady Kathryn and waited until the coach was moving before speaking. "I'm glad you accepted my invitation to the theater tonight. You've been shut up in Westover with Uncle Raymond for far too long. I fear for your own health, Aunt Kathryn."

"It's not been easy for me." The Countess of Kentington was elegantly attired in a flowered wine Chinese silk over a paler wine silk hooped petticoat. Her open skirt bore lace at the edges, and over her shoulders she'd draped a silk-lined velvet cloak of deep navy. She sighed and fanned herself. "It's so hot for May, dear, don't you think?"

The carriage picked up speed as the coachman cracked his whip over the lead animal and the team broke into a stylish trot.

"They say the play is dreadful," Lady Kathryn continued. "That awful actor . . ." She folded her ivory fan and tapped Charles's arm with it. "What's his name? The one with the pot belly? He's far too old to be playing dashing young—"

Charles clasped her wrist impatiently. "There's something of importance I must tell you."

"Not Raymond?" she began in alarm. "You haven't received—" Her fan tumbled to the floor.

"No, there's no news from Westover. If there was, it would come for you, Aunt Kathryn." Gritting his teeth, he retrieved her fan and forced himself to speak in a manner that sounded sincere. "I know I've not always lived up to your expectations, but—"

"Nonsense, Charles. You've been a second son to us. God knows Brandon hasn't always been a prize. Running off to the wilderness and coming home with— What were you about to say?"

"Brandon told me that she is carrying his heir."

Lady Kathryn sniffed. "Yes. He told me, too—this afternoon. I know I should be delighted, but . . ."

"She's not fit to be Lady Brandon, or to take your place, aunt."

"My feelings exactly, but Brandon will hear none of it. You know how he is. Nothing his father or I can say will persuade him to—"

Charles cut her off smoothly. "I've held my tongue to prevent a scandal, but when I heard Brandon proclaiming his excitement at her—" He cleared his throat loudly and drew himself up. "I've taken matters into my own hands, Aunt Kathryn. The truth is so sordid that I wanted to shelter you from—"

"I think you'd better tell me everything." Her voice lost its fluttery tone and took on an edge of steel.

"I've given Leah money from my own accounts and booked passage for her on a ship bound for the Colonies sailing this very evening. It's the reason I wanted you out of the house and why I took the liberty of giving most of the servants the night off."

"Charles! Brandon will—"

"Once she's gone, he'll be able to think sensibly. The woman's been . . ." He paused delicately. "To put it in common terms, she's nothing more than a slut. She's been cuckolding Brandon."

Lady Kathryn gasped. "Who is the man?"

Charles laughed wryly. "Rather ask who hasn't she shamed us with? I caught her with one of the grooms myself. I discharged him, naturally."

Lady Kathryn gave a choked sound. "A groom? A servant? My son's wife?"

"I'm afraid so." He patted his aunt's hand. "It's in her nature, I'm sure. After all, she's a red savage. Everyone knows they're totally without morals. She made indecent advances to me once when we were riding, and when I rejected her coarse suggestions, she threatened to tell my cousin that I had accosted *her*."

"I had no idea."

"How could you? It's Brandon I pity. But when I learned she was carrying a child, I knew I had to do something. She's been well paid. She can take her groom's bastard back to America."

"She was willing to go?"

"I gave the choice between leaving with a full purse or exposing her adultery to her husband. You know how servants gossip. How long could she expect to keep such behavior quiet?" He gave a long sigh. "I arranged to keep Brandon away from the house to-night. He and that accountant rode to Moorland House this afternoon. I've made certain they're delayed there until tomorrow." Charles took a snuffbox from the inner pocket of his coat and leaned back against the seat. "An annulment can be arranged, and Kentington's heir can marry someone suitable such as Lady Anne.''

"Oh, dear," Lady Kathryn worried. "Brandon will throw such a tantrum."

Charles sneezed delicately. "He will, won't he? It might be easier if we didn't tell him about our part in this affair. She's been whining ever since she arrived. He'll simply believe she left on her own."

"I think that's wise, dear," Lady Kathryn replied. "The less said about it, the better. With Raymond's health . . ."

"There is no sense in dragging the Wescott name through the pigsty, is there?" Charles caught his aunt's eye and smiled. "You have always been a woman of the greatest sense, aunt. It's what I admire most about you." He took a deep breath. "When Brandon demands to know where she's gone, you should be the one to tell him that she's left to return to the Colonies."

"I?"

"Who else?" He chuckled. "It's for his own good. In time, he'd thank us—if he knew the truth."

His aunt began to fan herself again. "I suppose you're right, Charles. It would kill Raymond. He's wanted a grandson so badly—to secure the title. Nothing against you, my boy, but you do understand."

"I've never envied Brandon's position as heir," Charles lied softly. "I wanted to protect you from this, but I simply couldn't stand by and see the by-blow of a groom assume the title."

"You did right," she assured him. "Naturally, I shall see that you are reimbursed for your expense.

It's only fair that the estate bear the burden of getting rid of her.''

"As you see fit," Charles agreed. "Now, let's not let this ruin your evening at the theater. Mistress Leah will be properly taken care of, and in a few months . . .'' He shrugged. "It will be as if she never existed.''

Leah stirred from her light sleep as the chamber door squeaked. "Brandon?" she asked drowsily. She'd remained in her rooms and eaten a light supper alone when Brandon hadn't returned. She would have preferred to go hungry rather than face the cool disapproval of Lady Kathryn or Charles's feigned friendship without Brandon at her side for support at the formal dining table.

"Nancy?" Leah sat up and rubbed her eyes. The scent of human perspiration came to her nostrils. It was dark in the room, but she thought she could make out two figures. "Who is it?"

" 'Tis Giles the footman, Lady Brandon. Ye must come down at once. There's been an accident.''

"Oh. Is it Brandon? Has he been hurt?" She scrambled out of bed and hurried toward the footman, wearing only a linen shift. She'd covered half the distance when suspicion set in. "Why haven't you brought a candle?" she demanded. "Where's my maid?"

The man lunged toward the spot where she'd been standing, but Leah twisted away. "Get 'er, Ben!" The second figure charged at her.

Leah rolled under the high bed and came up on the far side. She fumbled in the darkness for the letter opener that had lain there earlier. Her fingers closed around a silver candlestick, and she threw it at Giles. He cried out with pain.

"She's there, ye fool!"

The silent man came across the bed toward her. Leah found the brass letter opener and backed away toward the darkest corner of the room. Someone stumbled over a chair and cursed. Both men closed in on her. She waited, counting their steps, then dodged left. A man's hand caught the neckline of her shift. For an instant, Leah was caught, then she heard the sound of fabric tearing. Her head snapped back, and she gasped as her neckchain dug into her skin. She whirled and struck out with the letter opener.

Her assailant groaned, and Leah's neckchain broke as she pulled free. She dashed toward the door, unable to catch her amulet as it slid between her bare breasts and fell to the floor. She wrenched open the door and began to scream.

A heavy object struck the back of her head. Leah staggered to her knees as one of the men grabbed a handful of her hair and clamped a dirty hand over her mouth. She tried to defend herself with the letter opener, but her attacker seized her wrist and twisted it until the weapon fell from her numb fingers. Leah bit down as hard as she could on his palm, but he hit her again, a stunning blow to the side of her face. He clamped down on her nose, and she struggled for breath.

"Another sound and yer fishbait," the footman hissed in her ear.

Leah felt cold metal at her throat.

"Don't move, bitch," he threatened. "Kill ye now or later, it means nothin' to me." He pinned her to the floor facedown with his knee in the center of her back.

Heart pounding with fear, she lay still. When he took his hand away, she sucked in precious air in deep gulps. Seconds later, he twisted a rag across her mouth and bound her wrists tightly behind her.

"Ye've yer lord to thank for this. Dead 'e wants ye, as dead as them what dangles from Tyburn gallows. Ye and yer red bastard with ye."

Leah thrashed her head from side to side and cried out against the gag. No! No! Not Brandon! It was a lie! He wouldn't. No matter how much he wanted to be rid of her and her child, she thought frantically, he'd never have her murdered. She bit the gag in frustration as her attacker tied her ankles and rolled her into a blanket.

The pain in Leah's head washed over her in waves, each higher than the one before. It was hard to breathe in the confines of the heavy wool, and the gag cut into her mouth. She felt herself being lifted and slung over a man's shoulder. Then the blackness won, and she knew nothing more.

Leah was shocked back to consciousness as she hit the cold mud. She moaned against the gag and raised her face from the stinking ooze. It was still very dark. The moon was hidden by heavy clouds and the layers of coal smoke that smothered the city in black dust. She couldn't see clearly more than a few feet, but she could smell the river and hear the rushing current.

"Awake, are ye?" the footman asked. "Better for ye, bitch, if ye'd slept awhile longer.

His companion grunted, and it registered in Leah's

mind that she'd not heard him utter at word. Was he mute?

The air reeked of rotting garbage and human waste. Leah caught the scent of decaying meat and heard the rustle of small night creatures just beyond her line of vision. A wall or a building stood a few feet to her left, and in front of her she thought she saw a tumbled-down dock.

It was quiet for the city. Far off she could hear the rumble of carts and an occasional curse. The noises of the river were louder than human ones. The tide was running out, carrying the filth and refuse of London with it. And Leah knew with cold certainty that these men meant to murder her here on this muddy bank and throw her body into the Thames.

I have come so far to die here, she thought, in a death I would not give an Iroquois. She could not even cry out for help, and these two who had treated her so cruelly would be without pity. She wondered if they meant to rape her before they ended her life.

The fear she had felt so sharply in her bedchamber had melted away. She was exhausted and drained of will, her thoughts confused. Even her magic necklace was lost to her. I waited too long to use its power, she thought, and now the Eye of Mist is gone.

Her Shawnee instincts rose thick within her mind, urging her to sing her death chant and submit to the inevitable. Was death, after all, not the crossing of a river into the dream world? On the far side, she would find her mother and her dear grandmother waiting. Beyond this black, tumbling water would be gentle hands and soft voices. Dying would be like going home. There would be no more pain, or fear, or doubt.

She shut her eyes and tried to rid her mind of Brandon's face. If the man she loved had done this to her, she didn't want to go on living.

But her canny Scottish intellect surfaced, bringing with it a surge of icy rage. Would the daughter of Cameron Stewart surrender to death in a stinking mud puddle? The child of a man who had run an Iroquois gauntlet naked and spit in the face of a Huron sachem?

She twisted her head to stare at the two men and tried to talk. Her voice was muffled by the gag, but her tone was unmistakable.

"What do ye want?" Giles demanded. " 'Tis no use to beg. Yer lord has paid us fer yer dead body. Ye're no use to us alive." He rubbed his midsection. "Besides, I owe ye for tryin' to rip out me bowels with that dagger."

The second man, the mute, knelt beside her and cut the gag away with a knife. He caught hold of her hair and pulled her head back, then made a nasty sound and brought the knife to her throat.

"If it's money you wish, I be worth more alive," she said urgently.

The mute made a sound of derision and leaned closer, tensing his arm for the killing stroke.

"Wait," his companion ordered. "How so, slut?"

"I can get you money. I have a wealthy friend."

"Kill 'er."

"No," Leah cried. "Wait . . ." Her weary mind scrambled for the right words.

"Ye've nothin' to offer," the footman lashed back. "My mate 'ere, 'e don't fancy women—if ye take my meaning. I'd give ye a good tumble if it weren't for this 'ole in me side ye give me. It 'urts bad, and I'm for me bed and a mug of strong rum to ease the pain.''

"We're at the river," she said. "There must be ships bound for the Colonies. They take indentured servants to sell in America. If ye roll me down this bank into the river, I'm worthless, but ye could add to your purse if ye sell me as a bound woman.''

The mute growled. It was plain to Leah that he wanted to finish her and be off as quickly as possibly.

Giles laughed. "Smart, ain't ye, missy? We're to take ye to a captain, and ye'll scream ye be a bleedin' lady—the Viscountess Brandon. Ye mean to see us 'ang, is what. Do ye take us for fools, Ben and me?''

"Who'd believe me? Do I look like a lady?''

"And when ye get to the Colonies, what then?''

"Have ye ever known any bond servant who came back? They'd believe me even less there.''

"Hmmm." He motioned the mute to release Leah's head, and the two of them drew away to talk. Giles spoke in whispers too low for Leah to understand and Ben grunted.

Leah laid her cheek in the mud and waited, heart thudding, for them to decide what to do with her. The cold seeped up through her damp shift, and she began to shiver. She clenched her teeth to keep them from chattering. Out on the river she heard the chanting of boatmen and the rasp of their oars. A rat squeaked and scurried along the rotting wall.

"Well, bitch, it's time." The footman kicked her in the side, and she gasped. The other man laughed, a horrible strangled sound that made the hair at the back of Leah's neck prickle.

"Dead women bring no silver to your pocket," she argued.

"True enough," he said. "We ain't gonna toss ye in the Thames." He laughed. "We're takin' ye to Mother." He knelt and cut the binding that held her ankles together. "Ye can walk, can't ye?"

Leah staggered up, swaying to catch her balance with her arms tied behind her. She couldn't feel her hands. "I can walk," she answered stubbornly.

"Mother will know what t' do with ye," Giles continued slyly. "A shapely drozel like yerself—ye'll bring in a fine 'andful of coin every night, I wager." He gave her a shove. "Get on with ye! That way! We ain't got all night."

Sensing that any disobedience would only put her in more danger, Leah did as she was told.

Her captors forced her up an incline and along a narrow twisting pathway beside what she thought must be warehouses. As the streets were nearly deserted, Leah knew that it was very late at night or very early in the morning. Occasionally a shadowy figure would pass them on foot, but the stranger would keep his face averted and stay close to the sides of the buildings.

The stones were rough and cold against Leah's bare feet, and the night air was chill. They were still close enough to the Thames for the damp breeze to carry the smell of mud and decaying timber.

Giles led the way down an alley between overhanging houses. The space was too narrow for a horse and cart to pass, but still the paving stones were cut by a ditch of stagnant water.

Sounds of coughing and crying babies filtered through the dismal fog. Leah heard a dog barking and a pig grunting almost under her feet. She saw the dark shuffling form of the animal rooting at something in the ditch, and she stepped wide around it. The air smelled worse here than it had by the river. Leah's stomach rebelled at the overpowering stench of too many people packed too closely together.

" 'Ware," came a shout followed immediately by laughter over their heads. A cascade of liquid poured down into the ditch, splashed Leah's legs and filling her nostrils with the acrid scent of urine.

" 'Ware, yerself, ye old blowze!" Giles threatened. "I'll wring yer skinny neck if ye pour shit on my 'ead again!"

The old woman cackled and slammed her wooden shutter. Another shutter banged open on the far side of the alley, and a man cursed down at them. Giles cursed back, and the mute made filthy motions with his hands.

A furry animal ran across Leah's foot, and she bit her lip to keep from crying out. She started to the left and came down with her foot on something sharp. She winced as she felt blood trickle from her foot.

The footman shoved her again. "Keep goin'," he warned.

They turned left into another alley, then right. Leah gave up trying to keep a sense of direction. They seemed to be walking deeper and deeper into a human anthill. Now and then, she could hear wheels and horses' hooves on another street, but only those on foot could traverse the way they were taking. A man on horseback would have to duck to avoid hitting the overhanging houses above. The street was as dark as pitch; Leah knew that even in daytime little sunlight could penetrate such a maze.

As they rounded a corner, she saw the flare of lanterns and heard the raucous sound of voices. A woman's high-pitched laughter rose above the rest, followed closely by a loud crashing.

"That's Mother Witherberry's fer ye," Giles declared. "Always lively at Mother's, they be."

Leah's breath caught in her throat as the three neared what was clearly a tavern catering to the lowest sort of scum. The footman took hold of her arm and dragged her through the sagging doorway.

"Greetings, Mother," Giles shouted to a raw-cheeked woman in a dirty mobcap. "I brought ye some choice goods."

"Did ye now?" Mother wiped a froth of ale from her mouth and strode toward them on dirty, splayed bare feet. She was nearly six feet tall, with shoulders like a drover and hands like shovels. Her pale blue eyes bugged out of her horsey face, and her jutting chin—broken long ago and healed crookedly—was sparsely covered with bristling black hairs. "Cuds bobs!" she exclaimed. "Ain't ye just!"

Leah glanced around the low, smoke-filled room. Hard-faced men lounged against the wall and gathered around a long trencher table. One dull-eyed girl lay in the center of a table with her dirty yellow hair pinned to the scarred tabletop with a knife. The bodice of her cheap gown had been ripped away and a pair of dice balanced on her naked stomach. Two men eyed each other maliciously across her body. As Leah watched, one scooped up the dice and threw them again.

Another woman, dark-haired, dark-eyed, with the look of madness about her, ran her hands inside a sailor's striped shirt and swiveled her hips from side to side in dubious time to the tune played by a drunken blind man near the fire. An earless, noseless man dandled a girl young enough to play with dolls on his knee. She shrieked with laughter and reached for the fatty joint of mutton on the tin plate in front of them. Leah noticed that her face and the front of her filthy shift were greasy with fat.

Catcalls rose from the men as they stared back at Leah with hungry eyes. This can't be real, she thought. It's a dream, and I'll wake in Brandon's arms on our soft feather bed. But she knew it was real. With every sense acute, she stood motionless, judging the distance to the table and the knife holding the blond wench's hair.

Mother yanked Leah away from Giles's grasp. "Sweet boy, to think of Mother with such a peach," she said. "How much?"

The footman named a sum.

Mother threw back her head and roared. "Not fer me dear old father, rest his soul. Half that, and I'm givin' away me business. I'll die in the streets fer me kind heart."

"Look at the tits on 'er," the footman bargained. "She's strong. She'll earn more for ye in a week than these other sluts make in a month."

"Strip off that gown!" a sailor urged. He rose off a bench and began to clap. "Let us judge what ye're offerin'!"

"None o' that!" Mother censured. "Watch yer tongue! This be a decent establishment fer ladies and gentlemen." The crowd roared with laughter, and Giles nervously repeated his last offer.

"Take what ye kin get," Mother said. "Not a penny more will ye get from Mother, not if I was to be burned in hell. Take it with my good will, or ask

me more and try to get out of here alive with it!"
Again, the onlookers cheered.

Giles glanced at the mute. He shrugged and backed
toward the door. "Done," Giles muttered.

Mother Witherberry crushed Leah against her huge
sagging breasts in a monstrous bear hug, and Leah
choked at the woman's rank smell. "Please," she began. "I'm nay—"

"No need to take on," Mother said. "Ye're welcome here as any of my children." She leered into
Leah's face, showing broken, mossy teeth. "Be a
good girl and do as Mother bids ye, and I'll treat ye
as tender as spring lamb. Isn't that right, boys?"

Vile retorts filled the air and Leah blushed crimson, to the watchers' delight.

"Upstairs, me girl," Mother ordered sharply. "I'll
have a closer look at what I've paid good coin for.
And ye!" She snapped her head around to stare at
the footman. "Ye'll want to buy a round for the
house, now, won't ye?"

"I've not seen any silver yet," he protested.

"All in good time, all in good time." Mother
pushed Leah toward the staircase. "Up ye go, darlin'.
Ye look fair froze. We'll get ye some hot rum and
tuck ye in between the sheets."

"I'll warm 'er for ye!" the sailor shouted.

Leah clutched the railing and put one foot in front
of the other.

"Ye'll love it here," the big woman promised. "All
my children loves Mother's. And ye, sweet chick, will
see only the finest of my gentlemen."

"I'm no whore," Leah whispered hoarsely.

"All women is whores," Mother Witherberry
rasped.

"I can pay a ransom. Whatever ye want," Leah offered in desperation.

"Oh, I'll get what I want," Mother replied. "Mother always gets what she wants from her children. No need fer ye to talk o' ransoms. Ye'll make my fortune, darlin'. And Mother Witherberry didn't get where she is by lettin' no fortune slip through her fingers."

Chapter 19

Mother Witherberry shoved Leah up three flights of narrow, twisting stairs and stopped before a heavy wooden door with an iron bolt. "All me new children goes in the red room," Mother said with a cackle. She winked as she swung open the door.

A single candle burned in a holder attached to the far wall. The small room with peeling red paint was devoid of furniture. In a corner was a heap of rags.

"Where's yer manners, Maggie?" Mother cried. "Up with ye and greet our guest like ye been taught."

The rags stirred, and a red-haired girl sat up. Her eyes were red from weeping, and one eye was swollen shut. A scab marred the corner of her pretty mouth.

"Maggie's one of my children." Mother explained. "She'll be a sister to ye, and tell ye what's expected. Won't ye, darlin'?"

Maggie sniffed and stared down at her dirty hands. "I'm hungry," she said in a thin voice. "I ain't had nothin' to eat today. Ye promised I could have some bread."

"And bread ye shall have, me pretty." Mother pushed Leah toward the girl. "All them what works gets plenty of good food. I don't stint on my children,

I don't." She folded her arms across her sagging breasts. "Maggie's been a bad girl, Peach. She weren't nice to Mother's gentlemen, so she's stayin' here in the red room 'til she mends her ways—ain't thet so, Maggie?"

The girl stared at Leah.

Leah turned back toward the big woman. "I be a person of quality," she insisted. "If it's money ye want, I can give ye all ye ask for. I dinna belong here."

Mother threw back her head and shrieked with laughter.

"I am with child," Leah said. "And I'll not whore for ye, nay if it means my life. My husband is a great lord. He'll pay a fortune to get me back."

Mother's guffaws turned to snickers as tears of amusement streaked down her broken-veined cheeks. "Aye," she jeered, "an' I be His Royal Majesty, Prince George." She wiped her running nose with a sweat-stained sleeve. "Ye'll be a delight, ye will, Peach. As daft as a mummer!"

"She cares nothin' fer yer babe," Maggie whispered. "She'll give ye somethin' to wash it out."

"And if it don't work, it don't matter," Mother said. "Me gentlemen ain't so particular. Big bellies don't keep 'em from their pleasures."

Leah stiffened and her chin snapped up. "I tell ye that I be none of this," she said. "If ye dinna let me walk out of here, ye will live to regret it."

"Threats now, is it?" Mother roared. "Threats agin' her what means only yer best? Paah!" She hawked up a mouthful of phlegm and let it fly at Leah's feet. " 'Tis plain to Mother that ye need a few days here in me red room to think it over." She glared fiercely at the red-haired girl. "Talk some sense into her, Maggie, or 'twill go the worst fer both of ye." She waved a gnarled index finger missing the first joint. "Mother kin be kind to her children, or she kin be hard. The choice is yers, Peach—the choice is yers." She slammed the door so hard the wood groaned as she went out.

Leah heard the iron bolt rammed home. She turned back to inspect her companion.

"Have ye got anythin' to eat?" Maggie asked. Leah shook her head. "No? Damn the old sod. I hates her like poison. Ole witch." She pulled a dirty blanket over her bare legs.

"Ye be a prisoner too?"

Maggie nodded. "Not fer long. Mother's too tight to go without my earnin' fer long. It ain't the swivin' I minds. Any jade what survives the street as long as me knows they's times ye got to tip yer petticoat to fill yer gut. But I ain't one to stand fer the nasty stuff, an' that ole witch knows it." She grinned, exposing pointy white teeth.

Leah's stomach felt as though she'd swallowed a bucket of the Thames. The floor felt unsteady beneath her feet, and the pressure in her kidneys was growing stronger. "Be there . . ." she began. She looked around the room. "I have to . . ."

"There's a bucket behind that barrel," Maggie said. "Ye look wore out, poor chit. Drinkin' water in that pitcher, but not a crumb of food."

Leah covered her face with her hands. "It was true what I told her. I dinna belong here, and I'm not a whore."

Maggie pursed her lips. "No, ye don't sound like a London drab, and that's a fact. But I ain't no trug-moldie neither and here I be. I knew about Mother. I was warned enough times to stay clear, but I let a sailor with a pocketful of copper pennies whisper pretty words in me ear. He promised me roast beef and puddin'. Do what yer told and watch for yer chance to get away, is my best advice. It's what I aim to do."

Leah lowered herself to the floor before she fell.

"Ain't no use claimin' yer belly. Mother don't give a hog's trotter for yer brat." Maggie looked around and lowered her voice. "But if ye stay here long enough fer it to be born, she takes them away. I don't know if she throws the babes in the river or sells 'em, but I saw her take Meg's babe a week ago. Meg cried fit to have the watch around our ears, but Mother did it anyway. Snatched it out of Meg's arms, still wet from the birthin'."

Leah shut her eyes and tried to gather the will to fight. Her fingers moved to her throat in an unconscious and futile attempt to find comfort from her necklace. She breathed deep, ignoring the fetid smell of the dusty room. "I will escape," she said, more for her own ears than the other girl's. "I'll escape, and I'll take ye with me, if ye want to go."

"If words were pennies, beggars would eat sugar buns," Maggie chided.

"Nay. I will do it," Leah promised. "And I will make Mother rue the day she was born."

It was late afternoon of the following day before Brandon and the accountant returned to London. The affairs at Moorland House were as muddled as the rest of the Kentington finances. They'd been forced to spend the night at the manor due to a broken carriage wheel, and Brandon had used the extra time well. It was plain that someone had been blatantly robbing his father, and cousin Charles's name had occurred too often in the investigation to be a coincidence. Charles, Brandon decided, would have some hard questions to answer.

Upon arriving at Wescott House, Brandon went immediately to his and Leah's chambers. He was disappointed to find her gone, a disappointment that turned to anger and shocked disbelief when his mother informed him that Leah had left him to return to America.

"What?" Brandon demanded. "What did you say?" He'd found his mother with her friend Lady Rondale in the small parlor off his mother's rooms. The ladies were enjoying an afternoon of hot chocolate, sweetcakes, and—Brandon was sure—the latest London gossip.

Lady Kathryn's blue and white cup trembled in her hand, and she flushed. "Brandon, no scenes, please. Remember our guest." She indicated Lady Rondale, who smirked back at Brandon. "I've brought you up to have better manners," Lady Kathryn admonished.

Brandon took two strides and overturned the delicate tea table with one swipe of his hand. Porcelain cups and saucers crashed to the floor, and the sugar tongs rolled under Lady Rondale's petticoats. "Pardon, Lady Rondale," he said coldly, "but you will excuse us. High tea is over. My mother and I have something of importance to discuss."

Lady Kathryn gasped. "Brandon."

A maid squeaked and began to twitter.

Lady Rondale rose to her feet, brushing at the

spilled chocolate on her overskirt. "I never!" she declared. "I—I—"

"Out!" Brandon commanded. "Before I assist you." He glared at the nearest servant. The man was on his hands and knees gathering up the sweet buns. "All of you—out!"

Eyes wide and mouth gaping, Lady Rondale fled from the room as though pursued by hordes of Tartars. Two footmen and three maids followed close on her heels.

Shaking with fury, Brandon whirled on his mother. "What have you done with my wife?"

"I? I've done nothing."

Porcelain crunched under Brandon's boot as he drew near her chair. "Where is she?"

"Brandon, you're frightening me." Lady Kathryn fluttered her lashes and raised her hands. "You can't blame me if she realized how out of place she was here. She never—"

"My wife, Mother. My wife, and my unborn child." His tone softened, but the blue eyes that stared into his mother's were relentless. "I want them back. Now."

"For God's sake—"

"God has nothing to do with this, Mother. It smacks more of your hand—or the devil's. Leah wouldn't leave me like this, and if she wanted to, she wouldn't know how to arrange passage on a ship. No honest captain would sell her a ticket without contacting me first."

Lady Kathryn paled. "I can't help that. She told me that she wanted to go home . . . that you had quarreled, and that you both realized how impossible the situation was." Her mouth hardened. "She's not worthy of you, Brandon—not worthy of the Wescott name.''

"Don't attempt to judge Leah. You'll make me say things I'd regret. She's more of a lady than I deserve.''

"Nonsense. She's an uncivilized—''

Brandon picked up a Chinese vase and hurled it onto the floor. It smashed into dozens of pieces.

"Brandon! Have you lost your mind?''

"Not at all.'' He reached for a gold and white china shepherdess.

"No!'' his mother shrieked. "Not that! Your father bought me that when you were born.''

He turned back to her, cradling the statue in his hands. "Things mean more to you than people, Mother. They always have. If I have to destroy your precious possessions to find out what you've done with my wife, I will.'' He raised an eyebrow. "Well?''

"I've told you all I know,'' she protested. "I can't—Brandon!'' The shepherdess crashed against the marble fireplace. Lady Kathryn began to weep as Brandon reached for an ivory figurine.

The door banged open and Charles charged into the room. "Whatever are you doing? The servants said you'd gone mad.''

Brandon threw the figurine to Charles and he caught it. "Welcome to the entertainment,'' Brandon said. "Mother's just about to tell me where Leah is.''

Charles flushed and went to his aunt, putting an arm around her shoulders. "A bit rough on her, aren't you?'' he said. "She was afraid you'd blame her. What do you think we've done—stuffed your precious wife up the chimney? It's not your mother's fault. I took her to the theater last night, and when we came home, Leah was gone, bag and baggage.''

"Not quite." Brandon reached into the inner pocket of his coat and withdrew Leah's golden amulet. "I found this on her bedchamber floor. She wouldn't have gone two steps without this necklace—not of her own will."

"I swear to you," Lady Kathryn said, sniffing loudly. "I don't know where she is. I only know she's gone."

"I'm going to find her," Brandon replied. "I've got a lot to try to make up for. An when I do get her back, there'll be hell to pay if the two of you had anything to do with her disappearance."

"You can't talk to me like that," Lady Kathryn snapped. "If you value your inheritance—"

"Leah is what's important to me, not Father's damned money. You can take my inheritance and the title and give it to Charles or send it to hell, for all I care." Swearing, he stormed from the room.

Lady Kathryn began to cry again. "Oh, dear," she murmured. "I knew it would be awful. I just knew it."

"I'll go after him," Charles soothed. "Don't worry. This will pass."

"I don't know. I don't know if I should have told him—"

"You did exactly right. By now, her ship is at sea and we're well rid of her." Charles started for the door. "Don't worry, aunt. I'll keep him from doing anything rash."

"I just don't know. The girl really was impossible, but poor Brandon is so overwrought. He's never talked to me like that before . . . never been disrespectful."

Lady Kathryn looked around the room at her broken treasures and began to weep in earnest.

For Leah, the hours of imprisonment seemed like weeks. Without Maggie there, she knew she would have been on the brink of insanity. They slept on the flea-infested pile of blankets and straw, woke and talked, and slept again in almost total darkness. The red room was windowless, and when the single candle burned to a stub and went out, they had no other to replace it.

"Ye look dark as a gypsy," Maggie ventured as they huddled close together. It was raining outside. They would hear the wind and torrents of rain beating at the loose boards of the house, but they couldn't tell if it was day or night. "Are ye one of the gypsy folk? Can ye tell my fortune by my hand? A witch told me once I'd die by drowning—but I won't, 'cause I'll never set foot in a boat."

"Nay," Leah answered softly. She liked this tough English girl who'd offered her friendship and a share of her blanket without hesitation. "I be not gypsy."

"Scot, then. I've a mind to see Scotland someday. They say it's a fair land, with hills o' heather. And ye don't have to cross water to get t' it. A priest told me so."

"My father was Scot," Leah admitted, "but my home is in America. I be Shawnee—what ye call an Indian."

"Lidikins! Fer true? Ye'd not play fast and loose with me, would ye?"

Leah chuckled. "Nay. I like ye, Maggie. I'd nay poke fun at ye."

"If I get away before ye, I'll hunt out Davy the

Watch. I'll tell him Mother's got ye locked away fer her rotten trade. Most authorities is in the pay of Mother, but not Davy. I seen him give her a knock with his staff one mornin'. If we do get away to- gether, I'll show ye where—'' Maggie broke off. ''Shhh. Do ye hear that?''

Footsteps came up the last flight of stairs and stopped outside the door.

''Who's there?'' Maggie called. ''We're hungry.''

The bolt rasped and the door swung open. Leah blinked at the sudden brightness of the candlelight. A cadaverous-looking man set a bucket on the floor in front of him. His arms were overlong and so thin you could see the veins standing out on them; his fingers were stained nearly black and extended with yellowed nails that curved downward like the claws of a bird.

''Mother sends 'er best, lydies.'' His thin voice grated like cut tin and made gooseflesh rise on Leah's arms. ''Maggie, come get this light, if ye want it.'' His hooded eyes narrowed. ''No tricks, or I'll toss yer dinner down the stairs.''

Maggie scrambled up to take the candle. ''Mother still mad at me, Shanks?'' She grabbed a round loaf of bread from the bucket and broke it in half, tossing a portion to Leah. She tore into it with her strong white teeth and dug in the container for a wedge of cheese and some raw turnips.

''Mother?'' Shanks grinned, showing shrunken bony gums where his teeth had once been. ''Drunk as a lord since last night. Says ye both can come down, will ye go t' that Dutch merchant tonight with Meg.'' He scratched his right hip vigorously. ''The first mate was 'ere early; 'E swore ye bunters would be treated like quality, an' 'e paid Mother in 'ard coin.''

"Ye nitty knurl!" Maggie accused between bites of cheese. "Ye think me daft? I seen a draggletail come off a ship after the foc's'le was done with her. Dead as a plague-corpse an' still walkin'. Took the poor, bleedin' mawks a fortnight to stop breathin', but she were dead from the minute she set foot on the deck of that ship. I'm street canny! I'll not go, nor her." She threw Leah the remainder of the cheese. "And if ye're half a man, ye'll warn Meg. She's a slut, certain, but she don't deserve bein' throwed to those animals.''

"Meg's so drunk, she wouldn't know the difference," Shanks said. He scratched at his right buttock, produced a huge red flea, and cracked it between his teeth. "Mother won't like it if ye cause trouble, Maggie. Both of ye, she said. She promised three drabs and she took the silver." He belched loudly. "Ye'll go, the both of ye, if I got t' whack ye over the head and carry ye there." He leered at Leah. "Ye got the look o' a pigeon what knows 'ow t' please a man. Gi' me trouble an' I'll tumble ye myself, just t' make certain what the gentlemen be buyin'.''

Maggie made an obscene gesture, and Shanks backed out and locked the door behind him. "Ole coguey! Don't trust him, Leah. Sneaky bastard. It was him took Meg's babe away. He tries to act friendly to the girls, but he's Mother's cur, he is.''

Leah swallowed a mouthful of bread. "We must get away. I'd die before I'd let that human spider touch me.''

"Damned straight. Shanks is none to toy with. He's bad. Them fingernails—I heard he can pop a man's eye out with them." Maggie looked toward the door and then around the room. "We can't wait no longer. If there was a window . . ." she began. She pressed her ear against the door. "I kin hear Mother cussin'. She's comin' up, Leah. What are we gonna do?"

Leah crossed the small room and seized the wooden bucket Shanks had brought the food in. She stood to one side of the door and motioned to the far side of the room. "Ye get her attention," she said, "and I'll do the rest."

"Ungrateful sluts!" Mother roared obscenities as she pounded up the final flight of steps. "Tell me no, will ye!" She slammed back the bolt and flung open the door.

Maggie backed against the far corner. "I ain't goin' to no foc's'le, ye drunken ole bawd!"

Mother's bloodshot eyes scanned the room suspiciously, her gaze lingering for an instant on the heaped rags.

"Ye want them sailors so bad, ye lay with them," Maggie taunted.

With a cry of rage, Mother sprang at her. Leah smashed the heavy wooden bucket over the back of Mother Witherberry's head. The big woman groaned and collapsed like a split sack of wheat.

Maggie darted forward over top the prone woman and caught Leah's hand. "Quick!" They ran out of the door and hesitated at the top of the landing. "Up," Maggie whispered hoarsely. "We can't get out that way. Shanks is down there, and the public room's full of men."

The narrow hallway ended at another door. Maggie threw it open, and both women dashed in. A naked man and woman were rolling on a pallet on the floor.

Ignoring their cries of lust, Maggie picked up a stool and threw it through the rotting boards half covering the only window. "This way," she shouted.

Leah was only an arm's length behind. Before she followed Maggie out of the tiny window, she snatched up the naked man's tunic and breeches. Behind her, Leah heard men shouting and the thud of heavy shoe leather. The ledge was as rotten as the window shutters. The wood crumbled under Leah's weight, and she clung to the side of the house with every ounce of strength.

Maggie had her right foot on a board that ran from one house to the other across the narrow alley. "Give me a boost up," she urged. "I kin almost—" She put her left foot on Leah's shoulder and scrambled up onto the roof. "Toss me them clothes," she ordered.

Leah threw them to Maggie and followed her path to the slippery tile roof. Maggie was grinning in the gray morning light.

"Ain't it a fine day!" the redhead proclaimed. "And didn't Mother's head sound hollow when ye hit it with that bucket?" She threw back her head and laughed, prancing across the rooftop with the litheness of a cat. She put her hands on her hips and looked at Leah. "I'fackins! What ye got there, a blade?"

Leah discarded her ruined shift and pulled the man's woolen tunic over her head. She belted it at the waist with the leather strap that had been tangled in it and stuck the knife between her teeth.

"Ye're somethin' for a lady," Maggie said with glee. "Don't leave them breeches. We can trade them for some real food." She snatched up the pants.

"Good wool. I know a woman who'll pay sixpence for them."

Leah motioned back the way they had come and raised her eyebrows questioningly.

"You're right," Maggie agreed. "Them men is too big to get out that window, but they'll be up here after us soon enough. Follow me." She led the way over the ancient tiles and around the chimney pots to a spot where they could easily leap to the next house roof.

For nearly an hour, they climbed and jumped from roof to roof, wending their way farther and farther away from Mother Witherberry's establishment and deeper into the city. At last, Maggie slid down the sloping roof of a dilapidated addition and dropped into a muddy fenced-in yard.

The bare space was devoid of grass, occupied by a sow and her piglets, and a dirty-faced child. The boy stared and picked his nose as they climbed up on a barrel and dropped into the street beyond. Leah took the knife out of her teeth and tucked it into the belt. Her arms and legs ached from climbing, and her head felt light from hunger, but she was smiling. "Thank ye," she said to Maggie. "How did ye learn to do that? To use the rooftops as a path?"

Maggie's teeth flashed in an endearing grin. "I'm a London street rat, my friend. Them what don't learn ends in a pauper's grave quick enough." She shook her head. "Ye owe me no thanks. 'Twas yer hand with thet bucket what gave Mother her comeuppance." Her gaze became thoughtful. "Ye got a place t' go?"

Leah hesitated. If she went back to Brandon's father's house and it had been her husband who'd com-

missioned those men to murder her, she'd not get a
second chance. All that time she'd been locked in
Mother's, she'd tried to reason it out. Her heart told
her that Brandon was innocent, but her Scottish logic
refused to be silenced. If it wasn't Brandon, it had to
be his mother, or even his cousin Charles. How could
she point a finger if she didn't know who wanted her
dead? "Nay," she admitted to Maggie. "I dinna
know where—"

"Ye're with me," Maggie said warmly. She took
Leah's hand and squeezed it. "I'll find us a safe place
to sleep and somethin' hot to eat. Ye need rest, poor
thing—what with yer little one comin'. I've friends
aplenty in the street, and friends look after one another."

"I must find a ship to take me back to America,"
Leah said. "I've got to go home."

Maggie grimaced. "Ships. I hate the thought of
them, but it's my fate to drown, maybe not yers. It'll
be hard to find the passage money, but not impossible. All in good time. Fer now, let's sell these
breeches an' buy us the biggest breakfast in London."

Leah nodded. She was too tired and too hungry to
think straight, but she was free, and she was armed
with the knife. Later, she might try to find Anne, but
as Maggie said, "For now, let's buy us the biggest
breakfast in London." It seemed like wisdom that
even Amookas would have approved of. Leah
straightened her shoulders and followed Maggie down
the muddy cobblestone alley.

Chapter 20

London, England, June 1721

"**L**eah, I've been searching for you everywhere."

Leah opened her eyes and saw Brandon standing in the mist at the end of the street. With a scream of joy, she ran to him and threw herself into his arms. He caught her and pulled her against his chest, showering her face with kisses.

"My darling," he said, over and over. "I've missed you so." She tilted her face, and their lips met. She wrapped her arms around his neck and . . .

His lips against hers were cold. She touched his cheek, his mouth, his forehead. "Brandon?" she demanded. "Brandon mine, what's wrong?" She grabbed a lock of his yellow hair, and it slipped through her fingers.

"Brandon!" Leah cried aloud.

"Leah! Leah!"

Someone was shaking her. She gasped and opened her eyes. "Ohhh," she murmured. She covered her hands with her face as intense disappointment washed over her. "I be sorry," she said. "It was a dream."

Maggie's freckled face peered at her in the smoky torchlight. "Are ye all right?"

Leah nodded. "A dream," she repeated. "Go back to sleep." Maggie yawned and lay down, pulling a blanket over her head.

Leah rose from her bed of straw and glanced about the crude camp under the bridge. By the river's edge, Tomkin waved. She waved back, noting the heavy staff in his hand. Tomkin was a good guard; the others in the band could sleep easy, knowing that the husky boy would keep off bandits in the night. The burning torch and the practice of always posting a guard kept Cal's people safe.

Leah rubbed her arms against the chill of the dark-moving Thames. Maggie's brother, Cal, and three of the older boys were away tonight. In the morning, they'd be back with food. It was best not to ask where it had come from or how they'd obtained it.

There were fifteen members in Cal's band, sixteen if Leah included herself. Maggie said it was the best organized pack in the city. "No bloodsuckers," Maggie had said. "We look after ourselves. We take care of our own, and we don't pay off nobody." Of the original fifteen, eight were boys and seven girls. Four were children too young to care for themselves; Charity's babe was only three months old.

Leah had still not gotten over the shock of learning that hundreds of children roamed the streets of London without parents or relatives to care for them. Maggie's words had burned into Leah's mind like hot coals. "Poor folk throw their brats into the gutter like mongrel pups. Some children starve, some are snatched up by people like Mother Witherberry, and others hang fer stealin' a loaf of bread."

Maggie and her two brothers had been abandoned by their father when their mother died in childbed and the father took another woman to live with him. Maggie had been five, her brother Willy, six, and Cal nine. Willy had died under the wheels of a coal wagon, but Cal and Maggie had survived long enough to learn the rules of the street as Leah had learned the forest.

"Ye do the best ye can," Maggie had explained. "Ye fight fer a place to sleep and fer every crust of bread. Ye steal when ye got to steal and work when ye can. I've even begged, but beggin' is chancy. They's a beggars' brotherhood, and ye can die quick oversteppin' their rights. It was Cal decided we needed more hands and heads. Even children can be feared, be there enough of them. Each one has a say in deciding important stuff, but Cal's the leader. If it wasn't fer him and the big boys, they's plenty what would come in the night to rob and rape."

On Maggie's word, Cal and the others had accepted her into the band. They had given her a place to sleep and shown her how to secure food. Maggie had guided her around London to places and people Leah had never seen as the Viscountess Brandon. She'd stood in a crowd and watched the king of England pass in his gilded coach, and she'd listened to a condemned man recite a tale of his misdeeds before he swung from the rope at Tyburn Hill. She'd danced to the pipes of a strolling player and laughed at the antics of Punch and Judy puppets.

Only days after Leah had joined the band, Cal had taken her to Anne's mansion. She'd waited in the shadows of the carriage house while he had gone to the servants' entrance, claiming to carry a message for the marchioness. The cook had driven him from the back door with stout whacks of a broom to his head and shoulders. "Away with you, you thievin' guttersnipe!" he'd shouted. "Lady Scarbrough has nothin' to say to the likes of you. And if she did, she can't, for she's gone away to the country, and there's no sayin' when she'll be back!"

"Where in the country?" Cal had asked. He'd gotten two more blows from the broom for his audacity and a threat from the cook to call the watch.

Maggie and Leah had returned to Anne's house four times to look for her, but the house was closed and shuttered. And as the days turned into weeks, Leah had accepted the fact that her friend was really gone. Without Anne and without money to buy passage to America, Leah was at a loss as to what to do.

The moon had come full, melted to darkness, and come full again. Over a month had passed since Leah had escaped from Mother's house. Maggie had promised that she could remain with the band as long as she wanted to, but Leah knew that shortly her pregnancy would begin to slow her down. She must get home—home to her wilderness—before that happened. If her child was born here in the stench of London's back alleys, neither of them might live to see the forest. She might never feel her precious Kitate's little arms around her again.

If the sights and smells of London troubled Leah's days, her nights were worse. Again and again, she dreamed herself back in Mother Witherberry's evil house. She would wake, soaked with perspiration, still feeling Shanks's yellowed nails against her skin or hearing Mother's twisted laughter. And when she did not dream of her imprisonment, she dreamed of Brandon.

Leah pushed back the stray hair from her face and walked to the edge of the riverbank. Part of me still loves him, she thought. Part of me knows that Brandon could never have betrayed me to those awful men. He loves me and my child—I know he does.

It was that part of her that urged her to return to Wescott House and seek out her husband—to confront him with her charges. Twice she had written him a letter telling him what had happened to her. Yet she could not bring herself to send it.

What if it was true that Brandon wanted her dead? What if he had succumbed to his family's wishes and chosen the easiest way to rid himself of an unwanted wife and child? What if Brandon's love for her was as false as her father's? Could she wager the life of her unborn child's on her intuition? If she hadn't been pregnant, her decision would have been easy. Her heart bid her to trust her husband, but because she carried a babe, she couldn't take the chance.

The thought that she might go to Cameron for help had crossed her mind, but she had ruthlessly pushed it away. A man who had abandoned a five-year-old child and the woman who loved him would never come to the aid of that daughter so many years later. She still had her pride—too much pride to beg for crumbs from someone who had once been her whole life.

"I'd rather die than ask Cameron for anything," she murmured softly to the rushing tide. Anguished, she turned away and began to climb the bank to the cobblestone street.

Maggie appeared at her side. "Where do ye go, Leah? The streets are not safe at night."

"I've my knife."

"Ye'd be lost in ten minutes." Maggie trudged up the incline. "I'll walk with ye if ye're bound to play the fool."

"And risk yourself?"

"Two is safer." Maggie grinned. "Besides, we can always take to the rooftops."

Charles frowned, lowered the leather carriage curtain, and settled back against the padded seat. It was after midnight, and he and Brandon were riding into the city by coach. "You've gone on like this for more than a month. Can't you admit that your mother and I are right? She left you, cousin. She's gone back to the Colonies."

"With what? What money did she have? Some of her clothes were missing, true," Brandon said, "but I can't picture her trading her gowns for passage on a ship. I'm certain she's still here somewhere in the city."

"I think you contracted a disease of the brain in that wilderness. First you accuse your mother of stealing your bride, then you accuse me of robbing the family treasure house. God's wounds, Brandon, did you ever consider that you could be wrong? I've enough money of my own. I don't need to go to the trouble of stealing yours."

"I told you that I didn't want to talk finances with you until my accountant has completed his investigation." The case against Charles was becoming stronger day by day, but he didn't have time for that now. He'd spent the last weeks combing the city for any trace of Leah. He'd interrogated all the servants at Wescott House and informed the authorities of her disappearance. He'd even offered a huge reward for information leading to her safe return.

"You accused me of robbing Uncle Raymond blind," Charles said.

"I was drunk when I said it," Brandon lied.

"Is that supposed to be an apology, cousin?" Charles toyed with his snuffbox. "I don't know why I bother with you. I've been insulted, my honor impinged. You've not given me any chance to defend myself, yet here I am riding around London with you in the dead of night searching for a sailor who claims he might have seen someone who might be your missing wife." He took a pinch of snuff, sneezed, and put the box back in his inside pocket. "Mad as a March hare, the both of us."

"I didn't ask you to come with me tonight," Brandon reminded him. The coach horses' hooves striking the cobblestones made a lonely sound, and Brandon stared moodily out at the black Thames in the moonlight. "Maybe I am mad," he said, "but I can't shake the thought that I've failed her, and she's in terrible danger."

"She had money when she left Wescott House," Charles replied. "Your mother was afraid to tell you, but her personal strongbox with the household funds was missing. Nothing else was touched—not her jewels or her clothing. She thought she'd lost upward of sixty pounds."

"Now you're accusing Leah of being a thief."

"You didn't hesitate to call me a thief."

Brandon ignored Charles's sarcasm. "If you're so certain Leah took Mother's money and went back to

the Colonies, then why are we going to Blackfriars
Stairs tonight?''

"I've wondered that myself, listening to you revile
me,'' Charles answered sharply. ''Damn it, cuz.
We've been closer than most brothers. If there's a
chance Leah's still in London, of course I want to
help you find her.''

"You've been scant help the past weeks.''

Charles sniffed. ''You're entitled to your own opinion. I'm not without my own sources of information,
you know. I've sent out inquiries to various taverns
along the waterfront, asking if anyone remembered
seeing a lady matching Leah's description. An infor-
mant brought a message from this ship's mate who
claims he saw her talking to the captain of a colonial
merchant vessel. This is a rough section of the city.
I wasn't about to let you come here alone at night.''
Charles motioned to the back of the coach. ''It's also
why I brought along those two fellows.''

"There was a time when I would have trusted you,
but now . . . now I'm not sure,'' Brandon admitted.
''We're not boys any longer.''

"And who do you trust? Your mother? Your father?'' Charles made a sound of derision. ''You've
turned your back on your family, continuing to believe in a woman who told you she was leaving you.
No, don't protest. Your own words, cuz. You told me
the two of you argued that morning, and Leah told
you she was going back to America. Think rationally,
man. You're behaving abominably. I really do think
you're suffering from brain fever.''

The coachman reined in the team on Ludgate Hill.
''As far as I can go, sir,'' he called back. ''Yonder is
the street that leads to the Red Goose Tavern, but the

way's too narrow for the coach. Ye must walk from here, sir.''

Brandon and Charles got out of the coach. "Wait here," Brandon ordered the coachman. "John can stay with you and watch the coach.''

"Beggin' your parden, Lord Brandon," the coachman ventured. "Best take John wi' ye. He's a brawny lad and ready with his fists in time of trouble.''

"No need," Charles interjected. "We've these two men." He indicated Giles and Ben, both carrying heavy cudgels. "Your master has a pistol, and we are both wearing swords. I think we can walk down this street to the tavern and back.''

Brandon nodded. "We won't be long.''

"As ye wish, sir.''

Giles lit a torch from one of the coach lanterns and led the way off Ludgate Hill toward the water. Ben followed closely behind Brandon and Charles. A few hundred yards from where they'd left the coach, Giles turned into an deserted alley.

"This way, yer lordships," he said. "The Red Goose is offen this street.''

"Damnable spot," Charles grumbled. "I don't care for the smell." He kicked a dead rat out of the way. "I don't know how the poor devils can—''

When Charles mentioned the word *devils*, Ben leaped past him to slam Brandon on the back of the head with his club. Giles spun around, threw the torch to the ground, and attacked Brandon from the front with a wicked-looking knife. Charles flattened himself against a housefront as Brandon staggered to one side. He drew his pistol, but a blow from Ben's club sent it spinning away. Brandon pulled his sword and raised it to protect himself.

"Charles!" Brandon yelled. "Get the other one!" He slashed at Giles, and the thin man jumped out of reach of the flashing steel blade.

Charles withdrew his sword and ran it through Brandon's back. His cousin groaned and fell to his knees. Charles put his foot against Brandon's back and extricated his weapon. "End of game, cuz," he said. "Winner takes all."

Gasping, Brandon rolled onto his back. "You . . ." he managed. "You . . ." He began to cough.

"Fool," Charles pronounced. "I've waited so long for this—ever since Cecily. Do you remember her, Brandon? My Cecily?" He smiled. "Finish him," he ordered the mercenaries. "And don't forget that I'll need the body for his dear parents to grieve over." Charles turned away and walked back down the alley.

"Charles," Brandon whispered. The pain in his back was excruciating, and his breath came in strangled gulps. Two shadowy forms closed in on him. Brandon threw up an arm as he saw an oak cudgel descend. There was a flash of light, and then he felt nothing at all . . .

Leah and Maggie rounded the corner. Both saw the men bending over the prone body at the same time. Maggie gave a cry of alarm. "Watch!" she shouted.

Giles looked up and spied the women. "Shut them up!" he ordered. Ben whirled, torch in hand, and lunged toward them.

Leah and Maggie fled back the way they had come. Leah glanced back over her shoulder to see both men chasing them. The pursuer in front—the man with the torch—was one of the ones who had kidnapped her from Wescott House, the mute called Ben. She was sure of it.

"This way," Maggie urged. She threw open an unbarred door and dashed into an empty house. Grabbing Leah's hand, she led her through the trash-filled rooms and out the back door into a tiny yard. Leah followed her over a wall, down another alley, and up onto a roof. There, they threw themselves facedown and tried to catch their breaths.

"They were the men who captured me and sold me to Mother Witherberry," Leah explained. "At least the one with the torch was. He never talked. I think he was a mute. The other one was called—"

"Giles," Maggie supplied. "I know them. Thieves and scoundrels, the pair of 'em. Evil men. They murdered a whore in the shadow of St. Paul's last winter. Tomkin saw it."

"That man in the alley," Leah said. "They were robbing him."

"Right enough, love. And lucky they didn't catch us. I tole ye the streets wasn't safe by dark."

"We have to go back."

"What? Are ye witless?"

"That poor man. He may nay be dead yet, but he will be when they finish with him. Maybe we can help him."

Maggie shook her head. "Uh-uh, not me. I don't know him. He may be as bad as Ben an' Giles for all I know." She shrugged. "His bad luck to be in the wrong place. I say we get back to the bridge while we're still in one piece."

Leah sighed. "I canna. I owe those two. If I can steal away their prey, so much the better. I've got to go back and see if he's still alive."

"Ye'll get us killed too."

"Nay. You're too good a guide."

Minutes later, the two crept down the alley to the spot where the body lay motionless. Maggie stood over it, watching for Giles and Ben, while Leah knelt beside it. She put her hand on his throat to feel for a pulse, then laid her cheek close to his lips. "I think he's breathing," she whispered. She ran her hands over his body, shuddering when she felt the sticky pool of blood beside him.

"Come on," Maggie urged. "We have to go."

"We canna leave him."

"I'll go fer the watch."

"Ye shouted for him before, and not a soul poked his head out a window to see what was happening."

"Folks in this section know better. They mind their own business."

"I'm not leaving him for those two to butcher," Leah repeated.

"What if he's as bad as them?"

"I don't care," Leah said stubbornly. "I dinna like two against one." She tried to get an arm under the fallen man. "Do ye think ye can help me carry him?"

"Ye are mad. He's too big." Maggie began to back away. "We have to go. It's too dangerous. They'll come—"

"Maggie!" Leah threw her shoulder under his. "Help me," she commanded. She shook the man. "You've got to help us," she said. "Those men are coming back to kill you. You've got to walk."

The man moaned.

Maggie scooped water from the gutter in her hands and threw it into his face. "Wake up, rogue!" He sputtered and began to choke. Maggie grabbed his other arm. "Devil take ye, walk!" she cried.

Together, the women half dragged, half carried him back toward the empty house.

"I warn ye," Maggie said, puffing under the man's weight, "if I hear a sound, I'm dropping him and runnin' like hell." When they reached the house and managed to pull him inside, Maggie suggested they leave him and come back in daylight.

"He'll bleed to death," Leah said. It was ink-black inside the house, so dark that she couldn't see her own hand. The stranger's breathing was loud and strained.

"He may bleed to death anyway," Maggie said. "What if the watch comes and finds ye with him? They'll think ye murdered him."

"Ye go back to the bridge. I'll stay with him. Cal may be back. If he is, get some of the boys to help."

"Damn it. Ye don't even know him. Why risk your life—our lives—for a stranger?"

"I was a stranger, Maggie. Ye helped me."

"Ye'll rue this, I warn ye. It will bring nothin' but trouble." Muttering under her breath, Maggie slipped out the back way and climbed the wall.

Leah sat in the darkness and held the stranger's head. The scent of blood was strong in her nostrils. She drew her knife and waited, vowing that if Giles and the mute came, they wouldn't take her easily.

At that moment, a few yards away, Giles and Ben hurried back down the alley to where they'd left Brandon. "Where the 'ell did they get to?" Giles complained. "Two wenches. We were right behind 'em and they vanished into thin air."

Ben grunted and lifted the nearly gutted torch. Rats scurried out of the light and away from the pool of blood. The paving stones were stained dark red, but there was no body. He picked up Brandon's pistol and tucked it into his belt.

"By the king's arse!" Giles swore. "Where did 'e . . ." He shook his head. "Bloody 'ell. 'E's gone too. Maybe the watch did come, after all."

Ben grunted urgently and retrieved Brandon's coat and sword. They'd been in the process of stripping him of his valuables when they'd been interrupted earlier.

"Naw," Giles assured his companion. " 'Is lordship was dead, all right." He fished into a bag at his waist and came up with Brandon's signet ring and purse. "Lucky I got these afore them sluts came along."

Ben held out a hand, palm up, and tapped it with the other hand. His lips formed the words *Sir Charles*.

"Don't worry, Ben. Sir Charles's will pay what 'e owes us. We got the ring, the purse, and the coat. All we needs is another body t' put it on. Ye 'spose we could find a body?" Ben shrugged. "Find one or make one," Giles said. "Let's get out o' 'ere, before the watch comes back." He took the torch from Ben and tossed it into the gutter. It sputtered and went out, leaving the alley in blackness again. As silently as shadows, the two hurried away.

Leah wished for clean water to wet the stranger's lips and wash his wound. She knew he needed to be kept warm, even in the June night. But she had nothing, so she sat with his head in her lap and waited.

As the hours passed, he began to moan and toss his head. Leah felt the wound on his back. It had closed, but now that he was thrashing around, it was open again and seeping blood. She knew his life force

was draining away. At the back of the house was a
little moonlight, coming in the broken windows. Here
in this section, there was none, but she was afraid to
try to move him.

She cut a strip from the hem of her tunic and bound
it around his middle, trying to staunch the bleeding.
In wrapping the makeshift bandage around him, her
hand brushed an object in a pocket sewn on the inside
of his breeches. She slid her hand under his waistband
and pulled out her amulet and chain.

"Aiyee!" she cried. In Stygian darkness she would
know the Eye of Mist. Her fingers traced the familiar
incisions in the golden triangle as she realized why
the stranger had been so important to her. "Brandon!
Brandon, is it you?"

"Leah?" he uttered. His voice was so weak she
could barely make out her name.

She buried her face in his hair and inhaled his scent.
It was Brandon. How could she have not known?
"Brandon mine," she murmured, clutching her
charm between her fingers as her mind filled with
images she didn't want to accept. Brandon. Brandon
with Giles and Ben. The three of them together . . .
What could it mean? The awful thought that he'd come
to pay them for her murder rose in a dark corner of
her mind, but she pushed it away. It was too terrible
to accept. She had to believe in their love, no matter
what.

Tears filled her eyes and dropped onto his face.
"Brandon mine," she murmured again. "My husband . . . my love."

He began to cough and then to shiver. "Leah," he
gasped. His hand groped to touch her. "I . . . I . . ."

She drew in a deep breath. What did he wish to

tell her? That he was sorry? That he loved her still? Maggie had warned her that she would rue saving the stranger, that it would bring nothing but trouble.

"Alla gaski lewi," she whispered in her native tongue. It cannot be true. She lowered her head and brushed his cool lips with hers. Taking the amulet with both hands, she held it over Brandon's chest.

"Spirit of the Eye of Mist," she said fervently. "Hear my plea and grant my wish. If there be power in this amulet, let it come forth and save the life of this man. I, Leah Moonfeather Stewart, daughter of Cameron, call upon thee. Fulfill your promise, and let him live."

Chapter 21

Leah watched the first rays of morning light dance across the rushing surface of the Thames, changing the dark, foreboding river to a sparkling waterway of beauty. It was her turn to stand watch for Cal's band; everyone else was sleeping. She didn't mind. She couldn't have slept anyway, and the stillness of dawn renewed her strength and gave her an opportunity to listen to the counsel of her inner voice.

On the river, canopied tilt-boats manned by brawny watermen vied for position with the larger barges of oceangoing sailing vessels. The bloated carcass of a dead dog floated by, tangled with refuse from a poulterer's shop. At the water's edge, a scarred alley cat crouched to drink, while crows strutted up and down the muddy bank, cawing loudly.

Leah turned away from the river and looked back toward Brandon. A day and night had passed since Cal and his friends had carried him back to the camp under the bridge. Brandon was no better, in fact, he was worse. All night, he'd been wracked by high fever. Now he slept, but it was not a natural sleep, rather a fitful and dream-filled sleep that proved the extent of his injury.

Maggie had helped Leah tend to Brandon's wounds, but without medicine there was little they could do except wash him and bandage him tightly. Leah felt helpless. In the forest, she would have known a dozen plants to use. Mushroom spoors would have stopped the bleeding—here she was forced to resort to using balls of spiderwebs. Cattail, oak bark, or even the common plantain would have given her weapons to use against the Dark Warrior. She needed willowbark tea to bring down his fever and honey to mix with water so that he would not die of lack of fluid in his body.

Cal stirred from his pallet, rubbed his eyes, and got up. He went to where Brandon lay and looked down at him. Shaking his head, he came toward Leah. "He's dying," Cal said. "It's a wonder he didn't die in the night."

Leah's hand went to her throat where her amulet hung beneath the high neckline of her man's tunic. In the night, she'd nearly torn it away and thrown the necklace into the Thames. It was as empty of power as she'd feared. Her charm was useless—worse than useless, for it had caused her to have hope when she should have known what the outcome of Brandon's terrible injury would be. "He may not die," she said, denying her own logic. "He's strong."

Cal's brow furrowed. "Ye're Maggie's friend or I wouldn't o' brought him here t' begin with. He's a gentlemen an' thet's a danger t' the rest o' us, Leah. If he dies—and he will—it will bring the watch down on us. I can't let thet happen. He's got t' go."

"I've nowhere to take him," she argued. Brandon's mother might well be in on his attempts to murder her. If she tried to take Brandon to Wescott House, she might be imprisoned and killed. She didn't trust Charles or Lady Kathryn, or any of the servants. None of them had come to her aid the night she'd been kidnapped. "Ye canna turn us into the streets."

"I can and I will." He motioned toward the sleeping members of his band. "I've Maggie, and Charity, an' the others t' think of. Ye kin stay if ye like, but he goes."

"I've got to have more time. I'll think of something," she promised.

"No," he said. Cal's pale blue eyes met her gaze stubbornly. He was only a finger's height taller than she was and thin as a whip. His eyes, Leah decided, were too old for a boy who'd not yet reached twenty, and his muscles were always tense, ready to spring into action. "It's already gettin' light. People will be on the streets. He goes now."

She sighed heavily. "Wait. I do know of a place, but it's not close. I'll need a cart and a horse to carry him."

"Are ye daft? Why not ask me fer a coach and four?" He shook his head. 'Ye're mad, Leah—naught but a mad gypsy wench with wild tales of America."

"It be true, all that I told ye." She caught his hand. "I saved your sister's life, Cal. Ye owe me a favor. I know ye can get the horse and cart if ye want. Please, I'm begging ye."

He hesitated, and his prominent Adam's apple bobbed in his skinny neck. "If I do, then it's off wi' ye. Ye'll trouble us no more, not ye nor him. I'm weary of ye fillin' Maggie's head wi' yer nonsense."

"Do this one thing for me, and ye'll never see us again. I promise."

Cal scuffed the dirt with his square-toed shoe. "I

guess I kin try, but if I hang fer stealing a horse, I'll see ye hang wi' me, ye gypsy jade.''

The old gray horse clopped along at a maddeningly slow pace. Leah rose to her knees and leaned forward in the cart, straining for a glimpse of her father's great house. Brandon lay beside her in the crude two-wheeled vehicle. The borrowed farm cart smelled strongly of cabbage; a few wilted leaves still clung to the rough boards. It made a poor conveyence for a man with a sword wound, even if he was lying on a heap of straw.

Cal slapped the reins over the horse's back and urged it on faster. Cal and Maggie shared the high narrow seat at the front of the cart. Despite his complaining, Maggie's brother had insisted on coming along to drive the horse.

Brandon's condition was very bad. He was still burning with fever, and Leah could hardly see his chest rise and fall when he breathed. The movement of the cart had caused the wound to begin bleeding again. There was nothing Leah could do but hold his hand tightly and offer prayers that he would live long enough for her to get him proper medical treatment.

When Cal and two of the boys had picked Brandon up to put him into the cart at the bridge, he'd regained consciousness long enough to recognize Leah. "Tell no one where I am," he'd managed between cracked, dry lips. He'd gripped her arm so hard that his fingers had left purple bruises on her skin. "Promise me, Leah, that you'll tell no one . . . not Charles . . . not even my mother." She'd tried to learn why he didn't want her to send word to his family, but his words became lost in the ramblings of fever.

When they reached Lord Dunnkell's manor, Cal drove the horse and cart down a side street and reined in the animal. "I'll wait here fer the time it takes a kettle o' water t' boil over an open fire," he said. "Not a minute more. After that, we set yer man on the ground an' get."

Leah glanced up and down the deserted street. The iron fence surrounding her father's mansion was ten feet high and topped by spikes. She kicked off the clumsy leather shoes Maggie had given her and climbed the fence. Coming down the far side was even easier—she dropped the last six feet, landing on the thick, springy grass.

"Good luck," Maggie called.

Leah didn't look back. Remembering the problem that Cal had had at Anne's kitchen entrance, she decided to go in here by the front. A black-faced sheep raised her head from grazing and stared round-eyed at Leah as she passed. Leah held a finger to her lips and smiled at the fluffy white beast. The ewe, a tuft of green grass dangling from her mouth, continued to chew contently. Leah skirted a brilliantly colored peacock, then dashed around the corner of the house and up the front steps.

The front door was locked. She pounded on the brass knocker, and both guards on the other side of the iron gate turned toward the noise.

"Get away from there!" shouted one of the liveried blackamoors. The second threw open the gate and ran up the walk toward her.

Leah spun to face the huge angry guard. "Please," she began, "I must see Lord Dunnkell on a matter of life and death."

The man dropped his Turkish sword onto the grass

and advanced on her. His lips were drawn back in a snear and his teeth were bared.

"I must see Lord Dunnkell," Leah repeated.

The door opened a crack, but before Leah could react, it slammed shut. The guard lunged for her. Leah waited until he was almost upon her, then stepped aside. As the force of his attack carried him past her, she stuck out her foot and shoved him. The big man's head struck the edge of the marble step as he fell, momentarily stunning him. When he groaned and opened his eyes, Leah had one knee on his chest and her knife at his throat.

The door opened again, and a haughty man with graying hair and red and white livery stared at Leah and the fallen guard. "What's going on here?" he demanded. "Who are you, and how dare you assault Lord Dunnkell's servant?"

"Call your master," Leah demanded. "Call him or I'll cut this one's throat." The second guard had left his post and come to stand helplessly a few yards away. "I will see the Earl of Dunnkell," Leah said.

"What on earth—" Lady Dunnkell pushed past her butler. "Holy Mary, mother of God! What are you doing on my lawn, girl?" The pinch-faced woman stepped out onto the step. "Get up from there immediately and explain yourself." She glared at the other guard. "Have you been relieved of your post, Nathaniel? Do I pay you to stand gawking about like a milkmaid at a county fair?"

Leah's courage was fast dwindling. "I need to see Lord Dunnkell," she said again. Her voice cracked, and she blinked back tears. The man under her tensed his muscles, and she pressed the blade harder against his jugular vein. "Nay," she warned softly. "Dinna try."

"You're ruining Nehemiah's uniform," Lady Dunnkell chided. "Do you know what silk of that quality costs?" She clapped her hands. "Enough of this display. You've made your point. Let go of my guard and come into the house before I'm made a laughingstock of the city. I've a few moments before my mantua maker arrives, and I suppose you must be heard."

Leah looked from the blackamoor's stoic face to Lady Dunnkell's determined one. With a sigh, she withdrew the knife and scrambled to her feet, keeping a safe distance from the guard. He picked up his sword and looked to his mistress for instructions. Leah knew he would gladly have taken off her head if Lady Dunnkell would only give the word.

"Back to your place," the countess said. She motioned to Leah. "Come in, come in." She threw up a hand. "You don't have lice, do you, girl?" Leah shook her head. "Very well, let's get this matter tended to. I'm a busy woman. I have no time for silliness."

A few minutes later, Nathaniel and Nehemiah were carrying Brandon into the house by way of the servants' entrance. Leah had gotten no further in her explanation than the mention of Brandon's name and the fact that he was lying close to death by Lady Dunnkell's fence, than her ladyship had insisted that he be brought inside.

"We'll hear the rest of your story when Lord Dunnkell returns from his ride," she said. "I've heard rumors that Kentington's heir is missing. On the outside chance that you're not a madwoman or a liar, I'll not have Raymond Wescott's son die in my yard while we hedge over details. You should realize that you aren't the first to claim to be one of my husband's by-blows, but you certainly are the oddest. I never meddle in Cameron's personal affairs. We've been married longer than anyone else I know, and that's always been my policy. Cameron will certainly know the truth of the matter.''

Leah heard only half of what Lady Dunnkell said. She watched as Brandon was laid on clean sheets in a guest bedroom of the mansion. Maggie and Cal had gone when Leah got back, so Brandon was her only concern. ''I need warm water and soap,'' she said.

''I will call my personal physician,'' Lady Dunnkell said, ''and I will notify Lady Kathryn. She can send a servant to verify if this is, indeed, Lord Brandon.''

''Please, no!'' Leah cried. ''Lord Brandon insists that his whereabouts be kept a secret. Dinna tell anyone yet. Wait until I see my father first.''

''Very well,'' Lady Dunnkell agreed. ''It can't hurt to wait until Lord Dunnkell returns. You may remain in the room, but I warn you, my servants are very cautious. If you try to steal anything, you'll find yourself in Newgate faster than you talked your way in here.'' She dismissed Leah with a brisk nod and floated away, followed by a train of maids and footmen.

Leah busied herself with bathing Brandon and washing the wound. He had groaned when they carried him up the stairs, but he'd not opened his eyes. Leah hoped that Lady Dunnkell's English physician had more magic in his bag than she possessed. Otherwise, Brandon would die. And no matter what he had done to her, Leah wanted him to live. "I won't let ye die," she murmured stubbornly as she laid a clean wet cloth on his forehead. "Nay, ye shall not. Ye have too much to answer for."

"What is this nonsense about Kentington's heir?"

Leah turned to see her father standing in the doorway of the bedchamber. "If ye know him," she said boldly, "come and see for yourself. This be Robert Wescott, Viscount Brandon."

Cameron tossed his riding gloves and hat to a servant and strode toward the bed. "And you? Who are you? I've never seen—" He stopped, and Leah saw his composure crack. His eyes narrowed as he took another step in her direction. *"Sh'kotai?"*

Leah trembled as she heard him speak her dead mother's name. "Nay," she answered softly. "Dinna . . ."

Cameron motioned to the servants. "Out," he ordered, "all of you."

Leah waited.

"I'm sorry," he said. The familiar Highland lilt of his words made her eyes glisten with moisture. "I thought you were someone I used to know. You look—"

She forced herself to meet his gaze. "Dinna ye ken?" she said. "I be your daughter, Moonfeather."

"Leah?" He shook his head. "You can't be. My Leah was . . ." He trailed off as he closed the distance between them. "Is it possible?"

"Aye," she flung back. "I be that child ye abandoned—but a child no longer."

His gaze became shrewd. "If you are my daughter, what did I give you on the day I went away?"

Leah reached under her neckline and pulled out her

amulet. "This," she answered. "This worthless charm."

"My God." Cameron put his arms around her and crushed her against him. "Leah, Leah," he murmured. When he released her and stepped back, his cheeks were stained with tears. "Child." His voice was rough and gravelly. "I have no words."

"Well and well again," she said, "for it seems I have enough for us both."

"How are you here in England?" he asked. "And your mother, Sh'kotai, does she yet draw breath?" he demanded in the formal Shawnee phrasing.

"Nay." Leah shook her head. "It is a bad omen to speak her name. She has crossed over."

"Dead? But she was—" He was interrupted by a footman.

"Lord Dunnkell, forgive me, sir, but the physician is here."

"Send him in."

A mature man dressed all in black entered with his two assistants. Leah found herself hastily escorted to another room and left alone there with her father.

"Now," Cameron said, when she was seated near him. "Start at the beginning and tell me all."

Leah looked back toward the door. "My husband is near to death. Canna this wait?"

"McCloud is the best, but he has his ways. 'Tis best we leave him alone with the patient. How did you find—" He looked up at her. "That was you with Lady Anne that day in the carriage, wasn't it? I didn't get a clear look at you, but—"

"Aye. I knew ye. Your hair isna the same, but—"

Cameron pulled off his wig. Underneath, his close-cropped auburn hair was streaked with gray. "Leah, my precious little Leah. Remember, child, that I was a man grown when you last saw me. You were naught but a bairn, and now you've grown into a beautiful woman. You're the image of your mother.''

"She died giving birth to your child."

His eyes clouded with pain. "I didn't know. I wouldn't have left her if—"

"No? That's easy to say, isn't it—here and now. I begged you not to go, Father." Leah couldn't hold back the tears. "You couldn't stay with us . . . with me."

He sank his head in his hands. "I've regretted it a hundred times." He sighed. "The wilderness is a very different place than London. I thought this was where I'd be happy."

"With Lady Dunnkell?"

Cameron's head snapped up. "Margaret is a great lady, Leah. Your mother knew about her. I never tried to hide the fact that I was already married."

"You were as faithful to Lady Dunnkell as you were to my mother."

"More faithful perhaps." Cameron's features hardened. "I am a Stewart of Dunnkell. My blood is as blue as—hellfire and damnation—it's bluer than that German George who sits on the English throne. We were poor, Leah. There were crofters who ate better than we did at Christmas. I had a mother and brothers to think of . . . as well as those who lived on our land. My mother and uncle arranged my marriage to a wealthy heiress, and I accepted. I was sixteen when I wed Margaret—she was thirty. There's never been love between us, but there's been friendship."

"I told her that I was your daughter."

"She told me." He took Leah's hand. "She's a

good woman. Maybe if we could have had a child between us—"

"Lady Dunnkell is not the mother of my English sister?"

"How did you know you had an—"

"It has been too long, Father. Ye told me so. You said you were returning to another daughter in England."

He sighed. "So I did. No, Margaret isn't her mother. None of my children was born legitimate."

Leah stiffened. "I am Shawnee. I am my mother's child. Your English laws canna make me—how is it ye say?—a bastard."

"I never thought of you as being illegitimate. I loved you . . . I still do."

"Aye, so ye say, Father. But ye left me easily enough—and because of you, I lost my mother too."

"Sh'kotai and I . . . How can I make you understand? We loved each other, but it wasn't enough. I stayed with her seven years. She couldn't come back with me to my world, and I suppose I knew she'd only find unhappiness here if she did. And when I decided to return to England, I couldn't take you. She loved you too much, Leah. How could I take you from a mother who bore you? Stop looking at your hurt like a five-year-old. I didn't leave you because I didn't love you—I left you because I loved both of you too much to separate ye."

Leah shook her head. "I dinna know what to say to ye. All this time, I've hated . . . I used to wish ye dead."

"But you kept the amulet I gave you. You still wear it."

"Aye," she admitted. "I do, but . . ." She got up

and walked to a window, looking out at the mani-
cured lawn. "There be so much to tell ye, my father." She smiled. "I have a son. Kitate. He is
three—no, nearly four now. He is beautiful."

"So I'm a grandpapa and I never knew it. Is he
Lord Brandon's son?"

"Nay. I was married before I met Brandon, and
then widowed." She smiled through her tears. "But
I carry Brandon's bairn and heir now." Her hand went
to her belly protectively. "Things be not right between me and my husband, but that isna your fault. I
ha' wronged ye, I fear. In my stubborn clinging to a
child's heartbreak . . ." She shook her head. "Aiyee,
Father, I dinna ken where to begin to—"

"Start at the beginning, Leah. That's always best.
Start from the day I left, and tell me everything."

She nodded. "All right. Alex said that I—"

"My friend. Does he live still?"

She laughed. "Alex? Alex is immortal. He has . . ."
She began hesitantly, but soon the words began to
tumble out of her, rushing faster and faster. It was
as if the years had never been, as if Cameron had
always been her loving father. She'd never found it so
easy to talk to any man—not even Brandon.

She had reached the part in her story where Brandon had tricked her into coming to the dock at Annapolis, when a servant came to call them back to the
sickroom. Together, Leah and her father returned to
Brandon's side. She looked at him carefully and laid
her hand on his head. She could see no difference.

"I will stay with him, of course," the physician
was saying, "but his condition is very grave. He could
pass away at any time. The wound is infected, and he
has lost a great deal of blood."

"You are to spare no expense," Cameron instructed.

"And ye are to tell no one that he is here," Leah said. "No one. Lord Brandon commanded me to keep his presence a secret. Those who attempted his murder be still free."

The physician inspected Leah with cool eyes.

"You will do as the lady requests," Cameron said.

"You may count on my discretion," Dr. McCloud assured them. "I will do my best, but I can promise nothing."

Cameron turned to Leah. "You look as though you have not slept in days. Come, child, and let us see what we can do for you. If Margaret saw you in this . . . costume, 'tis a wonder she ever let you into the house."

"She didna exactly *let* me in," Leah admitted.

"I can't wait to hear it all. Come along. Let's get you properly attired for tea, and we'll join her in the small drawing room."

"No," Leah said. "I must stay with Brandon. He may wake and—"

"When he wakes, Dr. McCloud will call us," Cameron said.

"At once, Lord Dunnkell. *If* he wakes," McCloud corrected.

"You see. Nothing will be gained by you making yourself ill," Cameron said.

Outnumbered, Leah agreed. She was exhausted and starving. She knew she had to keep up her strength for the sake of her unborn child. Dutifully, she followed her father out of the room.

"You'll like Margaret," Cameron said. "She's a woman of uncommon good sense."

Leah yawned. Suddenly she was exhausted. Her eyelids felt as though they each weighed a pound. She rubbed at her eyes and suppressed another yawn. "The necklace is a fake, Father," she said. "I called upon it."

He stopped and looked down at her. "You what?" he asked.

"The Eye of Mist. You told me that it carried a blessing and a curse. I've had the curse. I'm here in England against my will. But when I called upon the amulet to save Brandon's life, it failed me."

Cameron nodded thoughtfully. "You asked for his life?"

"Aye, I did."

"Is he lost to you?"

"Nay, not yet but—"

"Then dinna give up hope, child. If I can hold you in my arms after all these years, then anything is possible. It may be that your amulet can give you your heart's desire as it gave me mine."

Chapter 22

Leah sat beside Brandon's bed and watched him draw one painful breath after another. He was hot to the touch, so hot she feared the fever would burn away his life force. He hadn't opened his eyes or spoken for six days. And for six days she had hardly left his bedside. "Dinna die, Brandon, please," she whispered. "Ye must fight."

Anger rose in her as she remembered how the English physician had wanted to bleed Brandon and purge him. She'd returned to the bedchamber to find McCloud's servant holding a bowl under Brandon's wrist while the physician prepared to open a vein with a knife. "Are ye mad?" she'd railed at them. "Has he not lost enough blood? Would ye murder him with your ignorant, barbarian customs?" She had wrenched the knife from the physician's hand and driven him from the sickroom.

McCloud had left the house in a cold fury, but she didn't care. What was he except another English fool? Her father had stood by her, agreeing that further bleeding would make Brandon's death certain, but her father's wife, Lady Dunnkell, had been shocked.

Leah rubbed her eyes and reached for the cup of

willowbark tea—a potion she'd prepared from ingre-
dients her father's servants had gathered. Willowbark
had the power to conquer fever . . . if she could only
get enough in him. "Drink," she murmured, lifting
the cup to his pale lips.

Her shoulders and back ached; her eyes burned
from lack of sleep, but if she slept, he might drift
away from her—and as long as she had breath in her
body, she would not surrender him to the Dark Warrior. "He's mine," she whispered into the quiet room.
"Mine."

If she could break the fever, she would give him
strong beef broth and honey water. Now all she could
do was continue to try to get the willow tea down him
and keep on washing the sword wound with salt water. In the night, when the fever was highest, she'd
commanded her father's servants to fill a copper tub
with cool water, and they had put Brandon, naked,
into it. At home, she had often seen children with a
fever bathed in the river. Brandon thrashed and cried
out, but the water did ease the heat of his tortured
body.

Leah's golden amulet felt warm against her throat.
"If you have power, show it now," she urged. "Make
him live!"

Brandon choked, and some of the willow tea spilled
down his chin, but most of it he swallowed. Leah
sighed with satisfaction and kissed his forehead
gently. "I do love ye," she whispered, "in spite of
all we have done to each other. I will always love
ye." She would not admit that he could still die, that
even Brandon might not have the strength to survive
that terrible wound.

Still, she could not forget that in all probability,

her husband had hired those awful men to murder her. Can't you see how much I want to believe in you? she cried silently. I want to believe in our love, but I do not want to close my eyes to the truth. Brandon had been in that alley with her kidnappers—and that had been no coincidence. To deny what she had seen with her own eyes made her a witless fool.

In spite of her lack of sleep and her worry over her husband, Leah's own strength had returned in the past six days. When she'd allowed herself to rest that first night in her father's house, she'd slept around the clock without waking. Physically she'd been exhausted, but she knew that her mental powers had been weak as well. She'd allowed the English surroundings to undermine her sense of self—she'd forgotten who and what she was. Now, those voids in her spirit had been refilled by meditation and prayer.

Day by day, her relationship with her father was growing stronger. Here at Brandon's bedside, they'd shared laughter and tears, reliving old memories of time gone by. As Leah heard her mother's name on Cameron's lips and saw the love in his face when he spoke of her, she was engulfed with a sense of peace. More than one person was being healed in this house, she realized. Pain and regret that had haunted her for so many years were replaced with warmth of Cameron's devotion.

Her father showed his caring in action as well as in speech. When he heard how much Maggie and Cal had done for Leah, he sent his coach to bring them to the house. To Leah's disappointment, the bridge camp had been deserted. Cameron promised he would have his servants keep searching for them, but it was obvious to Leah that Cal and his people were hiding because of fear. In so large a city, she was afraid that her friends would vanish without a trace.

Cameron had also done as Leah had asked and kept Brandon's whereabouts a secret. Her father had quarreled with his wife, Lady Dunnkell, over the necessity of hiding Brandon from his family, but he'd not weakened. "Brandon wouldna have urged Leah to hide him without good cause," he'd insisted. "We'll abide by those wishes until we've had the whole of this tale." Lady Dunnkell had been so angry, she'd threatened to pack up and move to one of their other houses in the country.

Brandon sighed and stirred restlessly. Leah broke from her reverie and moistened a fresh cloth for his head. To her relief, she saw that he was perspiring.

"Feels good," Brandon whispered. He opened his eyes and smiled weakly. "Afraid . . . I'd . . . dreamed you."

"Nay," she answered, breaking into a joyous smile. "I be real enough." Her knees felt so weak that she knew she'd be unable to stand if she tried to. He was awake! The fever had broken! She covered her mouth with her hand and blinked back tears of happiness.

Brandon licked his cracked lips. "I thought I'd . . . lost you, Leah," he murmured hoarsely.

"Who did this to ye?" she asked, trying to hide the lightness of her heart. Her reason fought with hope. Brandon was alive . . . He would not die. And she would not have to face a world in which he did not walk, and breathe, and laugh.

Still, it changed nothing between them, she reminded herself firmly. It would be foolish of her to expect more. They must still go their separate ways.

She could forgive him, but she wasn't fool enough to forget. She still loved him—she knew she would always love him. But there was nothing left of their marriage except memories of what had been and the babe she carried. Brandon had his life to live here in England, and she had another across the salt sea.

"Water . . ."

She poured more of the willowbark tea in a silver cup and held it carefully to his lips. "Drink this. 'Tis nay water, but it will make ye well."

"That's good."

She looked into his eyes and repeated her earlier question. "Who stabed ye, Brandon mine?"

He sipped more of the liquid gratefully. "Charles."

"Your cousin?"

He nodded. "Charles." His voice was low and raspy. "He brought along two . . . two ruffians . . . to help." Brandon took another sip. "But Charles did . . . the bloody work . . . himself."

A ray of hope rippled though Leah. "Charles hired them? What did they look like?"

Brandon shut his eyes. "Just common men," he said weakly. "Rough looking. One . . . one never spoke."

She began to tremble. "Why were you there in the night with Charles?"

"Mmm," he murmured. "Sleepy."

"Why, Brandon?" She grasped his shoulder. She had to know the truth. "Why?"

"To see . . ." He swallowed. ". . . see a sailor. Charles said . . . the man saw you."

"Brandon!" Heart thudding, she leaned over him and cupped his face in her palms. "Please, tell me. Did you hire those men to kill me?"

His eyes snapped open. "What?"

She released him and sank back in her chair. There was no need to hear his frantic denials—she had read the truth in his eyes. Brandon was innocent. He hadn't tried to murder her, and she'd misjudged him as badly as she'd misjudged her father.

"Leah! What . . . in God's name . . . makes you say—"

"Shhh," she soothed. "I know ye didna. It be all right now. I ken the truth of it all. Nay ye, but Charles . . ."

"You ran away . . . because you thought I—" He tried to rise, and she pushed him back.

"Nay, nay you'll hurt your wound. It was him all along, Brandon. Charles wanted me dead as well." She leaned over him again and kissed his damp forehead. "It's all right," she repeated. "I didna run from ye, Brandon. I was taken from your house by two men. And unless I be more stupid than I feel, by the same two who I caught standing over ye in that alley."

" 'Winner takes all,' Charles said. He left them . . . to finish me."

"Aye, and they nearly did."

Brandon's eyelids closed again and he sighed. "Keep a secret," he murmured. "Don't let them know I'm alive. I . . . I'll settle with cousin Charles."

"In good time. Sleep now." She squeezed his hand. "Sleep."

Some time later, Cameron found her still sitting beside the bed. Leah looked up as the door opened and smiled when she saw who it was. She raised a finger to her lips, then got up and went to the door. "The fever's broken," she told her father. "He was talking, but he's sleeping now." She accompanied

Cameron to the small sitting room off his own chambers.

"You tended him well, child. He's a strong man, but he'd never have made it without your loving care," Cameron said.

"Aye, I suppose, but I'd like to think it was his will to live that made the difference."

Cameron's eyes twinkled. "Or your amulet."

She changed the subject. "Ye be early," she replied, "I thought the dance was to last—"

"It does. Margaret will be the last one to leave. I left her with friends; they'll see her safely home." Cameron removed his scarlet coat and draped it over the back of the settee. His lace stock followed the coat. "The older I get, the tighter those damned things become," he complained. He went to a sideboard and poured a glass of brandy. "Would you care for some, Leah?"

"Nay." She chuckled. "Indian blood and firewater dinna blend well, Father."

"You're right, of course. I'd forgotten." He sipped his drink. "Life was so much simpler in America."

"I want to go home," she said. "Will ye help me?"

He nodded. "I wanted to keep you with me as long as I could, but you're unhappy here, aren't you?"

"I miss my forest and my son."

"And your husband, what would he say?"

Leah shrugged. "He loves me . . . and I him, but it be nay enough. He is a better man than I thought—probably better than I will ever know again. But I must go just the same. If I stay in this world, I will wither and die."

"Have you told him so?"

"Aye and aye again. Brandon has promised to take me home, but Lord Kentington is no better. I canna wait until Kitate has grown so old that he's forgotten me."

"And the child you carry?"

She smiled. "The Shawnee will welcome it, no matter the color of its skin."

Cameron drained the glass. "I should have stayed, child. Oh, not in the forest—I was never meant to be a Shawnee brave—but in the Colonies. Much of life here seems empty. I weary of the endless round of parties and balls. I weary of too tight fashions and men who think a new wig style the subject of an entire night's conversation."

"Father, I need to know. Will you send me home?"

"Aye." He nodded. "I'll take ye myself. Margaret will understand. I'll come, and I'll stay long enough to get to know that grandson of mine . . . and maybe to dandle this new babe on my knee."

"Oh, thank you." She threw herself into his arms. "When shall I book passage for?"

"I must make certain Brandon is well enough to look after himself. And there are things I must . . . Next month," she said. "Can we go at the next full moon?"

"Give me four to six weeks, Leah. I believe that will be time enough to settle my affairs here."

She drew back and looked up into his eyes. "Brandon will be angry with you if you take me. He is very rich. A viscount . . . He has power. He may try to stop us."

Cameron kissed the top of her head. "Don't trouble yourself, child. The Earl of Dunnkell isn't to be sneezed at." He laughed. "Your Brandon's family is rich enough, but Margaret can buy and sell them. If you want to go home to America, we'll go, and if we can't find passage to suit, I'll—''

"Thank ye, Father," she said sincerely.

He laughed again. "It's good to hear you call me that. Don't worry, I'll tend to it all. Now, it's best you get some sleep yourself. It's late. You spend far too many hours in the sickroom, and you've the bairn to think of. Off to bed with you. I'll send a servant to sit with your husband.''

"But I—'' Leah smiled. "Ye be right, Father. It is late." She caught the skirt of her blue-flowered silk and curtsied properly. "I must think of my child . . . and of others . . .'' Still smiling, she left the room and returned to her own chambers.

The next week saw Brandon's health improve by leaps and bounds. By the second day after his fever had broken, he was calling for solid food, and on the third, he was up on his feet and tottering unsteadily around the room.

Leah continued to supervise his care, insisting that he be bathed and his bandage changed twice each day. She went in to the garden and came back with herbs to brew different medicinal teas, and she sent servants out to the countryside for plants that she couldn't find near the house. She boiled fresh greens for him to eat and made flat Indian bread in the great kitchen. But as she tended her husband's physical needs and he grew even stronger, she forced herself to withdraw from him emotionally.

I have committed myself to leave him, she thought. I will love him forever, but I will do what I must do. I will keep the promises I've made here in England

. . . and I will go home for the sake of my own happiness and that of both my children.

At ten o'clock at night, nine days after Brandon's fever had broken, Leah crept silently from the house. Unseen by the night watchmen, she climbed over the iron fence at the far corner of the yard and jumped down on the far side. She picked up the bow and arrows she'd pushed through the fence and slung the bow over her shoulder. A pistol and a knife were tucked into her belt. Her hooped gown had been discarded in favor of the man's belted tunic she'd worn when she first arrived at her father's house; her hair was braided into a single plait and secured around her head with a black silk ribbon. High on each cheekbone, Leah had placed a streak of red paint.

"Too long have I forgotten my honor," she whispered into the night. "Nibeeshu Meekwon, Moonfeather of the Shawnee, is going to war." Only after she'd taken her revenge on the men who had kidnapped her and tried to murder her husband, after she'd repaid Mother Witherberry for her insults—only then could she go home to America. Only then could she tell Brandon's child what had happened without shame. Charles, she would leave to Brandon. It was her husband's right to confront his cousin and redeem his own honor. Charles was Brandon's, but the others were hers.

Cal and Maggie's camp under the bridge was deserted as Leah had expected. Only rats prowled through the meager belongings they had left behind. Leah had only come here because she guessed they might move into the empty house where she and Brandon had hidden from the assailants. Much of

London was still a maze to her, but she knew she could backtrack from the bridge to the house.

The streets were as foul-smelling and danger-filled as Leah remembered, but, armed, she feared none of the hulking figures in the mist. Most never saw her. She would flatten her body against a wall, or merely stand motionless. Once, a drunken sailor collided with her in the darkness, but she threatened him in Shawnee and nicked him with the tooth of her knife when he tried to hold her. He staggered away—more frightened than she was.

The fog was the worst she had seen, but it didn't matter. When Cal and Tomkin had carried Brandon from the empty house, they had made only five turns. One was at a public well; another at a spot where fire had destroyed two houses at an intersection. If she couldn't remember three turns in pitch blackness, she might as well take a cup and sit in the London streets and beg for a living.

When she reached the wooden fence that ran along the back of the empty house, she crouched and waited. In minutes, she heard a cough on the other side of the fence. "Tomkin," she whispered.

"Who's there?"

"Tomkin, it's Leah—Maggie's friend. Can I come over?"

"Are ye alone?"

"Aye."

"Come on, then."

She dropped down lightly beside the young man. "I need to see Maggie. Is she inside?"

"Naw, she ain't here. Ain't ye know? They got her back at Mother's again. We was attacked the night ye left with thet gentleman. The mute an' Giles an' a dozen or so street rats. They killed Gemmy and Charity's babe, and carried off Maggie an' Charity to sell to Mother.''

"Cal?"

"He's here, inside. He was all fer goin' after them, but Spots has got a broken arm. We ain't got much hittin' power.''

"Take me to Cal."

The public room of Mother Witherberry's was littered with the sprawled bodies of snoring men sleeping off the effects of raw gin and Jamaican rum. Dawn was still an hour away, and even the spit dog lay curled into a tight ball beside the smoldering embers of last night's cooking fire. A blackened joint clung to the iron spit, roasted to the consistency of old plaster, and a broken cask lay on the hearth, dribbling away the last dregs into the matted rushes that covered the ancient wooden flooring.

The dog stirred and whined in his sleep as chicken feathers began to float down the soot-covered chimney to land on the glowing white-hot coals. The dog sneezed and opened his eyes. Another clump of feathers drifted down and began to smoke as they touched the banked fire. The dog gave a series of short, puzzled barks, and Ben raised his head from the trencher table and threw a leather jack toward the noise.

The mug glanced off the animal's hind leg. He uttered a sharp yip, put his tail between his legs, and ran from the room into the adjoining shed kitchen. A three-legged table, heaped high with dirty wooden plates, leaned against the far wall. Under the table was a rat hole just large enough for the spit dog. The animal wiggled through the opening and trotted off across the backyard.

Tomkin emptied another sack of chicken feathers down the chimney, covered the top with a wide board, and slid off the roof on a rope to hang just outside a second-story window. He whistled once to signal Cal that the chimney stack was blocked and braced both feet against the crumbling windowsill.

Inside Mother's public room, smoke was billowing from the fireplace. Ben raised his head again and opened his eyes. The smoke stung them, and he began to choke. He tried to shout an alarm, but his muffled groans only angered the sleeping man beside him. The man struck out with his fist and overturned a pitcher of ale.

Ben blundered toward the barred door. By this time, other men were choking and stumbling in the darkness. Someone yelled "Fire!" and the room exploded into chaos. Ben tripped over a body on the floor, and two men climbed on top of him. A chair struck his head, and he smashed his nose against the floor. His nose began to spurt blood as he scrambled up and knocked a woman out of his way.

Outside, Tomkin and two of the boys in the yard took up a shout of fire. A girl screamed from an upstairs room, and through the house walls Tomkin could hear Mother Witherberry's cursing.

The public room door burst open, and three men staggered into the street. Unable to identify anyone in the darkness, the members of Cal's band fell upon the escapees with wooden clubs, showering them with blows. Ben was the fourth man from the house, and he cut a swath around him with a knife. He slashed one of the club wielders across the chest, but the boy dropped to his knees in front of the mute, and two more children struck Ben in the back. He went down and stayed down when Cal landed a solid blow to the back of his head.

Tomkin lowered himself to the ground. He and a second youth ran to the back of the house at the same time that Leah entered the house by the lean-to door. Men were still fighting their way out the front, and Leah heard foot thuds on the stairs. An unclad girl burst from the smoke and ran coughing past Leah into the backyard.

"Charity!" someone cried. "Where's Maggie?"

"I don't know," Charity wailed.

Leah took a deep breath and notched an arrow into her bowstring. She entered the smoky public room and crept cautiously around the overturned table, making for the stairs. Her foot struck a warm body, and she heard a man's deep groan. Still holding her breath, she stepped over him and moved toward the staircase.

Swearing at the top of her lungs, Mother Witherberry crashed down the final flight of steps with Shanks shouting right behind her. Leah knew there was no mistaking her voice or that of her human spider.

Leah's heart pounded as she drew back her bow. She wasn't more than six feet from the drunken bawd, close enough to smell the stench of her foul breath. At this distance she couldn't miss putting an arrow through Mother's black heart, even in the pitch dark. In the last instant before she released the arrow, Leah hesitated.

The big woman stumbled past, kicked a stool out of her way, and ran toward the door, still cursing

Shanks. Leah's chest was aching for breath, but she followed the sound with her bow, holding tight to the arrow's nock until Mother was out of range. I can't do it, she thought. Not to either of them—not in cold blood. Choking, she raced up the stairs.

Halfway up, she met a woman leaning against the wall, coughing. "Help me," she begged. "I don't wanna burn."

Leah grabbed her arm. "Go back to your room and open a window," she ordered the girl. "The fire's out." Still coughing, the woman jerked free and continued down the steps.

At the second floor landing, Leah ran into the nearest room and tore open the shutters, letting a gush of fresh air into the house. A candle burned in a wall sconce. Leah shielded the flame with her hand and carried the candle into the hall. In the next room she checked, she found two sobbing women.

"The fire's out," she repeated. "Where's Maggie?"

One girl stared dumbly, but the second pointed up. "Up there," she squeaked. "Red room."

As Leah started up the last flight, she heard Cal's voice calling his sister's name from the bottom of the steps. A man shouted, and then she heard a gunshot.

Leah reached the top landing. The door to the red room was unbarred. "Maggie?" she said. "Are ye there?" She threw open the door and raised the candle to illuminate the space.

A girl's still form lay on the floor. One arm was thrown over her head, and tangled red hair covered her face.

"Maggie?" Leah cried.

The girl raised her head, and Leah dropped to her

knees beside her. Maggie was naked to the waist, and the filthy gown around her hips was soaked with blood.

"Leah," Maggie whispered. Her mouth was swollen, her eyes blacked. "Be thet you?"

Leah dropped her bow and took her friend's head in her hands. "Oh Maggie . . ." A gore-stained knife lay a few feet away, a weapon with a leather wrapped grip. It was a knife Leah had seen before in Giles's belt. "Ye're sore hurt."

"No nasty stuff," Maggie whispered painfully. "Ye know I never allowed no nasty stuff." She brushed Leah's face with her bloodstained fingers. "Don't cry, Peach," she said. "We'll get away again. We'll go over the rooftops . . . just like before."

Leah bit her lip to keep from crying and lifted Maggie's torn gown to inspect her injury. Her stomach pitched as she saw the terrible gaping wounds, and she let the cheap material fall from her fingers. They'd come too late. By the looks of Maggie's injuries, she'd been stabbed hours ago. "Ah, love," Leah murmured. "What have they done to ye?" She blinked back tears and tried to focus on Maggie's face. "Are ye in pain?"

"Naw, I'm cold, is all." She touched Leah's face again. "It ain't too bad, is it?"

"Nay," Leah lied. "Not bad." She cradled Maggie's head against her breast. "Who did it?" she asked.

"Thet egg-suckin' Giles." Maggie coughed, and a trickle of blood ran from the corner of her mouth. "He had his fun . . . but he . . . he hurt me jest the same. Why, Leah? Why'd he do thet?" Coughs wracked her thin body, and she began to choke.

"Easy, easy," Leah whispered. The horror of her friend's dying made her feel as though her own blood had turned to ice.

"If . . . if we was near water . . . I'd be scared," Maggie said, "but . . . but I'm to drown, so I can't die now—can I?"

"Nay," Leah crooned. "Soon we'll be off over the rooftops, laughing back at Mother and Shanks and the whole pack of them."

"We will . . . won't we?" She began to choke again. "Bring the candle closer, Leah," she gasped. "I don't like the dark. I—" A gush of blood poured from Maggie's mouth, and she went limp in Leah's arms.

The ominous click of a pistol hammer sounded above Leah's sobbing. She turned toward the open doorway and stared into the steel muzzle of a gun.

"Couldn't stay away, could ye, ye red bitch?" Giles taunted. "Had to come back." He extended his arm and leveled the pistol at her head. Leah dived for the lighted candle as Giles pulled the trigger and the flint-lock roared.

Chapter 23

⌒⌒⌒

The room was plunged into darkness. Leah crouched low and held her breath, waiting for Giles to make the next move. Under her knee was his bloody knife—the blade he'd used to murder Maggie. It repulsed her, but she dared not move and reveal her position. She had a pistol in her belt, but she was afraid to fire for fear she would hit Cal or one of his people coming up the stairs. Below in the street, she could hear shouting and the sounds of fighting.

Giles rushed into the room. Leah drew her knife and waited. Fear tasted like cold ashes in her mouth, and gooseflesh raised on her arms.

"Where are ye, sweet?" he demanded mockingly.

She could hear him reloading his pistol in the blackness. Suddenly he lunged at her. She rolled away and he fired again. A second explosion followed the first. Giles cried out and slumped forward onto the floor. Leah rose shakily to her feet.

"Leah?"

She recognized Brandon's voice. "Here," she answered. "Be careful."

Cal's face appeared, illuminated by a lantern. His grin at seeing her safe contorted into a grimace of pain as he caught sight of his sister's sprawled body. "Ahhh, Maggie," he groaned. "Little Maggie."

Leah looked at Giles. He lay still, a neat round hole in the back of his blue wool shirt.

Brandon lowered his smoking flintlock pistol and held open his arms. Leah ran to him. "Brandon! How did ye know I . . . Your wound . . . !"

"Shhh," he soothed, holding her tightly. "Did you think I'd let you get yourself killed?"

"Ye shouldna be out of bed."

"I'll do well enough if you don't crush me to death."

She pressed her face into his chest and closed her eyes, willing herself away from this terrible room and the thick smell of blood.

Cal set the lantern on the floor and knelt beside his sister. Leah heard him weeping brokenly as she and her husband made their way down the crooked stairs.

Outside, the street was growing light. Armed men in her father's red and white livery stood in small groups. On the ground near the horses, Leah saw Shanks and Mother Witherberry tied and gagged. Mother was struggling, but the cloth around her mouth made her protests faint mumbles. By the door-sill, Ben the mute lay sprawled, obviously dead. There was another body, a man with a striped shirt and tarred pigtail. To Leah's relief, none of Cal's people were dead in the street.

Cameron rode toward them on a bay horse. His strained expression eased when he saw Leah. "Ye're safe," he said. "I'd have drawn and quartered the lot of them if you'd come to any harm."

Leah looked up at her husband and swallowed hard. Brandon's face was pale, but he'd kept step with her, and he hadn't let go of her hand since they'd left the red room. "Thanks to Brandon," she said. "He killed Giles. A few moments later and . . ." She squeezed Brandon's hand. "He belongs in bed, nay here hunting murderers."

"He does all right for an Englishman, this husband of yours," Cameron scoffed. "He ran that one"— Cameron indicated Ben's body—"through with a sword. The bastard tried to knife one of my men."

"How did ye know where I had gone?" Leah asked as her father dismounted and lifted her onto his horse.

Cameron waved to another servant, and the man led forth Brandon's mount. "You both belong at home. I'll have my master-at-arms escort you through the city."

"I know I wasna followed from the house," Leah insisted.

Cameron scowled. "I went to your bedchamber shortly after we parted and found you gone. When I went to Brandon's room and realized you weren't there either, I tracked you from the side door to the spot where you went over the fence. It didn't take me much longer to find you'd taken a bow and arrows from my collection."

"You tracked me?" she asked in disbelief.

"For seven years I lived among the Shawnee, Leah. Do you think me a complete idiot? You told me of Mother Witherberry and her filthy business. I meant to see her punished, child. Did you think your honor meant so little to me? Going back there on your own was a foolhardy thing to do—but something your mother might have attempted. I didn't think Brandon was up to riding, but he's as stubborn as you are."

Brandon reined his horse close to hers. "It took

time for your father to form up his retainers, and it wasn't easy to find this place in the dead of night. If we had come sooner, perhaps we could have saved the life of that poor girl."

"It pains me that you couldn't come to us—to one of us, at least," Cameron said.

"I was wrong not to trust ye," Leah answered softly. "Maggie was my friend. She died in my arms, but she had no chance. She was lost before I ever left your house. Her murderer—the man Brandon shot—was the same man who kidnapped me and tried to kill him. Giles was an inhuman monster. I only wish he could ha' died slower."

"Hush that, child," Cameron replied. "It's your savage Scot's blood talking. Dead is dead, and he'll harm no more women."

She nodded and looked back toward the house. "What will ye do with Mother and her cur, Shanks? Turn them over to the authorities?"

Cameron's eyes were hard. "I think not. From what you say of Mistress Witherberry, she's used to dealing with the law. If I give her to them, she may bribe her way out of jail and be back in business before we reach the Colonies. No, I have a better idea. There's a ship in the harbor bound for the West Indies. The plantations there are always in need of indentured servants to cut sugar cane. Seven years in the fields—"

"Can ye do that, Father? Sell them like animals?"

"It's better than they deserve. With luck, the fever will take them before they earn their freedom again." He put the mare's reins into Leah's hands. "Go home now. See to her, Brandon. I'll finish here. You'd best get back to the house before the city is awake and someone recognizes you."

"Could ye see that Maggie is given a proper burial?" She touched her father's cheek. "Cal has no money. He and Maggie saved my life. I want to—"

"Trust me in this, child. Off with you before the city watch comes. They can only stall so long." He signaled to his master-at-arms, and a half dozen men on horseback fell into position around Leah and Brandon. "I place the welfare of Lady Brandon in your hands," he said.

In single file, the horsemen trotted down the narrow cobbled street. Leah glanced back over her shoulder and saw her father standing over Mother Witherberry. Then her mare followed the master-at-arms around a corner, and she lost sight of Mother's.

Leah didn't ask Cameron any more questions about Mother Witherberry when she saw him at dinner that afternoon. She could tell from the expression on his face that he had finished the matter. The only other reference she ever heard him make to Mother was after Maggie's funeral two days later.

Cameron and Leah were leaving the small churchyard near St. Bartholomew's where Maggie had been buried. Since he wanted to "play dead" long enough to expose Charles, Brandon had stayed home.

Cameron stopped by the church door and shook Cal's hand. "I will be forever in your debt," he said sincerely. He glanced over at Leah. "I offered young Cal a position in my household," he explained, "but he said he prefers to enter the world of commerce. He wants to make a decent tavern out of Mistress Witherberry's establishment."

"Yeah," Cal said. "Maggie an' me was never used t' takin' orders from nobody." He crumbled his new hat in his hands. Cal, Tomkin, Charity, and the rest of Cal's "family" were all decently garbed in plain new clothing—clothing Leah had suspected her father had purchased.

Cal cleared his throat in embarrassment, clearly overwhelmed by the honor of receiving so much attention from a nobleman. "His lordship has generously offered t' lend me money t' buy ale an' get started. He said as long as the house was standin' empty, wasn't no reason why I shouldn't use it." He grinned. "They's room enough fer all o' us in the band. We scrub the place up a bit, you won't know it."

Leah said her good-byes to Cal and the others and walked away toward the waiting coach. As hard as it had been to see Maggie laid to rest, she knew it would wound her deep in her soul to take her leave of Brandon.

She paused and ran her hand along the low crumbling brick wall and stared down at the hard-packed earth, bare of grass. Not even weeds, it seemed, could grow here in London. Tears clouded her eyes, but she knew they were not tears for Maggie. Her sorrow was for the end of her marriage—for the parting that must be.

Brandon had kept himself strangely apart from her since the morning he had saved her at Mother's. "My father is taking me home to America," she had told him on the ride home. She'd expected him to berate her for saying so, or even to be angry with her for going off alone to seek revenge, but he hadn't.

"I won't try to keep you in England any longer," was all he'd replied. "I've done enough of that."

Since then, Brandon had been polite to her, even

kind, but he'd not spoken of their marriage again or of his child she was carrying. He'd not made any attempt to change her mind. Sorrowfully, Leah wondered if perhaps he was relieved that she was going home and leaving him to his own life. In spite of everything they had meant to each other, maybe he, too, realized that they were just too different to be happy together.

She closed her eyes as vivid memories flashed across her mind . . . She and Brandon in each other's arms at the waterfall. Their wild passion in the game room at Westover. Brandon kneeling before the fire pit in her wigwam. Brandon throwing a giggling Kitate into the air and catching him. She and Brandon charging the bear. And then, superimposed over those precious images of what had been was the enchanting face of a baby girl—a laughing infant with dark hair and startling blue eyes.

Lightly, Leah touched her swelling belly, knowing instinctively that she'd been given a glimpse of the daughter she would know and love, a daughter who would grow up without a father, as she had . . . But I had memories of Cameron, Leah thought sadly. This child won't even have memories of her father.

Memories . . . Soon, that would be all she had of her blue-eyed English husband. Heedless of where she was, or who could see her, Leah covered her face with her hands and wept.

"Enough of that, child," Cameron said. "It's hard to lose friends, but life is for the living." He waved to a footman, and the servant opened the coach door with a flourish. "You've had enough sadness," Cameron murmured as he helped Leah into the coach.

"Now let us think of the voyage home and the new life inside you."

"I want to see Kitate so bad," she admitted. "Will he remember me, do you think?"

"I doubt that his remembering you is anything you need to worry about, Leah. If he's anything like you, he has the memory of an old woods bison." Cameron leaned from the coach window and signaled the coachman.

Leah took a deep breath and tried to picture her son's face. If she kept remembering Kitate and how much he meant to her, maybe leaving Brandon wouldn't be so hard.

"Leah, we have to talk."

Leah looked up in surprise. It was the day after Maggie's funeral, and she was outside in her father's garden, kneeling on the grass. She had kicked off her red slippers, rolled down her silk stockings, and tossed them away just to feel the grass against her bare feet and legs. "Brandon?"

He was coming toward her, tall and broad, his handsome face set in hard lines. Behind him, neat rows of red and yellow roses were coming into bloom. Leah inhaled deeply of the sweet fragrance. Whenever I think of England, she thought, I'll remember this moment . . . the scent of those budding flowers and the way the sunlight glinted off Brandon's golden hair.

"I've been thinking this all out," he said gruffly, "and it's time we talked about it."

"Aye, if ye wish," she murmured. "Lady Dunnkell's roses be beautiful, aren't they?"

"Don't talk to me about roses. To hell with the

roses! Stop pretending to be an English lady. Yell at me. Throw something.''

"Ye'll be better off without me." Leah bit her lower lip and deliberately looked away. "Ye can have the annulment your parents wish," she whispered in anguish, "and marry someone who can make ye happy . . . someone like Anne."

"Damn it, Leah, you can't do this!" He caught her hand in his and turned it to place a lingering kiss at the pulse on her wrist. "I love you, woman."

She shook her head, unable to speak for the emotions that choked her. She wanted to tear her hand away from him, away from his touch, but she couldn't. Her lower lip trembled, and she blinked away tears. *You still want him,* her inner voice cried urgently.

"I'm not asking you to stay here," he said. "I just want you to give our marriage another chance." He kissed her wrist again, and a sweet aching spread like fire from the pit of her stomach through her body.

"Nay . . ." Her voice sounded strained and throaty. She drew in a deep, ragged breath as her throat tightened.

"If I come to America with you," he persisted, "if I come for good—will you forgive me?"

Leah moistened her lips and stared into his face. "It canna be, Brandon. There is too much . . ." She sighed and tried again. "When I told ye that I was carrying your child, ye were angry with me. I feared ye didna wish a son or daughter with Shawnee eyes and skin the color of copper."

Brandon flushed. "That was never the reason I was upset," he said. "I was afraid of losing you in child-bed. Your mother died that way, and someone . . .

someone I knew a long time ago.'' He exhaled softly. ''There was a girl, Leah . . . '' He shut his eyes. ''Cecily. She was the parson's daughter. We were both very young, and . . .''

Leah scrutinized Brandon's features in silence as he slowly related the story of Cecily and her tragic death. Sweat beaded on his forehead and his lips whitened as he described the stillbirth of her infant.

''The midwife said . . .'' Brandon's eyes glazed with pain as he repeated the careless words. ''The midwife said the baby was too big—it tore her apart.''

''And that's all?'' Leah asked. ''That is why ye didna want me to have your bairn?''

His lips thinned to a hard line, and he stiffened.

''Nay,'' Leah soothed. ''I dinna wish to make light of your agony, but ye must learn to accept that women do die in childbed. They also die of drowning, or of swallowing peach pits.''

''You don't understand. I was responsible. It was my child—at least I think it was.''

''And hers. Did ye force her?''

''God, no! But—''

''Shhh. Brandon, this be a woman's matter. Why didna ye go to your mother with this hurt? She could have told ye. Yes, we face death when we give life— but it is a burden of love. It is a risk women must take if life—all life—is to go on.''

''Cecily wasn't a woman—she was only a frightened girl.''

''And ye were nay a man, Brandon. Ye were both children. Ye meant Cecily no ill, and the Great Good Spirit, Wishemenetoo, would never punish you so long for such a boy's recklessness.''

"Charles loved her—more than I did, I think. He's never forgiven me for her death."

"Your cousin is twisted . . . nay, he is rotten inside like a worm-eaten tree. Ye canna judge yourself by his rules."

Relief flooded his features. "You believe me?"

"Aye, Brandon mine, I believe ye. Who else would be so foolish?" She smiled. "I may die in child-birth—who can know?—but you or any other man canna deny me the right to follow my own destiny. We canna hide from living, lest we would never drink for fear of drowning or never sleep for fear we wouldna wake."

"You forgive me, then? You'll give us another chance?"

"Brandon, I—" Her resolve slipped away, drowned in a sudden wave of joyous giddiness.

He pulled her into his arms, heedlessly crushing the fragile fabric of her costly gown. Before she knew what was happening, Leah found herself kissing him back, twining her fingers in his hair as he embraced her with all his strength.

"Leah, Leah," he murmured between kisses. "I'm so sorry . . . so sorry."

His mouth was hot and wet and demanding. Their tongues met and caressed, awakening deep longings that Leah had thought lost. The velvet sweetness of his mouth, the familiar man scent of Brandon, flooded her senses and drove everything but her desire for him from her mind.

His shoulders trembled as he pushed her back against the grass. "I want you," he said thickly, "here and now."

Hot desire stabbed through her as she gazed up

into his beautiful eyes, as blue as the sky over his head . . . English eyes, heavy-lidded with passion. *"K'daholel,"* she whispered huskily, I love you. They kissed again, and she touched his cheek and his throat, letting her fingertips caress his fair skin as the heat of his hard body permeated her own through the thin silk of her gown.

He lowered his head and deliberately kissed the sensitive hollow of her throat with tantalizing, slow, sweet kisses. "Leah," he murmured. "My woman . . . my wife."

She buried her face in his yellow hair and filled her head with the clean male scent of him as her hands stroked the contours of his neck and the top of his superbly muscled shoulders. The throbbing ache in her veins had become an insistent hunger, and she whimpered with pleasure as she felt the heat of his callused palm against her breast.

Brandon pulled her upright, and they kissed again as he fumbled with the laces at the back of her gown. His hot, wet tongue flicked against her bare shoulder, and then, as the laces came apart and her gown slipped down, he freed one breast from her garments and closed his mouth over her waiting nipple. She arched against him, wanting to feel him—all of him— against her. The yearning, the pounding in her veins grew to fever pitch. All that mattered was Brandon and the fulfillment of their love.

She rose to her knees, and he pulled her gown down. Her shift and petticoats followed, and then his breeches, and in minutes both of them lay bare in each other's arms. The thick, green lawn made a marriage bed as soft as any Leah had ever hoped for, and neither of them cared that garden hedges were the walls of their bedchamber and the open sky the only ceiling.

They kissed and touched and laughed. The shared caress for caress, giving pleasure and receiving it with utter abandon. And finally, when their passion reached its apex, Leah lay back against the sweet-smelling grass and opened her body to him. Eagerly, he entered her, filling her with the swollen proof of his love. Breathlessly, they strained against each other.

Whimpering with need, Leah lifted herself to receive each long, powerful thrust. She clung to him, feeling her body and soul swirling up and up in a whirlwind of sweet passion. And when they reached the crest of the mountain together, she cried out his name as he spilled his seed into her. Dark eyes bright and luminous, she fell back against the cushion of grass and pulled his golden head down to rest against her naked breasts.

"My darling Leah," he whispered. "My life began on the day I met you."

She lay motionless, savoring the aftermath of their rapture. So great was her joy that she was afraid to close her eyes for fear that when she opened them, this would all be a dream and they would be apart again.

After long moments of quiet happiness, Brandon broke the spell. He rolled over and sat up, smiling at her in the way that only he could, with that lazy, crooked smile that tugged at her heart. "You've done it now, witch," he teased. "You'll never be rid of me."

Leah sighed as all her doubts came winging back. "How can it succeed, *dah-quel-e-mah?* No matter how we love each other, ye wouldna be happy in my village, and I be not an English lady.''

He lowered his head to kiss her lips gently. "I'll think of something, I promise you. Will you let me come with you? I want to be a part of your life—a part of Kitate's and our child's lives. I don't want to be just a name without a face."

"What would ye do in the Colonies?" She sat up and tugged the torn shift over her head.

Brandon recovered his breeches and reluctantly pulled them on. "I'd try some of my ideas on Father's plantations. The economy of Maryland is built on tobacco, and one-crop farming can't last. Tobacco robs the topsoil of its richness. I have enough plans to last a lifetime, and the land there is untouched. Maybe I could do some good."

"What of your duty to your family?"

He grabbed her shoulders and pulled her against him, kissing her mouth hard. "To hell with them," he said. "You and the children are my family. Either I can manage the title and responsibilities from America or someone else can have it."

She sighed and wrapped her arms around his neck. " 'Tis a great sacrifice ye would make for us, Brandon mine," she managed between kisses, "but I fear I'd be nay happier as a planter's wife than as a countess. Our child would be half—nay, three-quarters—white, but I canna see Kitate following a plow. He is born to the forest and the wild ways."

"I'll think of a way, Leah. Just give me a chance. Let me come with you." He released her and stepped back, his eyes serious. "You know you still love me."

Leah smiled back at him. She forced herself to appear calm, wondering how he could not hear the beating of her heart. Joy bubbled up inside her and made her voice tremble. "I canna stop ye from taking ship to Maryland if ye wish."

"Tell me you want me to come."

Her lower lip trembled. "Ye know the answer to that. Ye've always known . . . since that first night I took ye from the torture stake."

"Say the words."

"Aye," she admitted, surrendering her heart to him once more. "Aye, my darling *Englishmanake*. I want ye to come with me to America. If ye can truly find a way—I want us to be mon and wife."

"Ah, love, you'll be the making of me." He grinned. "I will think of a solution."

"No more of your tricks," she warned. "I can leave ye as easily in Maryland as here."

"More so, I should think," he teased. He gathered up her shoes and stockings. "I think perhaps I need to get you up to your room. It would make a great scandal if the servants caught us here like this."

She smiled saucily at him. "And what would they say? Ye be my husband. To the English hell with servants, I say. It be what ye and I desire that matters."

An hour later, once more properly dressed, they found Cameron in the library. He looked up and smiled as he saw them standing hand in hand.

"From the glow on my daughter's face, I'd say you have news for me," he said.

Leah smiled up at Brandon. "He be coming with us, Father. We have gathered the scattered pieces of our peace pipe and mended it with tears and promises."

Cameron studied Leah's eyes and then turned his

attention to Brandon. "Are you both certain? I ken something of the troubles the two of you face. You come from vastly different worlds. There are some differences that love cannot cross, and there will be people both red and white who will never accept your marriage."

"Aye," Leah agreed. "That we ken all too well. The details be nay yet worked out, but I have faith in my husband. Some Englishmen be quite clever." She smiled mischievously. "For barbarians," she added.

"You have my blessings, then," Cameron said. He rose from his chair. "If you are attempting to reconcile your marriage, you may not want me coming with you to America."

Leah exchanged glances with Brandon, then tucked her hand into Cameron's. "Did ye believe our hearts so small that there wouldna be room in them for a father's love? Ye have given your word as a Scotsman, and we shall hold ye to it. Someone must teach Kitate and our daughter the proper way to speak the English tongue."

"Who says it will be a daughter?" Brandon asked.

"Never argue with a Shawnee peace woman," Cameron advised. "The odds are stacked against ye."

Leah's eyes grew troubled as her composure faltered. "I be nay a peace woman. I be unworthy of the honor."

Her father chuckled softly, and he smiled boyishly. "Your denial is the final proof. So Sh'kota, your mother, spoke when Mo-na Mskee-yaik-wee, her grandmother, declared her future. You have suffered, child, and you have proved your heart is pure. You have traveled far on a quest to bring wisdom to your people, and you have brought another human back from the claws of the Dark Warrior whom the English know as the Angel of Death.''

Leah shook her head. ''Nay, I didna.''

Cameron's gaze held her. His native burr grew thick as his deep voice touched her soul. ''You called upon the power of the Eye of Mist, and your wish was granted.''

''Nay,'' she protested. She looked from one to the other in confusion. ''I asked the spirits of the necklace, but it didna work.''

Cameron was relentless. ''You asked that Brandon's life be saved, didn't you?''

''I'm not sure what the two of you are fencing about,'' Brandon said, ''but unless I'm sadly mistaken, I am alive.''

''It wasna that way,'' Leah protested. ''I did ask, but nothing—''

''Is Brandon alive?'' Cameron caught her wrists and turned her to face him. ''You must accept, Leah. When Dr. McCloud first examined him, he told me privately that there was no chance. Brandon was a breathing dead man.'' He released her hands. ''The amulet was real, child.''

A curious whirling began in Leah's head. She felt dizzy, unable to breathe, but the sensation was not frightening—rather, it imparted the thrill of running the rapids in a light birchbark canoe . . . of seeing boulders looming up ahead and steering around them with the thrust of a paddle . . . of lying on her back in the damp grass and watching the majestic play of lightning across the sky. She sighed as she sensed the weight of a feathered mantle settle around her shoulders. And, from somewhere far off beyond the salt sea, she heard the piercing notes of an ancient melody played on a eagle-bone flute.

Brandon is casting off his responsibilities to this land, she thought with a curious detachment, but I am taking on a burden of love that I can never forget.

Gradually, the light-headedness subsided, and she became aware of the silk skirt twisted in her fingers, of the scent of tobacco and brandy coming from her father's clothing, and the faintest hint of rosebuds. She sighed and opened her eyes to find Brandon's intense blue ones staring into them.

"I should have been warned I was wedding a witch," he teased gently. "An Indian witch must be the worst kind of all."

"And the best," Cameron said. He patted Leah's arm. "You'll adjust to it, both of you. Her mother and I did." He chuckled. "After a fashion." His expression grew thoughtful and he leaned forward, giving his full attention to Brandon. "I was just about to come and find you. My messenger returned from Westover an hour ago. Your parents were overjoyed to find out you were still alive."

"What?" Leah asked. "No one told me of a letter to Westover."

"Once my fever went down enough for me to think straight, I realized Mother could never be in on the plot to kill either of us," Brandon explained. "No matter what I ever did, Mother supported me, even against my father's wishes. It was cruel to let them go on believing I was dead."

"We didn't send a letter," Cameron said. "There are too many ways a letter can be intercepted. I sent my trusted servant with instructions to speak only to

Lord Kentington or, if he was too ill, to Lady Kathryn. No one else in the household was to know that Brandon was still alive."

Brandon leaned forward. "Did your man say if my cousin Charles is at Westover?"

"Aye, he's there, but he was about to travel to London to retrieve your body. Your battered corpse has been discovered in Lambeth Marsh. Highwaymen crushed your skull so badly that a closed casket will be necessary." Cameron grinned. "Fortunately for your family, the authorities were able to identify your corpse by your ring, your sword, and your pistol."

Brandon nodded. "And fortunately for my cousin, the alleged highwaymen were stupid enough to leave my valuables so that my body could be identified. Without a body, my mother would never have believed in my death." He exhaled softly. "Did she take the news of Charles's perfidy hard? I know she loved him as if he were her son."

"The messenger said she wept and your father cursed," Cameron said.

"If the earl is well enough to work up a fury, he's not as close to death as his physicians think."

"He's capable of more than anger," Cameron replied. "Your father's hatched a scheme to expose Charles publicly. He's afraid your word wouldn't be enough, especially since you were attacked from the back in a dark alley. Your cousin is a verra rich man, and rich men have been known to escape justice before. He might spin any story, and you'd have to prove guilt without a doubt before a jury. The earl has planned your funeral at Westover in a fortnight. Dozens of influential people will be there, including the high sheriff. If Charles produces a body he claims is yours, he'll be arrested for attempted murder and kidnapping. Does that suit you?''

Brandon nodded. "Come what may, I'll be there. I'd consider it an honor, sir," he said to Cameron, "if you'd come with us."

"Done," the older man agreed. "I wouldn't miss this visit for an archbishop's fortune."

"We?" Leah asked. "Who said anything about we?''

"You have to come with me," Brandon urged. "You'd never forgive yourself if I got into trouble and you weren't there to help me out of it."

Her eyes narrowed suspiciously. "And what of our sailing date? Suppose we miss our ship?''

"We'll not miss it, child," Cameron said with a grin. "I purchased a likely schooner and I'm having her refitted for our needs. The *Jenny D.* Have no fear, the ship will wait for us, and I swear to you that you'll have Kitate in your arms before the pumpkins ripen and the wild geese wing south to the Chesapeake country."

"And you, *Englishmanake*," Leah challenged her husband, "do you swear to me also?''

Brandon held out his arms to her. "By the moon, love, by the moon and stars. If we live, you'll be sitting around a Shawnee campfire at first snowfall.''

"And what of Matiassu, war chief of the Shawnee? What will ye do about him, Brandon viscount?'' Leah demanded. "Do ye think he will have changed his mind about you?''

"Enough, woman. There is a time to speak and a time to be still. I'll deal with Matiassu when we're face to face." He grinned. "This is a time to be silent and kiss your husband." Laughing, she obeyed him, and Cameron wisely made a hasty retreat from the room, leaving them alone to whisper plans and promises between the delights of achieving a final reconciliation.

Chapter 24

Westover Manor, Dorsetshire, England, July 1721

The stone chapel at Westover was draped in black cloth from marble floor to vaulted ceiling. Hundreds of mourners filed past the closed rosewood coffin lying in state on a platform flanked by tall beeswax tapers. Incense hung heavy in the air, and the murmured prayers of the robed priests were accompanied by the sounds of weeping and the tolling of death bells.

Each mourner paused by the family pew to offer condolences to the bereaved parents, Lord and Lady Kentington, and their nephew Charles. The earl—still in poor health—had been carried to the church in a chair and was enthroned in cushions, his lap covered with a quilt. The countess was swathed and veiled in black crepe. So distraught at the death of her only child that she was incapable of speech, she merely nodded acknowledgment to the expressions of shared sorrow.

Outside the church, lines of coaches stood along the lane and crowded the stable and courtyard of the manor house. Black-garbed servants hurried to and fro, tending to guests and preparing for the formal reception and funeral feast which must follow the interment. Liveried footmen, coachmen, grooms, huntsmen, and armed retainers gathered in knots and waited while the elaborate rituals for Lord Brandon's funeral were conducted.

To the left of the church a stone wall bounded the graveyard. There, a broad-shouldered man and his two lanky sons were shoveling dirt from an open grave. Village children ran in and out among the tombstones, laughing and calling to each other, ignoring their parents' admonitions to remember the doleful reason for the gathering.

A black coach bearing the crest of the Earl of Dunnkell and drawn by four coal-black horses drew to a stop before the chapel door. Servants let down the steps and Lord Dunnkell appeared, accompanied by a slim lady in full morning attire. The two joined the grieving procession, first to bid farewell to the deceased, then to speak softly to Lord and Lady Kentington.

"You have my deepest sympathy," Cameron said. "It is an outrage that our finest blood should be cut down by brigands on the highway." The lady with him covered her veiled face with a black handkerchief and wept quietly.

"Thank you," Lord Kentington said. "I've made formal protest at the highest levels. You may be certain that the gibbets at Tyburn will be kept busy. We will punish my son's murderers if we have to hang half of London to do it."

Lady Kathryn blew her nose daintily. "It was good of you to come, both of you." She glanced at her nephew. "Lady Dunnkell is only recently back from Italy, Charles."

Charles nodded and fumbled with a black onyx pommel on his mourning sword. "We accept God's will," he mumbled piously, "but we shall never cease to lament the loss of my dear cousin."

Kentington cleared his throat. "Charles has consented to deliver a eulogy for Brandon before the funeral mass."

"Very fitting," Cameron said. He tucked his arm into his companion's and led her to a seat across the aisle and several rows back, hastily vacated by a baron and his wife. Cameron leaned close to his lady. "Are you all right, child?" he whispered.

She nodded, unwilling to admit how uncomfortable and frightened she really was. She'd insisted on coming to the church against Brandon's and her father's wishes. She'd not shame herself by complaining now.

"It won't be long," he promised, squeezing her hand.

Leah fought waves of panic. She felt smothered by the closely packed bodies around her, and she could hardly breathe beneath the layers of heavy black cloth. Her thick veil allowed her to see out without letting anyone view her face, but it also prevented any movement of air beneath the veil. Her head was spinning, and her stomach threatened to reject the fish and biscuits she'd eaten earlier in the bounding coach. Sweat gathered on her breasts and neck, dampening her undergarments and making her even more uncomfortable.

"Steady, child," Cameron murmured.

She clutched his hand and forced herself to try to

breathe deeply as her eyes searched the front of the sanctuary for movement.

From the back of the church, a musician began to play a golden harp, and the plaintive notes rolled over the crowd, stilling the murmurs and shuffle of feet against the worn stone floor. Swells of nausea engulfed Leah as she tried to ignore the stench of so many Englishmen and women in so many clothes crammed into such a small space.

Charles rose in the family pew and addressed the mourners. "We are come here on a sad occasion," he began, "to lament the passing of Robert Wescott, Viscount Brandon."

Leah's heart skipped a beat as she saw a narrow door open and a familiar man's form appear in the shadows A woman shrieked as Brandon appeared between the young priest and the coffin.

"But not so sad as it might have been, Charles," Brandon said loudly.

Several women screamed. One fainted into the center aisle. Angry men leaped to their feet and demanded explanations. Charles's mouth sagged open, and he staggered back as though he had been struck by a fist.

Brandon advanced on the family pew and pointed directly at his cousin. "I publicly charge you with the kidnapping and attempted murder of my wife, Lady Brandon. I also charge you with robbery and a foul attack on my own life." His scorching blue gaze flicked across Charles like the lash of a whip. "Guards," he shouted, drawing his sword. "Place Sir Charles Wescott under arrest."

Leah stood and tore away her suffocating veil as four armed men ran from the church entrance toward

Charles. Cameron dropped his hand to his own sword hilt.

"This is preposterous!" Charles cried. "A travesty of—"

Suddenly an altar boy stumbled into one of the tall candle stands, and it fell to the floor with a crash. Panic-stricken, the red-faced boy dived for the thick candle, tripped over the hem of his robe, and sprawled across Brandon's feet. Charles whirled and drew his sword with a single motion, placing the point of his weapon against Lady Kathryn's throat.

Kentington groaned and stretched out his arms to his wife. "In the name of God, no!"

Lady Kathryn squeaked in terror.

"Don't move, any of you," Charles threatened. "I warn you, I'll kill her."

"Put down that sword!" Brandon ordered. "Are you mad? You can't escape."

The chapel erupted into turmoil as frightened men and women shoved and climbed over benches to escape the threatened violence while others drew their weapons. Those in the front rows spilled into the aisle, preventing the guards from reaching the pew where Charles held Lady Kentington prisoner. Somewhere behind Leah a child began to wail.

Cameron's rapier gleamed in the candlelight as he moved to shield Leah with his body. "Get out," he said curtly. "There's a door halfway back on the side wall."

Fierce pride in her father shot through Leah as she eyed his unadorned steel sword. It was no gallant's toy in his hand but a warrior's weapon. For all his silk and satin, his gentlemen's manners, Cameron

Stewart was still a man to be reckoned with. She leaned forward and struggled to see around him.

"I said I want you out of here!" he repeated.

Leah's legs felt too weak to move as her gaze was drawn to Brandon. He stood like a rock with his upraised sword. Sunlight streaming through a stained-glass window tinged his beautiful face with gold and made him seem like some hero from an ancient Greek myth. Her heart rose in her throat, and she knew she'd never loved him more than she did at that instant.

"Don't add cowardice to your crimes, Charles," Brandon warned. His voice was low and controlled, but the unspoken threat sent shivers down Leah's spine. "You've shamed us enough already. Let her go and accept your punishment like a gentlemen."

"You're the coward," Charles shouted back. "You've hidden behind your name and your father's title long enough. Meet me outside—face to face—if you have the nerve."

"No!" Brandon's mother cried.

Charles seized her by the hair and tilted her head back, keeping the point of his rapier at the soft vee of her throat. "Your answer, cousin," he demanded.

"Nay!" Leah called out to Brandon. "Ye be not well enough to fight him."

"I'll fight you," Cameron offered. "Brandon's barely out of a sickbed. If you want to cross blades with someone, try me."

"Still hiding, are you, little cousin?" Charles taunted. "Would you like to see how it feels to be an orphan?"

"Let her go," Brandon answered. "I'll fight you, but not on holy ground. Outside—in the orchard beyond the graveyard."

"He canna," Leah whispered to her father. "His wound's barely healed. You must stop him."

Protests rose from the onlookers. "No!"

"The common dogsbody!"

"If Lord Brandon is ill—"

"You can't meet him on a field of honor!"

Kentington's face contorted with fury. "Don't give in to him, Brandon!" He shook his fist at Charles. "If you harm a hair on my wife's head, you little worm, I'll have you boiled in tar!"

Leah noted the stubborn set of her husband's features. She'd seen that look before and knew he was in no mood to listen to reason. She tugged frantically at Cameron's sleeve. "Father?" she implored.

He shrugged his shoulders. "I'm sorry. There's nothing I can do. It's a matter of honor, child."

"Honor? Madness, I say. The Shawnee are men of honor, but they dinna willingly face a crazed bear, unarmed."

"God help him," Cameron muttered under his breath.

"Stay close to him," she begged. Turning away, she moved toward the side door her father had pointed out earlier. She pushed her way through the throng, heedless of complaints from those she trod on or wiggled past until she reached the door.

The July sun was hot on her face as she stepped into the churchyard. She glanced around quickly to get her bearings, picked up her full skirts, and ran toward the stable courtyard where the servants were gathered.

In moments she was back with a protesting huntsman hot on her heels, his bow and quiver of arrows in her hands. There was no need to ask where Brandon was—the cheers and shouts of the crowd drew her to the edge of the apple orchard.

The ring of steel on steel echoed above the noise of the funeral guests. Leah found a hole in the spectators and plunged through, followed by the huntsman.

For a split second, it seemed to Leah that this was all a dream, and in her dream the world had come to a stop. She saw it all—the thick green grass glorious with sweet-smelling clover blossoms, the apple trees laden with immature fruit, the cloudless blue sky overhead. And Brandon . . . her Brandon . . . standing tall and proud. She heard the caw of startled crows rising above the yelling spectators and the buzz of bees among the clover. She could smell the bruised wild mint beneath the feet of the crowd and taste the mixture of fear and excitement in the air.

Then Charles's rapier began moving too fast for her eye to follow, and the streak of red that appeared along Brandon's left arm shocked Leah into reality. This was no dream, and Brandon was fighting for his life.

Charles was good. He was very, very good. Leah could see that in a moment, even though she had no knowledge of fencing. He moved like a dancer, in and out. His blade flashed like a living being.

Both men had thrown aside their coats and were fighting in shirts and breeches. Charles's full-sleeved shirt was creamy white; Brandon's bore two spots of crimson. Charles was quick; Brandon's movements were slower and more studied.

Charles was laughing, his gray eyes devoid of all humanity, as he parried and blocked Brandon's attacks. It was plain to Leah that Charles was a master of the sport and that he was taunting Brandon, playing with him. Charles could deliver a death stroke whenever he wished.

Brandon's face was pale; his eyes never left his cousin's as their blades clashed again and again. Leah watched the back of his shirt, expecting blood to flow from his own wound at any second. He was breathing hard, and each time Charles lunged, Leah was certain that Brandon's strength would fail him.

He was skillful, but even in full health he would have been hard-pressed to challenge Charles. Now, Leah knew, the battle was hopeless. Charles wouldn't be satisfied until he had driven his rapier into Brandon's heart.

Unless . . . She pulled an arrow from the huntsman's quiver and notched it to the bowstring. The huntsman shouted a warning, but she ignored him, waiting breathlessly for the right instant to release the arrow.

Charles launched another brilliant attack, feinting left, then right. Brandon went down on one knee, and Charles's blade dug a furrow down the right side of his neck.

Leah let fly her arrow. Charles screamed as the steel point buried itself in his left thigh. Stunned and bleeding from the neck wound, Brandon stumbled to his feet and raised his rapier.

Charles backed away, clutching the arrow. He spied Leah standing at the edge of the crowd. "You bitch!" he shouted. Blood soaked the back of his leg and dripped onto the grass. "You cheating bitch."

"Don't ye like it when the odds are even?" Leah cried. "Now you've a wound to match Brandon's."

The huntsman tried to wrench the bow from Leah's

hands, but she notched a second arrow and moved back, daring him with an icy stare to interfere.

Brandon was on his feet, weapon poised. His hard gaze flicked from Charles to Leah. He took a cautious step toward his cousin. "Charles," he offered. "We can end this without killing."

Charles staggered to the left and lowered his sword. "All right," he said hoarsely. He extended a bloody hand in friendship.

Brandon hesitated for a heartbeat, then nodded. He grasped Charles's hand. "I loved you like a brother," he rasped. "Why did you—"

"Brandon, watch out!" Leah screamed.

Charles slashed upward toward Brandon's groin with the point of his rapier. Brandon leaped aside, trying to block the blow with his own blade. Brandon deflected the force of Charles's attack, and the sword slid off to inflict a flesh wound on Brandon's inner thigh.

Brandon spun away and met Charles's slashing charge. Sparks flew as sword met sword in the glaring sunlight. The crowd hushed; even the children grew still. Every eye was riveted on the terrible conflict. Suddenly Charles feinted right and Brandon drove his rapier through the left opening in his cousin's defense a fraction of a second before Charles could carry out the same maneuver.

Charles was jolted backward by the force of the blow. He looked down in disbelief at the scarlet circle forming on his white shirt. His eyes widened, and his mouth opened and closed in silent protest. He staggered backward and crumbled to the ground.

Brandon stood over him for a long moment, then turned back toward the shocked throng spilling onto the field. "Leah," he called. Brandon swayed from loss of blood.

Men clustered around the fallen Charles.

"Leah," Brandon repeated. He passed a hand across his face and sucked in a deep, ragged breath. His blue eyes were dazed. Leah's heart went out to him as she ran toward him. Brandon saw her, stopped, and grinned crookedly. "Leah." Her name emerged as a whisper.

Only yards separated them now. Her feet flew across the trampled grass. Then from the corner of her eye, she saw Charles raise up on one arm and pull a pistol from another man's belt. He lifted it and took aim at the center of Brandon's back.

"He's got a gun!" someone shouted.

Sword in hand, Brandon whirled around, protecting Leah with his body.

"No!" Lady Kathryn screamed.

Leah dropped to one knee and drew back her bowstring, knowing all too well that her arrow would fly too late to save the man she loved. A gunshot sounded as she released the feathered shaft.

The arrow flew true, piercing Charles's chest, but he was already dead when the point struck. Cameron moved from a knot of men and stood over the body, a smoking pistol in his hand.

Leah dropped her bow and flung herself into Brandon's arms.

"It's over," he whispered, crushing her against him. "Charles is—"

"Dead," she finished. She had no need to examine Charles's still form as others were doing. Her anger and hatred had drained away when her father's bullet had halted his final attack on Brandon. "Come now,

Brandon mine," she urged. "Let us leave this field of death."

"The first arrow," Brandon said. "When you shot him through the thigh . . ." Uncertain, he looked down at her. "Men will say a woman saved me."

"Aye," she agreed, "they may say it. Would ye rather they said 'She let him die'?"

"No." He lifted her chin and kissed her lightly on the lips. "You have a different way of looking at things, chit."

"Practical," she replied. "I am practical. If Charles were a Mohawk, I'd have put that first arrow through his heart. I dinna have patience with English rules that would let a man like you die at the hands of a man like him."

Her father appeared beside her. "How bad is Brandon hurt?"

She smiled through tears of joy. "He'll live to be a trouble to me, I'm certain."

Brandon smiled at his father-in-law. "I owe you thanks."

"Any time," Cameron replied. "It does my heart good to rid the earth of scum like that."

"My son! Where's my son?" Lord Kentington's demand rumbled above the commotion. "Bring me my son!"

"My father," Brandon said.

"Hardly the voice of a dying man," Cameron quipped.

Kentington shoved aside the high sheriff and threw his arms around Brandon's neck, kissing both his cheeks soundly. "Proud of you, Robert," he said. "Your form needs some improvement, and you hold your rapier like a plowman, but there's hope for you yet.''

Leah eyes glowed with amusement. '' 'Tis good to see ye on your feet, father of my husband.''

"Damned physicians! Heads full of manure, the lot of them.'' He turned and bellowed to the nearest servants. "God's wounds, you maggot-brained louts! Bring my carrying chair! Would you see my heir bleed to death while you scratch your lazy arses?''

"I hardly need to be carried,'' Brandon protested. He shrugged off his father's arm.

Leah moved to support her husband's other shoulder. "Will ye take my help?'' she asked softly.

He grinned. "Whenever I can get it, love, for I'd not have you for an enemy—not for all the world.''

Three weeks later, Leah, Brandon, and Cameron stood on the deck of the schooner, *Jenny D.*, and watched as the last vestige of England vanished over the eastern horizon. Leah linked her arms through her father's and her husband's and inhaled deeply of the clean salt air. Overhead, seagulls wheeled and squawked above the snapping canvas sails, and beneath her feet Leah could feel the movement of the wooden ship.

"Regrets?'' Cameron asked Brandon.

"No.'' He shook his head. "Mother will get over her vapors, and I'll wager Father will live long enough to put his own affairs in order.''

"You're leaving a lot behind,'' Cameron said.

"Not as much as I'm taking with me. It's a new land, and a new life. Somehow, I think I'll find this one more interesting.'' He leaned down and kissed

Leah's forehead. She smiled up at him with her heart in her eyes.

"And you, daughter?" Cameron stepped away from the lovers. "Will you miss England?"

"Nay," she replied, "not England, but there is one thing I regret." She rubbed the warm gold of her amulet.

"And what's that?"

"That I never got the chance to meet my English sister."

Cameron chuckled. "But you did, child."

Confusion clouded her dark eyes. "Who? I . . ." Unexpectedly, understanding flooded through her. "Anne?"

Her father grinned and turned away.

"Father!" she protested. "How could ye . . ."

Whistling a Highland air, hands thrust deep in his pockets, Cameron strode off down the deck with a seaman's rolling gait.

"Your Anne," Leah murmured. "Did ye know?"

Brandon shook his head. "I had no idea, but with him nothing would surprise me."

Leah's lower lip quivered. "Well, I dinna like such surprises. Did she ken, do ye think? Nay . . ." She sighed. "He is a contrary man—as ye be, Brandon mine. Ye have talked your way onto my boat, and ye have talked your way into my bed—"

"And a fine bed it is, too. And us with so little to do on this long voyage but test the softness of our mattress."

"Enough of such goose feathers," she declared. "I have given ye time and time again. How, my husband, do ye expect to solve our problem once we get to America?"

Brandon grinned and pulled her close. He kissed her left eyebrow and then the right. "I will make a bargain with you, love," he said huskily. He kissed the right corner of her mouth and then the left. "If you will live with me on my plantation from the time the geese fly south to the Chesapeake until the Shawnee plant spring corn, I will be content. You can then take the children—all our children—and live with the Shawnee as you wish. You can spend your summers with your people in the wilderness and the winters with me. That way our children will know both cultures."

"Ye will not mind, truly?" she whispered.

"Damned right I'll mind, but we'd both have our heart's desire part of the time, wouldn't we? And I can always visit your wigwam if I get too lonely."

"I dinna—"

"Say, *yes*, woman."

"Yes, woman."

Brandon's mouth covered hers and his arms tightened around her. Leah leaned against him and let the happiness lift her spirit high above the rocking ship. She was going home—*they* were going home. And no matter what happened, she would always be secure in his love.

"Englishmanake," she whispered.

"Aye, wench, what is it now?"

"I think we should test that mattress to see if it be too hard."

Laughing, he gathered her up in his arms and carried her toward their cabin and a lifetime of loving.